I0757578

© KILLION
GROUP INC.

ESSENCE OF CHAOS

THE BOOKS OF THE CUARI
BOOK 1

MARIE ANDREAS

Acknowledgements

This story is a book of love that started a very long time ago and has gone through many incarnations. Thank you to Sandi Jordan for making me believe in this story and my writing again all those years ago. Keanin will always be yours.

Thanks to editor extraordinaire- Jessa Slade for her magic skills of helping me make sense and hunting down runaway plots. Thank you to Lisa Andreas, Patti Huber, Lynne Mayfield, and Fantasy Proofreads for trying to catch all the word shenanigans. And to Ilana Schoonover for working to keep me out of too much trouble. Any errors or mistakes that survived are completely mine.

A special shout out to Jonathan Jacob for coming up with the name for my big bad-Qhazborh, and for his ongoing support.

And a major thank you to Joolz and Jarling (Julie Nichols and Uwe Jarling) for an amazing cover and the Killion Group for the interior formatting.

Writing is a wonderful journey that takes a lot of support from folks around you. Thank you to everyone who has helped me, bought my books, let me cry on their shoulder, or helped in any way.

DEDICATION

This book is dedicated to the memory of Roxane Noelle Johnson.

You never got to see it finished and in print, but you will always be a part of it.

You are very missed.

OTHER BOOKS BY MARIE ANDREAS

THE LOST ANCIENTS SERIES
Book One: The Glass Gargoyle
Book Two: The Obsidian Chimera
Book Three: The Emerald Dragon
Book Four: The Sapphire Manticore
Book Five: The Golden Basilisk
Book Six: The Diamond Sphinx

THE ASARLAÍ WARS TRILOGY
Book One: Warrior Wench
Book Two: Victorious Dead
Book Three: Defiant Ruin

THE ADVENTURES OF SMITH AND JONES
Book One: A Curious Invasion
Book Two: The Mayhem of Mermaids

BROKEN VEIL TRILOGY
Book One: The Girl with the Iron Wing
Book Two: An Uncommon Truth of Dying

THE BOOKS OF THE CUARI TRILOGY
Book One: Essence of Chaos
Book Two: Division of Chaos
Book Three: Destruction of Chaos

CHAPTER ONE

JENNA REILLY WAS SWEAR-TIL-YOU-TURN-BLUE LOST. Not the making a left instead of a right lost, but the where-is-the-damn-road lost. She'd come out to just outside of Barstow, a desert town more known for being a stopping point to Las Vegas than for anything important, for what she thought was a newly discovered ancient burial dig site to gather supporting evidence for another dissertation. But there had been a large stand of trees, big ones, where there shouldn't have been anything larger than chaparral. Then her not so reliable ten-year-old car died, her cell phone gave its last gasp, and she'd brilliantly thought of walking the rest of the way to the location.

That had been two hours ago, and she not only hadn't found the location of the supposed burial site, she'd now managed to lose her monstrosity of a car when she gave up and turned back.

"It's here, I know it's here." The mantra was more for her own peace of mind than anything else. She was starting to get scared. And dizzy. The dizziness had started not too long after leaving the car and was getting worse. Logic said to sit down until it passed; emotion said to keep going until she found her way back. Everything she looked at had a weird double image to it, like a twisted afterimage that wasn't exactly the same as the original. The more she walked, the more the images differed from each other.

A thin shape brought her to a stumbling halt as it darted

ahead of her. The body looked like a distorted version of a greyhound. While she knew the animals were popular pets, she doubted anyone was letting them run wild in the backcountry of Los Angeles. A moment later another long, lean, and slightly blurred shape broke to the left. Her dizziness grew worse and she dropped to her knees.

"Is someone out here? This isn't funny." She reached into the pocket of her jacket. "I've got a gun and I'm not afraid to use it." There was nothing in her pocket beyond car keys and a dead cell phone, but hopefully it would scare off most people. Living in Los Angeles her entire life meant she would assume the worst, then be grateful if it didn't happen.

Her only answer was an increase in the blurs around her, closer, but still too fast for her to identify beyond vaguely dog shaped. The blurs made the dizziness worse, pain shot through her head, and then darkness overtook her, and she collapsed.

◆

Jenna's mind fought its way free of the darkness that engulfed it. Without opening her eyes, she took a few deep breaths and forced her mind to settle. The stabbing pain in her head gave way to a dull throbbing and the chaos diminished. Sucking in another steadying breath, she forced one eye open. When the world didn't explode in sparks of pain, she eased open the other eye.

At least the double vision seemed to have vanished. But in its place a surge of violent and distorted images slammed into her mind. Fangs and claws reached out toward her. The smell of blood filled the air and bile rose in her throat.

The visions vanished a heartbeat later.

Shaking off the last bit of adrenalin, she tried to figure out what had happened to her and where she was. Considering it didn't look remotely like the area she'd been in, she assumed that she'd started walking at some point. And fallen. She shoved aside the thought that she had no memory of going anywhere as she took in her new location.

Rugged sheer rock walls rose at least ten feet above her. The narrow ravine she lay in couldn't be more than six feet across, but it curved down beyond her line of sight. A quick glance around showed only small rocks, dirt, and a few torn plants that had most likely made the trip down with her when she landed here. Nothing that could be used to get out of the ravine.

The hand she held up wasn't hers. Jenna's heart pounded when she raised her hand to block the glancing light of the setting sun.

Far too thin, and the fingers were too long. Those faint white lines of old scars didn't belong to her. She moved the hand closer and tried to accept it as her own. Brushing the tattered sleeve further up her arm, she started shaking. It wasn't right either. The rest of the arm was pale, like it should be, but it was covered in additional fine, web-like scars from injuries she'd never had. She flexed the arm and hand. They moved under her command; she'd just never seen them before.

Panic growing, she looked down at her dust-covered clothing. She'd never seen the tattered, loose weave dress she wore either. However, a burst of relief hit her when she recognized the battered hiking boots and faded jeans she had put on that morning.

A hazy part of her mind stepped in and accepted the odd clothes and the scars, soothing her fears. The feelings of not recognizing her body vanished. She knew she should be worried for her sanity, but the vague, soothing essence in her head calmed her fears. It was like the one time she had too many pot brownies as an undergrad, reality was wrapped in a nice fuzzy cocoon of serenity, and right now her best option was to keep it in place as long as possible. She directed her energy to other things—like how to get out of the ravine. Judging by the sky above her, night would be falling soon, and spending it trapped in a ravine wasn't her idea of a fun evening. Hopefully, she could get out, find her way back to her car, and figure out a way to get it running.

First thing was to get the hell out of this hole. "Everyone always said I'd fall in a ditch if I didn't pay attention to where I was going. I never thought they meant litera—"

Her attempt at standing brought a scream and pain, as fire from her ankle shot its way up to her hip as she tried to put weight on it. Collapsing back into the dirt, she dug her nails into her palms until the waves of pain faded. She'd broken an ankle once before, right after high school, when she'd misjudged her landing while skydiving. This was the same pain. Minus the thrill of jumping out of a perfectly good airplane.

After two more failed attempts to stand, she yelled again, but this time with frustration and anger more than pain. She punctuated her screams by pounding the ground with her fists, but her efforts brought no relief to her leg or her situation. It did, however, bring an answering voice. It sounded male, but he wasn't speaking English. At that point she didn't care what he spoke. She wanted out of this damn hole.

"Down here! I'm stuck!" Possibly not the best thing to advertise if the person in question had ill intent, but she was willing to take the risk. This place terrified her, something far less rational than being in a strange ravine, injured, and with night falling.

The approaching voice continued to speak as it came closer, but she still couldn't make out what was being said. Light and musical, like a combination of French and Gaelic, yet it didn't sound like either. Nor could she understand a word of what the man was saying. A shiver made its way down her back. But she needed someone's help.

"Come on, you're almost here, I can hear you. I don't know what you're saying, but—" She froze as her rescuer appeared over the edge of the pit.

"Oh my God…what are you?" Her voice came out in an embarrassing squeak, but she couldn't help it. The face peering down at her was in no way human.

He was *humanoid*, with long, scruffy brown hair pulled back from an angular face with a thin band of cloth. Unfortunately, the cloth also kept the hair away from a pair of sharply tapered ears that Mr. Spock would have envied. And he studied her with wide, tilted eyes that couldn't be found outside of a Japanese anime film on elves. Worst of all, he started speaking again in that musical, elegant, and completely inhuman language.

Jenna swore. She'd hit her head harder than she thought when she fell. "You don't exist. Whatever you are, just go play in someone else's nightmare." She motioned the creature away, and then scuttled further back against the rocks.

Unfortunately, she'd forgotten her injured ankle.

The man pulled back a bit at her scream of pain, peering at her from the lip of the ravine until she clutched her leg and cried.

Dancing black circles obscured her vision as terrifying images of creatures chasing her tore through her head. Unseen smoke filled her lungs and one of the shadowy beasts reared up and reached forward, tearing into her dress before she could pull free again. The vision vanished as quickly as it came.

Reaching down, she felt the jagged tear in the dress. Whatever it was, it had happened. Somewhere, sometime, these images happened. She just wasn't sure when. Or to whom.

Shaking her head clear of the images, she noticed the

pointy-eared man looking at her with concern.

"…dark…" he said.

From the part of her mind that still pounded from the nightmare, she understood that word. The fact that she didn't think he was speaking any language she knew should have upset her much more than it did. That indistinct soothing recognition in her head kept her concern in check. Either that or she really was going crazy. Wiping away her tears of pain, she concentrated on his words, focusing that odd part of her mind to understand what he was saying. Visions of racing through the woods came back, but were weaker now; annoying, but not terrifying.

"I don't think you understand me." He still spoke the same musical words, but she understood them now.

"I do. You just said…but you still can't understand me, can you?" Try as she might, she couldn't form her ideas into the language she now could understand. A tiny part of her mind nagged that something was really wrong here. Again she shoved it aside. Survival over sanity.

"You act like you know what I just said." He paused at Jenna's frantic nod. "You do understand? Then why in the abyss can't I understand you?"

Jenna's shrug was lost as he peered up into the purpling sky.

He turned back to her with a frown. "We can't worry about that now. There are things out here at night that even I'd not want to meet without a good fire at my back." He pointed toward her leg. "Can you walk at all?"

When Jenna shook her head, he sighed. "Let me get my rope and come get you. I'd say stay there, but I don't see you have much choice."

The strange man didn't seem so unbelievable now. She was sure that wasn't a good thing. She shouldn't be seeing such things, let alone talking to them. This acceptance of him came from the same part of her mind as the acceptance of the odd clothes and the knowledge of his language. And the terrifying race through some unknown woods.

Try as she might, she still had no idea where she was, or how she got here. She knew who she was. She just couldn't figure out how she got from the Los Angeles backcountry to some pit in a forest. Or why certain limbs looked wrong, some clothes were wrong, and there was a pointy-eared man talking to her.

The strange man returned and lowered himself on a thick rope. From behind, he looked simply like a long-haired, human male.

Very long-haired, as his shaggy hair trailed to the middle of his back. His lean legs sported well-worn gray leggings and equally broken-in black knee-high boots. In the dimming light, she could almost believe he was just an eccentrically dressed human.

Until he reached the bottom and turned around.

The high cheekbones, huge slanted blue eyes, and elegantly tapered ears were too alien, and too beautiful, for humanity.

'Elf' flashed through her mind. Considering that elves didn't exist outside of fantasy tales and movies, her mind really shouldn't be going in that direction. But he looked the part. Tall, lean, exotic. But also scruffy and dirty. Somehow that ruined the elf image.

"Don't worry, I'll have you out of here and warming by a fire before you know it." He picked her up, carefully not jostling the injured leg. His smile was meant to be reassuring, and Jenna was sure it would have been had it been less alien.

Apologizing for the awkwardness, he swung her over his shoulder as they reached the rope.

Jenna would have forgiven any ignominy if she could just get out of this hole. The skin-crawling feeling about this place was getting worse, and the darkening sky wasn't making her feel any better.

As they reached the top, more images from a chase through the forest, and being hunted by those dog-like creatures, slammed into her head and she blacked out.

———◆———

Awakening slowly, Jenna noticed that her leg didn't hurt anymore. In fact, it was suspiciously numb. Ignoring the stabs of pine needles and broken nutshells in the palms of her hands, she pushed herself up, frantically checking to make sure her leg was still in one piece.

The leg of her jeans had been shoved up and away from her ankle, and her sock and boot had been removed. A strange, licorice-smelling, green-gray salve covered her from mid-shin to her foot. Aside from that, it looked fine.

"I've done what I could about your leg."

She jumped at the low voice behind her. For a moment she had forgotten her rescuer. She still understood what he said; and like before, when he spoke, faint images of being chased through the dark woods echoed in her mind. They were weaker than before, which she hoped was a good thing.

Darkness had fallen, but he'd managed to build a small fire. He had a rough camp set up around it, and a dark horse tied to a nearby tree. From the wonderful aroma, he'd prepared some kind of food as well.

"Better?" He squatted down next to her and gently prodded the area around her swollen ankle. "Luckily, I found some Earl's Bane to numb it."

He flashed a quick smile, and then shrugged at her obvious confusion. "Maybe your folk call it something different." He sighed. "I wish I could understand you. Are you hungry?"

"I'm starved." She was surprised he couldn't hear her stomach rumbling.

"Sorry." He shook his head. "All I get is a strange sounding mumble. You aren't from here, are you?"

Jenna gave him a tight smile and a shrug. She didn't think she was from wherever 'here' was, but she wasn't certain that he wasn't the misplaced one. Fortunately, that nice mental Prozac was still keeping her fears at bay. Things were going to get ugly if that weird soothing force in her skull ever left.

"Now I *really* wish I could understand you." The sharp angles of his face became more pronounced as the smile faded and his eyes narrowed. "We've had some odd things happening around here the past few months. You wouldn't be a part of all that, would you?"

Jenna shrugged again. She doubted it, but being as she had no idea where she was or how she got here, she honestly couldn't say.

"Never mind." His smile didn't quite reach his eyes this time. "I'm sure it has nothing to do with you. Now, about that food?" At Jenna's exaggerated nod, he laughed. "Right away, milady." Dusting off his hands, he turned toward the fire. He returned a moment later with two full wooden bowls.

"I can't believe how rude I've been." He shook his head after they'd both started eating. "Here I am dragging you out of ditches, fussing with your leg, and I haven't even told you my name." He gave a short bow. "I am Storm, woodsman by trade."

Jenna smiled and decided to give her name a try. She may not be too clear on where she'd been recently, but she knew who she was. "I'm Jenna." As she said it, she pointed toward herself.

Storm tried saying it a few times, but couldn't get the sounds right. "It's no use." He shrugged and gave a crooked grin. They finished their stew in silence.

He carried the bowls back to the fire. "We'll head toward the home of a friend of mine tomorrow. At the very least, Ghortin will be able to do something a bit more permanent about your leg. He might even be able to make you understandable. So, for now," he carried over a thick, woven blanket and tucked it around her, "good night."

Jenna nodded, and then snuggled deeper into the blanket. She still had no idea where she was, how she'd gotten here, or why she was able to see and understand a fairy tale creature, but she was full, warm, and sleepy. Her eyelids were drooping when she caught sight of a shadow behind the distant trees; tall, thin, and vaguely man-shaped, with a tall dog standing next to it. Both were semi-transparent, like they weren't fully there. They vanished completely before she could point them out to Storm. Jenna stared at the spot for a few moments, willing them to re-appear. When they didn't, she chalked it up to the horrific day she'd had and went to sleep.

CHAPTER TWO

———

JENNA WOKE UP IN A sweat the next morning as the fears from yesterday came pounding back. It took her a minute to figure out where she was, but then that nice soothing acceptance kicked in and she stopped worrying.

Storm raised his head from packing away the night's things and nodded to her. "Ah, will you now break your fast?" He brought over a small plate. "I'm afraid we have simple fare."

The fragrant red cheese, hard bread, and strange purple fruit he offered looked like a feast. She managed to give him a flash of a smile and refrained from bolting down the food.

The bread and cheese were standard and gone before she could fully taste them. The fruit, however, was amazing. It tasted like a combination of watermelon and grapes, with sweet crunchy seeds and a smooth purple skin. The instant she decided that she'd never tasted anything like it, a distant part of her mind recognized it as a ragbare.

Jenna knew that Storm had found it nearby; this was the season for them and they favored forest edges. She grabbed her head at the sudden stab of pain that came with the information. It vanished a moment later, as well as any further knowledge about the fruit.

She wanted to ask her companion about it, then remembered the one-way communication block they had. Storm sounded like he believed this Ghortin person could help. If so, they had better get to him before her mind surrendered completely. Providing she wasn't hooked up to an I.V. in some nice padded cell right now.

She had to admit, if she had gone crazy, at least she picked a handsome hallucination to share it with. Storm might be some sort of alien, but he was a damn good-looking one. Rustic, with his medieval woodsman–elf style, but attractive nonetheless.

"We'll make directly for Ghortin's." With no effort, Storm lifted Jenna atop his horse.

Panic filled her as she tried to get a steady grip on the horse. She never had been fond of the big things and the feeling was usually mutual.

"Now don't fret, those stories about Ghortin aren't true." He gave a smirk as he misunderstood the source of her panic. "Well, most of them anyway."

Although Storm's mysterious friend hadn't been the original cause of Jenna's worry and discomfort, he had her attention now. Did she want someone who had stories told about him, true or not, helping her when she was so vulnerable? She shook her head at Storm.

He patted her hand. "Ghortin isn't near as bad as the legends say. You know bards are always ready to embellish a tale. Especially when there's a mage involved."

He leaned down and gathered a longbow and quiver that had lain hidden behind his pack. For the first time, she noticed a dagger sheathed at his hip, and a pair of wicked-looking knives slipped into the tops of his boots.

That answered a few of Jenna's questions. Wherever she was, it wasn't technologically advanced. Nor safe.

They headed further into the forest, with Storm leading the horse and Jenna trying to stay atop it. She listened with growing discomfort as Storm pointed out local flora and fauna and some weird voice in her head made comments about it.

For instance, she knew she had never in her life seen the rose-like flower with the stunning golden hue they had just passed. Then a voice in her mind called it a natari and said that the delicate thorns were fatal an instant before Storm said the same thing.

This annoying double commentary continued every time they passed something new. Finally, she tuned him out and shut her eyes, forcing her mind to focus on nothing. It was working fine until Storm halted the horse.

"It seems I've put you off to sleep."

She opened her eyes with a start. She didn't want to upset him; right now he was the only link she had to whatever had happened to her. With an apologetic smile, she motioned for him to continue.

Storm smiled back, and then froze, staring closely at her face.

"What in the seven levels of the abyss?" he muttered under his breath. "Your eyes are gray."

Jenna nodded, trying to figure out what the problem was. Surely he'd noticed her eye color yesterday? Besides, how could some point-eared, elf thing act as if anything about her was abnormal?

He shook his head. "I said, your eyes are gray."

She nodded, slower this time, and leaned back on the horse. She didn't think he was dangerous, but he seemed upset.

"Aren't they supposed to be brown?" His own eyes narrowed.

She shook her head.

"They were brown last night." He sounded more as if he was trying to convince himself than anything else. Jenna shook her head again.

"Yes, they were." He leaned forward. "Dark brown. Now they're light bluish gray." He paused and tilted his head. "You knew they were gray?"

She frowned at her new companion, wondering if maybe she wasn't the only one with a tenuous grip on reality. One of them was mighty confused here. And while she would admit that there were more than a few odd things going on with her memories, she knew the color of her eyes.

"So we agree, your eyes are now gray." He spoke as one would speak to a slow child. Jenna narrowed her eyes at the comment, but nodded.

"And yesterday they were brown."

She shook her head sharply.

A worried look crossed his handsome face. He stared up at her for a few minutes, as if he could make her eyes change. He finally gave up and turned back to the trail. "What say we deal with this once we reach Ghortin?"

He continued deeper into the forest, but he refrained from making comments along the way.

After an hour or so they approached a clearing and a small, whitewashed cottage. Its thatched roof and crossed window shutters reminded her of a small Scandinavian inn. A circular double row of thin, white-barked trees gave the impression of guarding the cottage as the horse passed under their branches.

Jenna's stomach growled as the smell of roasted meat drifted toward them. The sound managed to shake Storm out of whatever thoughts he was lost in.

"Fear not, along with being a high and fearsome mage, Ghortin is a fair cook." Storm and the horse broke into a brisk canter, covering the remaining ground in a few minutes.

Storm plucked Jenna off the horse like a child and, without knocking, whisked them through the heavy door of the cottage and into a small parlor. Obviously Storm and this person were good friends. The part of her mind that insisted that mages existed knew they wouldn't appreciate intruders. She chose to continue ignoring the part that said mages, and beings like the pointed-eared man she traveled with, didn't exist.

Storm eased her down on to a crude, overstuffed orange

couch then took one of the rough wooden chairs next to it. Jenna thought his grin looked a bit too much like a cat bringing a new play toy home to its owner.

She shifted on the garish couch, wondering if it was too late to find someone else to help her, when a whirling circle of greens and browns opened up on the wall near the sofa. The swirls vanished, leaving in their wake a most un-mage-like person. Even though she had no memory of ever seeing a mage, she was quite certain that this stout man was not what she would have expected.

He was a few inches shorter than Storm, but his wide shoulders and deep chest made him look larger. He looked to be in his late fifties, with thick, straight, gunmetal gray hair that brushed the top of his starched collar and framed a round face with the beginnings of a beard. His dark brown pants were of a looser style than Storm's and they peeked out from a flowing floor-length vest worn over a simple beige shirt. If he was surprised at their arrival, his broad smile gave no sign.

"Well now, my friend, what foundling have you brought to my home this time?" His deep, warm rumble made Jenna smile in response. She smiled even further when she realized he had normal round ears and human features.

"Ah, lost little flower." The man's thick-callused hand swallowed hers as he bent over it gracefully. "You are most welcome to my humble home. I am Ghortin of the Mages, and you are?"

"Thank you. I'm Jenna." She smiled self-consciously and shook her head. "I forgot, you can't understand me."

"Why, my lady, you injure me. Of course I can understand you." His smile grew even broader as he answered her in perfect, unaccented English. She was surprised at how different it sounded. When Ghortin and Storm spoke in their language, she understood it, but it didn't sound like English, not even in her head.

"I don't understand why you can and he can't—" She broke off with a wince. Her ankle was throbbing again. "Can you help me? Maybe put some of that Earl's stuff on my leg again?"

Ghortin's dark eyes glanced to Storm in question.

Storm bent down and scooped her up. "I found her in a ravine at the western edge of the forest; she's injured her leg."

Jenna thought that he looked like he wanted to say more, but held his tongue. Whatever was going on behind those wide blue eyes, she could only guess at.

"Then what are we waiting for?" Ghortin's voice was still jovial, but his smile had faded a bit. "Come along, lad, bring her in."

He waved his left hand over his head with a flourish and the odd swirls on the wall reappeared. Ghortin marched through it and vanished down the newly created misty hallway. Jenna held her breath as they crossed into it. An instant later she was sucked into darkness.

CHAPTER THREE

THE CORRIDOR THAT APPEARED BEFORE her was long and formless, as if the walls themselves weren't quite sure if they existed or not. Faint outlines of doors flared against the blurry tan expanse as they walked by, fading again after they passed. Jenna wished that the mental commentary that had plagued her in the forest would pop up and explain all this as it had the local fauna. Unfortunately, only her own confused thoughts seemed to be bouncing in her head right now.

Ghortin halted in front of one of the flickering door outlines, his jaw muscles twitching as he glared at it. The outline grew stronger, and then finally held. Ghortin rocked back on his heels and gave the center of the new door a sharp rap with his knuckle. Silently, the door slid away into the wall.

"Damn elementals, always fiddling around." With a final glare at the doorway, Ghortin ushered them into the room.

The door slid shut abruptly. The doorway outline flared once, and then vanished. The wall was left as smooth as if the entrance had never been there.

Ghortin turned to Storm and Jenna with a grin. "Have to keep those vandals in line you know. House elementals are the worst."

Jenna nodded in agreement although she had no idea what he was talking about.

She was surprised to find they were in a library of sorts. Three walls were covered floor to ceiling by the most outrageous infestation of books she'd ever seen. Some were sideways, others upside down, and still more were backward. There were little green books, fat round lavender books, and monstrous black books. At least her mad fantasies came with good reading material. If she could read this strange language they kept speaking at any rate. And if she really was here and not in a home for the insane somewhere.

Storm gave the room a careful study before he sat her down in one of two well-worn leather chairs. He stepped back, quickly moving away from an odd furniture arrangement in which the desk hovered menacingly over the remaining chair. The desk was a monster, looking more like a flat rock with legs than a proper desk.

Ghortin marched across the room, stopping only when he was an inch away from the brutish desk. "I have told you before, *desk*," he pounded one of the few clear places on its surface, "leave my chairs alone."

Jenna tried to catch Storm's eye, but he was studiously looking the other way. Great, so the only person she knew here was afraid of furniture and his best friend liked to yell at walls and desks. Lovely.

Ghortin's voice rose as he continued berating the desk. "If you continue such behavior, I shall have no choice but to send you back to the prison quarry where I found you!"

The desk lurched away from the cornered chair. Jenna did a double take as the desk rumbled across the floor as if some small earthquake was taking place under its stumpy legs. Storm turned a nauseated shade of green, but still refused to look at the desk, Ghortin, or Jenna. Jenna took a long shuddering breath and forced this new event to join the rest of the problem thoughts lurking in a dark pit in her skull somewhere. Eventually this would all make sense. Just not now.

Ghortin paid neither the moving desk, nor the ill-looking Storm, the slightest attention as he pulled the freed chair out and settled across from Jenna.

Jenna glanced back and forth between Storm and the desk. Furniture wasn't supposed to move, but so many unbelievable things had happened in the past twenty-four hours that she was too overloaded to care. What was fascinating however, was how Storm was that pale sickly green all the way to the tips of his pointed ears.

Ghortin looked around and finally caught what Jenna was looking at. "Oh, him. Pay him no heed; our friend will be back to his normal self once the desk stops fidgeting." He smiled as the desk gave a violent shudder that was mirrored by Storm.

"Does all furniture move around here?" She wasn't nearly as disturbed about it as Storm appeared to be. Sadly, a moving desk wasn't the biggest problem she had right now.

"Nope, this one is my own special desk." He beamed, and then shook his head. "Alas, the tales will have to wait. You're in pain, and I'm sensing strange things from you."

"I have no idea what either of you are saying, old man." Storm's voice sounded as strained as his face looked. "Could we please get on with this?" He smiled tightly at Jenna. She guessed his reasons were equally about getting himself away from the desk as well as easing her discomfort.

"Oh, do sit down; it's bad enough without your long-limbed fidgeting." He shook his head and went to sit on the desk. "Kelars."

Jenna caught the strange term, but then that odd memory that knew their language told her that it was what Storm's people were called.

With one last glance at the now stationary desk, Storm took the vacant chair.

"Now that we're all settled," Ghortin said from his perch atop the desk. "Maybe you could fill me in on things so that I can fix them?"

Storm frowned at both of them. "Wouldn't it be easier if we all understood each other? It's great that you can speak her language; however, I lack your skill." Storm's sour mood had made his handsome face even sharper than before.

Ghortin made a show of laboriously getting off the desk, then came and stood next to her. "He can be a bit much, even for a kelar, but I suppose he's right this time." Hands clasped behind his back, Ghortin circled her slowly, nodding occasionally in accordance with whatever was lurking in his head. Finally, he stopped and stroked his scruffy chin. "Let's see if you're going to be able to help me with this." He laid his hands on either side of her head and muttered unintelligible words as he closed his dark eyes.

A weak blue glow surrounded Jenna and a distant part of her mind began to wail in primitive fear. She pushed Ghortin's hands aside.

The wailing stopped as soon as contact with him was broken. The odd blue glow, however, flickered, but then held steady.

Ghortin stumbled and backed into Storm. "My, my." He rubbed his chin slowly again. "You have an amazingly strong, albeit latent, gift of Power. You could quite possibly become one of my most successful protégés. Except for one great mystery." He paused, waiting for dramatic effect. When neither nudged him, he went on with a shrug. "The problem is that our lovely friend seems to be suffering from a massive, instinctive level, negative magic reaction." At their blank looks, even Jenna's memory-echo didn't have a comment about that, he added, "You instinctively block magic from working through you. I'm sure we can find a way around it, however." He gave a low chuckle. "I've never heard of someone so strong or so sensitive without training. That low-level spell shouldn't have triggered anything at all."

"Can you speak Common now?" Storm stepped around Ghortin.

"Ah yes, my young, oh-so-uncurious friend, she speaks Common now." Ghortin stepped forward, blocking Storm and cutting him off. "Actually, my dear, you speak your own language in your head." He tapped the side of Jenna's still stunned head. "But it will come out in our language, or rather the most basic of our languages, Common. Quite an intriguing, yet simple spell. H'song first created it nigh on 2,000 years ago. It was then—"

Storm stepped around the now pacing Ghortin. "Please say something, anything."

"What should I say?" The words still sounded English to her.

"Thank the stars. Now we'll find out how you got in that ravine." Storm smiled.

A twinge came from her ankle. "Do you think you could put some more of that bane stuff on my leg? This is great with the blue light, and you being able to understand me now, but this hurts."

Ghortin flushed with embarrassment. "My dear lady, I did go off and forget that ill leg of yours, didn't I?" He bustled back to her side. "Oh, and you can drop the mage light you know, just relax and let it slide away." He waved Storm forward as he headed for the desk.

"Now, you oaf, carry her to the desk, I'll need more room."

Storm didn't argue as he lifted Jenna onto the desk, but he backed away afterwards with amazing swiftness.

The sight of someone his size, and with his collection of well-used weapons, being so cowed by a desk, albeit an odd one, was enough to take Jenna's mind off her pain.

"Why are you so terrified of this desk? I don't think I've ever seen one move around before, yet you don't see me going all pasty faced." Jenna gave the desk an affectionate pat.

Storm went from green to white to red as Ghortin stepped forward. "There is quite a good tale behind that. It all started when Storm here was just a skinny kelar child."

"Her leg needs to be looked at," Storm snapped. "And we have things to talk about."

"Of course we do. We have to hear this good lady's tale." Jenna thought she caught a shared frown between the two, but then Ghortin was all smiles. "First, how would you like to hear about young Storm and the desk?"

"Actually, I've still got dinner to bring in. I won't be long." Storm cut in as he headed for the previous location of the door. The outline flared as he stepped forward. He was out the now visible door before Jenna had a chance to speak.

Ghortin grinned as the door faded behind Storm. "I figured that would clear him out. Now, would you rather hear about my illustrious life or Master Storm's fear of the bewitching desk?"

As he spoke, Ghortin lifted her injured leg. Jenna didn't feel any pain and wondered if he had numbed it at some point when she wasn't looking. With a quick movement he lifted her off the desk and lowered her feet to the floor. She gasped when the ankle held without pain.

"How?" She tapped forward with the formerly injured leg; there were no twinges, no stabs of pain. "This is amazing. Wasn't it broken? How did you do that?"

"All in a day's work." His smile was so smug Jenna was certain he often found use for it. "Now, how do you feel?"

"My leg feels great. But my head is another thing." She paused, unsure of how exactly to explain the weirdness that had been flitting through her head since she woke up in that ravine.

Ghortin frowned as he tilted her head around, looking for any external wounds. "You damaged your head? Something should have been said earlier."

"I didn't hurt it." She took a step back. "Well, maybe I did. I honestly don't know. It's like I have two sets of memories."

"Two?" He helped her back up on the desk. "Why, lass, even I only have one, and I've lived for quite a long time, let me tell you."

"I'm not explaining it right." She chewed her lip. She couldn't explain it to herself, so how could she explain it to someone else? "Okay, just now, when you fixed my ankle. I know you couldn't have done it. It was broken, and I know, unfortunately, how long it takes to fix a broken bone. And I know magic is impossible. At the same time, something in my head wasn't worried. It accepts that magic exists just as easily as I accept that credit cards exist. It knows you fixed my leg with a spell."

The mage laughed. "Of course magic is possible. You carry a great potential for it." He paused. "Do you mean to say that some strange force is making you disbelieve in magic?"

"I don't know how else to explain it." Jenna looked around for some sort of visual aid, but found nothing. "The other voice is the part that believes in magic. And kelars. That part isn't me. It shouldn't be here."

"No kelars either, eh? I'd say someone put a monster of a spell on you, except there's something else that I just can't pin down." His eyes lost focus for a moment, and then snapped back.

"No good, your magic block hinders my search." He pulled one of the chairs closer and sat down. "Why don't you tell me everything? Start with the non-magic memories, then move on to the other voice? Echo?"

Jenna nodded, that was a good description. As if someone had left messages for her in her head, but it was supposed to be her voice. "My name is Jenna Reilly; I'm

27 years old…" She paused, something was coming back, something important, but it stayed just out of reach. "I know that there's no such thing as magic and that Storm can't be what he seems to be."

The safe cocoon that had been soothing her fears of not belonging in this place was fading. "I know I've never seen this dress in my life and I can't imagine picking it out, let alone wearing it with a pair of jeans. And my hair is odd too. I haven't seen all of it yet, but it looks way too long; it was only to my shoulders. But now?" She waggled the end that clearly went five or six inches past her shoulders. "My hands and arms look wrong, and my body feels odd, but I can't describe it. And my eyes are gray."

"I can't say anything about the rest of what you've said, but I'll agree with you there." There was confusion in Ghortin's dark eyes, but curiosity was rapidly winning out.

"Storm said they were brown when he found me."

"That is odd." He peered closely into her eyes, "I can't say I've ever heard of eye color changing on a whim."

"I feel mismatched." There was no other way to say it.

Ghortin took out a quill and paper from the desk. "Now what about the second voice? The one that accepts magic is real?" He shuffled his papers around, muttering about his missing inkwell. After a moment he sighed and reluctantly placed the quill back on the desk.

"It's not exactly a voice. It's more as if I recognize things, things that I know I've never seen before. As if someone left their memories in my head but kept most of the details to themselves."

The blood drained from Ghortin's face. "Mindslaves."

The word meant nothing to Jenna, but her strange mental echo recognized it. It didn't clarify the term, but it chilled her blood.

"Like that. The echo, or whatever it is, recognized that

word. But I have no idea what they are."

"Victims of the worshippers of Qhazborh." He wet his lips. "Their minds are slowly sacrificed to give Power to their god, then to his priests and priestesses. However, if you're here you can't be a mindslave. You would be dead, not running around the countryside. Besides, the followers of Qhazborh have faded into small pockets of disgruntled hermits; even their most devout don't follow the old codes anymore." He patted her hand and tried to smile. "I'm sorry if I frightened you."

Jenna shook her head as more of her thoughts became clear. "I know I'm not a mindslave, whatever that is. I'm from Los Angeles." She gave a feeble laugh. "Although, from what they sound like, there are those who would debate the difference."

"What?" Ghortin pulled himself out from wherever his mind had wandered to and turned back to her. "You're from Losangeles, rather odd name for a town, don't you think? Was it named after someone famous?" He held up a hand. "Never mind. Although I do think that I have a dissertation on the followers of Qhazborh around here somewhere." He scurried over to the other end of the library.

"Ah-ha." He raised a thin red book high in the air, ignoring the shower of dust he got in the process. "It's been quite some time since I've been able to find, er, that is, since I've needed this particular book."

He nudged her over to one side of the desk. "Come, come, there's room enough for both of us atop this mammoth."

"I'm sure this is extremely interesting," Jenna said with growing discomfort, "but how is this going to help me figure out where I am or what happened to me?" The soothing feelings of recognition she'd had were almost completely gone now. Reality was setting in, and it wasn't looking pretty.

Ghortin finally forced himself to look up from his book. "My dear, you are in my forest, which is located two days' ride outside of the city of Lithunane, the capital of the kingdom of Traanafaeren. I'm certain that with time we'll be able to reverse the mind draining, if that's what it was, and get your sweet little head back in order. However, I don't believe that I've heard of your hometown. Is it in Traanafaeren?"

Jenna slammed his book shut. "Look, I'm not a mindslave. I'm from California, in the United States of America, on the planet Earth, which I am now damn sure is nowhere near Tranafar-whatever." She was shaking and couldn't stop. "I'm not from here!"

As she shouted the words, the enormity of what she said hit her like a slap in the face. She was in another world. Either that or this was a delusion. No, it wasn't a delusion, it was far too real. How in the hell had this happened? *What* in the hell had happened? Her breath started coming in short bursts as panic and terror slammed into her mind.

"Oh my god," her voice dropped, but the shaking grew worse. "I'm *not* from here."

"My dear?" There was worry in Ghortin's eyes, and he took her hand gently, patting it like one would a small child. "Maybe I can help. Planet Earth? United States? If you could just give me something tangible to go on—"

"Eight planets. There are eight planets in our solar system, or nine…never really happy they took Pluto away." She wasn't sure why she cut him off with that bit of information, but he'd wanted something more to go on. Besides, her brain didn't seem to be working right.

"Eight or nine, you say?" Ghortin kept rubbing her hand, clearly worried about her. Actually, judging by his expression, Jenna figured she must look raving mad. With a faint smile, Ghortin continued. "I've only counted six myself; mayhap your people have better equipment. How many moons do you have?"

"One, of course."

"There we have it." Ghortin jumped off the desk. "You *are* from another world. You see, we have two moons."

As he spoke he conjured up an image of the outside against the wall with the invisible door. The sun was giving way to a pair of bright golden moons. Moons that she'd missed seeing in the dense forest last night.

"We're not in Kansas anymore, Toto." The view of moons cinched what her mind had been telling her for the last ten minutes. She fought to keep from hyperventilating.

"Kansas? Is that another land you're from?"

"No." She rubbed the side of her face, jerking back when she hit some of the too long hair flowing over her shoulders. "It's just a saying where I come from. This couldn't all just be a dream, could it?"

"I assure you," Ghortin puffed up his considerable chest. "I am not a dream. A nightmare to some perhaps, but that is another matter entirely. Somehow, you managed to leave your homeland and come to ours." How he was so calm stating that horrific fact, she had no idea.

Jenna liked an orderly life, anxiety attacks had been a part of her life until she realized that keeping life slow and steady made them go away. This was too far away from slow and steady to even contemplate. "I'm in a strange land, with strange pointy-eared elf men, magic, a bunch of memories that aren't mine, a body that doesn't seem to be all mine, and you tell me that I'm not dreaming?" She forced her breath to slow down again.

"Easy, lass." He rubbed her shoulders. "Never fret, you've got a strong supporter in young Storm. Even if he is—" He pulled back and tilted his head. "What was it you called him? An elf man? And what of myself? You happen to be in the care of one of the foremost mages in the known world, I'll have you know."

Jenna sat there until the shaking faded and the feeling of loss worked its way out of her system. Rather, she was able to shove it into some dark corner to be dealt with later. Eventually she felt more like herself, or at least like the self she had been for the past day. "I'm sorry; this is all so strange." Which was the understatement of the decade, but about as good as she could do right then.

At some point Storm returned, but he silently hovered at the edge of the room.

"Never mind, my dear; you've obviously had a great trauma. We'll make sure that you find your way in this world, never you fear." Ghortin motioned Storm forward.

Jenna noticed that Storm's eyes widened at that comment, but Ghortin shook him off with a quick frown.

"But what will I do?" Jenna laughed weakly, thinking about the primitive equipment Storm had been using. "I don't have any job skills for this world." Which was true for her own world in a way. She collected college degrees the way some women collected shoes, but she still hadn't found a career she could live with.

"No skills?" Ghortin held her out far enough to get a clear look into her eyes. "My dear, you jest. Your mage potential is quite high, surely you knew that?"

"How could I know something like that when there's no magic where I come from?"

"Now then, I didn't realize your entire world was without magic. However do your people live?" Ghortin shuddered. "That's a tale for later, I believe. Magic-less though your world may be, you are a virtual well of Power; untrained of course, but it's there. The only sensible thing to do is for you to become my apprentice. You're a bit older than most, but I do seem to be without one at the moment."

Jenna opened her mouth to argue, and then shut it. What else could she do? Tendrils of panic worked through her mind. Strange world, no skills, and no way to survive? If Ghortin was willing to help her find a way to survive here until she could find a way back home, she had to be willing to take it.

Ghortin took her silence for agreement and propelled her toward the door. "First, I think you need rest. We'll bunk you down and see if some sleep doesn't sort out that head of yours."

"Thank you." A yawn hit her hard. Must be the changing world thing, bound to tire a person out. She was happy that Ghortin appeared to believe her story. She wasn't sure if she believed it herself, but it was nice that someone did. "Do you have any idea what is causing this weird echo in my head?"

"Alas, I'm afraid that I don't. Not as of yet anyway." Ghortin held up a dusty book. "But with these we shall find the answers, I assure you. As well as solve the mystery of your arrival here."

"Do you think we might be able to send me back?" She hadn't intended to ask that, the answer could shatter her current control over the panic.

"Ah, child, I honestly don't know. I can promise that we shall try." He nodded toward Storm. "Now come along, we must find a suitable room for you." He led the way down the hall.

Ghortin stopped in front of a doorway that wasn't there a minute before, then motioned for her to go in.

Jenna sat down on the small cot that took up most of the unremarkable room. Actually, it could have been the most remarkable room in the world; she was too tired to care. She just meant to rest for a bit, but quickly fell asleep.

———◆———

"Now that she's gotten herself settled, what say we go back out to the front room?" Ghortin didn't wait, and briskly walked down the hall.

"Settled?" Storm shook his head. "She was out as soon as she lay down. And of course you had nothing to do with it."

"Just a slight nudge, she was exhausted." Ghortin turned back with a grimace; there were far too many questions about this woman. "Which wasn't easy with that damn block in place. We'll have to work on that immediately, or we'll never get anywhere."

They continued down the hall toward the vortex, and Storm's sigh of relief at exiting the vortex was more audible than usual. Ghortin was glad he moved to get Storm out of the displaced area and on this side of the vortex quickly; his friend had never liked the undefined space beyond the vortex, but this time there was more than that going on.

One of Ghortin's first accomplishments as a master-mage had been to create his home at the mouth of a displacement vortex. The things were rare and infinite, folding into themselves in a way that even Ghortin couldn't explain. They were also notoriously unstable, which accounted in part for the lack of information about them. Ghortin had been the first, and the only, mage to successfully control one.

"How about some Stoutworth?" Ghortin tried to keep his voice light as he headed to the kitchen to grab the ale, but the tightening in Storm's face as he turned away showed that it had been a wasted effort. Stoutworth was too high-end to be had on a regular basis.

"That bad?" Storm asked from the parlor. "Is she mad or simply bewitched?"

Ghortin debated grabbing an ale of lesser quality and trying to play it down, but it was too late. Might as well make themselves happier with good ale.

He waited until Storm had his first sip before responding. "What would you say if I told you she's neither? That she does hail from another world entirely?"

Storm studied him for a moment; then finally he broke into a grin. "I'd say that one of you has been tipping a bit too much drink. How could she say that? I don't know about the odd leggings or boots, but that dress could come off any peasant in the field. Or do they have the same clothes there too?"

"I'm not sure about the clothes, and I'm afraid that she's not either." He studied Storm over the rim of his mug. "There are a lot of things she's not sure about."

"Her eyes." Storm shuddered.

"Ah yes, she said something about you mentioning them," Ghortin said. "There seems to be a fair bit that we don't know yet, but I believe she doesn't come from around here. I slipped in a truth spell along with the language one, and she didn't trip it once."

"How can someone be from another world? Or is she from one of the stars we see at night? Did she drift down to visit?" Storm waved a finger at Ghortin. "And if she was bewitched, wouldn't she believe her story well enough that she wouldn't trigger a truth spell?"

"I'll agree it's farfetched." Ghortin rose to his feet and began his customary pacing. His mind always worked better when he was moving. "Even bewitched she should have triggered some sort of response from the spell. Another issue, however, is her magic. If we believe her, and I do, she claims her land has no magic. Yet she has it in raw abundance. But untrained, totally untrained." He ruffled his scruffy beard in thought. "And she has the oddest drain on it, almost constant, yet I see no source."

"In what manner?" Storm leaned forward. "Not that I'm saying I believe you or anything."

Ghortin gave a rude snort. "Of course not." His pacing picked up speed. "The drain's an odd one, that's for certain. Appears to have almost a constant tap on her, as if she's magically pulling something or something is pulling on her. It's obvious she has no training at all or she would have stopped the Power loss immediately." Ghortin froze mid-stride. "When did her eyes change?"

"Last night or early this morning. Is it important?"

Ghortin resumed pacing. "It might be. Something's there, that's for certain. Let me think this through. What if her world is adjacent to ours?" At Storm's snort of disbelief he waved his hand and continued. "Not physically, but sort of shifted away from us. Close enough to cross over, but far enough to make it practically impossible."

"Even if such a thing were possible, why would anyone want to come over?" Storm laughed. "Wait, let me guess, she's the invasion force?"

"No, no, no." Ghortin's scowl jutted his chin forward. "Give me a moment. Once we tuned that odd echo out of her head she knew she'd never seen a kelar before, called you an elf or some such thing, and then said you didn't exist. What if her people don't look like ours at all? What if only her mind came through and somehow she's changing that body to whatever she was in her world?" He froze and spun, opening the vortex with a thought an instant before he charged into it. "Which may or may not be something we are ready to deal with. We need to see her. Now."

Storm was right behind him as he ran through the vortex. "Why the hurry? I don't think she's going to become a monster overnight."

Ghortin picked up his pace. "Think about it, my obstinate young friend; most body replenishments take place when the body sleeps.

Chapter Four

STORM PASSED GHORTIN AS THEY entered the vortex and got to the room a second before Ghortin did. Jenna was still in bed, but she wasn't sleeping well. Storm swore her flesh was twisting under the sheet, but he hoped it was just his imagination. "Ghortin, what in the eight hells is she?"

"Isn't this amazing?" Ghortin seemed far from worried; in fact, he appeared enthralled. "It's as if two bodies are fighting for the same space."

Storm grabbed Ghortin's arm as he turned to go closer. "What if there were two? What if the only way for her to come to our world was to take over another body? That echo in her head may be the remains of the murdered victim."

Ghortin removed Storm's hand from his arm, and then joined Jenna. "I don't believe for one minute that this poor lass is evil. And neither do you. However, there could be a grain of truth in your words nonetheless. Wake her up."

Storm shook his head and went to the other side of Jenna's bed. Arguing with Ghortin was pointless. The mage always won and Storm ended up with a headache. With a sigh, he sat down next to Jenna.

She didn't show the slightest sign of waking up until Storm shook her hard enough to almost drag her off the bed.

Unfortunately, she'd woken up before her memory did. Storm grabbed her hands after her first few strikes, but he couldn't do anything about her screaming.

"Would you do something?" Storm glared at Ghortin as the mage continued to watch. "I can't hold her like this forever."

Ghortin snorted. "Big, strong, kelar huntsman can't hang on to a simple thing like an apprentice. What are we coming to?" He gently reached down and took one of Jenna's fists from Storm's hand.

"It's all right, Jenna. Remember us?" He sat down on the edge of the bed, smoothing back her hair with his free hand. "Storm rescued you and I fixed that nasty broken ankle of yours?"

Jenna stopped yelling and warily glanced from one to the other. She finally shook her head. "Oh god," She freed her hands with a sheepish grin. "I'm sorry; I thought I was back home. I couldn't figure out what Storm was."

"Didn't like being awakened by an elf?" Storm was glad she'd finally realized who he was; he was going to end up with a bruise or two from her flailing fists. She was a lot stronger than she looked.

"Ghortin told you." She shook her head. "Actually, that was making the problem worse, because elves don't exist. Nor do kelars or mages." She gasped, clutched her head, and then collapsed next to Storm.

"What is it?" Ghortin pulled her back up into a sitting position with Storm's help. "What's happening? If you can tell us, we might be able to help."

"My head hurts." Her voice was little more than a whisper. "I can't see." Her eyes rolled back into her head.

Storm held her up with care. "What's happened?"

"I'm not sure what it was, but there was a flash of Power just a moment ago." Ghortin closed his eyes and gently laid his hands on Jenna's head. He opened them with a start. "She's dying."

"How? She was just talking to us." Storm stopped short of shaking her again, but he needed to do something.

The color drained from her face as he watched.

"I know, I know." Ghortin stood up and moved to the side of the bed. "Something is pulling her, draining her life as well as her Power. And I can't stop it." Ghortin's hands were a whirl as he formed spell after spell, none of them having any obvious effect that Storm could see. Her life was simply flowing away in front of them.

Minutes later, Jenna's heart stopped. Then it came back with a vengeance, and she pulled away screaming.

Fortunately, there was precious little air in her lungs so the scream was short. She looked toward Ghortin with red-rimmed eyes, fighting for breath.

"I was there. Home." She sat up in her bed and turned back toward Storm. "It wasn't a dream, I was in a morgue. Or what was left of me was." A shudder raced through her. "Cold. Broken. Dead." She collapsed.

Ghortin's gaze was fixed a foot over her head at a blank spot on the wall. "Hold her still. Make her pay attention to you—to this world. Do whatever you need to, but don't let her slip away again."

He didn't wait for Storm's acknowledgement before he shut his eyes and locked into a spell-trance. Storm shook Jenna gently, not wanting to hurt her, but all he got was more whimpering. Then she started shaking. Panicking, he tried to think of what else he could do. He tried shaking her, then slapping her lightly, then a bit harder. Since that failed to get her attention, and he didn't want to hurt her, he did the only other thing he could think of to get a response. He kissed her. Hard.

Her eyes popped open and she pulled away with a sudden alertness and surprising strength. "Of all the egotistical male things. Either slap a woman or kiss her; and you think that just because you're so damn pretty that any woman would want you." Her fist connected sharply with Storm's mid-section.

Storm pulled back as the air was forced from his lungs.

Jenna clutched her head and collapsed back to her pillow. He was just about to try shaking her again when Ghortin came out of his trace.

"Excellent job, my boy." Ghortin looked a bit frazzled, but he was smiling. "You tied her attention to this world extremely well. She's unconscious, but she won't be pulled back to her broken body again. See here, what have you done? You look for all the world as if you've been struck."

Storm grimaced. "She hit me. You said to keep her attention here and she kept slipping away. Shaking didn't work, so I kissed her." He scowled as Ghortin's eyes lit up in glee. He knew Ghortin wasn't going to let this go, not for a good while at any rate. "It worked, didn't it?"

"I'll most certainly grant you that."

"I assume from your smug face that everything is fixed now?"

The mirth faded from Ghortin's eyes. "I managed to end the drain on her life. She was causing it herself."

"She was trying to kill herself?" Storm studied the unconscious woman still in his arms. She certainly seemed like she had been fighting for her life.

"Not really, more like she was unconsciously trying to fix herself. Somehow, and I have no idea how so don't ask, part of Jenna came to our world, the rest of her however…" Ghortin shivered. "The rest of her didn't make it. The first time she slipped away from us she actually made it back to her world. If her body had been whole on that end, that would have been the end of the story. We would have lost her, but she'd be back in her home world now."

"I take it from the way she reacted that it wasn't?"

"No. Her world is strange, but I recognize a destroyed body when I see one. And there wasn't much of this one left to see."

"Oh gods." Storm brushed back Jenna's hair, her face wasn't relaxing in sleep. "No wonder she was screaming.

Is she going to be all right now?"

Ghortin helped Storm tuck Jenna under the covers. "I wish I knew. She'll no longer have the tie to her world that she had. I'd say we'll see no more physical changes."

Storm silently studied her. He didn't want to ask this question, but they needed the answer. "What happened to the original owner of this body? Before Jenna started changing things."

Ghortin resumed his traditional pacing, although it took an almost comical turn because of the small size of the room. "That is yet another problem, I fear. After going into her mind, I was directly exposed to that voice she hears—that echo. It is real. Sad to say, the body that Jenna was drawn into belonged to a newly made mindslave and a wildly magically strong one at that. Qhazborh's priests are back."

Storm slammed his fist on the mattress. "Damn it. I told Resstlin weeks ago that they had to be behind some of the problems we've been seeing lately. The bastard wouldn't send out anyone to check." Even at seventy years old, Storm was still a young man by the standards of long-lived kelars. Still, his family, or certain members rather, had no excuse for treating him like a wayward child. That was one of the reasons he spent as little time as possible at home.

Storm ran his fingers through his hair, and then sighed in surrender. "Will you get the word to them? Obviously nothing will happen if I do it, they don't take me seriously."

Ghortin patted his shoulder. "Sad to agree, but you're right. I'll get word to one of them. However, no one should be informed of Jenna's true nature. With all of the other nastiness of late, I don't want to throw in a woman from another world." He frowned in thought. "We'll say she's from one of the outlying villages near the Strann border. As my apprentice, they shouldn't look much past that story." That settled, he turned his frown on Storm. "And I believe we agreed that you would spend more time with your family?"

"No, you agreed. I sat there. However, you made some good points and I do intend to spend time with them." Too many things had been happening lately, deadly things. And making peace with his family wasn't a priority at the moment, no matter how important Ghortin felt it was. "Unfortunately, I had a pressing reason to be out this time, and a good one." He glanced from Jenna to Ghortin. "Is she going to be okay? Because I think it would be better if we talked about this somewhere else."

Ghortin hadn't missed the haggard lines that crossed Storm's face. But he had learned long ago that it was best to let Storm talk when he was ready. With a check on Jenna's pulse, he nodded toward the door. "She should be fine. I've set up a ward, and if she has any problems the spell will alert me."

Upon entering the parlor, Storm went straight to the couch and dropped down, his elbows on his knees, his head in his hands.

"Oklan is gone." His words dropped like stones and Ghortin felt the bottled rage behind them. "And his entire village with him."

Ghortin dropped to a chair. The past year had turned into a conglomeration of violent disasters. None large enough to point to any one person or group, but something bad was definitely growing. Brutish creatures, some no more than ancient myths, appearing with horrific consequences before vanishing again; the only proof of their visits, the dead bodies in their wake. Homesteaders from outlying areas disappearing. So far nothing as large as an entire village destroyed; or, he thought grimly, the appearance of a woman from another world whose real body was in shreds.

"Tell me exactly what you saw." When Storm rubbed shaking hands over his eyes, Ghortin realized how exhausted his friend was. Storm's stamina was exceptional, even for one of his race; it was rare that he was brought so low.

"I went out five days ago on the trail of those strange spiked dog creatures that have been reported out that way. I thought maybe Oklan or one of his wives might have heard something about them." Storm's gaze was fixed on a thinning spot on one of the bright rugs that covered the floor. "There were no sentries at all, which was bad, since they'd been doubling them since Goklin's lambs were killed. I went into the village slowly, but it was too late, far too late. They were all gone." He finally raised his eyes. "Ghortin, there's nothing left of that village but a burnt crater and rubble."

Ghortin sucked in his breath; that village held over two hundred souls. "Maybe they got out." The look on Storm's haunted face told him his answer.

"There were pieces." Storm swallowed quickly. "As I scouted the perimeter, I found shredded remains of the huts, livestock, and the villagers. Whatever did that hit them quickly and with a force beyond reckoning." He shook his head. "*I* sensed residue."

Ghortin swore under his breath. Storm was magic numb, he had not even the tiniest shred of magic sensitivity and never would. Someone or something had used a massive amount of magic in wiping out the village and hadn't bothered to shield it. Or there was someone with that kind of Power and the inability to shield it. He wasn't sure which was worse. His mind briefly went to Jenna. She possibly had more raw Power than he'd seen in decades. Could she have inadvertently destroyed the village upon her arrival?

Annoyed with himself for thinking it, Ghortin pulled

free his map from the ledge it had been hiding on. "Where exactly did you find Jenna?"

"Past the west side of the forest, in that ravine off the main trail." He shook his head as he pointed to the spot. "You don't think that Jenna—"

"No." Ghortin cut him off. That was exactly what he was thinking, but he didn't want Storm to be thinking it. Not yet anyway. There had been a time when all of Ghortin's intuitions held true. Unfortunately, those days were gone. He'd say nothing until he was positive. If the woman was innocent, she deserved a chance here.

"I was curious if she saw anything. She hasn't been able to remember anything of this place prior to you finding her. Maybe when she wakes up she'll have more of her memories intact."

Ghortin mentally measured off the distance between the village and where Jenna had been found. It was possible that she had accidentally destroyed Oklan's village with her arrival; although what a mindslave, and a newly made one at that, would be doing in the distant reaches, he had no idea. But the distance was daunting, it would have been a long steady jog for Storm, and he was a fully trained woodsman.

"There's nothing to be done for it, I'll have to head out there tomorrow." Running his hand through his hair, he swore when it got stuck on a myriad of knots that he didn't recall having. Damn elementals, they must have ransacked his hair while he wasn't paying attention. "However, I'm certain the Power signature will have become too diluted by then. Can you stay with Jenna while I go down there? I can't transport over, I don't want to disrupt anything." Not to mention heavier spells, such as transports, had been draining him oddly as of late, as if there was something wrong with the force of chaos from which all magical energy came. He'd spent his whole life with almost unlimited magical abilities; the fact that something or someone seemed to be limiting him was terrifying. Not that he would let anyone, even Storm, know that.

"I think it's the least I can do, being as I brought her here. Besides, you know home, they're more used to me being gone than being around." Storm interrupted himself with a huge yawn. "If you don't mind?" He nodded toward the short hall that led to the two non-vortex bedrooms in the cottage.

Ghortin's mind was already filled with the spells needed to retrace what had happened to the unfortunate village. "No, not at all. You've done more than enough to warrant a good night's rest." He waved Storm off, but the exhausted kelar was already gone.

Ghortin drained the last of his ale, still lost in thought. Things were changing too fast, but he'd told no one how serious he feared it might become. Partially because he was wary to start a panic, and partially because he was loathe to admit his inability to track down the cause. It was as if bits and pieces of the world were going wrong, slowly enough for most people not to notice. And unless he started putting the pieces together quickly, by the time the rest of the world figured things out it would be too late.

CHAPTER FIVE

ENNA WOKE SLOWLY, WHICH, WITH all things considered, was probably the most normal thing about the entire situation. As she stretched and snuggled under the warm blankets, bits and pieces of the events of the previous two days trickled through her mind. She'd always told her mom she wanted to explore a real unknown culture, something not examined to death by a million anthropologists. Guess Mom was right when she always said to be careful what you wish for. A stab of pain and sorrow went through Jenna as she thought of her family. If the timelines of the two worlds were in sync, then today her parents and older brother would be making her funeral arrangements.

The images of going back to her former body were vague and terrifying, but it had been clear that there was nothing left of her back there. She shut her eyes and let herself grieve. If she could find a way back, she would. This body was hers now. She'd do no one any good crying about her lost life. That Reilly pragmatism finally rose to the surface. She was here now, and finding a way to survive in this strange world was going to be difficult enough without worrying about what she had lost. She took a deep calming breath and bid her family, friends, and former home a silent good-bye.

Time to face her new world. She wiped away her tears and really looked around. The room was small, but the warm tan walls and undefined ceiling made it seem cozy instead of cramped. The ceiling matched the strange hall they'd come down, so she was still in the vortex. A simple desk and chair stood next to the cot, but unlike the library furniture, neither of them looked to be animated. At least they didn't respond when she said hello. All in all, it seemed to fit the bill of student quarters.

She hadn't seen anything that looked like a closet on her first visual inspection. Upon standing up, she remembered the elementals that Ghortin had used to call open the library door. Or maybe they *were* the door, it wasn't clear.

"Hello?" It was kind of silly talking to the air, but no more so than trying to talk to the desk or chair. "I'd like a door to my closet, or wherever the clothes will go." An open door against the far wall led to a bathroom, but a bath wouldn't be good if she had to put these filthy clothes back on. Hopefully a former student left a robe or something.

A faint collection of lines formed on the wall near her. As she approached, the outline of a small door came into focus. She gently pushed it to one side.

"Uh, thank you." She wasn't sure if it was appropriate to thank an elemental, but she figured she'd thank everything until she knew which things understood her. She couldn't be sure, but it seemed that the door's outline briefly glowed brighter.

Either the former student had been exactly her size, or Ghortin knew how to use his magic to size clothing just from looking at someone. The small closet was filled with clothes similar to what Storm wore, but in her size. A collection of new undergarments were in a small chest inside the closet. It took her a moment to figure out this world's version of a bra, but after a few twists she thought she could make it work. She took out dark gray leggings, a loose blue tunic, and soft black boots that hit mid-calf. She'd bathed and finished dressing when Storm knocked at her door.

"All ready for your first day in Ghortin's house of wonders?" Storm was clearly one of those wicked souls who was not only used to being awake at the crack of dawn, but was cheerful about it. He also managed to look even better than he had yesterday. His long hair was combed back, and, while still rustic, his deep blue shirt made his eyes more dramatic than they already were. "How does everything fit? I told Ghortin he should wait for you to wake before trying to do the sizing."

"They're not too far off," she said, still fiddling with the belt. She finally figured out how to wrap it without a buckle. "Not as far off as my stomach is right now. Do apprentices get fed in this deal?"

"Definitely. As Ghortin would say, you're of no use if you keel over." He led the way out the door. "I took the liberty of coming to get you this morning. Getting in and out of this warren Ghortin's created can be a bit difficult, even once you know it. But you should probably learn it quickly. No doubt Ghortin will let you fend for yourself when he gets back."

"Where did he go? Is it something to do with me?" She wasn't exactly certain of all that had happened last night. So much of it seemed like a dream. Most of it she wished was a dream.

"Actually, he's off running some mage errands. There was an emergency in a village a few days from here," Storm said. "I don't keep up on magic issues."

Was that bitterness Jenna detected? She couldn't be sure. Storm was smiling as he spoke, but there was a brief tightening around his mouth. She had been planning to ask him some of her questions concerning magic in this world, but maybe it would be better if she saved them for Ghortin.

They only took one wrong turn on their trip out, as Storm hit a dead end that whirled gently before them. Cursing softly to himself, he backtracked and finally got them out of the vortex and into the cottage proper.

Jenna smiled as she smelled what could only be this world's equivalent of bacon and eggs. She wasn't sure if she would recognize the animals they came from, but at this point she didn't care.

They walked through the parlor portion of the cottage, then into a small kitchen and waiting breakfast table.

"I can't believe how hungry I am." Jenna held herself back from running to the waiting food. But it was almost impossible.

"Ghortin is often hungry after over-using his magic." Storm motioned for her to sit at the small table. "After all that went on yesterday, I had a feeling you might be in a similar state."

She flashed him what she hoped looked like a grateful smile, then attacked her food. Maybe that was it—the whole magic thing was making her eat like a mad woman. She hoped so; she doubted this place had a weight loss program. Once she'd taken the edge off, she looked up to find Storm looking at her with what could only be admiration. Although her mouth was full, she managed to convey her question with a tilt of her head.

"Forgive me for staring. It's simply nice to see someone who will actually eat their food instead of daintily playing with it."

Jenna swallowed and shrugged. "I'm afraid I've never been one for false social modesties. I suppose I'll have trouble fitting in here." Although she figured that was probably the least of her worries.

"I don't think so," he said quickly. "Really it's only a small portion of the population that subscribe to them. For the most part Traanafaeren is full of honest people."

She couldn't help but pick up what he thought of the others. She decided to sidestep it for the moment.

"How big is Trana…how do you say it again?" The long middle was throwing her off.

"Trah-ah-n-ah-fair-ren," he said the name slowly. "Our kingdom is not quite as big as Khelaran, but larger than—" He caught her look and shrugged. "Sorry, you wouldn't know how big those are either. It takes forty days to ride from Lithunane to Irundail." He shrugged again. "They're the two major cities and they lie near opposite ends of the land. Widow's Rock is at the actual end, and it's a full day's ride past Lithunane."

Jenna nodded. Of course she had no idea of how many miles one could go a day on horseback. And somehow she didn't think he would be able to convert days to miles for her.

"I can't show you the entire land, but there is a vantage point in the forest that gives you a good sense of this area," Storm said. "I can take you when you're finished."

Jenna finally pushed away her plate. "We can go now if you'd like. I'm afraid I'm stuffed."

"Ah, then I have succeeded in my first task." He produced an elaborate bow. "Mayhap Master Ghortin will let me stay."

"I thought you lived here. Ghortin doesn't live out here all alone, does he?"

Storm turned as they went through the living room. "Alas, no, I don't live here regularly. I live in Lithunane, near my family. I've been trying to break free, but they won't have it."

He smiled when the sun hit his face as they got outside, and Jenna was struck again at how almost beautiful he was. Being stuck in a strange world with a stunningly good-looking man had to count for something. The day was warm and sunny with a hint of the coming autumn in the air. He motioned to the trees beyond the cottage's grove as they walked toward them. "Ghortin's forest is unique, to say the least. I'd wager there are some things living here that even he doesn't know about. He made quite a mess here when he set up that vortex. All sorts of things started coming out of it."

"What kinds of things?" Jenna froze. Had the fanged creatures from her waking nightmares come from this forest?

"Nothing dangerous, at least not anymore." He flashed her a soothing, if still alien, smile. "Huntsmen from leagues around came to prove themselves in his fabulous forest of dangers. Within a dozen years or so they'd killed or chased off all of the worst creatures."

They walked across the small clearing that surrounded Ghortin's cottage and into the forest. The double band of white barked trees were more striking than before. They also seemed to be a dividing line between the dark woods and the mage's cheery clearing. She said so to Storm.

"Good eye." He nodded. "They're more than just a dividing line though. Those trees were originally planted as a barrier against the local inhabitants of the forest after Ghortin's little creation. They're called Bakkera and they're rare. They act as magic reflectors and are almost impossible to break once they've been planted and set." He looked up at the closest silver-lavender leafed beauty as they walked beneath it. "Ghortin had a feeling that he might need them when he settled here. He doesn't sense them the way kelars do, but these trees have great souls."

Jenna inspected one leaf carefully. It was long and slender with a shiny lavender-tinged underside. But she'd have to take his word for the soul part. "So, where are we going now?"

"Not far." He paused, deciding between two pine needle-strewn trails. "The path to the vantage point has a few routes to get there, but I'll stick with the fastest."

They carefully pushed past a small clump of brush. The trail was wider here, but she was certain she wouldn't have seen it without Storm's help. This part of the forest seemed to have more old growth trees and was darker than where they'd entered.

"Just how messed up did things get around here when Ghortin created that tunnel thing?" Now that she'd let the thought creep in, the shadows had taken on a dangerous glint.

"From what I hear things were pretty bad," he said. "Not that Ghortin will admit to much these days. But the tales are still passed down of the tortured souls who tried to pass through this forest in those earliest days, and what they became. Many say they didn't die, but became part of the forest itself."

"He was letting those hunters kill *people*?"

Storm laughed. "No, even Ghortin wouldn't go that far." He turned back and shook his head. "Don't worry; they're only stories, exaggerated for effect. Besides, it all happened long ago. Any truth to those tales has long since died of old age. Come on, I think we should see the—"

He froze, staring deep into the forest. His stop was so sudden that Jenna bumped into his back. She tried seeing where he was looking, but she couldn't make out anything but more trees.

"What is it?" She lightly shook his arm. "Are you doing this to scare me? Because if you are—"

He turned and put one long finger over her mouth. "Listen," he whispered, still intently scanning the forest.

She strained to hear, but had no idea what she was listening for. "For what? I don't hear anything." She lowered her voice.

"That's what I mean." He studied the trees around them carefully. "No birds. There should be something. Anything."

"Maybe it's because of us?" It sounded feeble, even to her. A forest this size should be humming with animal and bird life. And up until a few seconds ago, it had been.

Storm studied her for a moment to make sure she wasn't going to panic. When it looked like she was calm, he nodded and led them both down a smaller side trail. Whatever was out here, it seemed to have moved to the right of them, blocking the path to the vantage point. Clearly, more than one animal or person was out there, and something was also behind them. They'd have to go further into the forest, and then go around it before they could go back to the cottage. Storm wasn't going to risk Jenna if it turned out to be something big. The hunting knife he carried wouldn't do much good against anything large. A year ago he would have shrugged it off as a bear or some other large animal out roaming. Too many strange things had been happening for him to shrug off anything at this point. Up to and including the slender woman following him.

Jenna stayed silent once she realized something was wrong. He was grateful that she followed his lead and didn't ask any more questions, nor break out in hysterics. He did notice she kept closer to him than she had before, however.

The forest stayed silent as they slowly tread their way toward a small series of caves. They weren't deep, nor far from the cottage, but they had some unique formations in them.

They were also easy to block from the inside if need be. Many an ancient hunter had saved his skin, if not his pride, by hiding in the Stone Angel caves. If they couldn't get around whatever was menacing the forest, Storm wanted someplace safe to hole up in. He briefly chanced a thought about Ghortin's earlier direction; the mage would have gone out the other side of the forest, but who could tell how far this danger stretched?

Jenna sneezed, frantically covering her mouth after the fact. She shrugged in silent apology to Storm, but he couldn't blame her for the sneeze. The strange smoky odor drifting toward them wasn't like anything he'd smelled before; but he'd heard of creatures who emitted that smell. It smelled like rusting armor left under a pile of refuse.

They reached the small cave entrance without problem. After that odor, Storm decided to wait this out. If his suspicions were right, they wouldn't make it back to the cottage.

He nodded for her to go in first, then rolled a nearby boulder to the cave mouth. There were more heavy rocks inside that he added to the entrance. As soon as the cave entrance was blocked, a glow rose from the damp walls.

"Is it supposed to do that?" Jenna whispered, tugging on the back of his tunic.

"Well, if it didn't, it'd be pretty dark in here." He wiped the dirt from his hands on his leggings as he turned to her and the rest of the cave. "I might be able to see, but I know you wouldn't." He motioned toward the back of the cave. "Might as well make ourselves comfortable." He looked back at the boulders blocking the entrance. "We might be here a while."

"What was following us? How long is a while?" She managed to blurt the two questions out so fast that they sounded like they came out at the same time.

"Keep asking questions like that and you might manage to keep old Ghortin busy." He led them to the back of the cave. It was larger than it looked at first, and an odd rock formation hid this back section from view of the entrance. A small wooden table, a pile of sturdy blankets, and some rushes lay in a corner.

"What's this, the family hovel?"

Storm held up both hands. "Let someone answer the first dozen questions before you hit him with the next." He sat down against the unnaturally smooth wall, stretching his legs out in front of him.

"First, I'm not sure exactly what was out there." Jenna

grunted at that, but said nothing. He wasn't completely sure what it was, and he certainly didn't want to explain that to her. Whatever was out there were predators, which was enough for now.

Storm continued. "This place could hold us for a few days if need be." He pointed behind her to a crevice running down the wall where a small but steady stream of water trickled.

"How can that be natural? For that matter, the placement of that glowing stuff is a bit too peculiar to be natural as well."

"Adding more questions again," he said. At least the questions would distract her from wanting to see what was outside. He admired her ability to be curious instead of terrified. "No, this isn't natural any more than it's my family hovel. The cave system itself is natural, but there have been modifications built in by Ghortin. He decided he wanted a place to hide out from some of his creations in the early years." He was going to add more when a loud crash sounded against the boulders.

Storm was on his feet in a second, with Jenna close behind. He glanced toward the pile of boulders at the front, and then back to her. "Stay here."

"I will not stay here." She glared at him. "I'm not some little flower that needs to be protected."

He folded his arms and stared down at her. "Oh? What weapons do you carry? Do you have skills of arms that I don't know about?" He took a step closer, forcing her to tilt her head back to look at him. "I'm being practical, not unfair. I'm sure with some training you'll be fine. But you said it yourself; you know nothing about this world."

Jenna sighed, blowing her hair out of her face, and slid back down to the floor. "Okay. Go kill whatever is out there. I'll be good."

Storm ignored the sarcasm in her voice. "I won't be long. I want to make sure the boulders hold." Satisfied she'd stay put, he went around the corner.

The crashing sounds stopped, but a low whiffing noise around the bottom of the largest boulder told him the animals who'd been in the forest were still there. Holding his knife ready, Storm waited to see if whatever was out there was large enough to force the rocks aside. He released a breath as the sounds faded away. He shoved the rocks aside. They'd have precious little time to make it back to the cottage before those things came back. They probably went for reinforcements when they couldn't bash through or dig under the rocks. He was guessing, based on intuition, but that had saved many a hunter—especially in this forest.

He was moving the final stone when Jenna ran into the front of the cave waving a short stick.

"Thank god you're all right." She skidded to a halt on the gravelly floor.

"And if I wasn't, what would you have done with that?" He shook his head. "I'll have to warn Ghortin that his new apprentice doesn't obey well."

"It's never been a strong point of mine," she said. "What was it? Is it gone?"

Storm finished rolling the outer stone into its original place. "Gone for now at any rate. But not for long I'd wager. Which means we need to get back to the cottage quickly." He held up a hand to forestall her questions. "No time. I'm not sure how far away they went. Come on." He turned and left the cave.

"They? As in plural?"

Storm was already off down the trail at a steady pace. "We've no time now, maybe later, but yes, there was definitely more than one out here."

He heard her start running behind him, swearing under her breath the entire way. As long as he could get back to his weapons, and those blessed Bakkera trees, they should be all right.

CHAPTER SIX

JENNA RAN AS QUIETLY AS she could. The skin-crawling feeling from the forest vanished the moment they passed under the double circle of Bakkera trees.

She slowed down at that point, but Storm jogged to the cottage. Whatever was out there, he clearly didn't trust the trees alone to be sufficient protection. She entered the cottage not far behind him, but didn't see him anywhere. She was about to go into the vortex to look for him when he came out of a hallway, pulling an elegant long sword out of its sheath.

"Where'd you get that?" She hadn't seen him with anything fancier than a bow and hunting knife. The long blade looked out of place on him, but by the way he held it, it wasn't a stranger.

"From my father," he said with a crooked grin. "I don't suppose you know how to handle a bow?"

"No." Jenna shook her head. "I'm confused. You didn't have that yesterday, and isn't it kind of large for a hunting weapon?"

Storm looked down as he slid the blade back into its sheath, so she only caught a hint of the odd look that flashed across his face. "I leave it here when I'm in the forest. It's *not* a good hunting weapon, but I don't want to only be carrying a bow and knife if our friends come back." He shook his head.

"That's the first thing I'm going to teach you once I'm sure things are clear—fighting skills. You probably won't be good with a long sword, might be able to eventually go with a long bow and short sword though." He was talking more to himself than her as he walked around her, as if he were judging her strength and agility on sight. "You wouldn't happen to be any good with throwing knives, would you?"

"Don't know." Jenna turned, trying to follow him as he continued his circle. "I've never tried; there's not a real big call for them where I'm from." She thought of all the nights she and her friends had hung out at the local pub. "I'm pretty good with darts though."

"Your people hunt with darts?" He snorted. "What do you hunt?"

"Dartboards." Jenna shrugged. "I didn't mean that I would use darts as weapons. You'd have to put poison or something on them, and I'd probably end up jabbing myself. I was saying that maybe I'd be good with throwing knives, since I seem to have good aim."

"Good thinking." He buckled the sword belt around his waist as they spoke, and headed toward the door. "Let's see if there's any sign of our guests." He held out his hunting knife for her to take and gathered up his longbow and quiver. "This knife isn't for throwing, but I'd rather not have you completely defenseless."

Jenna nodded grimly and took the knife. She wasn't squeamish about the concept of killing something if it was a matter of her or it. Particularly if it was anything like those things from her nightmarish visions.

They walked slowly out to the rim of white trees. A soft breeze brought with it the small forest sounds that had been missing earlier.

Jenna watched the tension leave Storm's shoulders. He continued past the ring of trees, but silently motioned for her to stay back. She almost objected. But if something was out there, she didn't want to hinder him. The knife he gave her was a little too unwieldy for her to have any hope of hurting something other than herself with it.

He hadn't gone far when he froze, nothing moving except for the wind picking up strands of his long hair.

He gave a slight nod, then turned and came back within the circle of trees. "They're gone, at least for now. And I'll know if they come back into the forest."

"What were they?" A shiver ran up her spine at his calmness. Whatever had been after them didn't seem to be something to be shrugged off. Most likely he was being overly calm to keep her from worrying. Which, of course, had the opposite effect.

"I recognized their scent eventually. They're called ertin."

When he turned and started heading to the side of the cottage, Jenna spun and marched after him. "Well, enlighten me. How am I supposed to learn if you don't tell me what ertin are?"

"Easy, easy." He held out his hands, warding off her attack. "Give the girl a knife and she turns into a warrior. I was just curious if that mysterious echo of yours would recognize the term. Is it still there?"

Jenna paused for a moment. "No, it doesn't seem to be there now. In fact, I haven't noticed it all morning. You don't think it's gone, do you?"

"I have no idea. I'm afraid that would be Ghortin's expertise, not mine," he said. "Unfortunately, he also knows more about ertin. I just know what I've heard, enough to recognize them on sight, or in this case, by smell. They're hunters, and little more than myths up until a few years ago. I've never heard of them being this far outside of the Markare before though."

As he spoke, Storm led her to the far side of the cottage. He went behind the wall and pulled out a well-used archery target.

"Now, your first lesson." He frowned when he realized she was still holding the knife. "That won't work. Wait here and I'll go get Ghortin's short bow." As he passed, he adjusted her hold on the knife. "It works a bit better if you grip it like this."

Jenna nodded and moved her hand; it did give her more control. "But I thought you were going to teach me the longbow?" She nodded to the dark bow he still carried.

"Ah, fearsome huntress, I shall. However, first you need to get used to archery. Besides, this bow is hard to pull back. You'll have to build up strength before you try."

He disappeared around the corner, reappearing minutes later with a much smaller bow and quiver.

"This is Ghortin's old set, perfect for an apprentice."

As he showed her how to string and draw the bow, an image invaded Jenna's mind. The shapeless, fanged forms from her terrifying visions were no longer so shapeless. "Storm, are these ertin all teeth, pale, with long pointed faces, and sort of dog-like?"

He pulled back in surprise at her description. "They would be much larger than our regular hunting dogs, but that would be an accurate description from what I've heard. Although Ghortin told me they're actually reptiles and they can be dark or pale. I thought the echo was gone, has it come back?"

"No." She shook her head slowly, not sure exactly how to explain it. "I don't think it's the echo. I think it may come from my own memories."

"They have such things in your world?" Storm's eyebrow rose at that.

"I think it may be part of what happened before you found me." She grimaced. "Before I fell into that pit. I remember being chased by those horrible things with teeth. They almost got me. It isn't any clearer than that. Just them, me, and the woods."

"Woods?" Storm looked toward the forest behind them. "*These* woods? Do you remember which way you were running?"

She shook her head with a sigh. The images were completely gone again. "I'm sorry, I can't remember. For some reason, I don't think it was these woods. I can't explain why though."

"All trees have a different feel to them. It could be that you're sensitive to it. Tell me if anything else comes back; and tell Ghortin. I think he's going to be quite concerned about two sightings of those things." He handed her an arrow. "But for now, we start turning you into an archer."

The rest of the afternoon went quickly. For Storm anyway. Jenna was starting to think her arms were going to fall off before the sun set. Finally Storm called an end to practice and they headed back into the cottage.

Storm toyed with going out and hunting something for dinner, but Jenna convinced him that whatever was in Ghortin's larder would be fine with her. Although there had been no sign of the ertin, she didn't like the idea of him going off this close to nightfall.

Jenna stretched out on the small couch, trying to work up enough energy to smear on a salve Storm had left for her sore hands and arms. She finally stirred herself and reached for the small jar, only to almost drop it once she'd opened the lid. "What died in here?" She glared suspiciously at Storm's back. "Are you sure that this is going to help me?"

Storm turned around from his attack on Ghortin's larder. "Would I lie to you? Well, I might, but not this time. One thing about Ghortin's concoctions; they work, but they're usually nasty about it."

He shrugged and turned back to his pile of ingredients. "It's up to you. Don't use it if you don't want to, but you're the one who won't be able to move a finger tomorrow. Hope you like stew; he's got a lot of stuff here, but not enough of any one thing."

Grimacing at the smell from the jar, Jenna gingerly rubbed on the ointment. She would admit it was soothing, as long as she didn't inhale. "At this point I'd eat a horse."

"Sorry, not this time." Storm came back to the parlor with a mug in each hand. "Water or ale?"

She thought of the aches in her body. "Ale, ale, and more ale."

Storm handed her one of the mugs and laughed at her expression. "I thought you might say that. But I'll warn you, you'll feel ten times worse if you're fighting off both a hangover and muscle fatigue tomorrow."

"Okay, then just ale. One, that's all." She took a deep drink and came up sputtering. "Good god, what is this, hundred proof?" She'd expected a nice beer and was hit with something that was much closer to two-hundred-year-old whiskey.

Storm smiled none too apologetically. "Sorry, I forgot to warn you. I thought a slight bit of Fire Lake might help you relax. The entire mug isn't full of it. Just a floater on top. By the look on your face, I'd say you probably got all of it."

"Do you people drink that stuff on a regular basis?" She cautiously took a smaller sip. It now tasted like a strong, warm, beer.

"It's a little strong for recreational drinking." From the way he drank, he obviously hadn't added the mystery liquid to his own drink. Jenna didn't think anyone could get so used to the stuff that they didn't flinch at all.

She stared into her mug for a few minutes. "You don't think those ertin things got Ghortin do you?" The question had been nagging in the back of her head all day, but she'd been too afraid to ask.

From his brief frown it had probably been on Storm's mind as well. "I don't think so. I saw three from a distance when I rolled back the rocks. Which might have caused us a problem, since we were basically unarmed. However, Ghortin was fully armed, and don't tell him I said this, but he's one hell of a mage. It would take more than three of those demon spawn to take him down." He rose and started setting a fire in the small hearth.

"Those things weren't really demons?" Everything was happening so fast; kelars, mages, ertin—she didn't think she could handle demons from some netherworld too.

Storm rocked back on his boot heels as he watched the logs catch. Satisfied, he went to check on the progress of their stew.

"Couldn't tell you," he said around a sampling mouthful. "I doubt it. Ghortin says it's almost impossible for demons to cross into our world."

That wasn't reassuring. "There are demons? And they could get here?"

"Of course there are demons, but they would have a hard time getting over here. I mean, it's a whole different world."

Jenna frowned at him. "I made it, didn't I?"

"Good point." Storm looked at her and nodded slowly. "I guess if they tried hard, perhaps they could duplicate what you did. You don't happen to remember what you did, so there's no point in worrying, is there?"

Jenna shook her head. He made sense if she just didn't think about it too hard. Right now, not thinking too hard sounded like a wonderful idea.

Finally, Storm pronounced the stew fit to eat. He brought two bowls out to the parlor saying he hated to waste a beautiful fire. Jenna was grateful that she didn't have to get up to eat, but too hungry to say anything beyond thank you.

They'd both finished their food, and Jenna was thinking about going to bed, when a distant howling could be heard from outside. It was so low and airy she couldn't tell at first if it was just the wind. The grim look on Storm's face answered the question for her.

"Stay here." He grabbed his sword from where he'd left

it by the door, tossing aside the sheath. "Don't open this door unless I call your name." The relaxed man he'd been moments before was gone.

"What if you're injured and can't call?" She followed him to the door, her muscles no longer in pain.

"If I'm not back at this door within fifteen minutes, go into your room in the vortex and don't come out until Ghortin gets you." His sharp face was tense, his tone serious. Jenna's gut tightened. He stopped with his hand on the doorknob and turned to stare down at her. "I mean it, Jenna, but I can't explain now. Just don't open this door."

Taken back by the intensity in his stare, Jenna could only nod. Then he opened the door and was gone into the night.

Jenna hesitated in shutting the door behind him, as she tried to see anything in the dark. All she could see was Storm rapidly disappearing into the night as he ran toward the line of Bakkera trees.

Sliding the bolt home, she leaned against the wooden door. What kind of world was this, where creatures could reach out of your nightmares and attack you?

After a few numb minutes, she went back to the fire and forced her mind not to think about anything, especially the rising howls she heard outside.

Within minutes she slid into a strange trance as the flames drew her in. She found herself floating through a gray fog. A primal anger that didn't feel like her own cut through it.

She wasn't sure how long she had been in the trance when a feeling of fury overcame her. Global at first, angry at everything, and then it slowly narrowed down to outside of the cottage. Her body moved without thought as she ignored Storm's warning and opened the door.

The scene was clear to her this time, even though it was still pitch black. A weird glow had taken over everything, as if her mind was getting the images without help from her eyes.

Storm stood no more than ten feet inside the circle of trees, fiercely fighting off what looked to be a group of large, dark, hairless dogs. Ones with disproportionately large fangs and heavy spikes down their bodies. When she focused harder, she knew they had to be the ertin. Most of the pack stayed on the other side of the protective trees, hissing and howling, but not crossing. Five had crossed the tree line and lay dead, their bodies twisted horribly in mute evidence to the lethal combination of the magic of the trees and Storm's skill as a swordsman. Six more were advancing on Storm, holding themselves awkwardly, as if fighting great pain as they crossed the row of glowing white trees. They advanced nonetheless. Storm was holding his own, but Jenna could tell from the way he stood that the jagged bite wound on his leg was taking its toll.

With her strange trance-like vision, Jenna saw an unhealthy red glow shining from the wound and that he was barely standing. One good rush from those creatures and he would fall. None of the participants noticed Jenna as she walked out the door.

She had no weapons, had no idea what she was going to do, yet she was compelled forward by a raging anger she'd never felt before. Something deep in her gut confirmed these were the creatures who had attacked her in her visions. At the same instant, three of the ertin circling Storm lunged forward. He skillfully slid his sword through the belly of one, and then turned to the next. Unfortunately, it was on the side with his injured leg, and he stumbled.

Intense fury at the ertin and fear for her friend engulfed Jenna's mind. She held her shaking hands out toward the lunging ertin around Storm and yelled. The ertin rolled back as if pushed, unable to do anything except remain upright as they were forced back by a spell coming from her, but not her. She continued to advance on the beleaguered animals, yelling unintelligible words the entire way. She wasn't sure what she yelled; it came out of something beyond her. *Something that wanted them gone.*

The ertin were all running now, and still she followed with her voice. It appeared to fill the animals with an insane fear, and they attacked each other as they fled the area. In her mind she could see them running, their numbers shrinking, until the last one made it past the far edge of the forest. A vague man shadow, like she'd seen the night Storm had found her, appeared, then also vanished.

Jenna collapsed in a heap. She sat, numb, for a few seconds before she remembered that Storm was injured. Unfortunately, along with the fleeing of the ertin, her ability to see in the dark had also left. It took a bit to locate Storm, who was much closer to the edge of the clearing than she had thought. He was trying to get up as she approached.

"They're dead. We'd better get you inside. Can you walk?" She heard the words, but she couldn't believe how calm she was being. Neither could Storm.

"Are you all right?" He got up shakily, but without assistance. "Are you hurt?"

His inhuman blue eyes watched her intently as she came close.

"I'm fine. I'm not sure what happened, but I'm fine."

Storm said nothing, but he did allow her to help him as they made their way back to the cottage.

She got Storm settled on the couch, then built up the fire. "It's got something in it, you know," she said matter-of-factly.

"What does? What in the eight hells happened out there?" He looked at her suspiciously. "Are you sure you're all right?"

"I told you, I'm fine." She came to the side of the couch. "Your leg has something in it. I can't see it now, but before whatever I did out there, I could see your leg in red. It didn't look healthy."

Storm grimaced as he moved it. "More than likely ertin spit. The bottle of Fire Lake is in the kitchen. Could you get it?"

Jenna nodded and came back a moment later with a dark green bottle. "Do you want a glass?"

"No." Storm took the bottle gratefully, opened it, and took a swig. Then set it down next to him and began tearing the legging off his wounded thigh. "Actually, it's for my leg. That stuff will kill anything, including whatever those creatures carry."

Jenna started helping him with the fabric. The skin underneath was flushed and the creature's teeth had left a jagged tear. Amazingly, there seemed to be no other injuries. "I'm surprised you only have one. Those things…" She let her voice drop; she couldn't vocalize what she thought of those creatures. They might not be from the netherworld, but they were close enough to demons for her.

Storm grunted noncommittally, and then poured some of the alcohol over his leg. Tears came to his eyes, but it was doing something as the wound burbled. "I wouldn't have made it at all if you hadn't disobeyed me. Thank you." He grimaced and clenched his teeth as the liquid flowed through the wound. "Although, I'm still not sure what you did."

Jenna sighed and sat down on the floor next to the sofa. "You're welcome, but I don't know what I did either. I was trying not to think of you out there fighting those things, when something took over. Maybe it was the echo fighting back." She shook her head. It didn't worry her, although she thought suddenly having powers that could come and go probably should. "I just knew I wanted them destroyed."

Storm poured some more alcohol over his leg, clearly

not worrying that most of it ended up on Ghortin's sofa. "Have you ever done something like that before? What were you yelling anyway?"

"Now who's asking all the questions?" Jenna smiled slightly as she idly tugged on a loose green thread from one of the rugs. "No, I've never done anything remotely like that. And I have absolutely no idea what I was yelling, or what language it was. I remember I had no idea while I was yelling it either. I was kind of hoping it was a language you recognized."

"I'm afraid not. What you yelled wasn't one of the four major languages, that's for sure. Maybe it was one of the mage ones." Storm took two more long drinks from the green bottle.

"D' you think you'll remember what you said for Ghortin? S'might be important." He was already slurring his speech. After her one sip of that stuff, she wasn't surprised.

"I couldn't remember them the second they were out of my mouth." He was fading fast as alcohol and exhaustion took their toll. But he wasn't going to give in before she did. She gave a yawn. "Look, I'm bushed, the door's bolted, is there anything else I should do before I head off to bed?" As she spoke she handed Storm one of the stray blankets that Ghortin had tossed over all of the chairs.

Storm took it with a grateful smile and suppressed his own yawn. "No, I think tha's it. I'm jus' gonna stay out 'ere a while." He didn't manage to suppress that last yawn, and Jenna nodded and took herself off into the vortex.

CHAPTER SEVEN

———◆———

JENNA AND STORM SPENT MOST of the next two days resting. Neither of them had much energy, although Storm's leg seemed to be healing unnaturally fast. Jenna wished she could call back that strange sight so she could make sure, but he insisted it was fine. On the first day he spent two hours sharing with her a seemingly endless list of serious injuries he'd gotten and how quickly he was up and about after them. Luckily, he tired out and fell asleep mid-story.

She decided not to bring the issue up again.

She hadn't been in a much better state, the events of that night had drained her badly. That she still had absolutely no idea what she'd done or how she'd done it wasn't making things better. It was as if someone else had done everything and she had just been along for the ride.

By mutual consent of silence, they both went to sleep that third night after the attack still not discussing what she'd done. However, occasionally Jenna would catch him looking at her thoughtfully. Jenna chose to ignore his unspoken questions. They were questions she asked herself and had no answers for.

Two days of doing nothing had been more than enough for Jenna. She awoke the next morning determined to find out what had happened and why. Whatever Storm could tell her would help, even if he didn't think it would.

She slid out of bed, quickly donning one of her many cloned outfits. Ghortin may have provided her with a wardrobe, but he certainly didn't give her much variety.

She managed to make it out of the vortex tunnel with only a half dozen wrong turns this time, and was quite pleased with herself by the time she got to the parlor. Her happiness slipped when she realized that Storm wasn't there. She heard clanking in the kitchen and smiled. He was clearly feeling more like his old self.

She turned the corner into the small kitchen, ready to surprise Storm, and was brought up short by Ghortin's broad back. She stopped just before running into him.

"Good morn, lass." He cheerfully called out as he turned and motioned her toward the loaded table. "Sleep well, did ye?"

Jenna nodded and slid down into a chair behind a plate of food.

Ghortin smiled as he took the other chair and began shoveling in food.

After a few minutes, he looked up to notice Jenna still staring at him, food untouched.

"Now, lass, don't tell me Storm's been filling your head with tales of my cooking? I assure you, he's not a connoisseur."

"Where is he?" She looked around, noticing a large bundle laying near the door. Ghortin couldn't have been home long. She took some eggs and chased them around her plate.

"Our Stormy friend has drifted away again. I finished my tasks, so I sent him home."

"But what about his leg?"

"He was wounded?" Ghortin wiped his beard with a ragged cloth. "Can't say I could help you there. The lad didn't tell me much as he lit out."

Jenna leaned back with folded arms and narrowed eyes. She had a hard time believing that Storm would have taken off without telling Ghortin about the dangerous visitors to his forest. And the notoriously quick healing kelar still had a limp last night. How was she going to survive in this place when no one would tell her any-thing?

"Now, lass," Ghortin began, not meeting her eyes. "He doesn't tell me a lot of things; you know? In a lot of ways he is simply a—"

"Are you afraid of me? Is that it?" Jenna cut him off. "Do you think I'm a spy or something?"

He looked up at her comment, a tuft of beard in his hands. "What? Oh no, not at all. It's that…I thought… more sausage?" He held up a dripping piece.

Jenna shook her head. "About what's been going on?" She prodded the rambling mage. "The attack in the forest? The fact that those ertin things made it past your trees?"

Ghortin studied her for a few minutes in silence. Finally, he gave a sigh and nodded. "I had hoped you might have thought it was a dream?" He shrugged. "You're right; as my apprentice you should at least have a glimmer of what's going on. However, you young ones don't need more than that. It'll just give you grand ideas." He stared at his empty plate for a few moments, then finally looked up.

"Hmm, yes. Well, for the last few months, we've noticed odd happenings here and there. Lately, they've been get-ting more serious. People are missing. Creatures of myth are out roaming. And now you've appeared."

"That's it? What about the ertin? What about my strange abilities?" She glared at him. There was no way that Storm wouldn't have mentioned the ertin attacks.

Ghortin frowned, but Jenna kept glaring. If he thought she would be intimidated because she was an apprentice, he was in for a rude shock.

"I was trying to spare you things you aren't ready for." He sighed. "I see that won't work. Shall we move into the library? I feel more comfortable discussing such bleak and dreary things among my weapons." He rose and motioned for her to follow.

"Weapons? I thought you only had books in there." She stayed right behind him. Maybe she'd finally get some answers. There was a difference between not wanting to know and not being told. She was getting fed up with the latter.

"Ah, lass." Ghortin turned and held up a finger. "Those are the most powerful weapons of all. Doubly so for the likes of you and me."

He waited until they were both comfortably settled in the confines of the library, and then told her what he knew of the ertin. Unfortunately, it wasn't that much more than Storm had known.

Physically, Jenna thought the creatures were built like tall greyhounds. According to Ghortin they actually were more of a warm-blooded reptile. Jenna thought of the raptor dinosaurs of her world and shuddered. "Thank god they aren't bigger. Are they trained, or wild?" The idea of domesticated carnivorous dinosaurs, no matter what size, was terrifying. A memory of the shadow man came to mind. "Would they have someone controlling them?"

"Mostly they're wild. They are difficult to control and often turn on their masters." He took out a small, lavender book. "But they have been successfully domesticated by a few."

He opened to a yellowing page, which showed a pack of nine ertin on chains held by a giant man. Looking closer at the painting and the text description, Jenna shuddered again. The animals' faces did look like the smaller raptor dinosaurs, like those scary things from that old Jurassic Park movie. However, their front limbs weren't the smaller arm type, but full forelegs like a dog. Their color ranged from a light gray to almost black, their tails long and whip-like. The long, pointed mouths bristled with a double row of small fangs. Their eyes were solid black balls, no discernible difference between pupil and iris, but the text warned that their night vision was unnaturally good. They had almost dog-like paws, but had an inch-long spur on the back of the two front legs.

"I think I saw a man out there, only in shadow, both when they were fleeing after the attack here, and the night Storm first found me." She was proud her voice stayed steady, which was much better than what her gut was doing. The more she looked at the drawing, the more convinced she was that they were the creatures from her terrifying visions. "Why were they chasing me? And who is controlling them?"

Ghortin shrugged and shut his book. "I wish I knew. I'd be willing to brush off one encounter with them as simply bad luck. But two? If these indeed were what chased you before Storm found you. I don't know, lass, but I'd say you're tied into this somehow. The ones that chewed up Storm were hunters." He paced around the room.

"Which would leave that they were after *you, Jenna,* directed by some unknown master. Or there was something extraordinary about this mindslave." He shook his head. "I can't think of what would be so special about a mindslave for Qhazborh's followers to use ertin to get one back. Do you recall anything of your arrival at all?"

"No, I'm sorry." She rubbed her arms as a chill ran through her. "So, the ones in your forest were after me. But how was I able to get rid of them? Storm seemed as surprised about that as I was."

"What do you remember?" He fixed his dark eyes on her closely. Very much like she had become a prized science project. Jenna thought, and not for the first time, that was what she was rapidly becoming. It wasn't a good feeling.

"Not much. Like I told Storm, it was almost as if I slipped into something that wasn't me. Could it have been remnants of the mindslave?"

"I doubt that. Magic doesn't stay once the mind is gone. Although…" He rifled through some old scrolls. "There could be something that was linked to the mindslave; something that you inadvertently triggered. Something like that is just tickling the edges of my mind. If I could recall what it was." He looked furiously through the scrolls, but finally gave up. "No, I'm afraid it's not coming to mind. The only way I'll know what happened to you is to work on your training. Get in your head, so to speak. And for that it might be best to start outside."

As they went outside, Jenna watched the friendly double ring of white trees surrounding the cottage. She didn't care what Ghortin said about the ertin being gone, she wouldn't have gone past that safe circle for anything today. They might not have been able to completely stop those creatures, but they'd slowed them down.

"Come, apprentice of mine, it's time to get started on your mastery of this world and magic." He led her around the far corner of the cottage.

"I thought I had some sort of negative magic reaction…thing."

He shrugged. "You seem fine now, and I see no reason to further delay the inevitable. Whatever it was you did to the ertin must have removed the block. Or it was part of your tie to your world. Either way, we should get started immediately."

He led her past the archery target of two days ago, and through a small gate at the back of the cottage. He carefully worked his way through a clump of fragile, spiky plants and into a mini grove of Bakkera trees and assorted blackened stumps.

Ghortin waggled a thick finger as he pointed to a tree stump for her to sit on. "Rule one. Always question authority. Unless, of course, it's a life or death situation. And I don't mean you have to balk every time someone asks you to do something. But what if their demand doesn't go with what you sense?" He shrugged. "It's your duty as a mage to question it. Some may say you're being cantankerous, but you just pay them no never mind." He tugged on his vest.

"The exception would be if a royal family member gave a *royal command*, those you must follow without question. In fact, you would be unable to refuse, because there's a spell built into the royal family and it's connected to all mages. Including you, now that you're here and have tapped into the chaos. But that hasn't happened in a long time. Trust me, they know better than to toss such authority around." He folded his arms across his broad chest.

"First, we need to work on some basic concepts, such as chaos. By its nature, chaos is a powerful thing. As thinking beings we fight it every day in our attempt to control and confine our sense of reality within the chaotic sphere."

Jenna hung tenuously to his words. Unfortunately, it reminded her of those philosophy courses that sounded great in theory, but that she never seemed to stay in past the first day.

"Take my vortex, for example." He waved toward the cottage behind her. "On a basic level, a displacement vortex is simply an unsecured sphere of chaos. In the brashness of my youth, I decided that one would make a perfect home—particularly for a great mage such as myself." He winked at her to show his opinion of that brash youth.

"Mages control the force of chaos. What I did with the vortex was to layer spells of control and direction upon it and harness the resulting Power. I was foolish, and I almost died for it. I'm sure you'll never have to deal with something as strong as a vortex, and if you do, run the other way. But it serves as an example of what can happen if one tries to tap into the deepest levels of the Power of chaos without fully understanding what it can do."

"So, when are you going to give me this understanding?" His conversation was fogging her mind over. She was all for knowledge, but this was akin to being dropped into a fifth-level physics course right out of grade school.

"Impatience has been the death of more would-be mages than anything else." He got up and paced around the small ring of stumps. "It will be quite a while before you get your understanding. All I can do is point you in the right direction. However, first I think a small experiment is in order." He stood in front of her.

"Now relax. What we call magic is simply an extension of the body's natural energy. It's as if magic users have another sense, one that enables them to manipulate the world around them with their minds. Now, no movement can occur without energy and it's the controlling of chaos that gives mages their energy. You might say every act of magic is actually two acts. First, concentrating on what you want to happen, and second, controlling the chaotic impulse of the universe to give your command energy. It's not something to be done half-heartedly, I assure you. Nor something that can be done if you lack that extra sense, like Storm."

Ghortin caught her frown. "Yes, our friend is a fearsome hunter and fighter, one of the best in the land. However, he is lacking the correct blood for magic. Most of his kind have at least a basic sensitivity, but he has none, it would take something of massive size and Power for him to even feel it. It's a sore point with the lad."

He held his hands in front of him as if he was holding water; he motioned for her to do the same. "Now for your first lesson. I want you to mentally gather a ball of energy in your hands."

"A what?" She couldn't sense any energy around her.

Ghortin held up a hand as if she were a skittish pony. "Easy, lass. Reach into the part of your mind that knows no bounds. The untamed, the borderless, the irrational."

That worked. She relaxed, closed her eyes, and reached out for the absurd; daydreaming was definitely in her skill set. Considering her present unreal situation, it wasn't all that hard. Chaotic energy pulled at her. Colors and shapes were all around her. Some went completely through her, leaving a strange tingling in their wake. She had just reached out for an interesting lavender tree when an intrusion shattered her new world and she found herself on the ground looking up at Ghortin.

"That was my fault, I should have warned you." He bent down to help her up. The concern in Ghortin's dark eyes scared her more than her fall had.

"What did you need to warn me about?" It came out more annoyed than she meant it to. "You told me to find the chaos, I was about to control some of the Power when you yanked me back here." She shook herself off and crawled back onto her stump. Her head was still spinning from her brief voyage.

"Aye, that I did. And you slipped into that ether like a master." He shook his head, but whether it was at himself or her, Jenna couldn't tell. "But a master wouldn't have cut off all ties with her body so that it stopped breathing and started causing me some serious concerns."

"Oh." She hadn't noticed that at all. Everything had all been so beautiful. "Next time I'll pay more attention."

"And you will. However, I think we'll be waiting a bit before your next time. You've an awful lot of Power and it'd be safer for all concerned if I teach you how to control it before I teach you how to access it." His eyes lost focus as something else came to him. He came back with a shake. "So, that being said, I believe I shall first teach you history and magic theory." He rose and dusted off the seat of his pants. "Things that can take place safely inside."

Jenna stayed seated. "I promise I'll be more careful; I

won't let that happen again." It had been so beautiful and thrilling there, she had to go back.

Ghortin frowned, there was a brief flash of serious concern before he schooled his face. "It's not that I don't trust you, my dear. But that place can be overwhelming for someone with too much Power and no knowledge of how to contain it. It can be a deadly addiction. And I don't want you trying to get there without me. Trust me, you wouldn't want that either."

"But," Jenna bit back her annoyed comment. The irresistible need she'd had for the place was fading. Maybe he was right. "You're right; I won't go there on my own."

"Excellent choice. Now, shall we?" Ghortin's smile returned and he held out his arm to lead her back to the library.

CHAPTER EIGHT

FOUR MONTHS LATER, JENNA WASN'T feeling so kindly toward Ghortin.

"It'll be easy." Jenna snarled to herself for the hundredth time that day.

Those words had become her mantra, given to her by Ghortin when he finally got around to teaching her spells instead of history. She'd repeated them to herself, at first to keep her determination up. Now, after four frustrating months, she repeated them to keep herself from committing mageicide.

The magic she had looked forward to during those dry history lessons had been anything but easy. Granted, four months wasn't that long, but by now she should be able to do more than simple hiding spells and blocking. She didn't even get any joy out of trips into that chaotic wonderland that she had fallen into that first day in the tree ring. Once you knew more of how magic worked, you didn't have to go to the source, so to speak, or at least not often. And the constraints Ghortin put on her when she did go ruined the thrill.

On the up side, she hadn't had any more odd reactions to magic. And she *was* proud of her blocking skills. Within the first three weeks of actual lessons, she was able to consciously block almost all low-level spells. Within two months, she could repel anything a mid-level journeyman mage could throw at her. Ghortin was impressed. Or he seemed to be whenever he happened to be paying attention.

After watching her like a hawk in the beginning, Ghortin had become distracted these last two months. Fall was well settled now, the days shorter and darker; and he claimed he had too many things to do before winter moved in. But Jenna had a feeling it had more to do with whatever was going on in this world magically, not naturally, that was causing him worry. Things like the ertin attack. Nothing had happened around her since then, but she also hadn't been further away from the cottage than the line of Bakkera trees. However, Ghortin wouldn't tell her anything of the goings on outside of their forest. For that matter, neither would Storm.

Storm usually came for a brief visit every week or so; far too infrequently in Jenna's opinion. However, whenever she brought up Ghortin's growing preoccupation, the handsome kelar simply danced around the subject. She wouldn't have thought a woodsman could be so verbally graceful. He was that way about their growing friendship too. There, but always holding her a bit at a distance.

And he seemed to have absolutely no interesting information about what was happening in the outside world. Not even an answer for why he always traveled with his sword now.

Unfortunately, Ghortin was also pushing her unreasonably hard. Unlike in the beginning when he was determined to take her lessons at a snail's pace, he now seemed to be pushing her to master status within the year. He would show up at breakfast, view her latest attempt, tell her what to do for the day, and then leave her to her own devices to complete the massive projects.

She knew she was probably far older than prior apprentices, but one would think that mage apprentices of any age shouldn't be roaming around aimlessly shooting off spells unattended.

Even Storm was getting worse. He'd been tense the

last time he'd come for a visit, barely nodding hello to Jenna before dragging Ghortin off deep into the vortex. Which in and of itself was highly suspect. Storm hated the vortex area—his going into it deliberately would be akin to her voluntarily going in for an unnecessary root canal. Jenna had given up trying to find them after four hours. When they finally did come out, Storm ran for his horse before Jenna could say anything.

That had been fifteen days ago, and Ghortin didn't seem surprised that he hadn't seen his friend since.

The continuing oddities of her two companions chased themselves around in her head as she absently chewed on a sprig of dying grass. She'd been pacing within the small circle of stumps outside of the cottage for over an hour and had finally had enough. This time Ghortin wasn't going to be able to hide. Resolutely, she stepped over the shortest stump and marched toward the cottage.

She wasn't surprised that the mage wasn't to be found in the 'anchored' portions of the vortex—her room and the library—or in the non-vortex areas like the front room, kitchen, and the spare bedrooms. Ghortin had been spending almost all of his time in the un-anchored portion of the vortex, making it impossible for her to track him down.

Until now.

She'd spent the last two weeks building up her allies— the house elementals. Ghortin berated them and Storm ignored them. So Jenna made friends with them.

At least as close to being friends as one could get with insubstantial fluffs of chaos.

She stood at the edge of the anchored portion of the vortex and willed herself to relax. Silently, she called her new companions to her. The elementals, by nature of their being, were all slightly different. But they all responded like bears to honey around directed mental energy. If they felt like it, the person didn't even have to have mage ability for them to respond.

A flittering began around the edges of her consciousness and she knew they had arrived. She hadn't made up her mind yet whether she wanted them to get Ghortin or to take her to him. Immediately sensing her desires however, the elementals made the decision for her and were down the hall in a flash.

A minute later, Ghortin came barreling down the hall waving his hands. Fortunately he spotted Jenna before he plowed into her.

"Here now. Clear way. Clear way. Those damn elementals have gone completely around the bend." The sturdy mage began shoving her back down the hall toward the cottage.

Jenna sputtered and batted him away, but it was like trying to stop the rush of a grizzly.

She finally planted her feet against the onslaught. "STOP." She directed the command at both Ghortin and at her over-zealous helpers. She couldn't say who was more surprised when his feet froze in place.

"No, wait. Un-stop."

Ghortin's feet came free a split second before balance became a serious issue.

"Now where did that come from?" Ghortin looked around as if he doubted his own ears. The elementals vanished like naughty children.

"I'm sorry." She bit down her smile and tried to look concerned. His gray hair shooting off in a thousand different directions left him looking more like a giant owl awakened too early than a powerful mage.

"I didn't think I could stop you like that. I wanted *you* to stop you."

"Me to stop me?" He shook his head and started patting down his hair. "First my elementals start trying to kill me, now my mere slip of an apprentice uses a command word. One, by the way, that I know *I* haven't taught her. What is happening to my neat, orderly world?" He kept glancing around as he spoke, as if watching for any straggling elementals.

"Sorry about the elementals. I've been working with them lately, but they have a mind of their own, so to speak. However, they do respond extremely well to commands they like, don't they?"

Ghortin's brows lowered. "What, pray tell, did you tell them to do? Tickle me to death?"

"Not in so many words." Jenna shrugged. It had seemed like a good idea at the time. "I got tired of you and Storm running around with your secrets. You're either somewhere deep in that vortex hidey-hole or locked in the library with that damn book." She pointed to the gray book in his hand. She hadn't seen him without it once in the last two months, even at meals, but he wouldn't let her even open the cover. "Something big is going on and, again, you are leaving me out of the loop. I'm not a kid."

"I guess it's my fault." He ran his thick fingers through his hair. "However, I'd rather not discuss this here if you don't mind. I feel better that those elemental misfits were acting under your orders, but there were still some uneasy moments there that I'd rather not repeat."

Jenna lost the rest of his muttering as he briskly moved out of the hall. Once in the cottage proper, Ghortin got her settled in the parlor and then went off to the kitchen.

He returned a minute later with two large wine glasses.

"Isn't that much better?" He handed her one of the glasses, then took over the chair directly across from her.

"What's happened now? More ertin?" She fought the shiver that went down her spine. Although her words had been flip, she was still having nightmares about those creatures.

"Yes. And more, unfortunately. No concentrated attacks like what happened here, but there have been more single sightings of them. No sign of your shadow friend though." Ghortin frowned and set down his glass. "Plus, we've heard of an increase in mindslaves being made. And the bodies of two women were found at the edge of the Markare. Their throats were cut."

Jenna choked on the sip of wine she had taken. That her body had partially belonged to a former mindslave increased her disgust of what happened to create more of them. "But why were the women killed? I hate to say this, but why weren't they made into mindslaves and taken with the others?"

Ghortin held her gaze for a few minutes before he answered, his dark eyes held pain and concern. Jenna took another long drink.

"I believe it was because they matched your physical description."

All the air left Jenna's lungs. People were murdered because they looked like her?

"Why? What's so important about me? Do they know who did it? Did they—" She couldn't ask if they had suffered; most likely they had. This world was harsh, and its deaths even harsher. She drained the rest of her glass.

"I'm afraid that we're not sure why, but the followers of Qhazborh want you, or the mindslave whose body you now have, back. And badly."

That wine was hitting her far harder than it should have. The world was getting fuzzy on the edges. Jenna stared into her empty glass. Finally she looked up. "Wha' do we do now?"

"We'll find out how this is all connected, never you fear. You're safe here in the forest with me. Moreover, if you've been practicing all of your spells correctly, you should be safe against most things outside of the forest as well. Unfortunately, women who look like you haven't been the only things under attack as of late. Illnesses have been hitting the outlying villages and towns, diseases that the best healers can't figure out. Eventually they vanish on their own, or the patient dies." His face was grim, but Jenna wondered why he was starting to lean sideways. "And then there's the Markare itself." His eyes drifted down to something only he could see, or something Jenna couldn't see at any rate.

And now the room wasn't just fuzzy, the floor was listing to the left.

Finally she gave up trying to make it hold still and coughed subtly to get his attention. Ghortin jumped at the sound. "Sorry, lass, I was just thinking. Any rate, the Markare has been faced with odd disappearances. Three within the last two ten-day."

"Three people, or three villages? H'can they know anyway? Thought you told me they were nomads." Jenna wished Ghortin would sit up right—he was giving her a headache.

"Whole villages, lass. They are nomadic, but still they follow set itineraries, there are only so many habitable places to live out there. These people haven't been seen. And the Border Watch mages felt them go."

"Go? Goh where? How could they just go 'poof'?" She tried snapping her fingers for emphasis but missed.

Ghortin rubbed his chin and looked at her closely. At least by leaning forward he wasn't listing so much. He looked at her, then at her empty glass. After a moment he gave a shrug. "They didn't go 'poof'. They vanished. I'm sure there was no poofing involved. Do stop that."

Jenna gave a guilty grin. She'd been trying to see if her snapping would work, but her missing had obviously upset him. Taking a deep breath, she tightly held both hands together and nodded for him to go on. That drink might have been called wine, but the buzz she was feeling was too intense for even a full day of wine drinking.

"Thank you. As I was saying, it was as if they were simply cut out of the essence of reality."

Jenna nodded as old movie bits floated around in her

wine-fogged head. "Like a million lives screamed out once in terror, then were silenced?" She held her hands so tight white lines formed on her knuckles.

Ghortin frowned. "I suppose something of that sort. Although a million lives would be far too large; more like a hundred."

Jenna lurched to her feet triumphantly, only to collapse back down an instant later. "Ah-ha. I know what your problem is. You've got a damn Deathstar in your desert." She reclaimed her glass for another drink, and then frowned when she realized it was still empty. Sadly, Ghortin didn't appear to want to give her more. Part of her thought that was probably a good thing.

"Now, now, dear." Ghortin stood up. "I know you're upset, we all are, but why don't we give back the nice glass, shall we?" He managed to free the empty glass from her fingers when a loud rap sounded from the door.

"Eh? What now?" He turned back toward Jenna. "You stay right there, don't move. Just let me see who's knocking."

Jenna tried to push herself upright when an extremely dandified Storm pushed aside the door the moment Ghortin freed the latch. He was a stunning example of a well-dressed gentleman and clearly was furious about it. Even to Jenna's blurred vision he looked good enough to eat. Storm's long dark hair was pulled back and styled with enough curl to hint at affectation, but it didn't in any way look feminine. A thin copper arch held his hair off his face instead of his usual cloth band. His royal blue velvet tunic and matching hose made his normally bright blue eyes luminescent, while a pristine white shirt and polished black boots finished the ensemble. Jenna thought the nasty grimace on his face did nothing to increase his sex appeal, although, to be honest, it didn't reduce it either. She couldn't figure out what he was doing, but it could all be a hallucination at this point, so she might as well enjoy it. Somewhere the back of her mind mentioned she was completely drunk and about to pass out. She told it to shut up and went back to staring at the stunning kelar before her.

"They did it to me again." Storm snarled as he stomped into the parlor, boot heels savagely pounding through the thin rugs. He looked ready to kill something. Or someone.

Ghortin wasn't even trying to keep from grinning. "Did what? Oh. Is that for me?" Ghortin spotted the decorated parchment roll that Storm was flinging about in agitation. Storm jerked it quickly out of his reach.

"Perhaps." Storm pulled himself up to his full height and glared down at Ghortin. Never mind that he was just a few inches taller than Ghortin. "Do I have the honor of addressing Ghortin al Tarn, Mastermage of Traanafaeren?"

The mastermage in question stomped his foot. "Damn it, you know who I am. Now let me have that paper."

"Easy, sir, I'll remind you not to rustle the royal messenger." Storm dusted off some imaginary dust particles from his tunic. Finally he looked back to Ghortin. "Much better, sir." Holding out the scroll, Storm read in a clear, practiced voice. "The royal family requests your presence, and that of your household, at a royal masquerade in honor of the coming T'faren and winter."

Storm tossed the invitation to Ghortin, and then flopped down next to Jenna on the sofa. He was more than a little surprised that she hadn't said a single word to him; she'd been so silent he hadn't known she was there until right before he sat down. She looked like she was thinking hard about something. More than likely she was trying to keep from laughing at him in his ridiculous costume. "I'm telling you, Ghortin, I try to spend more time with them and this is what they do to me." Leaning back, he noticed how wide-eyed and wild-looking Jenna was. She leaned close—examining the weave of his garments, it seemed—then leaned back and burst into giggles. He had expected her to laugh at him, but this wasn't her normal laugh, it was an actual giggle.

"Hi there, pretty boy." She waved at him, then frantically pulled herself back up as the wave threatened to dump her off the sofa. The smile she gave him would have been seductive, or so he supposed, if she wasn't listing badly to the side.

Storm stared at her in surprise, then glared at Ghortin. "It's the middle of the day and your apprentice is drunk? What did you give her?"

Ghortin nodded toward her abandoned glass, and then sat down to re-read the invitation. Storm took a whiff that almost knocked him off the couch.

"Gorgon ale-wine? What were you trying to do to her?" He looked in disbelief at the still giggling Jenna. Gorgon ale-wine was stronger than Fire Lake and never served in anything larger than a tiny glass. Jenna gave him a huge smile, winked, and waggled a lock of black hair at him. He would have been flattered if he wasn't shocked she was still conscious.

"Hmm?" Ghortin looked up from his reading. "Oh, I was concerned how she would take news of the recent events. So I thought she could use a spot."

Storm was vainly trying to keep Jenna from falling all over him. An upright position was no longer possible for her to maintain, and she seemed to be enjoying the feel of his tunic on her face.

"A spot is one thing, a whole glass is another. I know sailors three times her size who wouldn't be able to handle that much." Storm propped her up, trying to get her eyes to focus on him. They focused all right, but it looked more like a leer.

Ghortin frowned, pulling on his lower lip as he regarded Jenna. "I do suppose you're right. She isn't very big, is she?"

Storm shook his head in disgust and picked her up gently, batting away her hands. Without saying a word, he turned and carried her down the hall.

Jenna stayed awake, which in and of itself said a lot about her physical constitution. But she was definitely not going to be happy tomorrow.

"Soh, you're taking me to bed?" She pushed back the hair from his shoulder and was trying to reach the side of his neck. "Why, Storm, what will Ghortin say?" She found the side of his neck and was trying to aim kisses at it. Storm increased his pace and tried to dislodge her attempt.

"Jenna, you're not yourself right now—"

With surprising coordination she cut him off with a finger across his lips. "Shhhhh, I can be whoever you want me to be. After all, I'm not from here." She said the last in a conspiratorial whisper and her eyes remained closed so long afterwards he thought she was asleep. He was glad she probably wouldn't remember any of this. He needed to keep her at a distance, there was too much going on, and he couldn't get involved with anyone right now.

They'd reached her room, and she still hadn't opened her eyes. He gently laid her down on the bed, but her arm seemed stuck in his hair. As he tried to remove it, she woke up and kissed him solidly on the lips, "Goodnight, smexy." Then she fell back into the bed.

Storm gently untangled her arm. She might not remember this, but he certainly would. A second later a small army of elementals appeared and practically threw him out of the room. He shook himself off and headed out of the vortex.

"Have you noticed how close she's gotten to those

misbegotten elementals of yours? I'd no sooner laid her down than a whole herd of them chased me off."

Ghortin smoothed his hair unconsciously. "Aye, lad, that I have. But not until it was too late. That minx used them to flush me out of my laboratory earlier. She wanted to know what was going on and wasn't going to wait another minute for it." He grimaced at the memory.

Storm laughed as he resumed his seat.

Ghortin folded his arms and glared. "And she used a command word."

The laughter died in Storm's throat. Command words lay at the core of chaotic Power. Few magic users could tap into that rawness, let alone control it. "Are you sure?"

"Of course I'm sure." Ghortin snorted in disgust. "She used it on *me*. And what's worse, *I* didn't teach it to her."

"Then how did she learn it?" He folded his arms and glared at Ghortin. "I told you the lessons were too rushed."

"And you know very well why they are." Ghortin mindlessly fiddled with the royal invitation. "I can't keep her in here forever, and dangerous things are happening everywhere out there. I fear none of us will be safe, especially her. The least I can do is give the poor woman a chance."

"And I still say that between you and me there's more than enough protection. You've rushed her and now she's throwing around command words."

"I know." Ghortin gave in with a sigh. For a moment Storm thought his friend looked old, which, despite the mage's extremely advanced age, was something he'd never looked before. A second later it had passed.

Ghortin waggled a thick finger in Storm's direction. "That's no excuse for you to rub my face in it. I still say it had to be done. What if I'm not around? Things are changing quickly, more so every day. We aren't seeing it all yet. At some point she may find herself on her own."

He shrugged. "I'm afraid her use of a command word is yet another mystery. I didn't get a chance to ask her, but I gathered from her surprise she had no idea what she did."

"Like the night the ertin attacked. Afterwards she had no idea of what she'd said, or how she had done it." Storm frowned. "Could someone be working through her?"

Ghortin shook his head. "Doubtful. I thought of that when you first told me of the attack, so I checked. Anyone, even someone stronger than me, would leave residue if they were acting through her. I found nothing." He picked up the wrinkled royal notice from where he'd crumbled it unconsciously. "Now about this ball."

Ghortin and Storm spent the rest of the afternoon discussing the upcoming masquerade and, more importantly, the meeting the royal council was calling between the flowery words.

One the royal family didn't want the public notified about. Others in Traanafaeren had begun to see a pattern to the deadly events of the past year as well.

CHAPTER NINE

JENNA LOOKED BLEARY-EYED DOWN THE length of the cold, heartless floor that lay between her bed and the closet. With a groan, she let her head drag the rest of her body back to her pillow.

"Someone please end it now," she mumbled to the fuzzy ceiling. Normally she enjoyed the vagueness of the tan expanse overhead, but at present it was making her queasy.

"Finally awake, are we? Now what was that about ending things?"

"End my pain or my life, whichever is the quickest." She struggled yet again to fall out of bed. Never had she had such a nasty hangover. Never had it seemed so far to her wardrobe.

"Oh, come now." Ghortin's disembodied voice was less than sympathetic. "Normally I let my students wallow through such conditions; however, I realize that you may have had a lack of familiarity with the particular beverage in question. Consequently, I feel partially responsible. So, my dear, this one is on me."

An odd drink consisting of violently moving purple and orange swirls appeared on the floor next to the bed.

Fighting back the urge to choke at the sight of the thing, Jenna forced herself to crawl over to it.

"What am I supposed to do with this stuff?" She had an awful feeling she knew what he was going to say.

"Why, drink it, of course. You could pour it over your head if you rather, but I doubt it would have the desired effect."

Was that smugness in his voice? The last thing she remembered was *him* giving her some sweet wine, and he was smug? If she ever figured out how to crawl out of her room she was going to give him a large piece of her mind. Preferably the part that was trying to throw up.

"And what is the desired result? To kill me?"

"My dear," now Ghortin sounded peevish, "if you think you can pack and be ready to travel within the next two hours with your head coming out through your navel, then be my guest." He wasn't shouting, but the words were weighted perfectly, each one pounding like a stake through her battered skull.

Mindlessly, she reached out and clutched the swirling glass. Her first tentative sip made her rethink keeping the hangover and she tried to stop. The drink, however, had plans of its own and forced its way down her throat.

She threw the glass across the room and rolled to her feet sputtering.

"It crawled down my throat." She frantically looked around her sparse room for anything that could take away the taste of old tire rubber, swamp water, and fermented pineapples.

Ghortin chuckled. "It has to be bad; otherwise apprentices would be off getting drunk all the time. Stop sulking, get ready, and come have breakfast. As I've said, we've plenty to do today."

Jenna growled all the way into the bathroom. But she had to admit, even if only to herself, that the sludge had been better than the hangover.

———◆———

Jenna pondered the current situation as she wolfed down breakfast among Ghortin trying to pack. She'd gotten a little worried when Ghortin had casually told her about the formal ball. Supposedly she had been there when Storm delivered the invitation, but she certainly didn't remember seeing him last night. Most likely that wine had put her out before he'd arrived. What was more worrying was that this was her first introduction to this new society, and it happened to be a formal ball. She hated formal events in her own world; going to one in a completely foreign culture was almost enough to make her start looking for another glass of that wine. Ghortin had assured her that everything would be fine.

He paused, studied her frown for a moment, and then pulled up a chair. "I didn't want to tell you until we were on the road, but the reason we were invited is because the king's advisors noticed the same things I have. A council has been called, and not an open one." He was lost in thought, but didn't share it. Finally, he pushed himself away from the table.

"You need to go pick out what you want to take. Pack enough for a week as it's better to be safe than sorry. Warm clothes too, you never can tell what the weather will be like down there."

Jenna tried to follow his mental leap from the end of the world to her wardrobe. Finally she shook her head. "I don't have much to choose from."

Ghortin's smile succeeded in making it all the way up to his eyes this time. "Ah, but you do now, lass. It dawned on me that a young lady couldn't be making her royal debut dressed like an apprentice, even if she is one. I think you'll be happily surprised."

Even with the welcome new additions, it didn't take Jenna long to pack. Within an hour she was following Ghortin outside.

She took a deep breath as they walked around the corner toward the two horses. She still wasn't terribly fond of riding the big animals. They were beautiful, but they also scared the heck out of her. But Ghortin had pointedly explained to her that he wasn't about to exhaust himself, and possibly her, by using a translocation spell. Besides, as he pointed out, two days to get there wouldn't put too much of a dent in her posterior. She understood his point, but that didn't mean she was going to enjoy this.

Jenna let her eyes drift through the dark forest as they rode. Scattered streams of sunlight lanced in between the thick trees, lighting up small areas. The path was broader here, and she could make out one or two thinner trails within the path that showed where a single person, most likely Storm, had ridden recently.

"You know," Jenna wasn't going to spend two days atop a damn horse without any conversation, and Ghortin was getting ready to dive into his gray book. "You never told me much about Lithunane or the royal family. I'm going to be a bit of an embarrassment if I don't know anything about the capital city or the royals."

"You're *asking* for history lessons?" Ghortin looked at her closely for a minute, and then shook his head. "Lass, you could never be an embarrassment. But I shall be pleased to tell you a bit anyway."

He carefully slid the ever-present gray book back into his pack. "Lithunane is a new capital city. Up until eighty years ago, Irundail in the north was home to the royals."

Now, that was intriguing. Much better than identifying plant life as they passed. "Why did they leave? Was Irundail destroyed?"

Ghortin laughed. "Irundail? Not likely, lass. I've a goodly feeling that old monster will still be there when the world is long dead. No, the royals felt that after almost five hundred years of peace it would be safe to move to a more centralized location. Makes it quite a bit easier for me to visit as well. All of the royal family now lives in Lithunane, except for the third in line, Kaytine. She's a cleric of Irissanta and lives with the priestess. Although, because of her religious leaning, she's given up her place in the royal succession."

"Just how many offspring does this family have?"

Ghortin looked up in the air muttering names to himself as he counted. "Resstlin, who is the heir, Justlantin, Kaytine, Corin, Lilltkin, and of course the twins. Seven, yes, seven in all. Although I prefer to count the twins as one. The sweet little things are too young to be a bother, even to me. All in all, Daylin and Areania have raised a good brood. Resstlin recently turned one hundred and fifty-two and is working on learning how to run the kingdom."

Jenna adjusted her seat on the saddle. "The royals are kelar, I assume?" Unless humans on this world were as long lived as everyone else.

"Good, there's hope for you yet." He turned back with a wink. "Aye, they're kelar. But it was the luck of the draw that they were that. Ah, now that's an interesting tale, lass. I came that close to being king." He held up two fingers a hair's breadth apart. "Wouldn't have been a particularly good one, not like Kralin, Daylin's father. But, I could have been the king." He stared off into the forest as he spoke. "Kralin was an adventurer like me. Excitement, travel, distant lands. Not like today."

Jenna thought of the odd and deadly things that had been going on, including her own arrival and adventures with the ertin, and shuddered. If he didn't think the latest events were worthy of the past, she never wanted life to get that exciting again.

"There were six of us on that last trip; Kralin, Llitaan, Toshia, Oshrae, Carabella, and myself. Oh, the adventures I could tell you." His eyes were bright as he turned to her. Then he shook his head. "Another time, I think. But now we speak of that last adventure, the one that landed us here." He rocked back in his saddle.

"We'd made our home in a small village between the Strann and Khelaran borders. We were coming back from a particularly horrible battle in the Markare which had left us magically and physically drained."

His voice took on a distant tone, softer, as if he was afraid the memory would disappear. "Didn't think we were going to make it out of that last one. Not all of us did. Toshia didn't. Llitaan almost didn't." He shook his head, but Jenna couldn't see his face as he added softly, "Maybe it would have been better if she hadn't." He was silent for a few more moments. There was a distant pain there that hadn't healed, even after all those years. He finally shook his head and continued without prodding.

"I'm sorry, lass." He turned toward her with mist in his eyes. "I guess some things are better left forgotten. Maybe someday I can tell you about that last battle."

A ghost of old terrors crossed his lined face so quickly that Jenna almost thought she'd imagined it.

"As I was saying, we were beat, not literally mind you— even with our losses we still won the battle. Barely. We stumbled out of that desert on the wrong side, too weary to care. The land over here was wild and untamed. A land fit for the worst kind of monsters and outlaws. A few settlements struggled to survive, mostly in the midlands."

He nudged his horse forward; the big bay had almost come to a stop. Jenna swore the horse was listening to the story.

"We decided that we had little choice but to stop and rest a while. There was no way we could have made another crossing in our condition. Unfortunately, we were in the far north when we had to cross the Dragon range. No one in known history had ever crossed the range that far north.

"Although it would make for a better tale if I told you we went that way because we were brave, I shan't lie. We had no choice. The Winds were starting in the Markare and we had to cross or be swallowed by them. In addition, winter had begun. If we didn't make it over quickly, all the passes would be blocked. Struggling down from the mountains, we found ourselves in a magnificent emerald valley. Never before seen by civilized creatures. Now, winters up north are horrific at best usually, but within the valley it was almost spring." His horse had drifted back a bit so she could see Ghortin's face. The dreamy look in his eyes was something new to her. "The valley was amazing. Oh, don't get me wrong. Irundail of today is truly a feat. However, when we first found it? Ah, lass, it would bring tears to the eyes of the harshest campaigner. We set up camp and healed for the next half of a year." He took his water bag from his side, taking a deep swallow before going on.

"What we didn't know was that our last battle had been felt afar. I always believed that there was something beyond our understanding in that battle. People from all three kingdoms, Strann, Khelaran, and Derawne, came in search of us. They came for a new way of life, but couldn't seem to say how they knew to come. Over the years enough people had gathered that we began to have problems with thieves and criminals. We decided to stay and pull together a true kingdom. Besides, we'd buried Toshia in the valley and, even after ten years, Llitaan was in no condition to travel." He slipped back into silence.

"After ten years? What happened to her?"

He came out of his trance with a start. "Llitaan had been...captured is the best term. By the thing we'd fought in the desert. Only briefly. And we'd hoped we'd gotten her out quick enough. But when we rescued her, all she could do was wail and eat sand."

Jenna didn't say anything in the intervening silence.

Ghortin shrugged and went on. "Kralin had taken over as leader when Toshia died and he felt at peace staying in the valley and guiding the settlers. Carabella wandered off within the first three years."

He shook his head. "She never could accept that she

hadn't been able to completely save Llitaan. Cuari don't take defeat well, they aren't used to it. But I'll be the first to admit, none of us would have made it out if it weren't for that old vixen. She was the only one of us able to hold her own against that thing we fought. But once we decided to stay, we realized we needed a leader. We left it up to the people to choose their royal line." He snorted with a grin. "Wasn't a contest. Kralin became king."

Jenna looked up, noticing they were heading into a broader path and, beyond that, a clearing.

Ghortin urged his horse to speed up. "Thank the stars we've hit the way station. Now we can stop early for the afternoon. Well, lass, that wasn't so bad now, was it?" He turned to her with a grin, and Jenna noticed for the first time how late in the day it was.

She had been so caught up in Ghortin's tales that she hadn't realized how much time had passed. Unfortunately, as soon as that thought hit her, she realized how sore she was.

CHAPTER TEN

THE WAY STATION WAS AN attractive little building of wood and stone. It gave the appearance of leaning away from the road with the gangly additions in the back lording over the single story front. The front had a peaked roof with a stone chimney and smoke gently drifted up into the late afternoon sky.

Jenna was struck by how much it reminded her of an old bed and breakfast back home. The pang of loss she felt was like an old bruise.

Ghortin leaned over. "What is it, lass? Don't you care for our choice in lodgings?"

Jenna shook her head, banishing the lonely thoughts away. "No, I had a thought of home. My former home that is. I'll be fine."

Ghortin reached out a huge hand, engulfing her own for a moment. Then he nodded. "You'll feel better once we get some of Mugloon's stew in you."

He nudged his horse toward the station. The big bay went forward two steps, and then froze. Jenna's mare halted a foot behind him.

"Ghortin." Jenna tapped the horse's side a few times, but the animal wouldn't budge. "What's wrong with—?"

Ghortin waved her to silence, but kept his eyes on the thick clump of woods behind the way station.

"I should have been paying attention...damn me." He forced his horse to hold its place; it was clearly trying to bolt. Both animals now had their ears back and were shaking.

"What's wrong?" Jenna dropped her voice and stopped tapping the horse. If the horse bolted, she had no illusions about where she'd end up. "Do you hear anything?"

The mage turned slightly toward her. "No, do you?"

As he said the words, the incident with the ertin rose in her mind. And Storm saying those same words.

"Ertin?" She kept her voice calm, ignoring the terror that filled her stomach.

The mage shook his head. He had his eyes back on the silent scene before them. "I don't think so. The scent is different. But something is definitely wrong."

Just when she thought her nerves were going to break, a strange hooting broke behind the building. She couldn't tell if it was an echo, but the sound seemed to come from behind them as well—which explained Ghortin's reluctance in going anywhere.

Both horses strained to bolt, and arcs of Power flowed out of Ghortin's hands as he forced the animals to hold their ground.

A pointed head with huge ears rose out of the hedgerows in front of the station. There were stripes or some other markings on the dun-colored beast and its furred head was all wrong for an ertin.

Ghortin tensed as the front door flew open and a man with a short sword stepped out. Before Ghortin could shout, the vicious animal leapt out of the hedgerows and grabbed the man's throat. It was followed by two more of the previously hidden creatures. The man let loose a scream that ended in a sickly gurgle. Unseen hands slammed the door shut behind him.

One of the animals rose from its gruesome feast and stared right at her.

Its green, cat-like eyes glowed in the setting sun. The hooting began again, and the creature that had been staring at her went back to join its fellows.

Jenna frantically turned to Ghortin who seemed in

shock. He shook his head and briefly lowered his eyes. "Mugloon." He whispered it in eulogy but didn't look back to her. "The creatures are sciretts. Whatever you do, don't move a muscle until I tell you."

Jenna felt his magic as he reached out and identified the locations of the rest of the brutal animals. The one who had killed the stationmaster was still in sight, but the others had dropped back into the cover. It was about the size of a large monkey, and had elongated forelegs, but moved like a cat. The closest comparison she could come up with was a cross between a baboon and a panther. Although the shape of its ears and the dark russet stripes made her think of a hyena.

Ghortin drew in a huge surge of Power and flung it at the building. A faint glow settled over the station.

"Away!" Ghortin yelled as he released the hold over the horses. "I've protected the station, so they'll be after us now."

Ghortin's horse burst across the clearing with Jenna's mare right behind him. She clutched the reins, crouched down low on her horse's back, and held on as if her life depended on it. Judging by the speed of the sciretts, it did.

As they reached the far edge of the clearing, two sciretts leapt up and blocked their path. Ghortin muttered a spell that stunned the two monsters as the horses jumped over them. Unfortunately, the leap gave her a much closer look at the animals' inch-long canine teeth than she wanted.

Jenna felt Ghortin augment his horse's strength by feeding it some of his own Power. Jenna followed suit and drew in Power from the chaos that was threatening to take over her mind.

The sciretts stayed close behind. She shuddered and drew in still more energy to give to her horse.

The hooting grew louder. The much shorter legged

sciretts weren't having the trouble with branches and narrowing trails that the horses and riders were. Branches whipped her arms and face.

The hooting changed to howls after a few minutes, and Jenna took a risky look over her shoulder. One by one the animals dropped to the ground with exhaustion. From the ragged way many of them were going down, she doubted they would be getting up again. Some compulsion had forced them to run themselves to death.

Ghortin picked up on the animals' collapse and began slowing his horse's wild crash through the forest. After a few minutes they were at a complete halt. Both horses shook so hard that she was certain they were going to end up like the unlamented sciretts.

Ghortin crawled off his horse and immediately began feeling the animal's legs for injuries. Jenna did the same, though she wasn't exactly sure what she was searching for. It soon became apparent that aside from a myriad of scratches, all of them seemed to have come out of the chase intact.

"Keep moving. We've got a long way to go and I don't want anybody to freeze up. Our friends back there are sprinters; I'm amazed that they held on as long as they did." He gave the forest behind them a worried glance. "But they rarely hunt in packs either. And I know of no animal that will hunt prey past its own survival. Most of those that followed us are dead or dying."

Jenna couldn't help shuddering. She'd taken Ghortin's earlier warning to heart, but she hadn't thought she would have to fight for her life so soon. Judging by his surprise at the sciretts, Ghortin hadn't thought so either.

"But won't any that do survive go back to the way station?" She glanced back at the way they had come. "Shouldn't we help them?" She didn't want to ever see the sciretts again, but she couldn't think of abandoning those trapped people.

"I doubt they'll make it back, or even try to. I have a bad feeling they were waiting for us." Ghortin patted his horse as they walked. Both horses were exhausted, but they didn't seem to mind putting as much distance between themselves and those creatures as possible.

"And there will be help coming for them, never you fear. That spell I threw acts as a beacon as well as a shield. If you weren't so close to the casting of it you'd feel its call." He shook his head. "An important spell which I neglected to teach you, I now realize. I fear I shall have to remedy that before we get to Lithunane. The time is upon us for such spells."

Jenna couldn't help but look over her shoulder every few seconds. "What was it?"

There were other questions on her mind, like what were the sciretts, why weren't they behaving normally, and why were they after them? But she couldn't bring herself to ask those. She knew she wouldn't be able to handle the answers. Not now, so close after the attack.

Ghortin turned back to her with a nod. "More than likely, the best defensive spell ever created. If I do say so myself." He gave a half bow. "It actually adjusts to the attacking force. You didn't see it, but one of the creatures attacked the station as we took flight. The spell was triggered by that aggressive force and attuned itself to the sciretts' biochemistry. It then began emitting a repulse signal tuned to them. Plus, and this is the crowning glory, the spell sends out physical and magical warnings. Any travelers will stay clear of that area, unless they feel up to taking on the remains of an unnatural tribe of sciretts. Soon enough mages will be by to clear up any remaining problems."

"Are they part of whatever is going on?" In a softer voice she added, "Of my arrival?"

"They might be; most likely everything is related. But," he turned and looked at her intently, "your arrival is a symptom of the disease, not the cause. We'll nip that thought right now; you didn't cause the recent problems, they were here before you arrived. And I can't work with someone who's feeling guilty about being alive. Besides," he turned back to the darkening trail with a slight frown, "it'll clog up your Power. Emotions have a nasty habit of doing that."

Jenna opened her mouth to debate whether she was a cause or a symptom, but Ghortin whirled around with a dark look. So she raised her hands in submission instead.

"Okay. I believe you. I absolve myself for any of the strange things that have been happening in this bizarre world. Happy?"

Ghortin stopped and folded his arms. "Do you believe your words?"

She met his eyes, and then glanced away. "Almost."

He sighed and continued on. "That's a start. And no more than I could ask for given our present circumstances."

He slowed down his pace, peering into the woods on either side of the trail. "We should find a place to set up camp; even I won't be able to see much longer."

Jenna grimaced. She didn't look forward to spending a night outdoors in the woods. Particularly with those creatures in them somewhere.

"How much further to the end of the forest? Wouldn't it be better if we waited until we were out of it?"

"No. I doubt any of those things could have made it this far. Besides, past the forest is the Fyolden Plains, which will take a goodly portion of tomorrow to cross, and there is no coverage. And it's not something we can cross before nightfall." He started to lead them down a promising side trail. "Now, here's a test for you; why would anyone, particularly a mage, prefer to camp in the woods?"

Jenna thought about it for a minute, ignoring her

mind's demand to get the hell out of the damn trees and never mind the reasons.

"In here," she waved her arms at the thick trees. "You can't see anything." It wasn't meant to be an answer, more of a complaint.

Ghortin smiled; obviously he failed to pick up on the note of discontent in her voice. "Exactly. What you can't see, *they* can't see. Magecraft is a powerful tool, the strongest you'll ever have. But it has to be helped; you have to use circumstances to let it do the best it can. A portion of your Power comes from…" He turned and looked at her pointedly.

"From the earth itself; trees, and other natural energies. And a forest is a good place to draw from." She sighed in resignation. "It makes sense, but I still don't feel comfortable in here."

"Of course you don't," Ghortin said. A minute later they came out in a small hollow, surrounded by brush as well as the tall trees. "We haven't set up camp yet." He waved his hands to the clearing. Jenna felt a low-level probe coming from him as he magically scanned the area. Satisfied that it was clear, Ghortin nodded to her. "You'll feel much better once we've gotten some food into you."

He glanced around the area and cleared out a smooth corner, then turned to her with a sheepish grin. "I'm afraid that first I'm going to have to break one of my rules about not using spells for luxury. I was so preoccupied with things that I failed to bring adequate emergency supplies. So, unless you feel it would be better for us to sleep in the trees and eat berries…" He raised an eyebrow questioningly.

She was still less than happy with the camping situation, but suffering wasn't going to make it better. "By all means, break away. I'm too tired to care at this point."

Ghortin started to gather Power, and then stopped. "But don't tell Storm about this, all right? I'd never hear the end of it."

He went back to his work, and within minutes the formerly bare space was graced with two simple, but well-padded bedrolls, a satchel of food, and a pile of grain for the horses.

Ghortin turned to her with a smile and a nod, as if he'd done nothing spectacular. Just from the brief studies into magecraft she'd had, Jenna knew creating things out of thin air was not as easy as her teacher made it seem.

He smiled bigger. "Now, this moment is screaming for a lesson, I think. How would you go about anchoring these trees into a protection spell for our little camp?"

It took her three frustrating attempts, but after half an hour Ghortin was satisfied that she'd created a blind that no outside source would be able to see.

He studied the results and nodded. A moment later he gave a little sigh.

She looked up from where she was laying out her roll. "Is something wrong? Are they back?"

"Not likely. Now I already told you that, lass." He went over and began laying out his roll. "They won't be finding us. Not on this trip anyway. I was sighing at the way in which you are blossoming; I shall soon be in your shadow." He performed an elaborate bow in her direction. "But don't you let that make you cocky. You'll be my apprentice a bit longer. Now, off to the horses with you."

She nodded and forced her weary body up with a pang of guilt. She'd been so ready to drop that she had almost forgotten their companions. Ghortin had already taken their saddles off, combed them, and mostly settled them in for the night while she was setting her spell. All that was left was to check their water and grain.

Being too exhausted to look for wood, or cook anything, they didn't bother to set a fire.

Jenna lay back as soon as she finished her waybread, and

was asleep immediately after.

Early the next morning, she rolled over stiffly. She was barely awake, but was already fully aware of every rock, bump, and branch she'd failed to clear out of her sleeping quarters last night.

"Oh, shoot me now."

"Eh, shoot you with what? You certainly have troubles waking, don't you? All this talk of shooting and killing is not a healthy way to start your day."

She twisted her head to see Ghortin; she kept her swearing to herself when she bumped a particularly nasty bruise. He had for once been merciful; he looked like he'd been up for some time and hadn't done so much as peep to wake her up.

She stirred a bit more and could see that not only was he fully groomed and dressed for the day's ride, the horses were ready. At first she was grateful, and then she felt resentment that all that activity took place and her supposedly great magical Power hadn't so much as stirred her. Grumbling to herself, she looked over to see both horses were well past the range of her spell.

"Ghortin. The spell, it's—"

"Gone." He smiled down at her. "I had to take it down to give the horses some room this morning."

She forced herself free of the bedroll. "But shouldn't I have felt something when you took it down?" She tried straightening out the creases in her clothes, but soon gave up. "Isn't that the point? I mean, what if you were one of the bad guys?" She had begun to feel like she might have a bit of control over her own safety, but if her spells wouldn't hold she sure wouldn't last long.

Ghortin's head popped up from where he was rummaging through his pack. "Of course you felt something. You weren't completely awake. Think hard now."

She ran her fingers through her hair, trying to think through the misty vestiges of sleep.

Finally she shook her head. "Nothing. I didn't feel it go down at all. I still can't tell."

"You can't tell?" He stopped his fussing and looked up with a worried frown. "Did you feel it last night?"

Jenna nodded hesitantly. "Sort of. I could tell I was casting a spell. But I couldn't tell that it was there once I'd completed it. You seemed satisfied, and I thought maybe that was part of the spell." Besides she'd been so tired at that point she figured fatigue was making her miss things.

Ghortin was immediately next to her, holding his hands on either side of her head. He stared deep into her eyes. "Try to cast a spell."

His voice scared her. "Anything?"

At a silent nod from him, she tried to pull in Power. And almost fell flat on her face.

Ghortin grabbed her as she buckled. Shaking herself, she flung out for the Power again. This time a mind-shattering pain erupted in her head.

"Pull out. Jenna? Do you hear me? *DROP IT.*" He shook her shoulders.

Ghortin's use of a command word brought her back and out of the pain.

"I stopped; it's all right." She tried to push his hands away.

"What happened?" He pushed her down toward a log to sit. "You tried to reach for Power?"

She nodded miserably. "Nothing was there. It was as if…I can't explain it, it was gone." She couldn't explain to him the terrifying loss that had come with that blinding pain. It was as if the world around her was half of what it had been.

"Now, now. It's not the end of the world." He forced a smile. "I'm no mage healer, but I've seen symptoms like yours, usually in battle though. You've simply overdrawn your magic reserves." He sighed and rose to his feet. "It's my fault. I realized you weren't clamped down as tight as you should be. Magically, every mage within a fifty-mile radius heard you when you first started giving Power to the horse."

Jenna started to apologize, but Ghortin brushed her off.

"Now don't look like that. You're missing my point. It's my fault, you did nothing wrong and your magic will be back soon enough. You've got an awful lot of Power there, my lass. At times I forget that."

"I still don't understand. If I am so strong, how come I've lost my magic?" She wiggled her fingers in the air. At that moment it felt like something much more than magic had been taken from her. Something she hadn't realized was there before.

Ghortin took hold of her fluttering hands and pulled her up with a sigh. "I'm afraid I've sort of sped through a lot of your lessons. I might have missed some things. The stronger a student is, the bigger the risk for over drain. It would be far more difficult to rein in a war stallion than a colt, you know."

"So, I've been fighting myself? And I drained myself doing it?" She frowned; there was something wrong with his thinking. "I thought the whole thing to magic is creating energy, not restraining it."

Now it was his turn to look away. "Lass, for most magic users that would be true; although you still have to maintain control of what passes through you. For you—"

Jenna cut him off. "Wait, so now you're saying I'm a magic mutant?" Her brief bout with self-pity was tossed by the wayside.

He scowled. "I didn't say that. You are blessed with incredibly strong basic Power abilities. But you also seem to lose it, it flows through you when it should stay."

She chewed her lower lip for a few minutes, trying to follow this latest confusing addition. "So, I lost my magic because I carry too much Power with me and I leak?"

He nodded vigorously, gray hair flying. "Yes, yes. See,

now you understand."

She stared at him, then shook her head and began picking up the night's supplies. "I have no idea what you're talking about. How can I both leak and have too much Power?" She held up her hand wearily, this whole thing was getting too confusing. "Never mind, I don't want to know. Just tell me, will I get my Power back, and how can I keep from leaking if I do?"

"I think you'll be fine, just relax today, magically that is. If we have to run from anything, I'll take care of your horse. As for the leak, we can work on that while we ride. We can run some of my magic through your system to make sure those leaks are blocked." He picked up his bedroll, debating whether to send it back to oblivion. He shook his head and tied it behind his saddle. He motioned for her to do the same with the rest of their meager supplies.

"All set?"

Jenna nodded as she mounted her mare.

"Let's be off then. If we hurry, we can reach Lithunane before last bell."

CHAPTER ELEVEN

———

THEY CROSSED THE PLAINS WITHOUT any problems. Even so, Ghortin only let them stop once the entire afternoon. His unease intensified the further they went, and by the time the city walls of Lithunane were visible, as a dark line in the distance, she and the horses were jumping at butterflies. Jenna herself had even taken out her short sword.

She was about to ask him for any last-minute things she should know before entering the city when she noticed a figure riding out toward them. She smiled as the figure got closer. What she had thought was a short cape, was actually long hair.

Storm nodded as he pulled his gray horse up to theirs. His clothes were rumpled and covered in dust. "I just got back and heard about the attack on the way station."

Ghortin noticeably relaxed. "I am glad for the escort; things are a bit jumpy after that little adventure."

Jenna put her sword away. She hadn't gotten that good with it yet and felt a bit foolish with it out. "That beacon hit all the way out here?" Ghortin was right; she needed to learn that particular spell. Once her magic came back, anyway. *If* it came back. She quickly shoved that thought aside. Storm gave her an odd smile, as if she had said something completely different. Or he was thinking something completely different.

Storm nodded briefly as he turned to follow in their direction. "Sort of. Mage Acklan was on border duty and he has far-sense. He felt the disturbance as soon as

Ghortin cast his spell." He nudged his mount into a trot toward the city. Jenna kept up, with Ghortin trailing a bit behind. "What was it anyway? I just got back home a few hours ago and took off as soon as I heard which station was under attack."

"And you didn't wait to see who or what, simply grabbed that beastly sword of yours and ran to the rescue, eh, lad?" Ghortin sighed. "One of these days, my boy, you're going to run off blindly into something you can't handle."

Storm didn't answer, but she did notice he automatically adjusted the sword hanging at his side.

As he reached around, she noticed he was also armed with his long bow, throwing knives, and a small dagger. He may not have known what he was up against, but he was prepared for the worst.

After a few minutes of riding, Ghortin relaxed enough to pull out his gray book and completely ignored them.

Storm smiled. "How did you feel after your Gorgon ale-wine evening?"

The speculative look he'd favored her with from before was back. Jenna racked her brain for any memory of that night before answering. "Fine. Well, not so fine. Ghortin had to give me one of his evil concoctions so my head wouldn't split apart. I'm sorry I missed your visit."

"Actually, you were still up when I arrived. You don't remember?"

That couldn't be good. Jenna racked her brain some more. And came up with nothing at all, nothing past Ghortin telling her women who looked like her were being murdered. She shook her head tightly. "Not really. Why?"

Storm had briefly turned away, so she didn't completely hear him, but it almost sounded like he said "good".

"What did you say?"

Storm turned back, his grin a bit too broad. "I just said

no reason. You pretty much went to bed right after I got there."

Jenna narrowed her eyes, but he stayed silent. She thought about asking Ghortin, but her mentor was one of the least observant people she'd ever met. Unless it was related to magic at any rate. "I'm not planning on that ever happening again, but you'd tell me if I did something stupid, right?"

"Of course. I'd tell you if you did anything…stupid."

Jenna detected the pause right before stupid, but he kept smiling.

———◆———

Lithunane was further away than she originally estimated; the rolling plains played havoc with distance perception. It was well after sunset by the time they cleared the small city gate. A larger, more ornate gate hung closed to the right of it. Its intricately carved doors were bolted shut.

From the size of the crowd surging in with them it was obvious that many people felt it safer to spend the night within the city walls.

She looked to her companions for explanation, but neither seemed willing to comment. As usual. So she watched the crowd instead. There seemed to be equal numbers of kelar and humans, with a fair sprinkling of the short, stocky derawri added as well.

Jenna studied the derawri the most, this being her first look at the third species of her new home world. On the whole, they seemed no taller than about four feet high. They were solidly built, but it was all lean muscle. Many of the men wore sleeveless work shirts, which accented their well-formed musculature. Although Storm seemed to be the only one of his kind in sight with such long hair, with the derawri it appeared to be quite the norm. Many of the males had well-trimmed rounded beards, but none wore the mustaches that appeared common with the humans.

She happened to glance up in time to notice that her two companions, lost in their own conversation, had wandered ahead of her. Jenna broke off her study and nudged her horse to catch up.

A young rider arrowed his way toward them through the crowd. He dodged around a gaily painted derawri basket cart and paced his horse alongside Storm. He was a human boy of no more than fifteen, with long, unkempt black hair.

The boy was earnestly telling Storm something, his gangly arms flailing around as he spoke. Storm's face grew serious, and Jenna mentally cursed the crowd that had pushed her out of hearing range.

Ghortin was closer to them, and Jenna watched as the tale was repeated to him and his face grew somber. With a few terse words and a nod, Storm and the messenger whirled their mounts around and took off down a side road that seemed to loop back to the gate.

A small troop of kelar minstrels finally moved out of Jenna's way, enabling her to ride alongside Ghortin. "Shouldn't we be going with him?" She twisted to look in the direction her friend had gone, but he was far from sight.

Ghortin forced the serious look from his face, but it hung around his eyes.

"Now why would we want to go back out into that dark night when you're a guest of the king? Come, we must hurry, dinner will be within the hour."

Jenna folded her arms and glared.

Ghortin raised his hand. "Storm had to go run some errands. He said he'll meet you in front of the market after the second morning bell tomorrow and take you on a grand tour." At Jenna's continued look he added, "And it will give you and me a chance to relax and discuss things this evening."

They rounded a corner and found themselves on a fairly quiet roadway. It was broader than the one they'd left, and was cobbled in deep blue stones. The shops here were grander and fewer. At the top of the beautiful road was the castle.

It was inhumanly open and airy, and so unlike the ancient castles of Europe that Jenna at first almost failed to identify it as such. Tall, thin spires rose into the darkening sky. The castle's facade was almost entirely made up of huge stained-glass windows and pale luminescent brickwork that looked more like spun glass than earthen stone. A wide moat circled the entire building. The drawbridge was down and from the immobile look of the chains, that was its most common position. Six heavily armed guards stood at odds with the open lightness of the castle grounds. The guards recognized Ghortin as they rode closer and waved for them to pass.

Jenna pulled back with a start when they passed under the heavy walls and into the inner court. After the growing darkness of the city, the bright courtyard was quite a shock.

Jenna had no time to study where the light was coming from before two stable boys came and whisked the horses away. Ghortin and Jenna were handed over to the waiting hands of the palace seneschal, a wizened human who looked older than Ghortin. The men greeted each other heartily, Ghortin actually bowing slightly in honor before he embraced his friend.

He motioned for Jenna to step forward. "This is a happy meeting. Jenna, my apprentice, I would like you to meet one of my oldest friends and confidants, Tor Ranshal."

The grizzled old man took her hands in his own, peering down at her intently. She thought there was a flash of surprised recognition that crossed his finely lined face, but it was gone with the arrival of one of the most beautiful smiles Jenna had ever seen.

"I am most pleased to make the acquaintance of the pupil of my dear friend."

"I'm pleased to meet you." She thought about trying a curtsy, for there was something about this thin, gray haired man that led to reverence. She found herself liking him immediately.

"You must be starving." He kept his light hold on her hands, but nodded toward Ghortin. "If I know Master Ghortin, he went off unprepared as usual, and left you eating mage food. And after such a crisis." Tor Ranshal's eyes were an unusual golden color, and they glowed warmly as he poked fun at his long-time friend. Jenna was surprised to note that Ghortin actually reddened faintly.

The tall seneschal shook his head, acting as if Ghortin were no more than an errant page. "Now, my good Ghortin. You know mage food from nothing isn't good for you. We'll have to rectify that, won't we?"

He released one of her hands to take a hold of Ghortin's arm, spinning him nicely toward the castle's entrance.

As Jenna allowed him to lead her in, she had the distinct impression that the wizened old age look was mostly for show. There was an unusual strength under that calm surface.

Tor Ranshal led them immediately into a small room off the main entrance. Jenna was momentarily disappointed that she didn't get to see more of the castle first, but a sudden rumble of her stomach reminded her of what was important.

There were two men in the room already, sitting behind a low table laden with a varied selection of food. Behind them a small fire was crackling in a wide fireplace set deep in the wall.

The closest man was a tall human. Every strand of his shoulder-length blond hair was groomed to perfection.

His lean face rivaled that of a kelar in beauty, and he set it off artistically with a neatly trimmed Vandyke beard. Although quite striking, his burgundy colored velvet ensemble seemed at odds with the casual feel of the room.

The second man was a kelar, but, even for an age defying race, he looked young. His jet-black hair was cropped close, giving quite an amazing view of those long, tapered ears. Like all of the kelar men she'd seen so far, his dark, sharp face was smooth. Briefly Jenna wondered if the species had facial hair.

It was the second man who acknowledged their presence first.

"Ghortin, my good man." The dark-haired kelar smiled as he leapt forward. If Storm and the kelars she'd seen on the way in were a standard, this exuberant man was quite a bit shorter than average. He couldn't be more than a few inches above her own five-eight.

"Ah, another fair meeting. I had no idea you were back, Edgar." He sighed heavily. "Just another example of the seriousness of our situation if Daylin has pulled you from the field."

"I'm afraid so," the short kelar started to answer when a pointed cough broke in.

"Don't you think it would be best if this waited until the servants were cleared of the room?"

Jenna was shocked to see that the blond man was staring pointedly in her direction.

Ghortin moved forward. "Why, Ravenhearst, still as diplomatic as ever I see." He folded his arms and gave a tight smile. "If I may make some introductions?" He motioned Jenna forward. "May I present Lady Jenna, my *apprentice*? Lady Jenna, this is Lord Ravenhearst of Strann, and my good friend Sir Edgar, master spy extraordinaire."

Jenna gave a nod, but the blond noble barely acknowledged it. However, the wiry kelar spy bowed over her hand with a flourish.

"Oh, wretched my existence, that I never have such fair apprentices." He turned back toward Ravenhearst. "I'd say she has every right to be here. More so, in fact, than some people."

Tor Ranshal had held back, but he now moved into the room.

"Now, children, play nice. Of course the Lady Jenna must be here, so must Lord Ravenhearst, and many others before this is through. Shall we eat and save our bickering for the enemy?"

Ghortin and Jenna made their way to the table without further concern. The others stood back a bit until the new arrivals had settled in with nicely filled plates.

Jenna was glad that Ghortin had chosen seats far from Lord Ravenhearst. Even though he did not attempt to engage her in conversation, she did catch Ravenhearst giving her a few speculating looks from time to time.

Fortunately, from the reaction around the table, no one else seemed to like him either. She was surprised that this great meeting was made up of so few. She said something to that effect to Ghortin.

"What?" He looked up from gnawing on a drumstick. "No, no. This isn't an official meeting. More like a pre-meeting. Although two of these men are the most important in the land, next to the king himself."

Jenna spared a glance for Lord Ravenhearst. The noble was daintily picking through his food, as if eating it was beneath him.

She kept her voice low. They were at the opposite end of the table, and Edgar and Tor Ranshal were chatting, but it would be better if she wasn't heard. "I certainly hope that he isn't one of the two. Otherwise, this world is in more trouble than I thought."

Ghortin didn't need to look up to know of whom she spoke. "No, although he'd like to be. That's why he's here in fact; hoping to find things to add to his own glory." He shook his head. "Can't stand the man much myself. Why Daylin is involving him, I'll never understand."

Jenna nodded and went back to her food. Conversation drifted toward the incidents; most importantly, their encounter with the sciretts. From the first word, Lord Ravenhearst tried to discredit the attack. He stated, in heavily cloaked words, that perhaps their judgment had been in error. A pack of local dogs was the likely source.

Ghortin shot a disgusted glance at the nobleman. No one else acknowledged him, or his words, that much.

Jenna listened closely to the rest of the conversation, she couldn't help but notice that none of them seemed to be going deep into reasons or details. Obviously, Ghortin wasn't the only one who didn't trust the blond lord's interest.

A wave of exhaustion hit Jenna soon after she pushed her plate away. The men were deciding where to adjourn to as she practically fell out of her chair.

Tor Ranshal caught her before she slid off. "Child? Are you well?" The concern turned his magnificent eyes to copper.

"I'm sorry." Jenna shook her head. "I guess the whole trip finally caught up with me. I'm exhausted."

He patted her hand. "No need to apologize, child." He glanced toward Ghortin briefly. "I'm the sorry one."

She shook them both off with a yawn. "I'm tired. I think it was all that riding." She was too tired to glare at Ghortin.

"You need a good night's rest." The men spoke simultaneously. She grimaced, the last thing she needed right now was Ghortin in stereo. Even if she completely agreed.

As if their words had been a summons, a young human page came into the room. He peered through his too-long blond bangs at the seneschal.

"Jesop, good lad. Take the Lady Jenna to her suite." He turned and gave Jenna an elegant bow. "Good night, my dear, rest well."

Jenna nodded sleepily, said good night to Sir Edgar, and gave a curt nod to Lord Ravenhearst. She was too tired to be diplomatic.

"Don't forget you're meeting Storm at the market. And be back in your rooms by nightfall tomorrow for the masquerade."

Jenna nodded, though she knew he couldn't see her anymore. If she had more energy, she would have chastised him for being a mother hen.

Not many people were using the passageway they were walking down at present, as the mage lights were quite dim. Jenna kept close tabs on the short boy ahead of her, but found she was a little too close as she almost stumbled into his back. He had come to a halt in front of a pair of ornate red oak doors.

"Apprentice mage Lady Jenna a-Ghortin, the rooms belonging to your Master and yourself await. Do you have further need?"

His voice squeaked in a few spots, but Jenna managed to cover her grin by yawning. As the boy spoke he nudged the right door open so Jenna could enter.

"No, this is great. Thank you." Looking down for the first time, she realized how grimy she was. "Wait. You wouldn't happen to know where I could get a bath?"

"Of course, my lady. One has already been drawn and is waiting for you inside."

Jenna frowned. How had they known she would be coming up right now?

The page misunderstood her frown. "My lady? Is something wrong? You did say you wished a bath, did you not?" The boy looked terrified.

"Oh, yes. I did. I was wondering…" She paused as worry darkened his eyes. "Never mind. Everything is wonderful. Thank you." She tried to remember what Tor Ranshal had called him. "Jesop."

She smiled as the boy's face lit up. Obviously, pages weren't used to being identified by nobles. And judging from the decoration on the door, Jenna was ranking right up there. More than likely a mere apprentice wouldn't under normal circumstances, but she gathered that no apprentice of Ghortin's was a mere anything.

The boy ran off with a nod, and Jenna shut the door behind him. Leaning against the warm wood of the door, she surveyed their new quarters. The main sitting room was spacious and airy. Graceful forest scenes were richly displayed on the tapestries that covered most of the walls. Two bedrooms branches out on opposite sides of the front room, they looked the same, so she claimed the chamber closest to the door.

In the adjoining room was a sight she'd been looking forward to, even if its appearance was a mystery. A full bath with fragrant steam rising above it, and soft white towels beside it.

She let herself relax completely for the first time in days, but her mind kept drifting back toward Lord Ravenhearst. She couldn't shake the feeling that he was more than opportunistic. But since she couldn't explain it either, she let it get pushed aside for a while. Baths were meant to be enjoyed, not to worry in.

She found her things in one of a pair of bedrooms off to the side. Full, happy, and clean, Jenna tumbled off to sleep.

CHAPTER TWELVE

———◆———

THE BRIGHT MORNING SUNLIGHT WAS starting its journey across the stone floor when Jenna finally decided to open her eyes. She had been awake for the past fifteen minutes, but had been much too warm and content to think of moving.

However, from the scents she was smelling, some wonderful person had sent up breakfast. She quickly changed, then went out to the front room. Looking around vainly for her teacher, she realized he had not only snuck in without her knowing last night, he'd broken his fast and snuck back out again just as silently.

She was finishing up with a cup of amber tea and a piece of thick bread slathered with honey, when bells began to chime outside. Taking her cup with her, she wandered over to the arched window and peered down.

Somehow that page last night had navigated her up much higher than the three or four flights she thought they'd walked. At this height, Lithunane was spread out before her like a box of jewels. The graceful, multi-color pebbled roadways marked where one jewel ended and another began.

Here and there tall spires, some so thin they looked to be no more than gossamer threads, stretched up to the morning sun. Still others hung low to the ground, stating with elegance that grace can also be found in strength. From the diversity of the buildings alone, it would be apparent to any observer that more than one species called this city home.

The bell chimed again and Jenna shook herself free of the city's spell. She'd almost forgotten her meeting with Storm.

Hoping the housekeeper, or castle keeper, wouldn't fault them for the state of their rooms, Jenna bolted out the massive doors.

After a few false starts, she finally got pointed down the right stairwell. And after a few more, got herself out the gate and en route to the market.

The city was as beautiful at ground level as it had been from the tower, if a little bit less mysterious. But the wide variety of smells—ginger, cinnamon, and jasmine—drifting from every direction more than compensated for that.

The open-air market was perched atop a small rise a few streets over from the castle. It wasn't a permanent fixture; clearly the small shops packed up each evening. She found her eye caught by a tiny stall with crystals perched on the tip of the market's edge. She was allowing herself to be drawn to it when a low voice spoke softly next to her.

"Alas, my lady has already forsaken me for the wares of another man. And so early in the day, too."

Jenna managed to refrain from jumping out of her skin and glared at the sneaky kelar.

"Would you stop sneaking up on me?" Before he and Ghortin became so secretive back at the cottage, Storm had developed a fondness for sneaking up on her that bordered on the excessive. Out of habit she took her customary swing. She knew he'd keep out of reach.

"You insufferable point-eared goblin. You're always creeping up on people."

Storm laughed as he stepped back from another half-hearted swing. "No, just you." He stepped back further as she swung again. "I'm trying to get you used to kelar ways. We wouldn't want anyone to think you're not…" He leaned forward, a few stray hairs pulling loose of his customary cloth headband and falling across his face. "Shall we say, of this world?" His voice was low and serious, but his dark blue eyes were twinkling.

Jenna finally started laughing. It was damn hard to stay mad at someone this good looking. "Fine, you win again. But can we please call a truce while I'm here? I've got enough stuff to worry about, and I doubt that any of the local kelars are going to be sneaking up on me."

Storm relented. "Fair enough. Now how about a tour of the market?"

"Lead away." A thought hit her; she never had gotten a chance to ask Ghortin where Storm had gone, not that she'd be likely to get an answer. "Where did you go last night anyway?"

Storm shrugged causally, but he stole a quick glance around them. "I thought we could talk after the market, say a picnic? It's fairly close in here."

Jenna reddened a bit; he was right. Of course, if the people around her would just be more upfront about things, this wouldn't be an issue.

"Agreed." She managed to make it sound like that had been her intention all along. Taking Storm's arm, she led him toward the crystal cart she'd been aiming for before their encounter. "Are you going to show me this market or what?"

They made fairly good time, although Jenna was certain she could never have found her way through such meandering pathways. There seemed to be no rhyme or reason to the layout of the market area, although Storm acted like there was.

At one point Jenna could have sworn that Lord Ravenhearst stood a few stalls away. She tried to get Storm to follow when he darted away, but he refused, saying he wanted nothing to do with that particular noble. If it was him; the lord had people to do his bidding down here, he would probably never cheapen himself by appearing in person.

The noon bell began its chimes when Storm led them out of the market and down a small, dusty side road.

Jenna looked at him questioningly, but he just flashed one of his secretive smiles.

Finally he stopped in front of a small wooden cottage that was nondescript in appearance, but had the most amazing fresh baked bread smells wafting from it. Jenna's mouth began to water immediately.

"And for the final leg on your tour, I have arranged a picnic by the esteemed Madam Rachael, and a carriage ride to Sorrow's Sea."

Jenna looked closer at the small building, but she didn't see any sign marking it as an eatery. Deciding that she wasn't going to argue with those wonderful smells, she let Storm lead her inside.

The whitewashed interior was pristine, with small white porcelain ware along the top rafters. A tiny kelar woman bustled around, putting the finishing touches on a picnic basket. Jenna noticed with a start that the white haired woman was actually *old*. The first signs of age she'd seen in a kelar. A part of her was dying of curiosity to know how old an old kelar was. However, she refrained from blurting out her question.

"My boy." The sprightly little woman beamed at Storm as she wrapped her thin arms around his waist.

Storm returned the hug fondly. "How have you been, tiny mother?"

Jenna started for a second, and then realized his term must be one of endearment, not reality. The only thing they had in common was their species.

The smile faded from her lined face. She brushed a white hair back with a flour-dusted hand. "Something is going wrong, my boy. I'm not sure what it is, or where it's coming from, but mark my words, something has changed the pattern." She shook her head wearily. "I feel it in my marrow. Ghortin has come."

It was more of a statement than a question, but Storm nodded anyway. He was about to add something, when she spied Jenna.

Her diminutive face lit up immediately and she scurried over, enveloping Jenna with as much force as she had used on Storm moments before. Then she pulled back a bit, staring intently into Jenna's eyes.

"Ah, child, fate has taken you far from hearth and home. And given you a great task, one that has, and will, cost you much. Yet, you may be the answer." She nodded as if her nonsense was the most sensible thing in the world. "Yes, your coming, although not foretold, should not be unexpected." Sympathy touched her deep brown eyes. "But you may have to give up what you desire most, such as a return home."

Jenna froze in shock. "You know who I am?"

She looked up at Storm and saw the same look of surprise that must be on her own face. The woman's last words hit her a moment later.

"You mean I *can* go home?" She didn't dare believe it. Even thinking of home had been a pastime she'd outgrown in the past few months. The sight of her mangled former body still lingered in the back of her nightmares.

The small woman's face grew sadder. "Tsk. There I go again. I speak of things out of time. No, my child, I can't get you back, not yet." She glanced over to Storm with a smile. "And your secret was not betrayed by anyone. I have gifts. I see things others don't." Her eyes came back to Jenna as she sighed with a sad smile. "Don't fret; I'm old Rachael, the hearth mistress." Her eyes grew distant as she focused on something far beyond the little cottage. She snapped back, her eyes bright and inquisitive once more.

"Now is not the time for such dire talk and gloom." Her smile lit the room again. "Now is the time for young ones to picnic on the shore. Later things are for later times."

Storm came to Jenna's side and Rachael peered at the pair intently for a second. She grinned. "It's not spring by any chance, is it?"

Jenna was startled, the weather was pleasant outside, but it was obvious that winter was on its way.

Storm however, took the question in stride. "No, tiny mother, it's near autumn's end. As well you know."

A mischievous sparkle lit the woman's eyes. "Pity." She winked at Jenna. "Well, off with the two of you. And tell that old scoundrel Ghortin…" She paused as if listening to something. Finally, she waved her tiny hands at them. "Oh, never mind. He's with Tor Ranshal. I'll get two for one today." She cackled to herself, then shoved the fragrant basket into Storm's waiting hands and bustled the two out the door. Jenna tried to say thank you, but they found themselves outside before she could get the words out.

"I didn't get a chance to thank her."

A chime rang in the air above her. "You're welcome, my dear, now go play." The voice was definitely Rachael's, even if it came from nowhere. She clearly was more than just a hearth mistress, that term referring to dabblers in small magic.

Storm shrugged and led her around the corner to a small, open carriage. The gray horse hooked up to it greeted them as they approached.

"We might as well take her words to heart; I've found that arguing with Rachael is similar to arguing with Ghortin. You stand a better chance of winning an argument against the sea."

Storm helped her into the carriage, then took the reins and led them away.

"So she's a mage, right? Just how old is she? And, pardon my asking, but don't you have any friends without gray hair?"

Storm shook the reins, letting the horse have more freedom as they cleared the busy city streets. "Sort of. I have no idea. And, yes, but I find it easier to relax around elders sometimes. Happy?"

"How can someone sort of be a mage? That's like being sort of pregnant—you are or you aren't."

Storm shrugged. "You should ask Ghortin, he'd be able to give you a better answer. But I'm afraid he's not sure how she does what she does. She doesn't register as a mage on any known scale. I'm sure you didn't sense any-thing?"

Jenna shook her head; she wasn't ready to admit she couldn't sense anything magically right now. Although Ghortin assured her she'd be better soon, she'd believe it when she saw it.

Storm nodded. "See, no one can pick her up that way. And sometimes she sees the future as if it were the past." He flicked the horse's reins and they picked up speed. "But don't be too concerned about what she said to you back there. She's often wrong. Or way off, in terms of time. You could end up saving a small child when you're eighty, and that would fulfill her prediction. She's a sweet old thing, and once the mage council in Khelaran decided she was harmless, no one listens to her much."

Jenna looked out over the passing farm fields. They had left the city and were now in the agricultural portion of the land. Long rows of green neatly marked off the different crops.

The scenery was all nice, but she was still fascinated with Rachael. "How long has she been in Traanafaeren? She wasn't with Ghortin when they first came here, was she?" He hadn't mentioned her as being part of his band, but the fact that such a fascinating person hadn't been mentioned at all made her wonder.

"Ghortin's right, you've more questions than there are

grains of sand in the Markare." Storm nodded to a passing farmer. "No, she wasn't one of Ghortin's band. She was actually here before them. She helped the adventurers that first year. Ghortin claimed even Carabella treated Rachael with respect." He looked off into the distance. "You've not met her, have you?"

Jenna took her eyes off the greenery and looked at him sharply. "Carabella? Considering she wandered off almost a thousand years ago; no, I can't say that I have."

Storm's laugh startled a nearby cow. "Is he still trying to say no one has seen her? Honestly, one of these days she's going to come up and cuff his ears. You shouldn't lie about a cuari, even if she is your mother."

Jenna glared at Storm, but it was Ghortin she was mad at. "You mean he's withheld information again? He keeps lying to me."

"I don't know about again. But it's not really a lie. *Ghortin* hasn't seen or spoken to her since she stormed off all those years ago. But Carabella comes and goes, like all cuari. She doesn't visit when Ghortin is around. It annoys him to no end." His smirk showed her whose side he was on in this endless game of hide and seek.

"He hadn't mentioned that she was his mother." She shook her head. "Wait, so you're telling me that this immortal mother has spent the last thousand years *ditching* her immortal son?" This was something above and beyond perverse.

"Near immortal. Although, who knows, he may be immortal after all, he's been around for at least three thousand years. But if by ditching, you mean hiding from him, then yes, that's what she's been doing. She's been known to have Ghortin called away if he's at a function she wishes to attend." He shrugged. "I don't know what started it; I don't think they do either. It's become a great game for Carabella."

Storm had begun to slow the horse down and Jenna

noted with a start that they were coming upon a small beach. Behind her were low, green hills laden with groves of trees. Ahead lay the most beautiful coastline she'd ever seen.

"Takes your breath away, doesn't it? I've always thought this is the most beautiful place in all of Traanafaeren."

They were at a low point in the land; cliffs rose less than a mile away in either direction along the coast. The small, rock-lined cove they were at was little more than a break point. Low waves broke on the line of rocks that marched out into the sea. There were louder crashes where the cliffs rose in the distance.

"Oh, Storm." She couldn't think of words that could adequately describe this beauty. It brought home again, but less painfully this time, how far away she was from her own world. Nowhere on Earth could there have been a place that was as beautiful and pure as this cove.

"I know." He squeezed her hand, then jumped off the carriage. "Come on, let's break into Rachael's basket. I promise you, nothing in the palace can equal her food."

He untied the horse, speaking earnestly in its ear before letting it go graze on some nearby grass.

Storm studied the area for a few seconds before deciding on a perfect spot. He then put out a thick green blanket and began hauling out enormous stacks of food.

Jenna sat down next to him. "How many people was she planning on feeding?" She was amazed at the amount of meat pies, cheese sandwiches, rolls, fruit, and fresh fruit tarts that the basket held.

"Two." He smiled as he handed her a meat pie. "Of course, she knew one of them was me." He smiled contentedly as he took a huge bite out of his own pie.

The rest of the lunch was filled with silence as both paid serious homage to Rachael's culinary expertise. Jenna had to admit that everything was delicious. Even so, she was surprised at how much she ate, and truly amazed at how much Storm managed to put away.

Finally, Jenna allowed herself to fall back on the blanket with a sigh.

"This is absolutely wonderful." She closed her eyes, letting the sun warm her face. "I mean, Ghortin's place is great, don't get me wrong. But this is amazing. I've never felt so at peace. It's almost unreal."

Storm was silent, but she felt his eyes on her.

"Tell me about your world?" She must have tensed, because he added softly, "If it won't upset you, that is."

Jenna sat up, looking into those magnificent blue eyes. Eyes that didn't exist in her world. She smiled slightly. "It's different. No kelars for one thing. No magic. We're…" she paused and gave a slight shake of her head, "*They're* more technologically advanced. Yet this world has been civilized much longer." She shrugged. The chances of her ever going home were slim, better to focus on this world.

"It's crowded, noisy, and polluted." She wrapped her arms around her knees, forcing her eyes on the picnic basket.

Storm reached over and laid his hand on her arm gently. "And you miss it terribly." It wasn't a question.

Jenna nodded, blinking furiously to keep back her tears. This was stupid. She was over it. This was her home now. Somehow, her eyes didn't agree with her and the tears started to fall. Strong arms were around her in a second. Jenna found herself letting go of all the feelings she'd been blocking since her arrival. After a few minutes she pulled back, peering sheepishly at Storm.

"I'm sorry. I sure know how to spoil a day, huh?" She rubbed the back of her hand against her tear-stained face.

Storm smiled and wiped away a few stray tears she'd missed. He paused, looking intently into her eyes for a minute, then shook himself, and pulled back.

"I'm sure you've needed that for a long time." He gave her hand a quick squeeze. "I'm your friend, Jenna; I'll always be there for you, no matter what." He said it with such intensity that Jenna wondered if she'd missed something.

"Thank you." She couldn't figure out where such intensity had come from, so she couldn't think of anything more profound to say.

Storm looked at her for a few minutes, then began to pick up their supplies and returned the horse to its rigging. "We'd better start back. Ghortin will have my head if I bring his prize home late for the party."

Jenna nodded in agreement and climbed back into the carriage. The horse started down the trail with a single word from Storm.

"More than likely he'd have both our heads. You're going, aren't you?"

"Yes. And no, I won't tell you what as."

Jenna stuck her tongue out. "Fine, I wasn't going to ask anyway."

They were halfway back to the city when Jenna remembered there were other things she wanted to ask.

"You never did tell me where you went last night." This keeping secrets business was getting to her. She was going to have to work on both Storm and Ghortin to break them of that habit.

Storm looked ready to brush her off again, then nodded in defeat. "We think that someone has been smuggling something into Lithunane—or someones. We're not sure if it—"

He froze in mid-sentence as Jenna gasped, clutched her head, and crumpled into his right side. It felt like a hot poker had been rammed through her skull. Her magic was back, and it was flooding her senses.

"Jenna!" He pulled the horse up as he held her. "What is it? I don't see anything."

She shook her head and sat up straight. "I'm all right now. But—" she paused, finding herself drawn toward a group of low-lying hills they'd passed. They were set a bit away from the road, and Jenna couldn't tell that much about them, except that they were the source of her pain.

"Something's wrong over there. Really wrong. I can't explain what, but it's bad." She shuddered. That brief stab of pain she'd felt was enough to make her run screaming in the other direction. But whatever it was, she had a responsibility to find out—it was caused by magic.

Storm said nothing as he turned the carriage to cross the grass.

A small grove of trees lay at the base of the foremost hill. Wordlessly, Jenna nudged Storm's hand and reins toward them. The mare hesitated as they neared the trees. She came to a complete halt when they were about twenty feet away and refused to budge, even after Storm talked to her.

He turned to Jenna. "We'll have to walk in." He looked closely at Jenna's face. She was sure she didn't look much better than the horse. "Are you sure you should go in? Maybe it would be better if you waited here." He nodded toward the shaking mare. The animal hadn't bolted, and wouldn't, but it was only Storm's way with animals that kept her in place.

Jenna didn't answer, but shook her head and slowly got down off the carriage. Her eyes were glued to the grove. Whatever was wrong was magic, horribly twisted magic.

Storm followed, and Jenna noticed he automatically reached for his sword. His swearing reminded her he wasn't wearing it. She was grateful that her magic appeared to have come back, but aside from that questionable gift, and Storm's hunting dagger, they were unarmed.

Storm unsheathed the dagger and walked past her. Jenna followed, staying a bit behind and off to the left in case he had to fight.

A stench that could only be accomplished by an unburied corpse hit them as they got past the first line of trees. Overlaying that was a faint smell of sulfur, barely strong enough to notice.

Storm shot his arm across Jenna's path. Slowly, but with determination, Jenna pushed it aside.

Directly in front of them lay a large gray boulder that had been transformed into a crude altar. Upon it lay the mangled form of a dead court page. Although the boy's body was torn apart, his tattered sapphire and emerald uniform gave him away. Whoever he was, he'd been taken while on duty.

Other than the altar, there was no sign of why the boy was killed. But Jenna felt a lingering sense of evil in the area. She pushed her magical senses further, then pulled back with a jolt.

"That page," she grabbed Storm's shoulder. "He's the one who led me to my room last night. His name was Jesop." Bile rose in her throat.

Storm turned with a frown. "How could it be?" He nodded toward the body. "Trust me, that boy, whoever he is, has been dead for days."

Jenna pushed forward, ignoring Storm's protests as she tried to see the boy's face. She'd been so sure of what she had sensed. The residual aura of the murdered boy was Jesop.

She got to the other side of the boulder, where his face was turned, and dropped to her knees shaking violently and was sick.

The face had been ripped away. Whether from the sacrifice itself, or from wild animals afterwards, it wasn't clear.

Storm took one glance, then quickly looked away.

He helped Jenna rise and move away. "I don't know how that boy could have been the one with you last night; but I trust your abilities. But right now, we can't prove anything."

He turned away, looking in the empty air over the altar as if it could tell him something. "Could you hide the body magically? Just for a few hours."

"Hide him? We've got to take him back. He's got to be buried, and his parents told, and—"

"I know." Storm cut her off. "But we certainly can't take him back with Rachael's horse, it would bolt. Besides, whatever happened, magic was obviously involved. Don't you think Ghortin should see this?"

Jenna looked down. It seemed so wrong. As if leaving Jesop here compounded how he'd died. She finally nodded to Storm and silently began to call forth enough of a protection spell to keep the whole grove hidden for at least a day.

"It's done." She rubbed her arms roughly as a chill took her, one that had nothing to do with the weather.

They walked in silence back to the now calm horse; apparently Jenna's blocking spell even worked on her.

Storm went to help her up, but stopped with his hand on her arm. "I don't understand why you didn't sense that when we first rode down this way."

"I lost my magic after escaping from the sciretts." She shrugged. "At least we now know it was temporary."

They rode back in silence, each lost in their own thoughts.

CHAPTER THIRTEEN

BACK AT THE PALACE, STORM told Ghortin and Tor Ranshal about their grim find.

"Wise choice that you left the poor boy there; I might be able to pick up something that was beyond your ability." Ghortin paced around the small room they'd been in last night.

"What bothers me is that you said it was Jesop. I've had my people looking for him all afternoon. No one has seen him." Tor Ranshal rubbed his forehead.

"I know it sounds strange, but I felt him. It was Jesop," Jenna said.

"Couldn't it be a child who looked like Jesop?" Storm asked as he fingered the hilt of his sword thoughtfully. Arming himself had been his first piece of business upon their return; he wouldn't let Jenna find Ghortin until he had his sword.

"No." Ghortin had stopped pacing and stood near the long window, staring out into the late afternoon. "Whatever was here as Jesop had taken on the real boy's essence. Down to his psychic feel. Otherwise Jenna wouldn't have recognized the real Jesop when she came in contact with him."

"But I don't understand. What can make itself into an exact copy of another person?" Jenna's skin crawled at the thought.

"Demonspawn. Also called Helikin. It's been rumored that the higher-level followers of Qhazborh can bring them forth from other realms," Tor Ranshal finally said.

"Now, we don't know for certain." Ghortin tried to sound like he believed his words, like he desperately wanted to. But his pale face gave him away.

Tor Ranshal grasped his friend's shoulder. "What else could it be?"

Ghortin's grasp on the windowsill tightened until his white knuckles looked ready to pop.

"Do you think there are more?" Storm's face was paler than usual, but his eyes held a grim determination. Jenna knew him well enough to know he wanted to find something out there he could fight.

Jenna was lost. She hadn't heard of Helikin or demonspawn. But things were going from bad to worse quickly. Or maybe they'd been this bad since the beginning and she'd failed to notice. For once, Jenna didn't want to know what was going on.

Ghortin reached up and patted Storm's hand. "It's all right," Storm said. "I'm fine." He turned to Jenna, and she was glad to see some color was coming back to his face.

"I'd like to know more about this feeling you got when you originally sensed the boy." Ghortin came back and pulled out a chair next to her.

Jenna looked into those calm dark eyes and relaxed; maybe she had imagined the fear that had been there before. It was a nice thought, and she was going to hang onto it as long as she could. "I don't know how to best explain it. At first it was like…" she paused, looking for the right words. Nothing seemed to accurately convey that first stab of searing pain. She finally settled for something close. "It was as if someone had shoved a hot poker in my temple. It was just for a second, then it vanished."

"Was there anything else, child?" Tor Ranshal's golden eyes had grown copper with worry.

She started to shake her head, and then Storm spoke up.

"Right after you first collapsed; you said you felt something was wrong. Was that separate from the pain?"

Jenna shuddered as she remembered that brief, but terrifying, wrongness she'd sensed.

"I'd forgotten about that. No, it wasn't the same, it was almost worse than the pain. It was as if some extra sense had suddenly been created and was completely wrong. No, not wrong." She pinned down that horrible sensation. "Nothing. It didn't feel wrong, it felt like nothing. A horrible, empty, nothing. It was chaotic, but pushed so far into chaos that nothing was left." She could tell by their faces she was having minor success getting through. "As if you spun a color wheel too fast. Everything becomes nothing."

Tor Ranshal nodded in understanding. Jenna didn't want to think too hard about that awful feeling; she already had enough material for far too many nightmares.

"We'll have to get some people out there immediately." Tor Ranshal said. "I would go, but I must stay here for the preparations for tonight. And it would be best if any who do go were back in time for the celebration. We don't want whoever is doing this to know we are aware of them."

"I agree." Ghortin rose from his chair. "I'll take Storm and Sir Edgar. We should definitely be back—"

"What about me?" Jenna cut him off.

"Now, my dear." He patted her on the head. "You don't have to get in on every disaster, you know. Besides, you have lessons to work on."

"Lessons? When some poor child has been murdered?"

"I know it sounds crass, but life must go on. Your magic will be needed even more than before. Jesop would have—" Ghortin paused and peered at her closely. "Did that boy who took you up last night say or do anything odd?"

Jenna shook her head. "No, he was just a boy. Well,

there was the bath, but I'm sure someone else did that."

Now Tor Ranshal looked worried. "Bath? I left no orders for a bath to be drawn for your rooms."

Jenna looked at the two old men like they were crazy. "How could a bath be dangerous? I mean, no one tried to drown me or anything."

"Anything can be dangerous, even deadly, in the right hands." Ghortin's brow was creased with worry. "Jenna, stand in front of me and close your eyes." She obeyed without question; the tone of his voice terrified her.

He gathered in Power, and then a tickling sensation went from the top of her head to the bottom of her feet.

She held still for as long as she could before she finally had to scratch.

"I'm sorry, I couldn't help it." She shivered. "What was that?"

"You can relax, I'm done." Ghortin sat back down heavily. "I'm not sure what it was meant to do, but some-one cast an intense time-delayed control spell on you. And I think we should assume it was from the bath." He slammed his hand down on the tabletop. Fury reddened his round face. "Damn them! I couldn't read what it was; whoever cast it was at least a Master. Once my search spell triggered it, the whole thing disappeared."

Tor Ranshal stepped out of the room briefly, and then came back. "I've sent my second to go find everyone, especially our more notable guests, who had contact with Jesop recently. I'll have Adieon and the rest of the palace mages go over them one by one."

Jenna sat down hard, not noticing that she was only half on the chair. "Someone poisoned my bath with a spell?"

"I'm afraid so." Ghortin looked around the room as if it could give him the answers he sought. "I'm going to have to assign you a guard until I return. And I'll give our rooms a full sweep before I leave. Which I think we should do with all haste."

Jenna was still shaken when she got to their rooms to start her lessons. Dead duplicate pages, baths that were spelled, it was all hitting too close to their scirett encounter. And she hadn't recovered from that yet. She wandered over to a small desk set off to the side in her bedchamber. She was more than a little surprised to see that Ghortin had left his mysterious gray book lying open on it. She approached carefully, remembering scorched fingers from her previous attempt to look at the book a few months ago in the cottage.

A note in the mage's flowing script lay on top of the book. It said to study the two spells on the open page carefully. Jenna whistled when she lifted the note off the page. The two were Journeyman level defense and attack spells, both far above anything he'd ever given her before. She toyed with trying to see what lay on the other pages but didn't want to push her luck. Knowing Ghortin, he'd only spelled this page for her touch.

With a sigh, Jenna curled up on the armchair next to the desk, called up a practice beacon, and began working on the spells. She became so engrossed in the intricate spell work that she didn't notice the passage of time until Ghortin tentatively knocked on the semi-open door.

"Ah, excellent. All afternoon long, and you've stuck with it."

Jenna turned. "These weren't like the other spells you've taught me. They seem almost alive. Are the rest in here like that?"

"If you're a good lass, in ten or twenty years you might be ready to find out." He came over and closed the book, ending the discussion about it.

Jenna got up stiffly. She hadn't budged during her practice, as she was now finding out. After a few quick stretches, she followed Ghortin through the sitting room and into his bedchamber.

"Was it Jesop?" She had been able to push the horrible

event out of her mind for a while, but Ghortin's arrival brought it back.

He laid the book on his bed and turned around slowly. "Yes, I'm afraid you were correct on the identity of the boy." A long muscle on the side of his jaw twitched spasmodically.

"We don't know why, or who was responsible. Although Edgar feels that the followers of Qhazborh are behind it. He's seen some strange things in the outlands in the past year. But there's nothing to be done until after tonight." He looked up at her, and Jenna could see he was forcing a smile.

"Which reminds me, we have a formal royal event to be attending." He shook his head as he eyed her wrinkled clothing. "Now, you can't go in that."

"Should this ball be happening? I mean, someone planted a demon thing here and killed that poor boy; is a party a sensible thing to be having right now?" It felt wrong. This wasn't a time for gaiety, although she knew the ball itself masked deeper talks.

Ghortin hugged her tightly and then stepped back. "This hasn't been a peaceful trip for you, and I'm afraid it is going to get worse before it gets better. However, sometimes an important part of winning the battle is not letting the enemy know what you know. It lets them make a false step."

"So you're hoping that our knowing about the boy, but them not knowing we know, will weigh things in our favor?" She didn't feel like that was a good bet. So far, whoever the enemy was had been playing all the winning pieces.

Ghortin shrugged. "It might. It may not be enough, but if we cancel this now, they, whoever they are, will know we are aware of something. Besides, the ballroom is warded heavily; it would take a far stronger mage than myself to get in there uninvited." He pulled himself up proudly. "And there are few mages who could call themselves my equal, let alone my better."

Jenna studied his face for a moment, and then smiled. She couldn't forget what had happened to the boy, but maybe they had stopped a bigger plot and would be able to make the murderer show himself soon. "Understood." She held out her arms. "I do hope you brought me something to wear, unless a mage apprentice is a suitable costume?"

"And if I didn't? What would you do? Magic yourself something?" He tapped his chin, studying her for a moment. "That might be a good practice exercise actually. But no." He shook his head and some of the tension left his face this time. "I mean, what if you botched it somewhere, and the whole thing disappeared in the middle of the ball? Think of my reputation."

Jenna folded her arms. "Ha, ha. Your reputation indeed. My costume?"

"You simply don't appreciate the uniqueness of my reputation, my dear." Ghortin turned away and rummaged through his wardrobe. Without warning, he tossed a small bundle of what looked like feathers at her.

Jenna caught it suspiciously. "Is this all of it?"

"Yes, that's all of it." Ghortin turned with a sigh. "Trust me, you're a little thing; you don't need much material. Your mask is on the table in the sitting room. Now, scoot."

Jenna took her bundle off to her room. After a few unsuccessful attempts, she finally figured out how all the pieces went. He had been right; it covered everything, but only if you got it assembled right.

She studied her results in the mirror carefully.

Long black and purple feathers clung down her body, covering all that needed to be covered. Her long black hair was pulled up with an elegant silver tie with dangling tiny purple feathers. Delicate black slippers and an elaborate lavender mask completed the ensemble. She had to admit the results weren't half bad. As she turned, she noticed that small glimmer stones dotted all of the feathers, giving the whole thing a magical air.

Ghortin beamed proudly when she came back into the main chambers.

"Ah. I knew the Koye bird outfit would suit you." He spun around, showing her his brown and gold owl ensemble. Obviously, she wasn't the only one who'd noticed his similarity to an owl.

Jenna clapped appreciatively and took his arm.

"Come, my lady, we shall be the envy of all." Ghortin led her to the door and down the hall.

Other costumed guests drifted around them in the long corridor. Jenna noticed that fabulous bird and animal costumes seemed to be the most common. Ghortin let a few couples pass as they drew nearer to the ballroom.

Jenna halted at the arched entrance and gawked. It couldn't be helped, the hall was simply magnificent.

It was also huge. A football field would fit, with room to spare, within the rose marble walls.

Light from a thousand spiral glow holders caused silver veins in the walls to wink and sparkle. Halfway across the hall was a large, black marble dancing area. Scattered around were long, ornate, red-oak tables with delicate filigree chairs.

Flower garlands were strung everywhere and graced the beams of a series of spidery overhead walkways. The ceiling itself was some five or six stories up. But halfway between it and the festive floor hung slim paths lit by muted glows. There were few people up there at present, but Jenna was certain that would change before too long.

The guests outshone the hall if that was possible. Hundreds of brightly dressed, and in many cases underdressed, people milled under the magical lights.

As she and Ghortin entered the hall, Jenna was pleased to notice more than a few admiring glances. After being stuck out in the woods with Ghortin all these months, it was nice to know men still found her attractive.

"Truly spectacular, is it not?"

Jenna jumped at Ghortin's comment. She'd almost forgotten he was there. As it was, all she could do was nod. And try to keep her jaw from dropping.

"One thing kelars are extremely good at is creating beauty. Takes my breath away every time I come here." He froze. "There is that wretched Taffin. I've got a few bones to pick with that one." He patted her bare arm gently.

"Now you stay right here, I won't be but an instant." Without waiting for her reply, the feather-clad mage was off stalking his prey.

Jenna sighed and tried to keep out of the way. Looking around, it was obvious that some people were already well on their way to becoming joyously drunk. That, combined with the outrageous costumes, gave her quite a people watching opportunity.

One dandy caught her eye almost immediately. Unlike most everyone else there, he wasn't wearing festive colors. Long, lean, muscular legs were clad in white leather. A snug white tunic with golden lacing and a full white shirt topped it. Around his broad shoulders hung a shimmering short white cape. A thin golden dress sword completed the picture. Unfortunately, she couldn't see his face because his elaborate all white bird mask completely covered his head, trailing down to mid-back.

As she watched, a beautiful bead-clad woman came and possessively took hold of his arm.

Jenna watched them go. That one was definitely taken. She was re-immersing herself in people watching when Ghortin reappeared at her elbow.

"Drat that man." The mage adjusted his mask. "He's always wiggling out of our discussions."

Jenna was grateful that her mask covered most of her

smile. What Ghortin called discussion, other people would call a knockdown, drag out, verbal war.

The mage was elaborating on his latest victim's shortcomings when a clear horn rang throughout the hall. Within seconds, silence had fallen over the chamber as heads turned toward a long platform near Jenna and Ghortin.

Ghortin nodded at Jenna's unspoken question. "Our gracious hosts, the royal family. Don't fret, my dear; most of them detest official pomp. Their introduction, and the ball's commencement, won't last long."

Jenna nodded with growing excitement. She'd never seen royalty in person before. Certainly never non-human royalty. Luckily, Ghortin had made her stay in this spot; she now had a perfect view of the entire platform area.

The silvery horn sounded again and two small kelar children, obviously twins, came from a walled-off chamber, down a broad ramp, and onto the platform. They halted in perfect unison at the front of the dais as a crier announced them.

"Their Highnesses Princess Saysa and Prince Whealt."

The twins parted, moving gracefully to the outermost chairs on opposite sides of the platform. They turned to face the crowd as they reached their seats. They were absolutely adorable children, both with long, thick blond hair and clear green eyes. They looked no more than five years old, however they showed no discomfort at the cheering crowd. Both were dressed in simple outfits of light blue and green.

A willowy adolescent girl was the next down the ramp. Like the guests, she was clad in a gaily colored feather costume. Like her brother and sister before her, she wore no mask.

"Her royal Highness, Princess Lilltkin."

Jenna cheered with the rest of the crowd as the red

haired girl took her seat next to her sister.

The next person down the ramp paused before coming completely out. He seemed to be arguing with someone in the room beyond.

Jenna smiled at what she could see. At least she had good, if extremely unattainable, taste. The next royal was the white-clad dandy she'd spotted earlier.

Her smile fled, her hand tightening cruelly on Ghortin's arm, when the white-clad figure finally continued down to the platform without his mask.

"His royal Highness, Prince Corin."

Who also happened to be Storm. The normally relaxed kelar was moving stiffly, his usually mobile face frozen in a tight frown. Nonetheless, it was Storm.

Jenna squeezed Ghortin's arm still tighter as she watched her friend, now a complete stranger, take his place on the platform.

"Why didn't anyone tell me?" She hissed loud enough for the wincing mage to hear.

He peeled her fingers out of his skin before answering. "I didn't want to step into this. Storm said he would decide when to tell you—before this preferably—so I kept quiet."

Jenna was pissed. How could he do this? Her now unclenched fingers were itching to draw kelar blood. Almost everything about this world still unnerved her, but her friendship with Storm had gone a long way to make it bearable. Now she realized it was all a lie. *He* was a lie.

Gritting her teeth, she managed to keep from bolting as the rest of the royal family was introduced.

After Storm was Prince Justlantin. He was quite a bit shorter than his younger brother, but had the same rich brown hair, although he kept his neatly trimmed to the top of his shoulders. His large slanted eyes matched his hair, and the silver circlet on his head was slightly thicker than Storm's.

The next in the royal line differed greatly from her siblings. Most noticeably in dress. Kaytine, as she was announced, without royal title, was a delicate cleric garbed in the light green robes of the goddess Irissanta. No royal crown or band lay atop her silvery-gold hair, but she exuded a serenity that Jenna was more envious of than any crown.

As Kaytine took her seat, Jenna let her eyes slide over to Storm. Sitting between his brothers, he was stiffly keeping his eyes straight ahead, looking completely miserable. Jenna felt a twitch of happiness; he deserved it.

The pause was a bit longer before the announcement of the heir. Prince Resstlin was an imposing man, easily topping Storm in height, and outweighing him by a good sixty pounds, maybe more. Like Justlantin, his dark hair was cut shoulder length. The muscular man nodded to the crowd before taking his seat.

Two matching trumpeters stepped forward to announce the arrival of the king and queen.

King Daylin was an older version of the heir. His dark, almost black hair was beginning to turn gray. His piercing blue eyes were similar to Storm's, but the king and heir were both quite a bit thicker in build than her friend.

Queen Areania was a willowy woman with long masses of thick red hair. Her deep brown eyes reminded Jenna of a protective doe.

"The royal family of Traanafaeren."

As hurt and upset as Jenna was by Storm's duplicity, she couldn't help but cheer along with the rest of the crowd. She was cheering for everyone up there *except* Prince Corin.

"My good people." The king spoke amid the cheering. The crowd silenced immediately.

"I want to thank you for coming; may this be the best T'garen in our history. Let the festival begin." He held both hands above his head as the crowd roared in approval, then began to disperse and mingle through the hall.

Two dozen or so court hangers-on flanked the edge of the platform waiting to bend a royal ear, or just be seen with one. A heavily armed derawri woman loudly announced that the two youngest royals would be retiring to their rooms.

Jenna stood by sullenly as she watched a crowd form around Storm. Prince Corin, she corrected to herself. The name sounded odd, but it seemed to fit. Probably because it's his real name, her mind answered back.

Ghortin stood back, Jenna could feel him watching carefully. "I told Storm all along that he was making a monumental mistake in keeping this from you. But he wouldn't listen. I know he meant no harm."

"Meant no harm? For crying out loud, Ghortin, he's a different damn person. Everything he's said or done for the last four months was a lie."

Looking around the growing, curious crowd, Ghortin led Jenna toward an emptier portion of the large hall. She let him lead her. If she was going to yell, she'd rather not have it happen in front of the royal platform. She was so upset and annoyed that she wasn't sure she could control what she said.

"Now, my dear. I'll admit that he wasn't completely honest. But believe me; his Storm persona is quite real. More real in his mind than his royal one as Prince Corin. Now you can't tell me that you've told Storm everything about your past, back in your world?" He gave her a nudge. "Including those things you're not so proud of?"

Jenna's mind flashed on some of her less than brilliant moments. Like her short and doomed marriage. Three weeks of hell that she wouldn't share with anyone. But that was different from lying about who you are. Very different.

"I'm not letting you box me in on this one. This is not the same thing at all, and you know it. He's royalty, damn it."

She stopped as an awful thought hit her. "The market. That low down, slimy sneak. He must have had a grand time sporting me around the marketplace today. What did he do, command everyone to ignore him while he was with the stupid little apprentice?"

"Oh, now this is getting quite out of control." Ghortin took his most intimidating stance, arms folded tightly and legs spread. Jenna didn't lessen her glare in the slightest.

"First, let me say once again that *I* felt that our young friend was in error. Secondly, I assure you, he did not have the marketplace folk play games on you. Most likely most of them didn't have the foggiest clue as to his identity. People expect royals to always dress and act like royals. They don't look for a prince to be out shopping dressed like a common hunter. Thirdly, just because a situation seems like it should be ideal, that doesn't mean that it is."

The mage relaxed his stance and shook his head sadly. "That lad is miserable in court. Couldn't you see it on his face? He loves his family, but he doesn't want this life. He doesn't fit in." Ghortin's face softened. "Are you sure that some of that anger isn't directed at his female companion?" He nodded back toward the dais where the bead-clad woman had reattached herself to Storm's side.

Jenna felt the flush crawling up her face. "Are you saying I'm jealous? That woman could be the mother of his five children for all I care. *I don't like being lied to.*" She twirled around and stomped off in the opposite direction.

She heard Ghortin follow but he stayed out of striking range.

Jenna was so furious—at Storm, Ghortin, herself, and this asinine world—that she failed to pay attention to where she was going. Or to any obstacles too slow to get out of her way.

"What in the—?" Jenna's victim managed to get out before they ended in a tangled heap on the floor. Jenna herself was too stunned to say anything.

She struggled to free herself from the garishly clad arms of the kelar man she had bowled over.

"I'm so sorry." Jenna felt her face growing warm under her mask. Great impression at her first formal function.

She tried to help her victim up, but he ended up doing most of the pulling.

"Glad to see you ran into each other."

Jenna winced as Ghortin's voice boomed behind her.

She and her victim were standing now, and the kelar was removing his mask. That accomplished, he bowed over her hand with a sweep and kissed it.

"Keanin Plantarie, royal companion, at your humble service my lady."

Jenna stood there, staring at the shockingly handsome face before her. Long, pronounced cheekbones introduced his sardonic, yet sensual mouth. A tumble of wavy auburn hair had managed to fall rakishly across one tawny gold eye. Even in a race of beautiful people, this man stood well above the norm.

"Keanin, may I present my faithful, if a bit drifty, apprentice, Jenna."

Ghortin placed a soothing hand on her shoulder while she frantically regained composure.

She removed her mask, which was immediately taken from her by Keanin. He bowed over her hand again, this time with more passion than some of her former lovers made love.

The stunning man looked up with a brilliant smile. "The little magic one our Prince Corin found? The oaf failed to do justice to your beauty."

Jenna was feeling like she was going to blush this entire night. But her face stiffened when he mentioned Prince Corin.

"I wish I could say the same. He failed to mention anything." She hadn't meant to sound so bitter. This stunning man was more than likely a member of the court.

Rather than looking upset at her tone, Keanin looked intrigued. "He failed to mention even myself?"

Jenna's face settled into stone. "He didn't bother to tell me who *he* is. For the past few months I thought he was some forest idiot named Storm."

Keanin glanced up at Ghortin who nodded slowly. The auburn-haired kelar rubbed his hands gleefully.

"Oh, this is grand. He lied. Thought he could mislead such a fine lady as yourself, did he?" His bright smile was positively glowing. "Shall we go find his royal self so you can discuss this with him? I promise to hold him still if you wish."

She started to say no, and then changed her mind. "But aren't you his friend or something?"

"That is the reason I think you two should talk this out. Corin and I have been closest friends since childhood. And he's always prided himself on his honesty."

"Honesty?" Jenna spat. "That lying, deceitful, arrogant, son of a swamp snake."

Keanin smiled and patted her arm. "Exactly my point. Shall we find him now?"

With an evil glance at Ghortin, Jenna allowed herself to be led off.

CHAPTER FOURTEEN

STORM, OR PRINCE CORIN AS he certainly looked tonight, was surrounded by court lackeys, but his female companion from before had vanished. He hadn't bothered to put his mask back on and his annoyance at the people around him was obvious.

Keanin gleefully pushed the throng aside, Jenna's hand clutched possessively in his own.

"Corin old boy, I do believe Ghortin's apprentice has yet to be formally presented." He dropped down to a mockingly low bow. "Your Highness, may I present the Lady Jenna."

Jenna stepped forward with a glare that would have frozen boiling water.

Storm tried to smile, and then let it drop with a sigh.

"If the rest of you will excuse us, I must have a private conversation with Lady Jenna and Lord Keanin." He waved his hands at the surrounding crowd. "Go, dance, eat. Do whatever it is you people do."

The hangers-on drifted away like the petals on a spent flower. None of them appeared terribly shocked at their abrupt dismissal.

With the crowd gone, Storm held up his hands as if to ward off blows. "I know you're upset. But I felt it was better if you didn't know until you absolutely had to. I tried this afternoon, but it wouldn't come out."

Jenna's eyes narrowed and her arms tightened around her chest; she was afraid of what her hands might do if they were left on their own.

Next to her, Keanin mimicked her stance, but Jenna

could see him breaking into a huge grin every few seconds.

"Keanin, *what do you want*?" Storm said.

"Oh nothing, my glorious Prince." The graceful kelar gave another one of his florid bows. "I wait anxiously for your excuses concerning the charade you've been pulling on this lovely creature."

Jenna turned and smiled at the gorgeous kelar. "Thank you, Lord Keanin." She whipped back to Storm. "I'd like to know the same thing. I *thought* we were friends."

Storm pulled back as if physically struck. "We are friends. I never meant to hurt you." He paused, looking up at Keanin briefly. "I liked having someone who knew me as Storm, nothing more. Ask that grinning idiot next to you, I make a lousy prince."

"That doesn't make it right. If we're friends then I wouldn't have cared and you should have told me." She was still angry; she now realized she had counted on him. And that perhaps she was developing feelings for him, feelings that wouldn't be right for a prince who was obviously involved with someone. Her embarrassment was fueling the anger.

Keanin laid a hand on her shoulder. "If it's any consolation, he does make a perfectly awful prince."

Jenna studied them. She couldn't deal with this, not here. She was going to have to push all her anger and embarrassment aside for the moment. Finally she narrowed her eyes on Storm. "I don't think I forgive you. Not yet anyway. But at least I won't kill you. For now."

Keanin shook his head in mock sadness, auburn waves catching the glow from the thousands of lights. A nice distraction from her hurt feelings was watching this incredible man. He clearly had one purpose in life, to make women swoon; he was almost too beautiful to be breathing. A moment later that image was destroyed with a contorted expression. "If there isn't going to be any royal mayhem, then I suppose I'll be on my way." He looked over as a thin, human female started bearing down on them. "Oh. And look, there's one of my fiancés now. Tah."

He gave Jenna's cheek a quick kiss; then fled in the opposite direction of the woman.

"Fiancés? As in more than one? How many do you people have here anyway?" Jenna asked as the woman dashed after the fleeing Keanin.

Storm flashed his first real smile of the evening. "Normal people have one; Keanin, however, has never been normal."

Jenna found herself returning his smile against her will. "How many does he have?"

"Six at last count." Storm shook his head sadly, but Jenna noticed an evil twinkle in his eye. "Why, does the lady wish to become number seven?"

"Perhaps. He is good looking, isn't he?"

"As he will be more than happy to tell you."

A voice screeched out from behind them. "Cory honey. There you are. We've been looking all over for you."

At the sound of the high-pitched voice, Storm's face fell and a wary look darkened his blue eyes. Jenna turned to find the blonde, bead-clad kelar woman who'd been with him earlier bearing down on them. Two drunk male companions trailed behind her in some sort of game. Or perhaps that was the only way they could walk at this point.

"Oh, what an adorable child." The vapid blonde woman clapped her jeweled hands. Storm stepped in before Jenna could come up with a scathing, and more than likely embarrassing, retort.

"Lady Mikasa, I'd like you to meet the Lady Jenna, apprentice to Master Ghortin."

Lady Mikasa drew her perfect lips into a perfect 0. "You aren't a child. Silly me. I'm so glad that you've come along to help out Master Ghortin." She latched on to Storm's arm and pouted. "Now maybe my Cory won't have to spend so much time out in that awful forest."

Storm flinched, but didn't pull free of the woman's grasp. Feeling more than a little uncomfortable, Jenna started to edge away.

Storm noticed what she was doing, and gently disengaged Mikasa's arm. He forced a smile as he faced the blonde kelar woman. "You're missing the Trilane."

His voice sounded so tight that Jenna had to glance over to make sure it was him who spoke. His blue eyes were silently pleading with her not to leave. But she felt she'd had enough, dealing with this woman on top of everything else was too much.

Mikasa spun toward the dance floor, her beads whirling out provocatively. "It's starting." She tugged on Storm's wrist. He slid free of her grasp.

"I'm quite sure your friends would love to join you." He carefully pushed her toward her drunken companions. Fortunately for him, she was as drunk as they were and stumbled toward the dancing easily.

Jenna backed up, waving Storm off. "Look, Storm, or Prince, or whoever you are. I don't think we have anything to talk about. Storm and I were friends; this Prince Corin person is too complicated."

She turned to walk away, but Storm grabbed her arm.

"I'm sorry this happened. Really, I am the same person. I made a mistake; I should have told you about everything. Her too." He shot a disgusted look at the dancing blonde woman.

Jenna rubbed the growing pressure between her brows; there was no easy way out. Besides, in a sick way it was intriguing.

"So who is she? Wife? Courtesan? Strumpet?"

"Betrothed." Storm made a sour face. "She and I are to wed next year at Even Tide. But I don't love her. She is manipulative and rude to everyone who can't improve her station. I don't even like her." He added the last part quickly and with venom.

Jenna smiled slightly at the pathetic sound in his voice. "Okay, I give up. What is she, the daughter of an enemy king?"

Storm looked down, mindlessly fingering the peace knot on his thin dress sword.

"No, worse." He looked up despairingly. "The daughter of my mother's foster sister. We were promised before I was born."

Jenna's eyes narrowed. "And you can't find a loophole? Anywhere?"

Storm shrugged. "We probably could have. Except that *woman* decided she was madly in love with me the second she saw me. The whole court, including our parents, decided that love at first sight couldn't be denied. Never mind how I felt about it."

Jenna stood back and gave the kelar prince an appraising look. "Maybe she did fall in love at first sight. You aren't all that hard on the eye, and excuse me, but she doesn't seem too bright." Actually Storm was extremely good looking. Not on the same scale as his stunning rogue friend, Keanin, but handsome nonetheless.

Storm bowed extravagantly, mimicking Keanin's earlier flourish.

"Why, thank you, my lady. Would the lady be so kind as to accompany me onto the dance floor?"

Jenna's answer was swallowed as multiple explosions rocked the huge hall, knocking down party goers everywhere.

Storm ripped off the remaining threads of his sword's peace knot as the two of them ran toward the center of the room.

A huge robed figure stood in the center of a rapidly dissipating greasy smoke cloud. He was easily seven and a half feet tall, with splotchy gray hair drifting out from under the hood he wore. The robe he wore was of no color, yet of all colors. It was as if it had been created outside the normal realm of color. From the realm of chaos itself. Jenna's eyes were swimming after a few seconds of trying to look at it.

A horrible pressure build-up hit her. One that wasn't residue from the explosion. Something in the core of her being took over and she continued forward, angry beyond all reason. Her temples pounded and every part of her wanted to destroy that figure at any cost. It was the same feeling she'd had facing the ertin.

A yank on her arm brought her to a halt. Whirling with a growl, she prepared to blast whatever had stopped her. Fortunately for Storm, she broke through her killing rage and recognized him. Shaking in body and mind, she dropped her blast spell.

"What are you doing?" They shouted at the same instant. Jenna pulled free of Storm's grasp.

"Stay behind me. I can't protect you if you get in front," Storm yelled as he grabbed hold of her again, and this time his grip cut off the circulation in her arm.

"You pointy-eared moron. *You* stay behind *me*. I'll not be held responsible for his magicless highness being fried." The last was hissed out in a loud whisper. She knew how he felt about being without magic, but she wasn't going to let that pride get him killed.

He flushed at the comment, but didn't let go of her. All argument was swept aside as fighting broke out throughout the hall; horrifying creatures literally erupted out of many of the party guests, their disguises as party goers peeling off of them like shells. Many real guests were struck down before they realized that their companions hadn't been who, or what, they thought they were. Storm finally let go of her as he rushed for a tall kelar who'd used a previously hidden sword to slice through one of the guards.

At the same instant Jenna felt the queasy tingling that warned her of the impending release of a disruption spell. Ghortin had thrown small ones at her, but the way her skin was crawling, this was going to be huge. These spells could tear through bodies like paper. The figure in the nauseating robes crooked his fingers at the first wave of guards, all almost upon him, and they slammed to the floor and lay still. Then the figure turned toward her and Storm.

Without thinking, Jenna threw herself at Storm, tackling him low as he tried to reach the enemy. She also covered them both with the strongest energy shield she could create. A few seconds later a burning tingle went down her spine; then the wave was gone.

Storm twitched out from underneath her and rolled to his feet pulling her with him. "What in the hell were you…" He stopped in mid-sentence as he noticed the fallen people around them.

"My gods." He turned toward her, visibly shaken. Even some lesser mages had been felled by the wave. "Thank you—"

Jenna screamed as his words were cut off by a brutal blow to his left arm; one strong enough to knock him back to the floor. Soon the arm and the side of his tunic were covered in blood. One of the attackers had seen Storm and taken the fight to him.

With cat-like reflexes, Storm rolled out of the way, narrowly avoiding a blow that would have taken off his head.

Jenna screamed again as the blond 'kelar' that was attacking Storm began to change. Within seconds, a slime-covered creature that could only come from the depths of hell stood opposite the wounded prince.

Jenna tried to get closer so she could help, but she was afraid any magic she used would hit Storm. She picked up his discarded dress sword, but tossed it away a second later. She'd be better off with her sporadic magical skills than that useless stick.

She continued edging around the creature, keeping an eye open for a clear shot.

The thing was Storm's height, but most of that was in its long torso; thick, short, backward legs scrabbled furiously to keep it balanced on the blood-slick floor. What had appeared as a wicked-looking long sword in its kelar illusion was revealed to be an extension of the creature's right arm. Three-inch-long spikes glittered in the lights as the creature roared and advanced on Storm.

Storm tried to rise, but a snap of the creature's spiked tail brought him down with a bone-shattering thud.

In doing so, the creature had taken a shuffling step backward, leaving Jenna enough room to cast a spell. Her immobilization spell held the monster for only a few seconds, but it was long enough for Storm to regain his footing. He leapt over a nearby fallen body and freed a long sword embedded in its back.

Raising his new weapon, he blocked another near fatal blow. As the creature swung forward, Storm jabbed up with the sword. He managed to get a slice in, but the creature backed out of most of the thrust. Sickly green blood confirmed the thing wasn't kelar or human. It didn't have any real knowledge of swordplay either; whoever set it loose was not concerned about its skills; just about what havoc it could wreak.

Storm overreached as he swung his sword in a wild arc at the monster. The brute stepped in, grinning as he lunged for the kill. Storm snapped his arm back up and skewered the creature.

The creature couldn't pull back fast enough and screamed in a twisted chorus of a hundred voices as the blade pierced its thick hide. With a final wail, the monstrosity vanished in a blinding flash, leaving a stunned and bleeding Storm in its wake.

Jenna rushed forward as the tall kelar prince crumbled. Half carrying, half dragging, she managed to get him out of the way of the fighting.

At least fifty different monsters that Jenna had a bad feeling were actual demonspawn had appeared in the hall. And from what she could see, Storm was a lucky one; shredded bodies littered the formerly elegant hall. A few oozed green, showing some demonspawn had also been killed.

Storm twitched; then regained consciousness as Jenna got them secured behind an overturned table.

"Have to get to the king." His voice was rough, his breathing short and rapid. Obviously there was something other than blood loss affecting him. Most likely some of the creature's slime had gotten into his wounds.

Jenna ignored his comment and tried to concentrate on his injuries. She knew some healing magic, but she feared she didn't know enough.

Something from within the gashes was blocking her magical probes, but she was able to stop the bleeding. When she finished, Storm passed out again.

Moments later he was conscious and struggling to rise. The fact that Jenna was able to thwart his attempt was a strong testament to his condition. After a few attempts, he finally did succeed at batting away her hand.

"We must protect the king. Ghortin…" His voice was weaker now and Jenna feared he was going to go under again.

"Ghortin is doing fine without you, I'm sure. You're in no shape to help anyone, let alone your father."

"No." His pain filled eyes cleared for a moment. "But you are."

"Me?" Jenna looked at the destruction around her. "My magic's half-baked, I couldn't hold that thing that attacked you at all. Besides, I can't leave you here."

Storm grabbed her arm with his uninjured hand, showing a strength that surprised her. "You must protect them, Jenna. You must."

The intensity in his eyes scared her. He had to realize that without her he was totally defenseless.

"Royal command, mage." His face was tight and pale, sweat glistening sickly.

Jenna glared at him and blinked away a frustrated tear. She knew he was right, now with that command she had no choice. Refusal of the command wasn't an option; Ghortin had told her that the Royal Command, when issued by a royal, acted like a command word. It was already starting to crawl into her consciousness; if she fought it, she'd black out, or worse.

She frantically looked around for someone who could watch the injured prince. Unfortunately, the only people left around them were in no condition to watch anything anymore.

Storm shook his head. "I'm going with you." Shoving his bloody hair free of his face, he shakily arose. A small, unarmed child could have beaten him at this point, but at least he was standing.

Jenna finally gave up. "Fine, but you lean on me. And don't worry; at the first sign of trouble I'll be more than happy to drop you off." She was trying to joke, but from the determination on his ashen face, Jenna understood that if trouble did come, *he* would leave *her*. Jenna vowed they would stay clear of trouble until they reached the king's side.

Their progress was slow but steady; most of the fighting had ended in the area they were in. As they reached the royal dais, the malevolent figure threw back the last free-standing mage before him. The remaining eight mages were linked with Ghortin in a final shield between the giant figure and the royal family.

Unsure what to do, she pulled them up as close as she felt was safe to the dais. She kept them low, behind another shattered table; she didn't want that rogue mage realizing there was an unshielded royal out, since they seemed to be his target.

She spotted Sir Edgar helping Tor Ranshal across the room. Like she and Storm, they were out from the protective circle of the mage shield. But she was relieved to see that both men were moving.

The robed figure raised his hands and Jenna felt unbelievable amounts of Power flow into him. Gasping, she realized he was drawing from the mages he had already disposed of. Whether they had been dead when he started, Jenna had no way of knowing. They were now.

Ghortin's face contorted in a feral grimace. He too understood what was happening. He also obviously realized he couldn't stop it if he wanted to maintain the shield over the royals.

Storm had been laying still, and for a moment Jenna thought he'd lost consciousness again. Then he stirred at her elbow.

"Must get closer."

Jenna looked down at him in exasperation. "That thing out there just sucked up the lives and magic of a score of mages. How in the hell do you think I can fight that?"

Storm struggled to shake his head, but his eyes were starting to roll back in his head. "Just get closer. Don't attack."

Jenna looked around for any way she could move them closer without being seen. There was none. The floor between the dais and their hiding place was bare.

A burst of painfully raw Power lifted her off her knees and slammed her to the ground. Shaking, she peered around the edge of their table. The three outermost mages in the shield had been literally blown to bits. Ghortin and the others were shaking with fatigue and she could see they wouldn't be able to hold for much longer. She started to pull in Power, unsure what she was going to

do; the over-riding urge to destroy that she had felt at
the first attack was gone now. Unfortunately, so was her
magic. Like in the forest after the sciretts, she felt nothing
when she tried to draw Power in. Collapsing, she turned
to Storm just as all hell broke loose.

An earth-shattering blast shook the room and a stabbing glare momentarily blinded her. Straining to see
through the pain, she saw that the wall of mages was now
gone. The rogue mage had gathered Ghortin's body like
a rag doll. A woman's hysterical scream broke out as the
figure reached for the king. Next to her, Storm swore
under his breath and managed to cover Jenna with his
own body in a final burst of energy. She had the vaguest
sensation of things rushing at her. Then the world went
black.

CHAPTER FIFTEEN

———◆———

JENNA'S EYES FELT LIKE SHE had fallen asleep face down on a beach. She tried to raise her hands to wipe them but neither arm would respond. Gritting her teeth against the throbbing pain, she forced her eyelids open.

A dark form hovered over her. After a few panicked blinks she finally realized that it was Keanin's worried face that filled her blurred vision. She tried again to force her hands up, but it was as if they weren't hers.

"Now, now, my lady. Everything is fine." Keanin was trying hard to force some lightness into his voice. But he wasn't good at lying. "Maggie said you are to rest. Don't worry, your body will let you know when it's time for moving about."

"What…" Her throat felt like sandpaper and sounded the same.

Carefully supporting her head, Keanin held a small glass to her lips and gently let the fluid slide down.

Jenna took a moment to enjoy the coolness on her throat, and then tried again. "Thank you. Where am I?" A memory flashed through her confused mind. "Storm? Where is he?"

"Easy, Jenna, easy." Keanin glanced around the sparse room; then leaned in closer. "Do you remember anything about the transfer?"

Jenna tried to shake her head and found that it was as immobile as her hands were. "What transfer? Keanin, where am I?"

"You're in Irundail. Corin was holding on to you when

the rescue beacon was activated."

"Rescue beacon?" She remembered something triggering Storm's final burst of movement. "A woman's scream?"

"The queen. See, you are remembering. I knew you would." He looked around again, his movements suspicious.

"Why wouldn't I? And who are you looking for? Where's Storm?" Her voice rose as her strength came back.

"He's here; like I said, you two came through the transfer together. That was two days ago, and you're the first one to wake up. He's still unconscious. Maggie is the head healer; she let me in even though the mages all said your mind was more than likely burnt out."

"Great." Jenna looked at the ceiling. She couldn't remember anything after the scream. But what happened prior to it was coming back in pieces. "What happened to Ghortin?"

Again Keanin furtively looked around, and Jenna realized that he more than likely wasn't supposed to be talking to her, providing she recovered well enough to be talked to. The local mages must have figured she'd blown something important in her head. Thank goodness experts were as fallible here as they were in her world.

"The rogue mage who attacked the ball took Ghortin and the king. And before you ask, I don't know much more. The final blast took out all the mages at the Lithunane end, and those here were drained pulling the royals and friends through. I think—"

The door behind Keanin opened. "You think what, my quiet-as-a-mouse seducer?"

Jenna found she could now turn her head enough to see the speaker. She was a large human woman with broad hips and flyaway gray hair. Her thick hands were on those hips and she looked less than pleased to find

Keanin talking with one of her supposedly comatose patients.

Keanin hopped off the bed and bowed to the imposing woman. "Maggie. I was coming to tell you, she's up. And she seems to be all here too."

"Lad, what am I going to do with you?" She was frowning, but there was a smile in the woman's friendly brown eyes. "Well, my lady, I am glad that this stuffed peacock was right for once. Can't say as I agree with those mages when it comes to healing anyway. If you'll pardon, you being one of them and all."

She turned back toward Keanin. "Now what was this grand idea I heard you voice, pretty boy? I might be willing to listen since you were good enough to keep our lady company."

Keanin looked hesitantly from Jenna to the healer. "I thought that maybe Jenna might be able to help with Corin's healing. She might know something about how he got his injuries."

Maggie studied Jenna for a few moments. Then shook her head. "No. I won't have you risk injury to one patient for another. It'll wait."

"I could at least talk about it. I'm feeling better already."

Maggie started to shake her off, but Jenna forced herself up into a semi-sitting position. "I was with him during the fight. I threw a spell at the creature that attacked him." She looked away with stinging eyes. "For all the good it did." One thing for certain, the bitterness at having her magic first be too weak, then disappear entirely, was going to haunt her.

Maggie rubbed her hand on her chin, reminding Jenna of Ghortin thinking on a problem. "Hmm. Do you know what kind of creature it was? None of the royal family got a good look at any of them. Except for Corin."

Jenna nodded slowly. That monster would stay in her memory almost as long as her guilt did. "I think it was what Storm called a demonspawn. The thing was disguised to look like a kelar guest, but it burst out of the illusion once the fighting started. I think some of its slime or something got into Storm's wounds. I tried healing him, but I couldn't do much." She looked away again. What was the point of having Power if you couldn't count on it?

Maggie sat on the bed next to her, taking one hand gently. "So you were the one who did that. You probably saved his life, you know. That is, once the stubborn boy wakes up. You stopped the bleeding and slowed whatever had gotten in." She smiled with a nod. "And aside from your being Ghortin's apprentice, Corin must think fondly of you. He spent the last of his energy making sure you came through the transfer with him."

Jenna felt her face go warm. She had thought he was trying to get her closer to fight, but he was trying to make sure she was caught up when the eventual rescue beacon was cast.

"I wish he hadn't. I mean, I'm glad he did, but maybe if he hadn't he would be better off right now."

Maggie gave her hand a little shake. "Now don't you be beating yourself up. It wasn't pulling you through with him that got him in his present state. Something got inside that poor boy when he fought that demonspawn. You slowed it down, but we can't stop it."

A strange and intangible feeling crossed Jenna's mind. "Could I go see him? I know my magic isn't working, but I think maybe I could help him somehow." She had no idea why she had that feeling, but she did. She knew she could help him if she could see him. Maybe Keanin had been on to something.

Maggie shook her head; then stopped and stared at Jenna's face. Obviously something was there that gave her hope. "Do you think you can get up? Keanin, give her another sip of the silberia. Now, drink it all."

Jenna found she was able to sit up completely and hold the clear glass without help. She drank the whole thing, feeling the last numbness flee from her limbs as she did. "I think I can walk." She glanced at Keanin. "I might need a leaning post?"

He smiled. "I am but to serve." The stunning kelar bowed low as Maggie snorted and shook her head.

"Aye, always for a beautiful woman you mean. Oh, lad. Away with you." She shooed the bowing kelar out. "You can come back when your ward is properly attired."

Jenna managed to swing her legs over the side of the bed by the time Maggie returned with a suitable outfit. "Why was I unconscious for so long? I gather that Keanin got here the same way, and he seems fine."

Maggie handed her a skirt, loose shirt, and soft slippers. "We're not sure as to that. Could be a lack of familiarity with the transfer spell or trying to defend Prince Corin. Keanin said he was certain you'd never experienced that in your homeland."

Jenna managed to hide her start of surprise. Surely Storm wouldn't trust her secret to Keanin? He was nice, but rather flighty to be trusted with something so important.

"I have a feeling that you were weakened by that mage's attack; the backlash could have struck you before you were pulled out of there." She helped Jenna with her clothes, and then stood back with a smile. "There now, pretty as a picture. You're certain you feel up to this?"

Jenna nodded; if she could do anything for Storm, she had to try. Ghortin would have wanted her to. She waited for the stab of loss to leave before moving toward the door. Ghortin wasn't dead. He couldn't be dead. Once Storm got better, they'd go find the old mage. She refused to let her mind think about what would happen if her only two companions in this world were lost beyond her reach.

Maggie took hold of her arm. "Lass? Are you all right?"

Jenna forced a smile at the honest concern. "Yes, but I'm worried about Storm and Ghortin." She wished she had someone, anyone, who she could confide in right now.

Maggie nodded and motioned for Keanin to come back in and take Jenna's other arm. "That's more than understandable. Now you say something if you get too tired."

The walk to the room wasn't far, and although Keanin tried to make small talk, Jenna wasn't paying attention. The slim white door ahead was her main focus. Keanin took a deep breath, and she felt the tension in his arm as he held the door open for her.

Jenna gasped as she stepped through the doorway. Storm was lying on a large white bed; unfortunately there was little difference between the snow-white coverlet and his pale face. His dark brown hair fanned out in an almost black halo above his head. His face had always been angular, but now it was gaunt, sharp bones jutting out everywhere.

Jenna hesitated a second before rushing inside the stuffy room. She carefully lay her hand atop one of his, wincing as she felt the protruding bones underneath. His long black eyelashes fluttered a tiny bit, but there was no other movement.

A soft scuffing noise brought her attention away from her dying friend's face. Two women were off to the side, one leaning heavily on a chair. It took Jenna a few moments to recognize Queen Areania and cleric Kaytine. Both women looked almost as bad as Storm did, with the addition of dark circles under their eyes.

Kaytine forced a tight smile and motioned for Jenna to take a seat by the bed. The queen looked ahead blankly, clearly not seeing anything other than her son's wasted face.

"I'm afraid we were never introduced. I am Cleric Kaytine and this is my mother, Queen Areania. You must be the Lady Jenna that my brother spoke of so fondly." Her voice was so soft and soothing that Jenna found herself relaxing immediately. She nodded, and then looked to the queen.

The queen gave no response until Kaytine leaned forward and spoke in the older woman's ear. Jenna couldn't hear what was said, but a flicker of awareness flashed across the queen's delicate features.

"My daughter tells me you were with my son during the attack." It was a statement not a question.

"Yes. I tried to help him. My magic wasn't strong enough." Jenna bit her lower lip to keep her eyes dry. "I'm so sorry."

Kaytine gave her an encouraging smile. "I'm sure you did what you could. In fact, if I know my stubborn little brother, you had your hands full convincing him he couldn't fight anymore."

Jenna felt her own smile come back. "Even when he could barely walk, I had to practically carry him."

Kaytine shook her head with a grin, and even the queen gave a small smile.

"That's my brother." She gave her mother's shoulder a little squeeze and got her settled into the large chair. "You always did say he was the most headstrong kelar in the land."

"As a child he was worse." The queen looked back at her unconscious son and her smile faded. "It seems he never grew out of it."

A voice came from the partially shut door behind them. "I hate to interrupt your majesty's premature grieving, but I believe the Lady Jenna has something that could help your son."

Jenna started at the new voice. Maggie and Keanin were still standing by the door, but two new people had entered. It was the taller of these two brown robed figures that had spoken.

"Forgive my companion if we startled you." The second figure stepped forward, extending a small hand. From the lack of height and low voice, Jenna guessed the second hooded figure was a derawri male. She took the shorter man's hand. "I am Dantil, a helaermage. And this is my companion, Ailane. As she said, we have sensed something in Jenna that could aid in the prince's recovery."

Jenna had no idea who they were, or what a helaermage was for that matter. "I couldn't stop that demon thing from attacking him in the first place. My magic fled when I needed it. How do you think I can help him now?" Never mind that was what she'd come there for. She heard how hopeless it sounded coming from another.

Ailane held up her hand. "Not just you, my child. Your mentor will help you. If what I sense is true, it shall be Master Ghortin's skills and Power you will draw upon."

Jenna looked from one robed figure to the other with a skeptical eye and dropped her voice. "How can I draw on someone who isn't here? I don't know what you're trying to do, but I don't think it's right to hold me up as a false hope in front of his family." She couldn't face the queen and Kaytine.

"We wouldn't say such a thing if we thought it could not happen." Dantil came forward. "We have reason to believe that Ghortin may have transferred his essence into your mind prior to his capture. Although difficult, it would be within his range of skill, and it would explain why none of us have felt anything from his consciousness since the battle. If he were dead, we would have felt his leaving. Besides Ailane *Felt* something in you, which is what drew us here. She's never been wrong about a *Feeling* in her life."

He took hold of Jenna's hands. "You will have to relax completely. Whatever he's done is going to be disorienting for both of you, and it's going to feel strange having another consciousness in your mind." The derawri man squeezed her hands gently. "You must stay calm, no matter what you feel. Although he's the one that initiated the transfer, he may not have much memory of what happened. At least not at first. This is a rather unexplored skill, I'm afraid."

As he spoke, Jenna felt part of her mind pull away from the rest. A thin wall blocked out the room around her. With a jolt, she heard Ghortin's voice coming out of her body.

Actually, her mind heard Ghortin; her ears heard her own voice.

"Dantil. Damn it all, man, what are you doing here? I thought you were still holed up with the rest of your strange crew in Irundail. Well, come along quickly, man, something's after the royal family."

Jenna's body convulsed as Ghortin's mind tried to make old physiological connections in a new body. She felt Ghortin look down.

"Apprentice. How'd you get here? Or rather, how did I get here?"

Jenna tried, but found that she couldn't reach her vocal cords. Her thoughts must have been clear to her mental roommate however, as she felt him smile.

"Of course. I'm in Irundail, correct? Or rather, we are." Jenna could almost see her teacher rubbing his chin in thought, although she didn't think she had actually done so physically.

"It's coming back. Well, Jenna's mind is flashing back for me. That bastard." The last word was spit with a growl so low Jenna was surprised it came from her throat.

"If I'm in here, then that thing still has my body. At least he hasn't killed it yet." Ghortin searched the scholars' faces through Jenna's eyes. "Was anyone else taken?"

Ailane had pushed back her hood and glanced at the

queen. "The king was also taken. From what we've been able to gather, you two were the targets." The tall helaermage continued briskly. "There is nothing you can do for him at present; but you can help his son."

Jenna felt her hand go to her head. "Gods, did they get Resstlin too?" Even as Ghortin asked the question, Jenna's mind said it was Storm.

"Nay, the heir is ruling in Lithunane, the rest of the royal family is here." As Ailane spoke, Ghortin forced Jenna's body to turn toward the bed and the pale kelar in it.

Instinctively, Ghortin stuck out a hand to assess the damage. It jerked back as if burnt a second later. Jenna felt a flash of pain, but couldn't tell if it was from Ghortin or herself.

"What has happened?"

Faster than anyone could get out a verbal answer, Jenna's mind flashed through the thing that had attacked Storm, and her less than successful attempt at healing. Ghortin's appreciation flowed through her.

"Thank you, my dear. I think, with what you just showed me, I can heal him through you. Then I'll go away and give you back your body while I figure out a better way for our new partnership." Nothing was said out loud, but Jenna heard him as clear as if he was right next to her.

Ghortin moved Jenna's body next to the injured prince as he reached forward again. Through Ghortin, Jenna saw the internal damage done to Storm's body. His systems were shutting down one by one as a greasy, black fluid flowed through them and overpowered them.

A surge of healing magic flowed through her. Ghortin's skills pulling forth energy reserves she hadn't known of.

Storm tossed as the healing magic attacked the dark fog that had taken hold inside of him. Jenna rocked back as more and more energy flowed through her and Ghortin and into Storm's battered body. The demonspawn residue was slow to leave, fighting to hang on until the end.

But by then Storm had recovered enough to start fighting back. Although he lacked magic, Storm's will to live was fierce, and he succeeded in pushing the last dregs of the infestation away.

Ghortin's mind-voice was weak from the fight. *"I must rest. Storm will recover, and so will I. But I can't stay to explain things right now."*

Jenna felt refreshed, not exhausted like she thought she would be. *"You will be back, won't you?"*

"My dear, I have nowhere else to go. I'll return, fear not."

All of Jenna's senses slammed back into full focus. She swayed as the flood of light caught her unaware.

"Catch her."

"She's in a faint."

Maggie and Keanin rushed forward to grab her. Jenna let them set her on the edge of Storm's bed, then she shook her head.

"I'm all right. Things were spinning there for a moment."

Dantil's bearded face was tight with concern as he came forward. "That's you, isn't it, Jenna?"

"Yes. Ghortin's left for the time being. I think that's what made me unbalanced. It was as if a veil had been lifted."

Ailane looked over from her monitoring position near Storm's head. "That is consistent. You and Ghortin are sharing your body for now; when he took over, he pushed your sensory information aside."

Jenna nodded. "I thought that was probably it." Storm's breathing was steadier, but his eyes were still closed.

"Is he going to be all right? Ghortin chased out all of the black stuff, shouldn't he wake up?" Maybe they hadn't gotten it all.

"He's had a serious injury," Dantil said, as much to Jenna as to the queen and Kaytine hovering nearby. "He'll be fine, but I'm afraid it's going to take some time."

A gravelly voice cut in. "Not too long. I've got to get the son of a snag who brought those things in."

Everyone crowded forward as Storm's slanted blue eyes cracked open. He gave a weak smile as he looked at the faces of those around him. He frowned when he realized that two others weren't there.

"No." It was more of a hoarse whisper than a shout, but it was enough for Ailane to pull everyone back.

Dantil read the prince's thoughts on his anguished face. "Easy, lad. Your father and Ghortin have been captured. But we have no reason to believe either of them has been killed."

Storm let his eyes slide closed. He opened them again, catching Jenna's eye with a curious look. "But I heard Ghortin. I know I did. He was inside me, helping me fight."

"He is here, sort of." Jenna shrugged. "They haven't quite explained it to me either. But somehow he's taken up residence here." She tapped her temple. "I'd ask him to come out and say hello, but he was fading away after we healed you." She looked toward the two helaermages. "And I'm not sure how to call him up anyway."

"Don't you worry about that." Dantil patted her hand. "Once old Ghortin gets his second wind you won't be able to keep him out." He turned back toward Storm. "I must say, young Corin, you gave us quite a scare."

Storm opened his mouth to answer, but was smothered by his mother and sister. The queen took hold of her longhaired son and kept rocking him back and forth like a small child.

Storm finally managed to pull back. "I'm all right, Mother. Really." He sighed heavily as his mother showed no signs of letting go.

"Kaytine, please make her understand, I'm—"

"You're going to be all right!" Keanin's exuberant shout cut him off, and within seconds the graceful kelar noble was taking over where the queen missed. Kaytine had pulled back and was laughing at the three of them. Soon everyone but Ailane was chuckling at Storm's long-suffering looks. The female helaermage's serious face showed clearly what she thought of such behavior from the royal family.

Finally the queen and Keanin pulled back. Storm let himself slide back into his pillows with a sigh. "I promise, after I get Ghortin and Father back, I'll never pick another fight with anything that even faintly looks like demonspawn. Will that make you people happy?"

Keanin and the queen looked ready to start swooning over him again when he looked up to Maggie with pleading eyes.

The healer came to his rescue. "We must give the poor boy some rest. He'll be up and about soon, but only if he rests. Even you, Your Majesty. You may come back later, but I would be remiss as a healer if I let you stay. Particularly when you're as worn out as he is."

Kaytine laid her hand on her mother's shoulder. "She's right, we can come back. I know I could use some rest."

The queen rose without argument, gently leaning over and placing a kiss on her son's forehead. Turning to leave, the tall woman paused in front of Jenna.

"Thank you. I wish I could think of more to say, but thank you with all my heart."

Jenna smiled awkwardly, embarrassed by the raw emotion in those huge brown eyes.

Queen Areania smiled back. "You shall always be counted as a friend of the royal family." She gave Jenna a quick hug, then left the room.

Kaytine also paused in front of Jenna. The green-clad cleric leaned forward conspiratorially. "Don't tell him this, but that rascal has always been my favorite brother. As a cleric of Irissanta, I thank you as well." Laying her hands on either side of Jenna's head, she sang a few soft words. A feeling of peace and strength overwhelmed Jenna. Kaytine was gone before she could recover enough to thank her.

"But it wasn't me. Ghortin saved him." She didn't like basking in a false glow.

Dantil stopped as he was pulling up his hood. "Nay. The mage may have had the technical knowledge, but you had the Power, and the heart."

Out of nowhere, Jenna found herself swallowed in a tight embrace, her face smashed against Keanin's chest. "Thank you. He's my closest friend." He pulled back from his hug and there was real gratitude and concern in those magnificent golden eyes. "Now the proper way to thank you is for me to take you under my wing and show you the wonders of Irundail while our erstwhile prince doth repair himself." There was now a playful, and slightly wicked, gleam in his eye.

"What about me? If you two are off and about all the time, who will keep me company? Not that I'm planning on staying here long," Storm said with a stifled yawn. He was trying to be playful and light, but his fatigue was showing.

The two helaermages headed for the door. Dantil stopped briefly. "I'm more than certain you'll have many visitors."

Ailane bowed her head as she left. "Rest well, Prince Corin.

Maggie herded Jenna and Keanin toward the door.

"Wait. Can I talk to Jenna alone? Briefly?" Storm added the last when Maggie looked ready to shake her head.

The large healer sighed. "Briefly. And I'll escort this rogue out." She took hold of Keanin's arm. Then turned back to Storm with a scowl. "And I want you asleep the instant she leaves, do you hear, scamp?"

"Promise."

Jenna went back and sat next to him on the edge of

his bed.

Storm reached over and took one of her hands. "I want to thank you." He raised his hand at her mute protest. "You forget, Jenna, I was in here while you two were working. I felt what you gave. And back at the ballroom, I wouldn't have made it out alive without you." He squeezed her hand weakly.

Jenna gently squeezed back. "What was I supposed to do? Let a royal prince be skewered by some badly made-up monster? They might think I did it deliberately."

He gave a crooked smile. "You aren't still upset, are you?"

"I think I'll get over it; all of this has put things in a different perspective. For which you should be eternally grateful, you difficult, obstinate, giant elf."

Storm gave a weak chuckle. "Well, thank you again. For everything." He looked intently into her eyes for a moment, and then broke away as if exhausted. Which he more than likely was. "I'd better let you go, or Maggie will be in looking for you. Just be careful around Keanin, and if he tries anything, tell him I'll give him one hell of a sword lesson when I get well."

Jenna tilted her head coyly. "What if I like it?"

"Then I'll give both of you a sword lesson." He tried to sound gruff, but he coughed and blew the image.

Jenna leaned forward and gave him a gentle kiss on the forehead. "Thank you."

Storm gave a yawn as he slipped lower in his bed. "It's fair; you saved my life, so I'll save your virtue."

Jenna laughed as she slipped out of the room.

Chapter Sixteen

M AGGIE WAS THE ONLY ONE waiting in the hall when Jenna came out. She had half-expected Keanin to be there as well, and was surprised at the twinge of disappointment that she felt.

"I'm certain you're fine, however, in light of what you did, and who you have floating around in that pretty head of yours, I'll be keeping you in my House of Healing for a few days." The solid healer's stance plainly said that argument would be useless.

Jenna cast one last look around for Keanin and then let Maggie lead her down the hall.

"Tsk, tsk. That scoundrel's already got you watching for him." She clucked as she headed toward Jenna's room. "Don't you be looking for that scamp, I chased him off. I won't have that rogue hanging around and wearing out my patients." Maggie sounded gruff, but the crinkles around her eyes gave her away. She was as charmed by Keanin as everyone else was.

Jenna hid her smile behind a cough. "How long do you think it will be before Ghortin shows up again?"

"Couldn't say for certain." Maggie shrugged. "Ailane and Dantil didn't know, and I'm afraid what you've got is more in their field than mine."

"But I thought this had been done before." An awful thought snuck up on Jenna. "This isn't going to be permanent, is it? Other mages *have* gone through this before, haven't they?"

Maggie put her arm around Jenna's shoulders. "Everything's going to be fine. To be honest, I'm not sure that any mage has ever actually completed what Ghortin did. But, fear not, that's never stopped him before."

"So I've noticed." Jenna's stomach flip-flopped. She was glad that Ghortin was still around in a sense. She realized how much she cared for the gruff man when she thought he was beyond her reach. But she didn't relish living the rest of her life with him in her head.

Maggie looked over and frowned. "Child, I'll not have you work yourself up into a dither until I say you're ready. I'm sure that Ghortin can answer all of your questions after you have gotten some rest." They stopped in front of Jenna's room. "Or do I have to give you something to help you rest?"

Jenna held up her hands in surrender. "No, I think I'll be fine by myself. Thank you for your offer, but I—"

Maggie broke in, grinning wickedly. "Had some of Ghortin's healing drafts before, have we? Never fear, my medicines are nowhere near as bad as his. But if you don't think you'll need them, I'll be off." She turned as Jenna's hand was on the door handle. "It's almost time for dinner. I'll make sure the kitchen sends you up a nice big plate. We've got you, might as well get some meat on those bones."

Jenna stifled a yawn as her stomach chose that second to rumble. She was tired, but she now realized she was also starving. "Thank you, Maggie. For everything."

The jovial healer grew serious for a moment. "Thank *you*." She shook her head, gray hair sticking out like quills. "Prince Corin *was dying;* there was no question of that. After two days of trying, all we could do was watch him go. I watched that rascal grow up. To a lot of people here, you've become a heroine." Her smile came back. "But enough of that. Off to your room, eat some food, and then off to sleep. Healer's orders." With a nod to make sure Jenna understood her commands, Maggie turned and marched down the hall.

Jenna slipped into her room gratefully. Lounging sounded good right now, it was shocking how exhausted she felt. She went to the small set of drawers and pulled out a nightdress. Looking through the drawers she saw that someone, most likely Maggie, had managed to collect a small wardrobe for her. Which was good since she'd come over wearing that flimsy bird costume.

Settling herself into bed, she tried to recapture the feeling of Power that had flowed through her when she and Ghortin were working to heal Storm. But try as she might, she couldn't get it back.

An attendant from the kitchen knocked once before she came in with a tray. She was covered in the full habit of the religious healing guild. The woman managed to get the tray over to Jenna's bedside with a few spills. That in itself was suspicious. Someone used to carrying trays certainly wouldn't make those spills. And why would a healer be doing kitchen drudgework anyway? Jenna was wondering if she should call for help when the attendant lifted her head.

"Keanin. I thought Maggie chased you off?"

The auburn-haired kelar smiled mischievously under his habit. "Oh, she did. Yes, the mistress of the House of Healing was quite adamant that no young male hooligan was going to disturb her patient." The last was done in perfect imitation of the healer's deep voice.

Keanin shrugged helplessly. "Is it my fault that my other personality is a female member of the religious guild?" His golden eyes opened wide for effect.

Jenna laughed. She was pretty sure Maggie was on to him.

"I wanted to make sure you were given enough food." Keanin said. "And to see if you had any plans for tomorrow?"

Jenna uncovered the huge mound of food on her tray.

Obviously Keanin was planning on dining with her. "All this for me? Or was I to have a dinner guest?"

Keanin didn't answer, just helped himself to a piece of meat.

Jenna joined him. "I do have some questions." She knew the bigger ones, like what happened at the ball, would be far out of Keanin's reach. But there were other, more mundane ones, he could help with.

He removed the habit and perched on the edge of her bed. "Ask away. As far as I know I'm not supposed to stay quiet about anything. Or at least anything I remember." He waved long, graceful fingers in her direction. "Just remember, my fee for answers will be your company tomorrow."

"It's a deal. First off, I don't understand how we got here. I know my geography of this—area isn't as strong as it could be; but aren't we at the other end of the country?"

She watched Keanin closely to see if he'd caught that pause. She had almost said this *world*, instead of this *area*.

Keanin caught the look, just as he had caught the pause.

"It's all right." He gave a self-deprecating smile. "Believe it or not, there are some secrets I can be trusted with. Corin told me of your unique place of origin." He leaned forward. "Now that is one thing I'd like to talk about sometime. But not now." He leaned back, laughing at Jenna's expression.

"So you knew all along that I'm from…" She let it dangle.

"Another world. Yes. And it's good of you to be cautious. I don't know much of what goes on outside of Lithunane anymore, but dangerous things are afoot. The fewer who know about you the better."

"In a way I'm glad you know. I felt sort of alone, not having anyone around who I could trust with my secret."

Keanin flashed one of his heart-stopping smiles. "See? I

am good for something. Now, about your question." He broke off a large piece of bread, nibbling as he thought.

"You're familiar with translocation spells?" At Jenna's nod, he continued. "Well, the royal family sort of has a built-in one. Actually, it's built into all of their primary audience and living areas in Lithunane. When called upon by a member of the royal family, it will transfer the whole bunch back to the safety of Irundail. It also works on a few select hangers-on." He gave a self-mocking bow. "And anything, or anyone in your case, they happen to be hanging on to. Corin must have grabbed hold of you when he knew the spell had been triggered."

Jenna nodded slowly as she picked at some bread. "I heard a woman's scream before Storm grabbed me."

"The queen. She's always been a bit high strung, although in this case I'd say it was justified. The whole lot of us got dumped here. Resstlin's the only one who was sent back. He's acting as king now."

"Why didn't it get triggered when the attack first happened? I mean, wouldn't it have been better to have evacuated when the fighting first started?"

Keanin nodded. "They tried it when the fighting started. But for some reason, it didn't work. I'm no mage, but I gathered that things were pretty out of sorts, magically speaking, for a while there."

"The disruption spell." She shuddered; that was one spell she never wanted to feel again. "It must have done something to the rescue beacon. It must also be what prevented Ghortin and the king from being brought along with us." It made sense; any spell that was on call constantly would have to be extremely sensitive. The mage may, or may not, have known about the rescue spell. She chided herself. That whole event was too well planned out; he must have calculated the rescue spell's strengths and weaknesses into his plan.

A shiver went down her spine. That delayed action spell

that Ghortin had found on her; it must have been part of the attack as well. Someone had targeted her. Either they knew who she was, or they were taking care of Ghortin's apprentice to get to him. Who knew what that spell could have made her do?

"Are you alright?"

Jenna shook herself and smiled weakly. "I think so. I just realized that I had been targeted too. Although I think I was probably meant to be an assistant to the attack, not a victim." She briefly outlined the whole incident with the fake page and the bath. She didn't tell him about finding the real boy, or any of the other things. She wasn't sure who could be told what, and she was going to play it safe until she talked to Ghortin again.

Keanin grew quiet as the talk turned toward the missing king.

"Are *you* all right?" Jenna watched as Keanin played with his food where moments before he'd been wolfing it down.

"Of course." He looked up and met her eyes. "No, I'm not." He ran long fingers through his thick hair. "My parents died when I was young, and the royal family raised me as one of their own."

He tried to smile, but Jenna noticed that the tension and loss of the past two days was finally surfacing. "In fact, King Daylin used to joke that I was his real son, and that Corin was a foundling. When it looked like I was going to lose both the king and Corin…" His voice tumbled off and he looked sightlessly down at the bed cover.

Jenna took one of his hands in hers, the food tray forgotten off to one side. "Storm—I mean Corin, is going to be fine. And you know he won't rest until we get them back."

Keanin squeezed her hand tightly. "Corin's going to be all right because of you, my lady. I shall never forget that."

A wry smile lit his elegant face. "And he'd probably like it if you continued to call him Storm. He does wish that were who he was."

Jenna nodded in agreement. She was having a hard time getting used to his real name anyway. "One more question, then I'll let you go until tomorrow. What about Mikasa?"

Her wish to switch to lighter subjects worked. Keanin rolled his eyes. "That one. Met her, did you? I'm afraid our Corin has gotten himself trapped with a royal disaster. Not that she's not beautiful; heaven knows, she's lovely to look at. But I swear, if I hear 'Cory honey' one more time, I'll break that beautiful little neck myself. She's trouble, stay clear of her if you can."

Jenna chuckled at Keanin's flawless imitation of Storm's bride-to-be. Hanging around the court constantly certainly gave him a lot of fuel for mockery and imitation.

"Like the rest of Storm's real life, I don't know anything about the two of them. Except that he claims to be unhappy."

Keanin's sadness vanished completely. "Unhappy? Lady, that boy is miserable. The official engagement began last year, announced before the two met. Corin figured he could talk her out of it once they met in person. He couldn't believe that any intelligent person would want their partner for life picked out for them. He didn't stand a chance." His hair fell across his face as he burst out laughing. "She took one look into his big blue eyes and swooned. Literally, right there in the courtyard. When she came around, she swore to all who would listen that she would never be parted from her gallant prince."

Jenna couldn't help but feel sorry for her friend. It probably had never dawned on him that his bride-to-be would *like* being promised sight unseen. "But that's awful, they'll both be miserable."

Keanin patted her hand. "Never fear, he'll waggle out

of it somehow, he always does. And Mikasa's too caught up in court life to be miserable. She's not looking for true love, she's looking for power." He carefully peered into her eyes as if searching for something only he could see. "Why, are you a bit smitten with our fair prince? To hear tell, Corin rescued you from the Abyss."

"Actually, he accused me of the same feelings toward you. I'll have you both know, I'm quite happy with the status quo at present, thank you." Jenna shot him a frown. "And I'll also have you know that he plucked me from a ten-foot-deep ravine, not some pit of hell." She didn't add that she still had nightmares about what could have happened to her if he hadn't rescued her.

She tried to stifle a yawn, but the sharp-eyed kelar caught it anyway.

"Maggie would have my hide if you turn up all tired out tomorrow." Rising gracefully, he bent over and gave her a quick kiss on the cheek. "Off to sleep with you. I'll be back in the morn to start that tour of ours. Sleep well, my lady." Then he was gone.

Jenna slid under the covers. Lying there, she tried mentally reaching out for Ghortin. It wasn't a serious attempt; her mind sort of drifted that way. But then she started to panic. What if he never came back? What if he never left? What would happen if that king-napping mage killed Ghortin's body? Would he be with her forever? Or would he just pop out of existence?

She shook herself free of the dark thoughts. Exhaustion was making her paranoid and irrational. Besides, if she did want to reach Ghortin, she certainly couldn't do it with a fear-clouded mind.

As she slowed her thoughts down, she focused tightly on her own sense of balance.

Finally, as if he was speaking to her from far away, Ghortin's voice came to her.

"Lass, you couldn't wait, could you? Well, now you've got me,

what did you want?"

It was harder than it had seemed in Storm's room to focus her thoughts into concrete conversation. Probably because they were both still exhausted. *"I wanted to make sure you were still there. No one seems to know much about what you did. How will I know if anything's happened to you?"*

"You'd feel it." His voice was grim. *"But don't worry about me; I'm a tough old bird. I'll make it through. But how is everyone else?"*

"Storm's feeling better. He woke up after you'd gone. I think he's already making plans to go after you and his father."

An odd wave of concern flowed through her mind. Sharing Ghortin's emotions like this was going to take some getting used to. *"He'll need to be careful with himself for quite some time. I don't need to tell you how close to dying he was. But I'm sure Resstlin will curtail him long enough. How is Areania?"*

There was a peculiar tone to his voice with the question, but Jenna couldn't tell if it was from her or him. *"Not well, and probably getting worse. She was hanging on to Storm like a lifeline. Now that he's going to live, I think she'll be forced to think about the king."*

Ghortin was silent so long that Jenna feared he might have slipped away again. When he spoke, the voice in her head was grim.

"I'm going to tell you things that you mustn't tell anyone. Not even Storm." His tone was low, as if he didn't want to say it at all. *"I don't know for certain that the king is still alive. And I get no feeling from my body at all. Theoretically, I should be able to sense something, but since this has never been done before, there's no precedent."* Jenna sensed a mental shrug.

"Worse yet, I get no feelings from the attacking mage. I didn't when he was in the ballroom, and I don't now. Just the sheer energy he used to call forth those demonspawn should have blasted his location to any mage in a hundred miles. Never mind disguising them and planting them in the castle."

Jenna shivered. She hadn't thought about that. She was too new to this whole mage thing to have thought about trying to pick up on the attacker's magical signature.

Mentally, she flashed to her first sight of the attacking mage; perhaps something in her memory would register for either her or Ghortin. She could see the mage, but her mind's eye refused to focus on him at all. It was as if that robe of his was disorienting her mental eye as it had her physical eyes.

"What do we do now?" There was so much information, she couldn't process it enough to be terrified at the moment.

"I'm afraid there isn't much we can do right now. I'll stay out of your consciousness as much as possible, but I'll be here if you call. Hopefully I'll be able to come up with some answers soon. Meanwhile, learn about Irundail. And don't let on that Resstlin may be king in truth and not just interim. I don't yet know what we're up against, or how we can stop it; but panicking people more than they already are certainly won't help."

The pessimism in Ghortin's mental voice unnerved her. He was the most optimistic person she'd ever met, on either world. If he was this worried, she didn't want to think about the consequences.

"Isn't there anything I can do to help?" She hated feeling helpless.

Obviously the emotion-feeling bit went both ways. *"Easy, lass. Things aren't that lost yet. It's difficult because you're seeing my internal doubts now, ones that normally no one would see. The best thing you can do is keep people calm. By this time tomorrow, it will be common knowledge that I'm living in here. If people see that you're upset, they'll believe that I'm upset. Besides, I think keeping Storm here long enough to completely heal will be task enough."*

Jenna felt the emptiness of his leaving before she had adequate time to retort. Which was exactly as he had planned.

She leaned over and turned down the glow light. It would be hard to appear carefree tomorrow, and after, but Keanin was the person to help with that. Banishing her nightmares away until she could deal with them, Jenna slid off to sleep.

———◆———

A firm shake jerked her awake a moment after she had fallen asleep. Or that's what it felt like. "Am I going to see your face every time I wake up while I'm here?" Jenna growled at the smiling Keanin above her. She disliked early risers, and if Storm and Keanin were any indication, kelars were a whole blessed race of them.

"I'll have you know, there are more than a few women who would kill for such an honor. Up, up, up. Healer Maggie has let me come to take you away for a day of fun and excitement."

Jenna responded by pulling the blankets up and over her head. "G'away. It's too early."

Keanin gave a few tugs on the offending blanket, but Jenna's grip was like rigor mortis. He might be the most amazingly good-looking man she had ever seen, including in the movies, but sleep was a valuable commodity. Besides, he wasn't trying to drag her into bed; he was trying to drag her out of it.

With a shrug, he surrendered the battle and went for a different approach. He scooped her up, blanket and all, in one lighting fast move.

"Hey." Jenna squealed from within her pile of blankets. "Put me down." She started thrashing about, not caring if she knocked Keanin over. Fortunately he, like most kelars it seemed, had amazing balance.

"Tsk. If you don't behave, I shall have to take you out around the city like this."

Jenna pounded on his chest. And to think she used to get upset when her roommate woke her up by gargling too loud.

Keanin laughed, finally losing his balance and tumbling both of them onto the bed.

"Having to win them by force now, are we?" Maggie's dry voice cut through their laughter.

Jenna tried to jerk herself free from the tangled blankets. "It's not what it looks like. Really. He, ah, was trying to drag me out of bed."

Maggie settled her hands on two solid hips. "Doesn't look like he made it too far." She glanced pointedly at the pile of intertwined limbs on the bed.

Futilely, Jenna attempted again to free herself. Keanin hung on all the tighter, looking up with a tortured face. "Alas, she has found us out, fair one. Mine virtue is at loss."

Maggie finally burst out laughing as she smacked the prostrate kelar in the head. "Sir. I'll take it kindly if you refrain from making my patients squeal." She gave a nod to Jenna. "And I do hope you can protect yourself from this ravisher. I'll still need your help with the prince. I'm afraid it's going to be a little while before he's ready to be up and about."

Jenna sobered as she slid out from under Keanin. "How is he? Has he gotten worse?"

"His Royal Shagginess is resting peacefully at present. But fear not, you'll be the first notified should his status change. In fact, that's why I'm here."

She reached for something that had been hidden in the bun of hair on her head. At first glance, it appeared to be a small, gray mouse. At second glance, tiny delicate wings were noticeable. The small creature's whiskers jutted forward as it explored the healer's hand.

"This is Ivan, she's a scree. Let her sit in your hand for a bit." Maggie slid the soft creature into Jenna's hand. The mouse whiskers wiggled in earnest as it got to know its new host. "She'll be able to find you anywhere now that she knows you. If something happens, I can call you back immediately."

Jenna was fascinated by the little scree stretching her wings. They looked like they belonged on a bird. They were dark blue with small magenta dots on the tips. All four legs were there like a normal mouse. The wings seemed to have been added on as a genetic afterthought. One of Ghortin's earliest lessons came to mind. "She's a created being, isn't she?"

Maggie nodded as she took the tiny creature back. "Aye. Although the scree are very old created beings. They can't breed without magical assistance, but they've been around for at least two thousand years." She watched as Keanin got to his feet. "But enough of that, I see your escort is itching to depart." She grabbed Keanin by one pointed ear with her free hand. Not an easy feat since he was a good foot taller than the healer and his ears were hidden by all that hair. But Maggie managed with a surety that spoke of practice.

"*You* can wait in the hall. I'm quite sure our young friend can get dressed without your assistance."

Once they'd departed, Jenna wasted no time dressing. Who could tell how long Keanin would stay out?

CHAPTER SEVENTEEN

———◆———

THE BRIGHT MORNING LIGHT CAME as a shock. Although her rumbling stomach told her it was morning, it was easy to forget the time in the windowless wing of the House of Healing. It was also a bit disorienting stepping out of a building she'd never stepped into.

All her thoughts of disorientation were washed away as the splendor of Irundail rose before her. The House of Healing lay adjacent to the most solid looking building she'd ever seen. Huge, thick towers rose from the corners of dark gray walls made of bricks as tall as her. Dagger-like arrow slots were the only breaks in the solid gray.

Two guards stood at attention at the open gate. Like the royal guards in England, they looked more like stone than humans, or kelar in this case.

"Ah yes. Our tour begins with Castle Irundail, the most heavily fortified construction in the known world. And where, might I add, we shall later have to see about finding accommodations for you. Once our esteemed Maggie has deemed you well enough to move out of her House of Healing, that is." Keanin's mischievous grin told Jenna that he was also staying in the castle.

"But we can deal with that later, right?" The day was too beautiful to deal with looming, dreary castles.

"Why of course, my lady. You have but to ask and I shall obey." He swept down in one of his trademark bows. "On with the tour." He led them away from the House of Healing and the castle. The two buildings, plus another fair-sized one on the opposite side, were on the uppermost level of a group of huge stone terraces.

The buildings all looked out over a long green valley dotted with small clusters of farms. The rock terrace trailed out behind the buildings to a sharp drop into that same valley. They slowly made their way to the edge near the road, with Keanin letting her gawk in silence. As they reached the turn in the road, Jenna realized a good-sized town was at the end of it. Not only would it provide homes and supplies for people working in the castle and supporting buildings, but in an attack, it would be the first layer of defense. Irundail was obviously built at a much more dangerous time than Lithunane, which lacked such defensive measures.

"Have there been many attacks on the castle?"

"Not many." Keanin smiled as if it was all his doing. "And none have ever made it past the Keepers."

Keanin chuckled at her obvious lack of understanding of the term. "Ghortin is getting remiss. An apprentice mage who has never heard of the Keepers?"

Jenna felt that she had to defend her teacher. "He didn't have that much time, you know. He had to forgo some history so that he could make sure I wouldn't accidentally fry somebody."

"Now, don't you think about bespelling me. I was teasing. I'm certain his cragginess did a fine job. I'll explain about the Keepers when we can see them."

"How far are we from the Markare?" Ghortin's descriptions of the massive desert didn't make her want to go there, but seeing it from a safe distance would be fine.

Keanin jerked his head up, his golden eyes wary. "We're not close, thank the gods. Bad things go on in the Markare. My parents were killed there."

Jenna squeezed his hand. "I'm sorry." It sounded weak, but there wasn't much else she could think of.

"It was a long time ago. I was just a baby." He shook his head and pulled her along with him. "But let the past stay in the past. I think we should enjoy ourselves."

Jenna forced a smile. "Agreed." Clearly Keanin had some demons of his own, but he wasn't going to deal with them today.

She gave a large white building careful study as they passed. More of the mysterious helaermages wandered in and out.

"That's the Helaermage House." Keanin noticed her interest. "Since the helaermages are an order of religious wizards, they all have various levels of magecraft, but they have also devoted their lives to the neutral god DOL. It's a secretive order, but they seem to be up for doing good deeds, even if they claim not to take sides. They often disagree with unaligned mages over matters of theory and practice. But, as you saw yesterday with Dantil and Ghortin, most of them get along well enough on a personal level."

"So they can do the same things mages can?" They didn't have the same feel she got from Ghortin. But with the sporadic manner in which her magic had been working lately, she didn't know if she could trust her sense about it.

Keanin shrugged. "I'm afraid I have no more than a rudimentary knowledge of magecraft myself. I'm not gifted." He kicked a small loose stone as they continued their walk. "I do know that there is some sort of internal difference in the way the two classes work magic. I'm not clear as to what it is. There aren't many helaermages down in Lithunane because the DOL temple is in the mountains outside Irundail. The helaermages refuse to be far from it for any length of time; I think it has something to do with their Power."

The town was more congested than Jenna had previously thought. Houses seemed to lean precariously into each other, although Keanin assured her they were quite sturdy. People barely acknowledged them, which, after the over-attentivness from everyone around her the past few days, was a relief to Jenna.

"Oh, I almost forgot." They were halfway through the twisting streets when Keanin pulled up short. "The Keepers." He backtracked them down the street. He looked down each side street carefully, as if he was trying to jog his memory. Finally he nodded to himself and squired Jenna down a thin, dark path. Within minutes they arrived at a small hill of grass behind the buildings.

Pulling Jenna along behind him, Keanin crossed the grass and walked to the top.

"Can you see way down there?" He pointed toward the south.

Huge cliff-like walls of deep black rose majestically into the sky. Squinting, Jenna could make out two white towers sitting on either side of a chasm between the walls. The walls were easily eighty feet tall, and the two towers sitting upon them were another twenty or so feet from top to bottom. With the cliffs behind the town, this gap would be the only way in or out.

"Those towers are the Keepers. The most amazing mage achievement outside of Ghortin's mystical abode," Keanin said.

"What do they do?" She had a hard time believing that anything could be as impressive as Ghortin's home.

Keanin's face fell a trifle. "I knew you would ask me that. I'm afraid my knowledge of their exact abilities is somewhat limited. But they do it well."

"You have no idea what they do?" She folded her arms and gave her new teacher a scowl.

"I didn't say that." He drew himself up with mock pride. "I know what they do; mainly keep raiders, miscreants, and hooligans out of the valley. I lack the knowledge of *how* they do it. But they are impressive, aren't they? They have never been breached, and never will be. We're safe here."

They wandered back toward the center of the city slowly, Keanin pointing out odd places of interest along the way. By the time they got there, Jenna's stomach was making some undignified noises.

"I say, I never did ask if you had breakfast," Keanin said.

"I usually get out of bed to eat, and in case you hadn't noticed, I was in bed when you got me. I think that means you owe me breakfast, or lunch, or whatever meal they're serving right now."

"Ah, my lady. How could I be so remiss? Come, come. We shall seek nourishment for your fragile bones." He led the way down a twisting side street.

The tavern he led her to looked more reputable than most on the street. The inside of the place was neat, if well worn. The small wooden tables were plain, but at least they were clean. Even if they looked more like someone had slapped pieces of wood together rather than actual woodworking.

A portly human man poked his head out from the kitchen. "Be with you shortly. 'ave a seat." He disappeared behind the swinging door without waiting for a response. As Jenna's eyes adjusted to the dim light, she realized the place wasn't empty like she had at first thought.

Two off-duty female guards huddled in a corner, inhaling their food.

Oblivious to her observations, Keanin plunked down at a nearby table. "This place has gone downhill a bit since I was here last, but it's still better than most at this end."

"There are better places at the other end?" Jenna was hungry, but she would be willing to wait for a better inn.

"Now don't sound so worried. This place may have slid in looks, but I recognize the innkeeper. He's as good a cook as you'll find this time a day. Many of the places, including the expensive ones at the other end, don't open until later."

"And w'at will you folks be 'aving today?" The inn-keeper was back and his smile was sincere enough. But Jenna knew it was directed at the wealth of their clothes, rather than them personally.

"What have you got for a fair lady's breakfast, my good man?" Keanin asked.

"Last night's roast, good and lean. Some fresh bread and fruits." His head gave a slight bob as he spoke.

"We'll take two servings of it all. And keep it coming until my companion has had her fill."

Jenna looked away at Keanin's theatrics. The outrageous man couldn't even order lunch without making a show.

The stout tavern keeper bobbed his head again and bustled back through the swinging doors.

A movement in the corner caught Jenna's eye, and she looked up to see that one of the guards was almost at their table. She seemed to give no attention to Jenna, but zeroed in on Keanin like a hunting falcon.

"Say, fair face." Her voice was low, and Jenna realized with a shock that the woman was quite drunk. And quite well muscled.

"My mate and I don't recall seeing you 'round here before. How about you coming over and introduce yourself properly."

The undisguised lust in her eyes seemed to surprise Keanin, but only momentarily. Rising smoothly, the kelar noble took the woman's scarred hand, bending over to kiss it as if she was of noble birth.

"Ah, alas, as much as I would like to join you two fair flowers, I fear my honor and duties forbid it." He gave a weary sigh and glanced over to Jenna. "I am nothing more than a royal servant, but the queen has entrusted the daughter of a visiting dignitary to my care. My life should be forfeit if I fail to keep her entertained and safe."

The guard pulled back, favoring Jenna with an assessing stare. Jenna did her best to appear meek and a bit stupid.

The woman pulled in close to Keanin, running one long finger down his face and down to the top of his open shirtfront. "But my friend and I could make your forfeited life very pleasurable. It has been a long time since I've had such fare."

"Ah, if it weren't for my duties." He shook his head wearily. "Mayhap I can find you later?"

The guard stepped back. "My name is Marta, of the seventh regiment. When you've finished your responsibilities, come find us. We spend our eves at the Ox and Hound." She wrapped her arms around a startled Keanin and planted a passionate kiss. She pulled back with an evil smile. "Until later, pretty face." Without another look at either of them, Marta stumbled back to her companion.

Keanin sat down with a thump, his golden eyes wide and vacant. Finally, he shook his head and turned to Jenna. "Are you ready to go on with our tour now?"

Jenna shook her head. The amorous noble had met his match.

"Keanin, we haven't been served yet." She paused and glanced meaningfully toward the two guardswomen. "Or at least I haven't."

"Of course. I knew that. At least I think I did." He looked like a man who had taken a much longer journey than he had intended. "Quite interesting clientele the place has."

"Keanin, if she had kissed you much harder you would have sold me into slavery and followed her off a cliff somewhere." Jenna laughed. It had been tense there for a moment, but the woman fortunately wasn't belligerent, just amorous. "Pretty face." She folded her hands under her face and batted her eyelashes in mock adoration.

"Stop that." He swatted at her hands. "I'll have you know I was in complete control the entire time."

The keeper was back with their food before she could respond.

Fortunately, once they'd realized their prey wasn't able to play, the guardswomen finished their meals and left. But not before Marta gave a slow raking stare over Keanin's lean form. Jenna managed to keep a straight face until the women were well clear of the place.

CHAPTER EIGHTEEN

T HE REST OF THE AFTERNOON was a relaxing one. Jenna continued teasing Keanin about Marta and he continued to deny any attraction to the woman. But not entirely convincingly. Female soldiers might not be his regular fare, but he was pondering it. That must have been one hell of a kiss.

At one point, late in the day, she saw someone who looked suspiciously like Lord Ravenhearst. But, like when she had been at the market in Lithunane with Storm, by the time her companion turned around, the cloaked figure was gone.

"I know *that* one wouldn't have been picked up by the rescue beacon." Keanin wrinkled his slender nose. "The only reason he's allowed in the royal castle at all is because of his wretched ambassador status."

Jenna didn't say anything more about her unease, but she kept a close eye out. She was certain that it had been the blond nobleman she had seen. And furthermore, she was equally certain that he had seen her.

It was almost dark by the time they worked their way back up to the House of Healing.

According to the apprentice healer on duty at the door, the prince had been biting and snapping at everyone while he awaited their return. "Shall we, my lady?" Keanin held out his arm formally, assuming the role of court lackey. "I do so hate to keep royalty waiting, don't you?"

Storm looked better than he had the day before, but

he still was a shadow of his normal self. His grayish skin looked like it was stretched too thin. He was also being supported entirely by a huge pile of pillows, although he was trying to make it appear that he was sitting up of his own power.

"Maggie told me you two had left; I thought you would never get back." He tried to sound gruff, but his voice was still too weak to pull it off. "So, what's the news?"

"Shouldn't you be resting more? Like asleep?" Jenna asked.

"Ah, I fear he is too ornery for rest." Keanin moved forward, slowly pulling out a seat for Jenna and one for himself. "Even when it's obvious he's weak as a fledgling."

Storm favored his friend with a fleeting glare. "Pah. I'll be out of here soon enough. It's just a scratch."

Jenna raised an eyebrow at that, and Storm quickly amended his comment.

"All right, it was a deep scratch." He frowned. "What's the news? Have they found Ghortin and my father? Are there any clues as to where that evil mage has gone?"

Jenna was momentarily chagrined. They'd spent the whole day out as if nothing was wrong. Then she remembered that Ghortin had told her to do that very thing. She felt recovered, but judging by the reactions, she had been close to dying when she arrived here.

"Ghortin is still in my head. As for your other questions, I have no idea. I'm sure your royal mages and lackeys aren't going to fill Keanin and me in on what's happening."

Keanin stepped in smoothly. "Besides, you know no one is going to do anything until Resstlin comes back and gives the royal word."

Storm tried to slam his fist on the bed. The feeble result was shocking to Jenna and she had seen how badly he was injured inside. Averting his face, Storm drew the twitching hand back toward him as if it hadn't happened.

"Damn it." He growled, as angry at his weak body as he was at the situation. "Now's the time to strike, while there's a chance that the demon mage is weak—there's no way what he did wouldn't take a toll."

Keanin held out a comforting hand. "I know you're upset. We all are. But what's the point of fretting about things we have no say over? None of us are going any-where for quite some time, I think."

Storm looked ready to argue, but seemed too tired to carry it out. "I intend to be up in a few days. If Resstlin isn't back by then, I'll go find our father and Ghortin's body without his approval."

Another image drifted into Jenna's mind. "Storm, would Lord Ravenhearst have been picked up by the rescue beacon?"

"No." Storm shook his head. "Unless someone was hanging on to him, like I was holding you. Keanin? What of it?"

The handsome kelar shook his head. "Jenna already spoke to me of it." He shrugged. "To be quite honest, I have no idea whether he came through or not. It was quite chaotic when the transfer was finally completed. I suppose he could have come through, then disappeared before I saw him."

"I know what I saw." Jenna paced around the small room. "It was him. He took off before Keanin could see him, but I know who it was."

Storm's eyebrows rose. "Again? Are you certain? What was he doing?"

"Yes, again." Jenna growled; she didn't like the tone of disbelief in his voice. "And for all I could tell, he was just standing there. It was outside one of the sword shops, one with a lot of off-duty guards outside. Anyway, one min-ute he was there, the next he was gone. But I know he saw me." It almost felt like she should recognize some-thing about the blond nobleman, something that stayed just out of reach.

Besides her growing unease about Ravenhearst, there had also been some elusive thing wandering through her mind during their walk. For some reason, she felt like there was something missing, something that she needed to remember. She found herself staring mindlessly at the grayish skin on Storm's hand with a frown. Suddenly it came to her.

"Ghortin's book."

Both kelars looked at her oddly.

She waved her hands at them. "No, this isn't about Lord Ravenhearst. Not directly anyway. Something else had been nagging at me today, and I remembered what it was. Ghortin's book. Surely that thing has some answers. He was obsessed with it."

Storm's face, which at first had been as blank as Keanin's, cleared up. "You mean that gray book he kept lugging around with him?"

Jenna nodded enthusiastically. "Yes. Right before the ball he let me study two of its spells. Judging by the pages, they were the lowest level in the book, but way above anything I'd ever done before. The language was odd too." She renewed her pacing around the room. "That book must have something to do with all these strange happenings; why else would Ghortin be so obsessed with it? I'm sure when he comes back he'll have us go get it."

"Easy, easy." Keanin raised his hands as he glared at Jenna. "You're getting as bad as Corin. We can't go darting all over the country. Winter's practically upon us, and I know there isn't enough mage ability left in either Irundail or Lithunane to light a match, let alone transfer a bunch of adventurers. And you cannot seriously think of traipsing all the way down to Lithunane on horseback." The stunning nobleman shuddered.

"We can't just do nothing; couldn't we have someone send us the book? It would be smaller than sending a person." Jenna couldn't help it, the more she thought about it the more she knew that they needed that book.

"It's not that easy." Storm was the one talking her down this time. "I don't think they would waste the energy even if they had it, which I doubt. Plus, I know Ghortin, and more than likely he's got enough wards on it to blow Lithunane sky high if someone tries to take it without his tricks."

"So, as soon as you get better, we'll go after it," Jenna said as she ignored the pang of fear that followed. She knew they needed that book, but going back to the scene of the attack left her cold.

Keanin looked at them like they had lost their minds. "Didn't you hear me? Winter? And after that, floods in the plains? This part of the country is wretched to travel through for months. You know that, Corin." He fiddled with the edge of his tunic.

Jenna couldn't blame him, but they needed the book. Hopefully, with Ghortin's essence inside her head she'd be able to safely open it. And Storm's reasoning about attacking while the enemy was still recovering made sense. They needed advice though. Reaching inside her mind, she called Ghortin's name. Just mentally shouting for him seemed rather unprofessional. But she couldn't think of a better way.

She felt his presence before he spoke. Like his visit last night, he stayed strictly in her mind. Apparently he wasn't going to take over her body every time he came for a visit.

"*Yes, child?*" His voice was vaguely foggy, like he had been sleeping. "*Did you have a nice time with that young peacock?*"

"*Yes. But we were wondering about your book.*" She was still having trouble directing her thoughts internally; she wasn't sure how to push them toward him without yelling.

"Which book?" His voice sounded stronger now. *"Why am I getting so many nervous-edgy feelings from you? Has something happened?"*

Jenna gave a tiny mental sigh of relief. She hadn't been sure if Ghortin had complete access to her thoughts and memories. Thankfully he didn't unless she let him. Life would have been uncomfortable for them both if he were rummaging around in there all the time.

"Nothing's changed, if that's what you mean. Although I did see Lord Ravenhearst out in town. Storm and Keanin don't believe me." She briefly flashed the image of the person she had seen. Ghortin's recognition sealed it; it was Ravenhearst all right. *"I got to thinking and realized that we should have your gray book. Don't you need it or something?"*

Ghortin's mind had been expressing concern as to the arrival of Ravenhearst. He grew more concerned when she flashed the book in her mind.

"Lass, I don't recognize that book at all. You say it's mine?"

Jenna's stomach clenched. It never dawned on her that Ghortin might not remember the book. How could someone forget something he'd carried around for months and not forget anything else? She thought mental images of him pouring intently over the book.

"You have to recognize it, you carried it everywhere. Don't you remember having me work on those two spells right before the ball?"

Ghortin's confusion grew. *"As far as I know, I've never seen that thing in my life. But your images are true."* He faded off for a moment, and then came back. *"This is a grave concern. If I have forgotten something like that, who knows what else I've forgotten?"* An overwhelming fear started to spread throughout Ghortin's consciousness. He let it flow over him briefly, then fought back and subdued it. But she still felt his unease. His mind had always been his greatest weapon. Suddenly that weapon wasn't trustworthy.

She was about to try and comfort him when she

became aware of being shaken.

"Jenna?" Keanin said worriedly. "Are you all right?"

Jenna shook her head, realizing with a start that she had been leaning over on Storm's bed with her eyes closed. They must have thought she'd been struck numb or something.

"Yes, I was talking to Ghortin." Her face went hot. She should have told them what she was doing instead of drifting off like that. "I didn't mean to scare you." Judging by both angular kelar faces, that was exactly what she had done.

"Ghortin doesn't remember the book." A wince from inside her head told her that Ghortin may not have wanted them to know. But whatever was going on, they were all involved in it. Ghortin's mental lapse was something they needed to take into consideration.

"Well, I'm sure he has lots of books, and besides, that leap to your head may have jarred him," Keanin said hopefully.

Storm shook his head weakly. "He's been with this one book almost exclusively. And Jenna is right; he did believe it was connected to what's happening. But you may be right about the jump loosening his thoughts." He turned to Jenna. "Does he know why he may have forgotten this?"

"We were discussing it when Keanin shook me. If you give me a second, I'll see if he wants to talk to you." She closed her eyes and called for her teacher again. His thoughts were still distracted, but he answered immediately.

"*Maybe that would be best.*" His voice sounded uncertain, and she could tell it would take a while before he felt settled about losing his memory.

"Hello, lad." Jenna heard his voice and hers in unison. It was an odd feeling, but at least she didn't feel quite as blocked out as she had the first time the mage had taken over.

"Ghortin?" Storm said a bit awkwardly. This was his first conscious encounter with the Ghortin/Jenna conglomeration.

"Who else?" Ghortin said wryly. "Don't answer that. I think it would be best if we didn't let many people know about my missing memories. We'll tell Maggie and Dantil. They're the two best chances we have for getting my memories back, but don't say anything to anyone else."

"We're going to find your body," Storm said with brutal finality. Jenna knew that soon, healed or not, he was going to find his father and Ghortin.

"I've been trying to convince them that others will take care of it and the inadvisability of travel within the next few months." Keanin looked down at Storm like he was nothing more than an errant child.

Jenna wanted to argue that statement, but had to be content with arguing in her head. Ghortin heard her quite clearly.

"My apprentice seems to argue against your wisdom, Keanin. But I think you're right." Jenna's hand went up to forestall Storm's angry rebuttal. "You may have to go. But now is not the time to decide. Like it or not, you must heal before we do anything."

"But what if Jenna's right and that book of yours holds our answers? Or at least points us in the right direction?"

"That's a chance we'll have to take, I fear. An ill-advised trip would be worse than none at all. However, I am concerned with the appearance of Ravenhearst. I never have liked that man, and I can't think of a single good reason for his being in Irundail. If he was sent anywhere after the attack, it should have been back to Strann." Ghortin's mind flitted across ideas far faster than she could follow.

"Keanin, I'd like you to use your connections to find out if anyone knows why the ambassador is here. And don't be obvious about it."

The handsome kelar bowed. "Am I ever? Although I can't think of any reason why he'd be involved in these misdeeds. He's not my favorite individual, but he's rather harmless."

"So he's let us believe." Ghortin's mind was already thinking about other things, and their contact was starting to weaken. "Now, I want you to rest," he pointed at Storm, "Keanin to spy, and Jenna to study." He'd almost gone when another thought struck him.

"Do you know if Tor Ranshal and Lord Edgar came through?"

"I don't think so," Keanin said. "But I'm afraid I haven't spent much time in the castle."

"It could be helpful if they were here." A subtle touch in her mind told her that he'd gone off again. She sighed.

"I hope you didn't have any more questions, because he's gone." She studied her companions. Keanin wanted no part of any of this. He was a court flower and he liked it that way. Storm still had fight in his eyes, but the wearied lines down his face spoke of his inability to follow through.

"I'll be up sooner than he thinks," Storm said. "Are you with me?"

She rolled her eyes. "Of course we're with you. But you're not going anywhere until spring, and neither are we."

Keanin followed her out. "You heard the lady, rest."

Storm let his hand fall on the coverlet. It was still the closest he could get to slamming his hand down. But Jenna noticed his eyes were shut before she closed the door.

CHAPTER NINETEEN

THE NEXT MONTH FLEW BY for Jenna. She studied harder than she ever had in her life, even preparing for her final papers in graduate school. Her echo had eventually come back, but it didn't respond to much in Irundail. Most likely the former mindslave had never been this far north.

Jenna also began training with Armsmaster Garlan. The half-breed kelar-human took to her right away—once she'd proven she had some basic training. She seemed to do best with bow and knife, but was also working on the sword. She shocked the entire castle by designing and using a weight set to help her build strength for fighting and drawing the long bow. Soon, her methods were being surreptitiously copied throughout the castle.

Storm's strength came back with agonizing slowness. Actually, it was agonizing for him, but Jenna was glad that her friend couldn't get out of his room. Their visits were strained as Storm's need for revenge, and his frustration at being physically trapped by his own body, became obsessions.

Keanin had become Jenna's only stable influence. The flashy kelar was always outrageous and managed to do quite well at lifting her spirits. But he'd found no clues as to the whys of Ravenhearst's appearance. No one in the castle had seen the nobleman in Irundail, and however he got here, it wasn't with the rescue beacon. Jenna thought she had seen him twice more, but she couldn't get close enough to be certain.

"Forget it." Jenna slammed her fist on the desk. As if injuring herself would make the spell she was working on any easier to learn.

"*Now, I told you this wouldn't be easy.*" Like the others, Ghortin's temper was getting short. He still hadn't been able to figure out how far his memory could be trusted, so he had to rely on the memories of others and hope he wasn't missing too much. It was making him more testy than usual. "*You have got to hold it steady; if you don't, the whole thing will blow up in your face. Try it again.*"

Jenna growled at her internal tormentor. The lessons had been getting, in her opinion, entirely too advanced.

The one they were working on now, for instance. It was supposed to enable her to stun everyone within a fifty-foot perimeter. Used correctly, it would make a mighty weapon. But one slip up and she could end up turning all that Power on herself. As she found out yesterday, the mildest result of such action was being blasted unconscious and waking up with a headache that went down to her toes. That she was still nursing the remnants of that same headache didn't improve her spirits. And Ghortin showed no pity at all.

"Look, isn't there something less dangerous that I could work on?" She didn't care that she was whining. "My head is killing me, and you said yourself that this isn't a spell to be taken lightly."

Ghortin gave a mental sigh. "*I usually wouldn't be so adamant, but I fear that even this spell may not be enough in the times to come. But I suppose a short break is in order. If you kill yourself, I won't have a home.*"

Jenna made a face, but it lost her intended effect since she had to make it at herself. "Thanks for your concern." She knew before she finished the last word that Ghortin had disappeared into the dark corner of her mind that he'd made his own.

Sighing, she walked out into the bright afternoon

sun. Winter had been short and mild and spring already showed signs of coming. She wandered around the garden grounds in no direction, glad to be out of the stuffy cottage.

Ghortin had moved their practices outside when he realized that Jenna's control over her magic wasn't as good as it could be. Then he commanded local workers, via the castle household of course, to build them a small workroom cottage when it became obvious that too many people were finding time to sit around and watch the unusual practice sessions.

Jenna was thinking about getting some food when a magical bolt surged through her. It was some distance away, but it still sent goosebumps up the back of her arms.

She spun in a slow circle, trying to determine the location of the surge. It hadn't felt threatening, but Powerful.

A gentle tug pulled her toward the grassy edge of the terrace toward the Keepers and the cliff walls. She wasn't the only one who felt the surge; small groups of people began to come out of the castle and the House of Healing. A few mages broke free of their studies and made an appearance, but there were no brown robes of the helaermages among them.

Even Keanin came out, which was a bit of a surprise since he kept adamantly denying any magical ability. Of course he could have simply followed the crowd. The auburn-haired kelar liked to stay abreast of happenings, as long as he wasn't too close to the center.

"What's all the ruckus about?" He amiably slipped one long arm around her shoulders.

"I don't know." She paused, looking closely at the tall kelar. "Did you feel it?"

He started to shake her off, then frowned, and nodded. "Yes, I did. But you can't tell anyone, especially not your mental companion. It's just a tiny bit of ability."

Jenna started to ask why, then seeing the seriousness in

his eyes, she let it drop. She had found out a little about Keanin's parents. They'd been part of a magic research colony in the Markare. One in which something had gone so horribly wrong that no one had survived. Or survived long at any rate. His mother had dragged herself to Irundail only to die after getting the king and queen's assurance that they would raise her infant son. Both of his parents had been low-level mages. Keanin didn't relish any magical tie between himself and what killed his family. Jenna knew he couldn't suppress it forever, but *he'd* have to decide when it would come out.

There was movement in the distance. A group of guards and two others had come past the Keepers and was now entering Irundail through the ravine and heading toward the city. The surge of Power that had drawn her was gone, but now her curiosity was engaged.

"Come on," She tugged her companion toward the roadway down to the town. "Let's go see what it is."

Keanin leaned back enough to slow her down; he was slender, but his height gave him leverage. "Why rush? Whatever is down there will come up here in due time. You and Corin are too much alike, always rushing into things."

"Yes, but they may not let us see what's going on if we wait." She continued tugging him.

Keanin sighed and allowed her to lead on.

A mass of curious people was getting to the city level when Jenna and Keanin caught up with them. Castle guards were holding the people back from a battered pair of travelers who were making their way in. Jenna edged her and Keanin forward through the crowd. A bearded guard started to yell at them until he saw who it was. It was common knowledge that mastermage Ghortin was somehow sharing his apprentice's body. And since most people weren't sure when he was in there, they tended to treat Jenna with solicitous respect whenever they met her.

"Greetings, my lady." The guard bowed stiffly. "I hate to bother you, but we have some people who are in dire need of aid."

Jenna leaned forward to see their condition and pulled back with a gasp. Two barely conscious figures; a tall, white-haired human man, and a short, dark kelar in torn black garb, were being supported on two guard horses. She almost didn't recognize Tor Ranshal and Sir Edgar in their current conditions, but it was certainly them.

She rushed past the guards, mentally calling Ghortin as she did so. This was no time for heroics. These men needed help and she wasn't confident enough in her abilities to try it without Ghortin.

"*Back already, lass?*" His voice was merry until Jenna forced him to see through her eyes.

"What mayhem is this?" The voice was hers, but it was Ghortin who was now in charge. Jenna held back, watching from the back of her mind.

"Greetings." The bearded guard seemed to know that he was now definitely talking to the mastermage, and his bow was a bit deeper. "We don't know what happened to them, great one. They triggered the Keepers, and when we went to investigate, we found them collapsed at the foot of the cliff."

Jenna felt her hand take hold of Tor Ranshal's. Ghortin was seriously shaken by the condition of his friend, but Jenna was bearing the brunt of it. The mastermage kept all his misgivings locked up with her.

"Tor Ranshal? Speak to me, old friend."

If Lithunane's seneschal was disturbed at being called 'old friend' by the young woman, he gave no sign. He wearily opened one eye. "Did we make it? Are we in Irundail?"

His voice seemed to stir the battered Sir Edgar into movement. "We're surrounded. Back. I can still fight."

His voice drifted off, and his battle stance had been little more than a spasmodic jerk toward his empty scabbard.

"Yes, my friend, you've made it. With many tales, I'm sure." Jenna's body turned toward the captain of the guards. "We've got to get them up to Maggie's immediately. Stand back." Jenna felt Ghortin gather Power through her. She also felt the workings of a spell with such intricate chaotic weavings that it made the one she'd been working on look like child's play. Seconds later, a tingle surged through her body and mind. There was a flash of light, and suddenly she and the two injured men were in the middle of the large hall in the House of Healing. There was a momentary delay before Ghortin spoke.

"Are you alright, lass?"

"Yes, I think so. You did a translocation spell, didn't you?" She didn't add that he sounded a lot weaker than he had moments before.

"You're developing an ear for the subtleties," he said wryly. *"I'm afraid I didn't have time to consult you; with whatever they've been through, they wouldn't have been helped by the blasted long trip up this monolith."*

"You don't know what's wrong with them?" She was getting worried at his voice; he was fading fast, and she certainly didn't want to face all those people and tell them Ghortin had disappeared.

"They are showing blood loss and a few broken bones. Edgar has a grievous head wound that isn't externally apparent—that's why I had to get them up here immediately. It will be up to you to find out how they got this way." He broke their mental contact, speaking to the alarmed healers pouring in from every side.

"Get the Mistress Healer. These men need care immediately." He grabbed hold of the nearest journeyman healer. "I'm going to be gone for a while, Maggie will understand, the strain was too much. You are to obey my apprentice as you would me." He was gone before either the startled healer or Jenna herself could respond.

"What would you have us do, my lady?" The healer motioned toward the two unconscious men.

"You heard the mastermage, get Maggie." She looked around, grabbing two of the largest healers. "See if you can get stretchers for them." She managed to keep the panic out of her voice; quite a feat since she hadn't thought Ghortin was going to vanish. Obviously, he'd had little choice. That added still more worry, which she roughly shoved to the back of her mind. One worry at a time.

"What's happened?" Maggie's booming voice cleared a circle around the injured men.

Jenna's heart lightened at the sight of the solid healer. "They were found outside Irundail. Ghortin said Sir Edgar has a head wound that's not visible and they both have broken bones."

"Bring them in here." Maggie held open a door for the stretcher-bearers. "I'm not sure what you can do for them now, child. They probably won't be waking for a while, not if I can help it. The best healers have been notified. I can call for you in your rooms if anything happens."

Maggie had couched it politely, as if she was asking Jenna if it was all right if she was excluded. But Jenna knew it wasn't a question. She also knew she heartily agreed with the healer.

"That would be fine," she said steadily, keeping the relief out of her voice. "I'll be waiting in my rooms in case you need me." With a nod, she hastily vacated the crowded room and headed straight for her rooms in the castle.

She hadn't realized how tired she was until she sat down on her bed. That little translocation trick Ghortin pulled had saved the men quite a bit of discomfort, if not more. But it certainly took its toll on her. For the first time since Ghortin had popped in her head two months ago, Jenna truly realized that it was her Power that he used when he worked magic.

She had assumed that when he took over, that it was him doing all the work. If she hadn't been so tired, the realization probably would have greatly disturbed her. As it was, she shoved it to the back of her mind with all the other waiting worries, and then slid off to oblivion.

A soft but insistent tapping at the door roused her from her dreamless slumber. She jumped up at first, thinking it might be a summons from Maggie, but then stopped. If the healer needed her, the summons wouldn't be quite so subtle.

She wandered to the door, trying to clear the sleep from her brain. She patted down her mass of sleep-tossed hair and debated again whether to get rid of the excess length. For some perverse reason, she felt changing any-thing else of this new body of hers would be unfair to the poor former owner.

"Thank the stars." Keanin barged in. "I was beginning to think you'd run away or something."

Jenna shook her still fogged head. "No, I took a nap. That thing that Ghortin pulled wore me out."

Keanin didn't seem to be listening as he strode over to her set of chairs and held one out for her. "So I gath-ered from your appearance. Here, my lady, you don't look quite yourself yet."

Jenna sat down gratefully. Being jolted out of sleep like that was never her favorite way of waking. "Did Maggie send you?" She was still sorting out who was where in her head.

"No. Actually, when I tried to go into the House of Healing, she had one of her people chase me over here. I was hoping you might have some answers."

"What? The great Keanin *wanting* to get in the middle of something?" She stretched, trying to get the rest of her body awake.

"I didn't say that. I always want to know what's going on, I just don't want to get involved in it. Too easy to get injured that way."

"Oh, fine. But someday you're going to find something you'll have to get involved with."

The kelar shook his head. "Don't you be laying curses on me; I'm your friend, remember? Now what's happened? That was Tor Ranshal and Sir Edgar I saw through the crowd, wasn't it?"

Jenna nodded. "Yes, but I'm afraid I don't know much more than that. After Ghortin and I got them here, Maggie all but chased me out too." One of her stifled worries came back. "I think Ghortin may have overdone himself this time. He vanished right after the transfer was finished."

"Hey, no long faces around me." He leaned forward, taking hold of one of her hands. "I'm sure he's fine." Keanin screamed and jumped forward.

"What happened? Are you okay?" Jenna jumped to her feet but couldn't see any injuries.

Keanin turned red. "Sorry if I startled you, but our friend here startled me." He reached up into his hair and pulled out a small, chattering scree. His response had startled it as well and the small creature was scolding him most thoroughly. He handed it over to Jenna.

"She must be from Maggie." She looked around the furry thing for a note or message. "Well, Ivan, do you have something for me?" She didn't expect an answer and almost dropped the poor thing when it spoke.

"Mistress Maggie requests your attendance in the Healing House." The creature's voice was high pitched and distant.

"How did she…" She held the scree up, searching for any sort of mechanism.

"That's how scree relay messages. Or so I've heard. I've never been privy to one giving its message before. They repeat words trained into them. I don't think they've the intelligence to understand what they're saying though."

The scree turned and resumed scolding Keanin in its own language. Jenna started laughing, careful not to jolt the creature still sitting in her hand.

"I'd say she's smart enough to know when she's being insulted." She petted the chattering animal with a forefinger. "It's okay, Ivan. You've done a good job, you can go now."

The scree rumbled gratefully at the petting, then flew off through the open window.

"Shall we go? You did say you wanted to know what was going on, didn't you?"

Keanin nodded. "You've got me. Just don't let me volunteer for anything dangerous."

Jenna waited until they were out of the castle before she tried reaching for Ghortin. She didn't want people watching her while she was looking around in her head. Unfortunately, she got no response. A slight surge from the echo in delayed recognition to the scree, but no mastermage. She kept her attempt, and the lack of results, from Keanin.

Keanin noticed anyway. "What's wrong?" He peered at her closely. "You tried reaching Ghortin, didn't you?"

Jenna looked away, then finally nodded. "Nothing. Please don't say anything to anyone, not even Maggie. I don't want to give them more things to worry about."

Maggie and two other healers were closed in around a bed as they entered the room. A single healer monitored a still form in the second bed. Moving closer, Jenna recognized the wan face of Sir Edgar. He looked better than he had a few hours ago, but his short black hair sharply accented his thin, pointed face and the unhealthy pallor on his normally dark skin.

Maggie noticed them at that moment. "Come in, dear. Someone has been asking to see you." She stood back a bit and motioned them forward.

Tor Ranshal's face was waxen, but he managed a smile. "Ah, child. I'm so glad to see you again."

Jenna moved closer. It was more than a little disturbing to see the formerly energetic old man look so ill. She never had found out how old he was, but right now he looked older than Ghortin's three thousand years.

"How are you feeling?" She could see the answer, but it was the first thing that came out.

"As good as can be expected," he said. "I hear I have you to thank for getting us up here?"

"Ghortin actually." She bit her tongue as soon as the words were out. She hadn't wanted to bring him up. More than likely Tor Ranshal would want to speak to his old friend as soon as possible. How could she tell any of them, least of all him, that she couldn't find the master-mage floating in her head?

Tor Ranshal's golden eyes sparkled, giving his face a hint of its former vitality. "Ah, but I'm sure you were the driving force. Let that scamp go play somewhere else. I want to enjoy your company."

Jenna briefly wondered how the old man had known, then brushed it off. Tor Ranshal was familiar with magic and the strain it took. He must have known that either she or the mage would be tired.

"What happened? Why were you two out there?" The questions blurted out of their own accord.

"That's a tale that will be long in the telling, my lady." He looked up at Maggie. "Would you be so kind as to find chairs for all? I've much to tell, and it may take—"

"Tor Ranshal? What are you doing here?" Everyone in the room turned at the new voice. Storm glared at them from the doorway. He looked pale, especially still wearing the long, heavy, white hospital tunic, but he was standing without trouble. "And why didn't anyone tell me?" The last was pointedly directed at Maggie.

Maggie deflected it with a flick of her hand. "Until I say you're fit to leave, you're no more than another one of my patients. You need rest, not updated reports of comings and goings." She held firm for a moment, then relented with a sigh. "But since you're here, you might as well stay." She flagged down a passing apprentice healer. "Get us some chairs if you would, and bring a blanket for his highness."

Storm looked sharply at her tone, but continued into the room nonetheless. His movements weren't as graceful as usual, but for a man who'd been resting in bed for a month, he was moving exceptionally well.

"Tor Ranshal and Sir Edgar arrived a few hours ago. The seneschal just awoke."

Storm turned away from Maggie, noticing the still figure on the other bed for the first time. "Is Edgar all right?"

"He will be. We've treated his internal injuries and both of their external ones." She faced Tor Ranshal with a heavy frown. "Which reminds me; I will cut this so short it will make heads spin if I think you're tiring yourself out. Am I understood?"

The smile that graced the ancient man's face was warm. "Of course, mistress, I will abide by your rules in your House." He shot a wry glance over to Storm who neatly refused to catch it.

The chairs, and a woolen blanket for Storm, were brought in, and Tor Ranshal settled in for his tale.

CHAPTER TWENTY

—◆—

"I DELIBERATELY BROKE LOOSE OF THE Beacon when the queen triggered it so that I would not be pulled through. I knew Edgar and I would be needed in Lithunane to investigate the attack. The real guests who had been replaced by demonspawn were all found murdered in their rooms." Tor Ranshal stopped for a sip of water. "There were also a few guests who were not demonspawn, but appeared to be helping the mage who attacked us. And there were Qhazborh symbols left near the dais." He let all of that sink in.

Jenna and he shared a look at the mention of guests who helped the invading demonspawn. There was little doubt now as to what that spell in her bath had been intended to do.

Tor Ranshal continued. "We did manage to track down two more pages who weren't what they seemed. Unfortunately, they escaped before we could catch them. They were under the house of Ravenhearst, but we couldn't find the Lord anywhere."

"He's here," Jenna said.

The old seneschal nodded wearily. "I had feared as much. Although, I am at a loss to explain how he got here or exactly what his involvement is in this. He was gone by the time we realized his connection to the pages."

His brow furrowed. "There were also strange mage callings and signs for the first two days after the attack. They seemed to come from the east, somewhere toward the Markare, but I could tell nothing more. The border mages near there felt them as well, but then the feelings stopped. I had hoped that somehow Ghortin could guide us with the Book of cuari. I'm afraid things are happening that are beyond my unworthy abilities."

Jenna winced at the mention of a book. "Is this Book of cuari gray by any chance?"

"Yes, child, it is. And very old. Much older than the mastermage himself, although he felt he could conquer it." He stopped when Jenna frowned. "It is here, isn't it? We were unable to find it in your rooms back in Lithunane."

"It's not here," she said. An unsettling thought crossed her mind. "Ravenhearst couldn't have gotten it, could he?"

"No. He wouldn't have been able to get past Ghortin's safeguards." But the crease between his brows told Jenna he didn't quite believe his own words.

"Do you think he could have gotten past them if he had help?" Storm asked grimly. "The sort of help that the rogue mage had the night of the ball?"

Tor Ranshal hesitated, and then met Storm's eyes with a frown. "Yes, I suppose. Since we don't know exactly how that mage was able to do what he did, anything could be possible."

"Come now." Keanin jumped out of his seat. "You don't think that Ravenhearst was in league with that *thing*? He's a questionable individual and all, but I don't think he'd go that far." He looked at the somber faces around the room. "Would he?" he added faintly as he slid back into his chair.

It was bad enough to be attacked in your own home. But to be attacked by someone you regularly socialized with was entirely something else.

"I am afraid we have no idea what Ravenhearst is truly up to." The seneschal rubbed his forehead. "As for the book, I assumed that Ghortin had found a way to move it here when no trace was found." He looked up at Jenna with a deepening frown. "And you say Ravenhearst is here?"

"Yes, but no one seems to have seen him but me."

"I don't think he'd be here if he had the book," Storm said, "provided it's that important and that he knows about it. We're not sure how he is involved with this."

"He's been associated with some demonspawn pages, he's vanished from one castle and is lurking unannounced near another," Jenna said. "I'd say he's up to something. And if the book is that important, don't we have to assume he knows about it? And what if he has it, but can't get it open? Wouldn't he come looking for someone who could?" Jenna couldn't keep the fear completely out of her voice. Maybe there was a reason why she had been the only one who'd seen him.

"Unfortunately, that is possible as well. But we may be over-reacting." Tor Ranshal took hold of Jenna's hands. "I didn't want to ask this, as I know how tiring it must be for the both of you, but could you ask Ghortin where he hid the book? We may be worrying needlessly. Perhaps it was too well protected in Lithunane for our remaining mages to find it."

Jenna looked around the room. She knew Ghortin hadn't wanted anyone to know about his memory loss, but there was no way around it; Tor Ranshal and these others needed to know. Everyone in this room could be trusted. "He doesn't remember the book at all."

At Tor Ranshal's jolt, she quickly went on. "He doesn't remember seeing such a book, let alone studying it. He thinks that some of his memories may have been lost when he transferred into my mind." She looked around the room, her eyes avoiding Maggie's, but settling on Storm's, she knew he'd be on her side. "I think we have to go see if the book's in Lithunane. Maybe going back there will free Ghortin's memory."

"I agree that something has to be done. This is grievous news of Ghortin's infirmity. But I think you should wait until you hear our tale before any rash decisions are made." Tor Ranshal took another long drink from his glass, then settled into a pose that reminded Jenna of Ghortin when he was teaching her a long lesson. She briefly wondered who stole it from whom.

"Once things had been as secured as they could be in Lithunane, Edgar and I determined that we needed to come up here to get the book and to see what else we could determine about the attack. Transporting this far with the current condition of our mages was out of the question, so with Prince Resstlin's begrudging blessing, we departed from Lithunane on the fifth of Aven, nearly four weeks ago." His golden eyes drifted off into the past. "We wanted to keep our numbers small so that we could pass quickly and with stealth; there have been reports of ill-happenings in some of the distant towns. The prince wouldn't hear of it. We finally bargained him down to fifty handpicked guards. Ki' Crell returned to Lithunane two days before we left, she decided to lead our group as soon as she heard you were up here." He nodded to Storm.

Jenna thought the name sounded familiar, but she wasn't sure. She knew that *Ki'* referred to a derawri honor guard. Judging by the concern on Storm's face, she was someone close.

Keanin was stunned. Whoever this warrior was, the fact that she hadn't completed the trip hit them hard.

Tor Ranshal had noticed it also. "Don't worry, I'll tell you more when I get to that point, but I don't think she's gone." A shadow crossed Tor Ranshal's weathered face. "I wish I could say the same for the others who were with us. But I'm getting ahead of my story.

"We had no trouble for the first two days; even the weather seemed to be on our side. Then we were ambushed by a suspiciously well-trained pack of ertin. They hit us a day's ride before the Hills of Dhom, where we had no coverage.

"Five good people died that day. Six more were gravely injured in that attack. We wanted to leave them in a village, but we found none that were suitable. The troubles of this past year have been slowly leading to an exodus from the smaller towns; particularly those near the Markare. Two villages were nothing but cinders."

Storm's fist clenched tighter on his blanket, but he said nothing.

"We tried everything we could to save the injured, but they all died within days of the attack. The beasts had some sort of poison on their claws and fangs. Those of us who had minor injuries from the attack were sick for a day or so. The weather turned at that point. Rain followed our every step; cruel winds, unnatural in that area, hounded us day and night.

"At the far side of the Hills, we met a pride of sciretts. At first they seemed content to follow us. Edgar led our group in the most evasive maneuvers he could, but they always seemed to be there when we finished. They hit us outside the remains of Grindal; the village looks to have been abandoned some months ago. A group of the followers of Qhazborh were hiding in the deserted village and they and the sciretts trapped us in between them. That was the first time the mage wind blew."

The old man grew paler, reaching a shaking hand for the glass of water before continuing. "I have some low magic, so did six others in our group. As we drew our sources together to hold back the attackers, a strange wind overtook us. It ripped the six of them to shreds on its first pass." He was speaking by rote now, as if he could distance himself from the horror.

"It knocked me senseless. By the time I'd recovered enough to be of any use, we'd taken heavy losses. Out of the fifty who started, only ten lived to see the Scareani Mountains. Only Ki' Crell, Edgar, and I saw the other side."

He sat lost in his thoughts for more than a few minutes. Finally, he shook himself and looked around the room with a grim smile. "Ki' Crell was the strongest of us. I had lost most of my magic and was barely able to walk; Edgar had shattered ribs, a broken wrist, and had taken a heavy blow to the head. Crell decided she would go ahead of us and bring back help; Edgar and I couldn't make it another step, we never would have gotten here."

He looked straight into Storm's eyes. "When she had been gone a week past the agreed waiting time, I took it upon myself to try my failed magic one last time. I gathered my tattered Power around me, then flung Edgar and me as hard as I could, to here." He gave a wry smile. "I almost made it."

Jenna sent a brief probe, but she'd have to take his word for his previous magical abilities. He was now as magic-dead as Storm. She shuddered. Ghortin had described this kind of overload before. By reaching out to gather from around him, when his own skills were weak, if not completely gone, he'd destroyed his magic ability. Unlike when she over-taxed herself during the run with the sciretts, it was quite likely that the seneschal would be magic-dead for the rest of his life.

The room was silent for a few moments.

"Which way was Crell headed?" Storm's question sounded simple, but there were lines of worry and determination closing in around his eyes. He'd been itching to go do something since he'd woken up. Tor Ranshal's tale, and the disappearance of his friend, was enough to nudge the kelar prince past rational thought, not that he hadn't been close to it the past few weeks. He was going out, with or without their help or blessing.

Tor Ranshal shook his head. "Not yet." He fixed his

strange golden eyes on Storm's tense face and held the prince's glare until Storm finally looked away. "You're in no condition to rescue anyone."

A sharp groan dragged everyone's attention away from the two. It had come from Edgar, who was now awake and slowly trying to sit up. His healer kept pushing him back down.

"Now, you must stay still. What will Healer Maggie think?"

"Too late, we've spotted him." Maggie sighed as she walked to the dark-haired knight's side. "Edgar, I swear, I'm going to think you kelars know nothing about staying still until you're better."

"Mistress Maggie," he said, still struggling to sit up. "I knew you wouldn't be far. And see, your excellent care has already paid off; I feel like a new man."

"Good try." She waggled a thick finger at him. "You've been in my excellent care for only a few hours. I'm afraid even my abilities aren't enough to mend broken ribs or a damaged head in that short amount of time. Bone takes time to knit. Your head injury is healing but you still need rest." She raised her other hand to emphasize the point when the thin, sharp-faced kelar looked ready to argue.

"I think the best thing for my newest guests is rest. I'm sure the castle will be sending someone over soon. I'll tell them what Tor Ranshal has told us and they can talk to you directly, in the *morning*." Her pointed look encompassed the entire room.

"I do believe that's our cue." Keanin held out his arms, one for Storm, and the other for Jenna. She didn't think Storm would take it, fearing it was a sign of weakness. But he rose with a flourish worthy of Keanin and took the proffered limb. Jenna took his other arm and the three left the room.

In celebration of Storm's newly established mobility—Maggie couldn't well confine him to his room now—they had a lavish supper together in Jenna's little workshop.

Storm made no comment about Tor Ranshal's tale, and he seemed almost as carefree as Keanin. His flirting with her actually almost made Jenna blush once or twice.

Jenna didn't believe him for a minute. He was planning something; that was for certain. What exactly it was, or when it would take place, she had no idea. She wanted to ask about this Crell person, but even if Storm's cheeriness was only an act, she didn't want to destroy it. It had been too long since she'd seen him laugh.

As the night drew to a close, Jenna found herself listening to the two bantering kelars with only half an ear.

"I hate to be the one to poop out first, but it's been a long day." She covered a yawn. "I'm going to go to bed."

Keanin gave a stretch and winked. "Want some company?"

"He asks the same question every night, and every night he gets the same response." Jenna shook her head and looked at Storm. "You really would think he'd come up with something new after all this time."

"He's not used to having to come up with something new." Storm smirked. "He's never had to ask more than once before."

"Ha, ha," Keanin said. "I'll have you know, I do it because it's expected of me. And Jenna is an attractive woman. Besides, I can't resist a challenge." He started for the door, and then turned back to Storm. "Do you want us to walk you back?"

Storm shook his head. "No, thanks. I can manage by myself. I just want to stay out here for a bit more."

He didn't look tired, or ill for that matter. Jenna realized that he might not be as weak as he appeared. Kelars *were* quick healers; and prior to his injury he had been an extremely healthy individual. And fewer people would be keeping an eye on him if they thought he was still recovering.

Jenna tried to convey her concern to Keanin the entire way back to the castle, but he wouldn't listen.

"Corin's not that devious." She scowled, and he gave in with a sigh. "If you're that worried, I'll go follow him and make sure he stays put. We can tell Maggie about your paranoid delusions tomorrow."

Jenna gave him a grateful smile.

"Now, are you certain I can't come in?" He leered at her from the door. He was amazingly good looking, but she certainly wasn't about to make her already complicated life more so by getting involved with the kingdom's Don Juan.

She sighed. "Good night, Keanin." The auburn-haired kelar barely got his foot out of the way of her door as she shut it.

———◆———

Later that night Jenna tossed in her bed as yelling and screaming burst through her dreams. With a jolt, she realized it wasn't a dream. And that the yelling was coming from the lower levels of the castle.

Throwing on a shirt, leggings, and boots, she grabbed her dagger and ran out the door. It wasn't until she was two flights down and could hear swords clashing that she realized she might be being a bit overzealous.

She detoured toward Keanin's room. He might not be much of a fighter, but suicidal charges looked silly with one person.

Keanin clearly had the same idea. She rounded the corner to find him barreling down on her. "Jenna. We should be back in your rooms." Well, almost the same idea.

"With the whole castle under attack?" As she said it, she realized the enormity of her words. No one should be able to get to the castle, let alone compromise it. Unless they got in by magical means. Visions of invading demonspawn ran through her head. "Come on. We've got to do something."

Keanin pulled back. "But I'm unarmed."

Jenna rubbed her head. "You ran out into this without *anything?*"

"I didn't think we'd go fight. I thought I'd go make sure you were barricaded in your rooms. With me preferably."

"I'm a mage, remember? I'm supposed to defend people, not hide. Here, take my dagger. At least I've got my magic." Or so she hoped.

"Ghortin's back?" Keanin kept pace with her easily. And although he didn't seem pleased about the sharp dagger in his hand, he clearly knew how to hold it.

"I can do it without him," she snapped. She didn't want to tell him that no, Ghortin wasn't back.

And that she wasn't sure her on-again, off-again magic wouldn't let her down. But she had to do something. At least she'd armed Keanin. Hopefully he wouldn't die because of her folly.

The noises were coming from the main hall. Jenna and Keanin burst down the last stairs in a blind rush. Men and women were locked in gory fights, but she didn't see anything that looked like demonspawn. In fact, most of the attackers, a wide assortment of kelars, humans, and derawris, who looked like they should be in town going about daily business, were fighting with little care. They didn't seem to notice what wounds they took. Their eyes were vacant and their jaws were slack, but they continued their bloody onslaught with force if not skill.

Holding back, Jenna saw that the castle guards were doing their best but there weren't nearly enough of them. Their sapphire and emerald tunics were splattered in blood. Fighting alongside them was a group of men and women dressed in forest greens and deep browns. At their forefront was a small snarling derawri woman with long red hair.

Jenna nudged the stunned Keanin in the ribs. "Who is that?"

Keanin's relief was evident as he followed her finger to the red-haired woman. "Thank the stars! That's Ki' Crell." His face fell a second later. "No!"

Jenna looked to see what had shaken him, and caught a glimpse of familiar long brown hair. Storm had been fighting a tall human who seemed determined to keep fighting until he was hacked to pieces.

Storm had dropped to one knee, which was what had frightened Keanin. But, as Jenna watched, the prince drove his sword through the slack-faced attacker's chest. A second later, Storm rose and engaged another. She had been correct about Storm's real condition. He was pale, but he was definitely more than holding his own, and from the muscular condition of his shirtless torso it would seem he had been building up his strength for a while.

"Stick with me," she said to Keanin as she made her way to Storm's side. If they were going to go under, they might as well go together.

Keanin hesitated, then muttered to himself and followed her. They were attacked twice before they reached the kelar prince and Jenna flung their assailants back with her magic. She began to feel a glow of pride that her magic hadn't let her down. Just as soon as it started, she chased the thought away. The fight wasn't over yet, no point in jinxing herself.

"How did they get in?" she yelled to Storm.

"I don't know. I was talking to Crell when we heard the screams. Luckily she had brought some of her people back with her." He moved back as a pair of slack-jawed derawri lunged forward. Storm chopped down one, Crell grimly dispatched the other as she moved into the center of the room.

Jenna held back. Her magic would be more of a hindrance than a help in such close quarters.

A second later she was knocked off her feet by a dead-eyed, heavily armed woman. Jenna flung a shock spell at her face, startled into throwing it without restraint, too much Power surged out of her, and she couldn't regain control of it. Within a heartbeat, the woman was nothing more than cinders.

Jenna didn't have time to worry about what she'd done, as three of the attackers broke free of the melee. They shoved past whoever was between them and the stairway viciously stabbing and slicing with their knives, until they reached the closest stairway and started climbing. Unlike the rest of the invaders, these three moved with purpose.

Jenna was confused by the fight and wasn't sure which stairway it was they were going up. Storm, however, recognized it immediately.

"They're going to the royal chambers!" All of the guards who were able to fought their way to the staircase. Storm tore through the crowd with Jenna and Keanin fighting to keep up. Even Crell was hard pressed to match the prince's mad dash.

At the top of the stairs and down a short corridor, they came upon the remains of the guards that had protected the queen's rooms. Jenna averted her eyes, but grimly jumped over them with the others. She also began to draw in Power directly from the realm of chaos.

The main doorway to the royal wing was shattered. Jenna sped up until she was next to Storm. They froze at the doorway to the queen's chamber. The tableau before them wasn't good. The queen lay on the floor of her chambers, her eyes were closed, and blood was seeping out from a blow to her head. Jenna sent a tight probe. The queen still clung to life.

Beyond her, two battered and bloody royal guards were fighting a derawri man, a kelar woman, and a short human mage. The three they'd been following.

Jenna's mouth went dry, and a shrill ringing filled her head. Somewhere in the back of her mind Jenna felt the echo become aware. And something else, something too deep for her to understand. This triad made her blood race. They were more than they seemed, even if she had no idea what. *She needed them destroyed, the same way she'd needed the ertin back at Ghortin's cottage to be extinguished.*

Barely able to maintain control, she turned to Keanin and pointed at Storm who had charged into the fight. "Keep him out of my way. Don't argue." She was fighting the urge to obliterate the trio so hard that the tension in her neck was almost unbearable; they had to die. Keanin was pale, but he nodded. A second later he'd leveled the prince with a flying tackle and started dragging him back. Even in his weakened state, Storm was stronger than him, but Keanin was taller, and had managed to knock the wind out of Storm for the moment. Crell had obviously worked with mages before, and kept her own people back.

Jenna let the strange urge take over. She didn't have a choice. At least Storm was now out of the range of fire.

The short human mage turned around as he felt her Power. He snorted in contempt when he saw the single person that faced him. Waving his companions aside, he stepped forward.

It was the last move he ever made.

All the tension in Jenna, all the anger she instinctively felt at this magic fueled monstrosity, flowed out of her like an avenging fire. The mage's body imploded so quickly that his face still held the look of contempt as it vanished. His two associates had a second longer before their insides went through the same contortions.

Some part of Jenna's mind felt revulsion at the violence of their deaths. But mostly her mind felt an overwhelming vindication. She could do anything. Nothing could stand before her.

A second later the Power backlash hit her and she lost consciousness, dropping her to the floor like a discarded rag doll.

CHAPTER TWENTY-ONE

———

JENNA SLOWLY AWOKE, AND FOUND she was back in her room in the castle. As soon as her eyes opened Helaermage Dantil handed her a glass filled with a murky white substance.

"What is this?" She took a sip and almost spit it back out. The chalky stuff stuck in her throat.

"I know. Tastes awful, doesn't it? But it's the best thing for a backlash headache. And I gather you've got a huge one." Dantil smiled.

Jenna peered over the rim of her glass. "The whole thing?" At a nod from the helaermage, she forced the rest of it down. Perhaps Ghortin learned his potion making from the mysterious helaermages.

"Is everyone all right?" She knew many weren't, but she was worried about her friends.

"We lost eight people. It would have been worse if Crell and her band hadn't shown up." Maggie answered from the other side of the bed. "The queen is seriously injured, but she still lives. Justlantin believes that they were trying to take her, not kill her. Keanin and that idiot Corin came out no worse for wear." The healer frowned heavily. "I told Corin I would tie him to his bed if he ever tried to do something so weak-brained again. Did you know he'd built a training area in an unused room in my House?"

"How did the attackers get in here in the first place? At least one of that final three was a mage, and I think the other two were linked to him somehow. Shouldn't the

Keepers have been triggered or something?" Jenna was still unnerved by her reaction to the trio she killed.

"I'm afraid we aren't exactly sure," Maggie said. "Tor Ranshal thinks that they snuck in when he and Edgar triggered the Keepers. No one would have noticed a few extra people in the crowd of onlookers and guards that surrounded them."

"As for the rest, we think they were expendable troops, most likely locals who were spelled, whose sole purpose was to distract the guards and kill as many as possible," Dantil said. "None of them survived; they killed themselves rather than be captured."

Maggie took the empty glass from her. "You seem to be fine, but if you notice any strange side effects, I want you to find Dantil or me immediately. Am I understood?"

Jenna nodded weakly. Exhaustion was taking over. That, and more than likely there was something in Dantil's drink.

She struggled to stay awake; she wanted to tell them about the strange presence that had appeared in her head during the fight. But she found it impossible to keep her eyes open, let alone get any words out.

———◆———

She didn't wake again until after the first noon bell. Unlike the chimes of Lithunane, the heavy bells of Irundail were quite loud, and she was amazed that she had slept through the first bells of the morning. Stretching tentatively, she mentally pushed where the headache had been. She sighed as no pain flared up to greet her. That drink of the helaermage's may have tasted awful, but it did the trick.

She left the castle as soon as she was dressed, wanting to get away from the silent tension that prevailed there. She didn't want to go to the Healing House either, she just needed to be alone, to sort out what she'd done to that trio, so she wandered in the outer garden. She was so lost in thought that she didn't notice Keanin sitting on the grass until she almost stepped on him.

"How do you feel?" His voice was so subdued Jenna had to check to see that it was really him. There were lines on his angular face that hadn't been there yesterday, and the dark circles under his eyes told her he'd gotten no sleep.

"Tired." She tried to catch his eyes, but after his initial glance to see who had stumbled on him, Keanin stared off into the distance.

"You, on the other hand, look awful," she added as she sat down next to him. Being alone could wait.

"If my ladies in Lithunane could see me now." He forced a tight smile.

"Keanin? Are you hurt?"

"Only in heart and spirit."

As he spoke, she remembered that the royal family had raised him as one of their own.

She took one of his hands. "The queen will be all right. She's got the best healers in the world here."

He finally looked up, tears filling his eyes. "I hope so. But it's not just her, it's everything." He shook his head. "All I ever wanted was to live in the court, happily surrounded by friends and family. Everything I love is falling apart."

That, Jenna thought to herself, was the understatement of the century. She wished she could lie to him and say everything was going to be all right. But she had never been that good of a liar. So, she changed the subject instead.

"Did you get a chance to talk to anyone? When did Ki' Crell get in?"

"She and her band arrived after midnight. She was coming here to gather some healers to head back, when she heard that Tor Ranshal and Edgar were already here."

He gave a shudder. "I hate to think what would have happened if they hadn't been here."

"Where were the rest of the guards?" It hadn't appeared that there were more than thirty or so in the fighting last night. There were a few hundred stationed around the palace grounds.

"They were drugged. Even those in the guardhouse. Maggie thinks that it must have been an airborne poison since it took almost all of them out. They'll live, but they're all in sorry shape today."

The lines in Keanin's face were still deep. Jenna rose to her feet, dragging him with her. "Come on."

"Where are we going?"

"To see Storm and Tor Ranshal. I think we have to start making plans now."

"Prince Justlantin has already called a meeting. Tor Ranshal isn't there because Maggie said he was still too weak. She told him you were too weak, too." He folded his arms. "Which is good, since otherwise they would have called for Ghortin."

Jenna met his gaze with a frown. "You didn't tell anyone that he still hasn't come back, did you?"

"No, but you're going to have to tell them soon. They need to know. What if he's gone for good?"

"He can't be. He's got nowhere else to go." But she didn't believe her own words. "Fine, I'll tell them when we go talk to them. Are you coming or not?"

"Do I have a choice?"

"Not really. You're in this with the rest of us now."

"Well, then," he straightened his rumpled garments with a glimmer of his normal flair. "Let's go find the rest of our suicidal bunch."

Storm was in his room talking quietly with Crell. The small woman's flame red hair fell past her waist. She was thick and muscular, like most of her race, but had an alien grace. Her bright green eyes flashed as she chuckled evilly at something Storm had said.

"Hey, can anybody join in, or is this for sword-wielding maniacs only?" Keanin asked as he pulled Jenna into the room.

"You evil scamp." Ki' Crell ran forward, almost knocking Keanin down with her hug. "Still an eye for the ladies, I see." She gave Jenna a warm smile, and then tipped her head. "Wait, aren't you that mage who took out those bastards last night?"

Jenna nodded. "Apprentice mage, actually. I'm Jenna."

"Crell, at your service." The derawri fighter turned back toward Keanin with a sly smile.

"Mage apprentice, eh? Pretty boy, I think you're out of your depth. Don't mess with this one; I'd hate to see your gorgeous face blown to bits."

"I'll have you know, the lady Jenna and I have an understanding—"

"He keeps asking, and she keeps knocking him down." Storm cut him off as he nodded to Jenna. "I'm glad you came up. I wanted you two to meet. Crell is one of my oldest friends, and Jenna's my newest."

Jenna was touched by his sincerity. The frustration and anger inside him seemed to have calmed, at least for the moment.

"Are Tor Ranshal and Edgar awake?" Jenna asked.

"Probably by now. Maggie dosed them both with her juice after the attack last night." His eyes held the same worries Jenna's mind did. They needed answers; otherwise the whole country was going to be torn apart before they realized what they were up against. And they needed Ghortin's book.

"You should probably call Ghortin back," Storm said.

A light dawned in Crell's face. "You're the one. Well, that explains it then, doesn't it? Any apprentice of that one would have to be able to hold her own. Where is he? And why wasn't he out there last night?"

Jenna looked at Keanin. He wouldn't tell, but she would have to.

"I'm not sure what all Storm has told you." From their reactions Crell was someone to be trusted. "But Ghortin has sort of transferred himself into my head. It happened during the attack in Lithunane when that bastard grabbed Ghortin and the king." She sighed; there was no easy way to say this. "However, ever since the translocation spell for Tor Ranshal and Edgar, I haven't been able to reach him."

Storm gave a low whistle. "Then that was all you last night?" He shook his head. "I thought he'd taken over again. Can you reach him now?"

Jenna closed her eyes, but she knew it was futile. She opened them slowly. She'd felt nothing but an echo of her own thoughts. "I'm sorry."

"Hey." Storm got to his feet and took hold of her hands gently. "It's okay. Maybe he's resting. Don't worry. Come on, let's go talk to Edgar."

At first Jenna was confused by the lightness in Storm's tone. Then she understood the reason for it. Like her, he must have realized that something, finally, was going to be done.

Edgar and Tor Ranshal were awake and talking quietly over a late breakfast in their beds. Both of them looked up as the foursome entered the room.

"And how are the fierce warriors today?" Edgar asked.

"Fine. And how are the fierce adventurers?" Storm answered, mimicking the knight's tone perfectly.

"Ouch, that hurt." Edgar winced.

"I think I'll be staying away from adventuring for some time, thank you," Tor Ranshal added wryly.

Storm's face grew sober and he shut the door behind him. "That's what we're here to talk to you about."

"Our adventure? We didn't have a chance, as Tor Ranshal told you," Edgar said.

Storm looked around the room. "We're going after Ghortin's book, and then we're going after the bastard who started this." His face was grim.

"But you don't know who, or what's, behind this," Edgar said, picking at his plate. "Didn't you listen to what Tor Ranshal told you? Everything is falling apart out there."

Storm was surprised. "You'd rather we sat here until whoever or whatever it is tears this land apart?"

"No, I just don't want you going off in a rush like you usually do." His steady black eyes looked into Storm's clear blue ones. "And I don't want you to go without me."

Storm relaxed with a crooked grin. "I'd never dream of it."

"Don't we need to talk about this, work things out, plan, etc.?" Keanin frowned.

"He's right," Tor Ranshal said softly. "And you know Justlantin is going to make you wait until Resstlin comes back up here."

"That's why we aren't going to tell my beloved brother." Storm snorted. "You know Resstlin wouldn't approve it. ' Not until we're sure what we're up against' is his battle motto. Besides, did he show any sign of leaving Lithun-ane soon?"

"Not until summer." Tor Ranshal turned to Jenna. "What does Ghortin say to all this?"

"That's a problem. I've lost contact with him." She met his eyes squarely. "He hasn't come back."

"That isn't good. He should have recovered by now." He looked closely at Jenna. "The things I heard that you did last night; it was you, not Ghortin?" His voice was unusually sharp, as if he'd tripped over something.

"Yes, it was me. I'm not sure what happened. Something just took over, but it wasn't him."

"Hush, my dear." Tor Ranshal leaned forward and took

her face in his hands, muttering to himself. The others couldn't hear him, but Jenna picked out bits and pieces. "Could it be? After all the searching?" He held her face and turned it to one side. "Hold still, my dear." Jenna felt him trying to draw in Power, then stop. There wasn't any for him to draw from. "Oh, stars, I'd forgotten I'd tapped myself out. Jenna, you say you have no idea what you did? Has this happened before?"

Jenna almost didn't want to answer because his intensity was so unnerving. "Yes," she said finally. "Against the ertin, back at Ghortin's cottage. I sent them away to die, as opposed to blowing them to bits." While she was grateful both times for whatever Power stepped in and destroyed the attackers, it was disturbing that it seemed to be growing. And that she still had no idea where it was coming from. Or, she feared, how to control it.

Tor Ranshal smacked himself in the head. "Right under our noses. That's what we get for not confiding more in that blessed mage. Oh, how I wish Rachael was here."

His voice had dropped down low again and Jenna couldn't hear all of what he said, but she did catch the name. Surely the palace seneschal didn't confide in a hearth witch from the bad side of the city? But, as Storm said, she wasn't what she appeared to be.

"Do you mean Rachael the hearth witch in Lithunane?"

"What?" His golden eyes flashed as if he hadn't been aware that he'd spoken out loud. "Yes, dear. I'm sorry; I thought I was talking in my head. I think you're right, Corin, you must get Ghortin's book immediately." He turned to Jenna, clasping her hands tightly. "As much as I want you to stay, you must go as well. But promise me you'll go to see Rachael the minute you get into the city. Before you go anywhere near the castle. And don't give up on Ghortin; I'm sure he'll find his way back."

Jenna frowned, what they didn't need now were more

mysteries. "Is there anything I should tell Rachael?" She was going to feel foolish popping in on the old woman for no reason.

He made a quick little movement with his hands, then nodded. "Tell her I sent you. She'll figure it out. Now, as Keanin says, we must make plans, but you should all go as soon as possible. By tomorrow, I'd say."

Keanin's face had brightened when Tor Ranshal spoke of making plans, and crashed when he said tomorrow.

It was dinnertime when Jenna finally went to her room to pack. Storm had come to the castle with her to see how his mother was. Keanin had trailed listlessly behind. Jenna had a feeling she was going to have to make sure he didn't wander off; the poor thing wasn't handling any of this well. He'd broached a plan with Tor Ranshal, of him staying, and taking troops down later, after the winter storms and spring floods. Tor Ranshal seriously considered it, then shook his head.

"I strongly believe in coincidence, my boy, and I think you've fallen in with these people for a reason. For good or ill, you must go with them."

From that point on, Keanin sulked. Jenna had tried a couple more times to reach Ghortin, but after giving herself a massive headache, she decided to let it rest.

She had everything packed by the time a light knock came at her door. She opened it to find a sullen Keanin and a somber Storm. "Your mother?"

"She still hasn't woken up. We said our good-byes." Storm looked around the room as they entered. "Are you packed?"

Jenna quelled the butterflies in her stomach. "Yes. Are you certain this is going to work?"

"You tell me, it's your spell that's going to cover us. Do you want to practice on the packs on the way out?"

"Might as well." This was why she had a twisted stomach. Try as they might, they couldn't figure out a way to get clear of Irundail without being seen that didn't involve magic. Tor Ranshal was, as he put it, 'tapped out at the moment'. But he helped Jenna work on adapting her cloak spell. She'd have to pay close attention to everything around her and keep the group in tight formation, but, theoretically, she should be able to hide them as they left Irundail. The theoretical part was what got her.

If this failed, at the very least it would make it impossible for them to try again. She didn't want to think what the worst case could be. She briefly wondered what the penalty was for kidnapping a prince.

Storm patted her arm. "Come on. Tor Ranshal showed you how, and we all know how much Power you have. This will be simple."

Jenna winced. "I have Power sometimes, but it's not consistent. What if it cuts out as we're passing the guards?"

Storm shrugged. "Then we'll run for it. No one is going to be looking for us to sneak out."

"Can we stop all this chit chat and get on with this?" Keanin frowned as he slid down on to a chair. "I know this has to be done, but why can't it be some other group? I don't want to see my closest friends skewered, stabbed, or blown apart."

"Calm down." Storm squeezed his friend's shoulder. "You're with the best of the best, so cheer up."

"Can we move on to the Healing House now? Before I do something stupid like run screaming down the halls?" Keanin asked.

Jenna mentally reached out for the swirling chaos. She didn't need much at this point; hiding their packs wouldn't be that hard. But it was reassuring to feel the Power out there.

She couldn't help jumping every time someone greeted them on the way out however.

Storm finally took her arm, holding her steady as they continued their evening stroll through the grounds.

Edgar met them first, he was dressed head to toe in black, looking much more like a spy at this point than a knight of the realm. She meant to ask him about that at some point on their journey south. Somehow, being both a knight and a spy seemed odd. One was forthright and honorable; the other was sneaky and devious. Edgar was both, and was very good at both from what she'd gathered from Storm.

Crell was dressed in muted dark browns and greens. A tall human male standing next to her was dressed likewise. She and the rest of her people would join them once they got out of Irundail. Her band of hunters wouldn't be remarked on if they left, and it would ease the burden on Jenna's spell.

"I see we are assembled." Tor Ranshal looked over the group. "Crell, I think you and your companion can go join your people now."

The flame-haired derawri warrior nodded, then turned to Edgar. "At the base of Trundlin, then. We'll expect you by noon tomorrow." Flashing a smile at everyone else, she and her companion left.

CHAPTER TWENTY-TWO

A FEW MINUTES AFTER MIDNIGHT JENNA set the spell exactly as Tor Ranshal had told her. But she still wished she could be sure it was working. The seneschal told her she would feel a slight tingle when it was in full coverage. She thought she felt it, but she couldn't be sure it wasn't just nerves, the echo acting up, or any of a variety of other things. For all she knew, they looked as they were; a small group marching toward the border of Irundail for the entire world to see.

"Would you stop fidgeting? I'm sure your spell is working fine," Storm whispered.

"What if it's not? They'll think we're kidnapping you or something," she whispered back.

"Actually, my lady, since we're surrounding you, it looks more like you're the kidnapping victim," Edgar said amiably from the front of the group.

His pace was a bit more hesitant and stiffer than usual. But considering the condition he'd been in the day before, it was amazing he was up and moving at all. The injury to his head had been healed with a few hours of work by a half dozen mages.

For the most part, they didn't see anybody. When they got down to the city, the only people they saw were drunks, either on their way home or on their way for another drink. Jenna didn't take their lack of reaction to heart. She doubted that any of those sops would have seen them even if they were standing unspelled right in front of them.

The fact that the guards didn't come out at the entrance to the city should have made her feel better. But it didn't. She realized her thoughts were becoming paranoid, but she couldn't shake them. At least she didn't share them with the others.

"All right, we're almost to the gate," Keanin whispered, speaking for the first time since they left the House of Healing. "Last chance for rational thought to kick in." No one bothered to answer him, but Storm turned around and shook his head.

Jenna felt the sweat beading up on her forehead. They had added guards to the main gate, although there was less evidence that last night's attack came from outside than originally assumed.

She held her breath as the four of them walked silently through the row of guards. She continued holding it until they'd gone past the Keepers.

Of course, that was a rather long walk, and she swayed to the side a bit when they reached the end.

"What's wrong?" Storm whispered as he steadied her. "Did something get through?"

Jenna was glad that the darkness hid her embarrassment. "No, I…the strain and everything. This spell isn't easy." She sure as hell wasn't going to tell him she'd almost passed out because she was holding her breath.

They continued in silence for another twenty yards, until they came to the edge of the forest.

"You can drop your spell now, my lady," Edgar said. "I think we're past them. As long as we stay quiet, no one will see us in here."

Within a few hours of walking through the woods, Jenna and Keanin found themselves lagging behind Storm and Edgar. Which should have been embarrassing, since they were recovering invalids. But neither Jenna nor Keanin particularly cared at that point. Besides, Storm and Edgar were both in their element now.

Keanin froze. "What was that? I heard something."

Jenna slowed down and tried to listen, but she heard nothing. Keanin's sharp intake of breath told her he still did.

"Storm, Edgar. Back here." She whispered as loudly as she felt safe. Keanin might not be happy about being on this trip, but he certainly wasn't going to start making things up. And, like all kelars, his hearing was exceptional.

Storm and Edgar turned around sharply, both keeping their hands on their sword hilts.

"What is it?" Storm said softly when they got close.

Jenna gestured behind them. "Keanin heard something behind us."

"Could it be Crell?" Edgar whispered from the darkness.

"I doubt it; it's too early, but we are almost at the meeting spot," Storm said as he nodded to Edgar. "But we should see who is making that much noise. You two stay here."

Keanin and Jenna waited, standing back-to-back and peering into the darkness. It was times like these that she envied the kelars for their superior sight; straining to see into the darkness was doing nothing for her nerves.

Finally, a group of about twenty people approached. As they moved closer, it appeared that they were palace guards. However, since she'd been in two supposedly safe castles where grievous fighting occurred, Jenna wasn't willing to trust appearances anymore.

Then Storm and Edgar came forward, wrapped up in an argument with a tall guard captain.

Storm stepped into the center of the dark clearing. "I think we should stay here a while. At least until sunrise. It's too far for us to go tonight, whichever direction we go," he said pointedly to the man he'd been arguing with. Then he turned and began gathering firewood. Although dawn was not far away, it would be impossible to set up any type of camp without some light.

Once they got a small fire going, Edgar and Storm continued their argument with the captain.

Keanin gasped as the troops moved into the firelight. Directly across from him was the soldier, Marta, who tried to seduce him on their tour of the city a month ago.

"Oh no." He turned to Jenna with a dismayed face. "Jenna, you've got to convince Corin to send me back. I can't travel around with that woman after me."

Jenna spared a glance for the embattled Storm and Edgar. "I think we may not have a choice. I've no idea how they found us out so quickly, but I'll wager that none of them get much sleep tonight."

"Oh, stars. Hide me." Keanin practically jumped into Jenna's shadow. He looked rather ridiculous as he topped her by over a foot.

"My lady, my captain bids me to make you and your companion comfortable. I've set up sleeping quarters for the two of you off to the side." Marta's smile was polite, but she showed no recognition of Jenna. "This way, if you please."

Keanin peeked out from behind Jenna. His face was half visible in the firelight, but Marta didn't seem to recognize him either.

"My lord?" she said hesitantly, as if unsure of how to treat a belligerent noble. "I assure you, we will not harm you. It will be much warmer where we've set your bed. I'll wager a pint, *they* won't have figured out what to do until far after daybreak." She finally noticed the odd way Keanin was looking at her. "Do I know you, my lord?"

"You don't recognize me?" Keanin said as he came out fully into the firelight.

The soldier shrugged. "I do not. But I haven't been part of the palace guard very long. Previously I was of the seventh regiment. Might I know your name?"

Keanin drew closer. "Keanin. You don't remember me

from the tavern a few weeks ago?"

She shook her head, "A few weeks ago? What was a lord doing in a tavern? I'm sorry, my lord, I truly don't know you. But will you come take your bed? The captain hates it when people don't do what he thinks they should."

Keanin looked like a landed fish. Jenna stepped in front of him. "We would be more than happy to collapse anywhere you say. And thank you for setting it up for us." She latched on to Keanin's sleeve. "Come on, Keanin, thank the nice soldier, and let's go to sleep. I'm sure tomorrow's going to be another horrifically long day."

Keanin sputtered along behind her. Finally, when they were both set up in their bedrolls, he turned to Jenna. "She's faking it, that's all."

Jenna was already drifting off and turned back to him sluggishly. "What? Oh, Marta. Face it Keanin, you're not as memorable as you thought you were." She quickly slid into sleep, forestalling any further conversation.

———◆———

Nearby, Storm and Edgar weren't having much luck with the captain. "Look," Edgar stifled a yawn, "we're not hurting anybody, and this has to be done. Or do you like fighting off invaders in the heart of your castle? I, for one, do not."

"That is not the point, Sir Edgar. And well you know it," the captain said stiffly. "You didn't bother to ask the prince."

"Of course not. We've got one with us. I thought one royal person was enough for such a small group." The spymaster-knight grinned as he slid a knife free of its wrist sheath and began flipping it in elaborate loops.

Storm rolled his eyes at his friend's actions; he did that sort of thing solely to unnerve whomever he was speaking to. "I'm not going back, Kern. You know as well as

I that if we go back then nothing will be done about any of this until Resstlin gets up here and they have a dozen meetings on it." He knew that Kern was following orders, but those orders were wrong.

Captain Kern shook his head and began to marshal the same arguments he'd used since he'd found them. Storm cut him off. "Before we go through this entire farce of a discussion again, will you answer me one question? How in the bloody stars did you know that we'd left?"

The dark-haired captain started to shake his head, then shrugged. "I suppose it can't hurt to tell you. Your mother, the queen. She regained consciousness not too long after midnight. She was frantic with worry that her son was going into danger. No one believed her until we checked and found you missing. When we realized who else was gone, we began our search. We never did see you. Just happened upon you here."

Storm nodded and mentally kicked himself. Somewhere in her unconscious mind she must have heard him when he said his farewells. They weren't going back, and that was final. But he was in no condition to fight at present. And Edgar looked as exhausted as he felt, even if the spymaster hid it well. "We're not going anywhere at this point. Let's get some sleep and figure things out in the morning."

Captain Kern studied Storm for a few moments and his pinched face grew tighter. "You're going to have to go back. By force if necessary. Your brother outranks you, and your group of four can't stand up against my twenty."

Storm smiled politely. By morning Crell and her band would be here. The odds would be a bit more even then. "We all must do what we have to do. Good night, Captain." He and Edgar rose and went to their bedrolls.

———◆———

Jenna woke to muffled grunts. Opening one eye, she

saw that the camp was under attack. Her gut tightened and she started to pull in Power.

Opening both eyes, she realized that the palace guards were being pinned down by a familiar looking group of brown and green clad archers and swordsmen.

"Good of you to join us, Crell." Storm's voice came from out of her range of vision, but she didn't want to move and possibly confuse Crell's people.

Storm came up and helped pull her to her feet. Jenna still got up slowly, but it was more due to stiffness rather than concern of becoming a target.

Storm turned to Captain Kern, who was now tied up. "What were you saying about us going with you by force? I believe we've decided that for you."

"What happened here? You decided to play with some guards?" Crell looked curiously down at one held near her foot.

"No, our enthusiastic prince said a bit too much to his mother on her sick bed and the good woman woke up and alerted the troops," Edgar said. "They were becoming quite persistent that we go with them."

"I don't like interfering with palace politics, but this time I must insist," Crell said. "No one here is going with you, Captain Kern. We'll leave your ropes loose enough so you'll get free before nightfall, but I can't have you following too closely."

"You'll have to do more than tie us up, Ki' Crell. I can't go back to the royal family and say I discharged my duties so wrongfully." Kern twisted his bound hands around to a more comfortable position.

Crell fingered the hilt of her curved sword. "I've never taken on palace guards before. I wonder who would win?"

Jenna felt a familiar, and welcome, tingle in her mind. *"Ghortin?"*

"Aye, lass, what's going on here?"

She quickly passed on everything that had happened while he was gone, carefully leaving out how worried she was that he'd never make it back.

"*Well, I've missed quite a bit. And I do think Tor Ranshal was right about getting this mysterious book of mine. I wish I knew what his other mutterings meant. But that can't be helped for now. Stand aside, missy, I've got to avert bloodshed.*"

"I don't think there will be any need to test such a thing today, good Ki' Crell." Jenna had that strange double voice feeling she got when Ghortin spoke through her.

"Jenna? What are you doing?" Crell asked.

"No, I'm afraid you all get to deal with me now. And since, as a mastermage, I outrank everyone here, and quite a few not here, I order all of you to stop this foolishness right now."

Captain Kern looked at Jenna with narrowed eyes. "I know they've said that Mastermage Ghortin is somehow residing in this young lady's head, but isn't this appearance rather sudden? How do we know this isn't simply the apprentice trying to get rid of us?"

"Kern, Kern, Kern. Ever the suspicious fellow. You have a mark in the shape of a deer on your left flank and a—"

The captain flushed. "Enough. I believe you. In a way, I'm glad to hear you, my lord. Please talk some sense into the prince."

Jenna's body turned toward Storm with a shrug. "Nope, won't work. Believe me, I've tried on many occasions." They turned back to Kern. "Besides, on this, I side with him. We can't tell you all the reasons, but we must get to Lithunane as soon as possible. I'm sorry to do this, but I'm afraid I'm going to have to commandeer your troop. We'll send word back to Justlantin, he'll know it wasn't your fault."

The dark-haired captain sputtered. "But you can't overrule a prince. And the queen."

"Sad to say, yes, I can." Jenna sensed Ghortin's smirk and she hoped it wasn't showing. "In matters of State in which magic has come into play, in this case by attacking the royal family, I can overrule anyone, including the king himself. Convenient little law, actually. Kralin set it up for me when he drew up the charter. I'm surprised Justlantin didn't realize it when he sent you after us."

"Then why didn't you say anything last night?" The captain's eyes narrowed again.

"My dear sir, I don't take over my poor apprentice every moment of the day. Besides, I truly hoped that you all would be able to settle this without my intervention. But you can't. So, I'm taking over, and I'm bringing you with us."

The captain opened his mouth to argue, but closed it again when one of his men stepped forward; one who was not bound by ropes. Jenna was startled to see that it was Garlan, the Armsmaster.

"Kern, I'm afraid he's right. I went along with you on this, but we've no choice now but to obey orders."

The stunned captain looked from one to the other; finally, he gave in with a sigh. "I turn over myself, eighteen soldiers, and Armsmaster Garlan. What is your will?" He nodded.

"You shall come with us to Lithunane. I assume that your contingent is comprised of carefully selected, and eminently trustworthy, guards?"

At Kern's nod, Ghortin continued. "Nothing that you see, hear, or do can be repeated to anyone outside our present group. Ki' Crell, that goes for your people as well. I'm not sure what we'll see on the way down, but I don't want rumors or panic spreading."

Both Kern and Crell nodded.

"Then let's get on our way. We've a long way to go and speed is of the essence."

CHAPTER TWENTY-THREE

AS SOON AS EVERYONE ACCEPTED the addition of Kern's group, Ghortin nudged Jenna back to the forefront. She tried to catch him before he disappeared, but he was too fast. With a sigh, she finished stowing her bedroll and went to see how Keanin was doing. The kelar noble was half-finished because he kept watching Marta whenever he thought no one would notice.

"Has it been this cold the whole time, or did the temperature just drop?" She struggled another tunic on and topped it with her cloak. She didn't want to bring up the soldier woman again; besides she was startled at how cold she'd become.

"What?" Keanin jerked his eyes away from Marta. "You probably didn't notice last night, but it's been awful since we left the shelter of Irundail." He darted another glance at the soldier. Fortunately, Marta was busy getting things ready and hadn't noticed him yet.

"What's the matter, can't you stand being forgotten?"

Keanin reddened slightly. "I don't understand it. No woman forgets me, especially after she's kissed me. There's something else going on, mark my words." There was quite a large dose of wounded pride in his voice.

"Isn't that a little bit egotistical?" She started helping him with his pack. How he could get it so messed up in one night was beyond her.

Keanin frowned. "Not at all. It's factual. She simply must be lying." He didn't sound convinced though.

Jenna laid a hand on his shoulder. "I know this whole

thing must be quite a shock to you, but I don't think she's acting. Besides, she was extremely drunk that day."

"True." Keanin burst into a beautiful smile. "I hadn't thought of that. Why, she probably kisses lots of people in that condition and doesn't remember a single one. Thank you, my lady. I feel much better now." Whistling, Keanin got his pack together and on his back.

Storm came over to see how they were doing. "Does Ghortin have any ideas on which way we should go?"

"He's vanished again. He didn't leave any instructions—" She cut herself off as something bubbled to the surface of her mind.

Whether it was from the echo, Ghortin, or some other source, she wasn't sure. "Is there a temple of Irissanta nearby?" The urge to go to one was strong.

Storm nodded slowly. "Yes, out on Cathedral Island. Why?"

"I can't explain it, but I think we should go there first." As soon as she said it, the nagging in her head stopped. Since Ghortin was her primary source of nagging headaches these days, she assumed the idea came from him.

"It won't be too far out of the way, and I guess following your hunches is the best plan we have. Besides, it will let us bypass many of the abandoned villages that Edgar and Tor Ranshal faced on the way up. I'll notify the others." With a nod to Keanin, Storm went back to the small group of leaders. Even though Ghortin would have final say, Storm was sharing his leadership of the mismatched group with Crell, Kern, and Edgar; it was easier than fighting.

The collective leaders called a halt a few hours into the trip. Storm and Edgar both claimed they were fine, but Crell still sat them down and made them rest.

"We're not going to carry you two oafs the rest of the way because you wore yourselves out during the first full day march; now down with you. We'll move on when

I say so. Unless you think Ghortin would object?" The small warrior looked up at Jenna with a wink.

"Not at all," Jenna said, blithely ignoring Storm's glare. "In fact, I think he'd agree whole heartedly. Especially since it is well known that certain kelars don't know when they're tired."

Storm vented his frustration on a stray lock of hair hanging over his face, and then dropped down on a log. Edgar shrugged good-naturedly and sat down to re-wind the splint and bandage on his wrist. There was still some tendon damage that the healers felt should heal naturally. It didn't seem to slow him down at all though.

Keanin was grumbling again. Now that his distress over Marta was appeased for the moment, he returned to fretting about their journey.

"I don't see what your problem is, Keanin," Jenna said, finally fed up with his prophecies of doom. "I saw you handle that dagger in the castle." She gave a nod to the longbow slung over his pack. "And Storm assured me that you are a master with that bow when you want to be."

"In tournaments." Keanin shook his head. "I've never been in any type of fighting situation. I've never wanted to be. To be quite honest, I'm not completely sure I won't run off screaming at the first sign of a battle."

Jenna looked at him intently. It was obvious that he really feared this. "But you didn't in Lithunane. Or, as I recall, in Irundail. You weren't happy, but you held your own."

Keanin winced. "Must you remind me? Irundail was the first time I'd ever killed a person." He gave a shudder. "You don't know because you'd already blacked out. But once you'd taken out that unholy trio in the royal chambers, I all but fell apart. I managed to pass it off as stress and concern for the queen. But *I* knew what it was." He looked up with serious concern filling his eyes. "How do I know that fear won't take over if something should attack us?"

Jenna took his hand in hers. She looked at it for a few minutes before speaking. His hand was long and delicate, like most of his race, but it lacked the hardened strength of Storm's.

"I don't think anyone likes fighting." At his nod toward Storm and Edgar she gave a tight little smile. "No, not even those two. I can't speak for Sir Edgar, but I think Storm fights because he can't stand feeling helpless; not because he takes joy in killing."

Keanin looked at his lifelong friend. "I suppose you're right, he isn't a violent soul at heart. But they can't possibly be as afraid as I am. Even you, a newcomer to our world, have shown more courage than I." He hung his head.

"I haven't had a choice. Ghortin ingrained the mage's motto into my teaching. Literally. I have to help others, I can't help myself. And there's something more." She looked over to Keanin, but he still wouldn't meet her eyes. "I don't know if they told you about how I arrived here."

Keanin looked up at that. "No, they didn't. Which isn't too surprising, I'm often left out of those things."

"Somehow—and don't ask, even Ghortin isn't sure how—part of me was thrown into the body of a mind-slave." At Keanin's sharp intake of breath, she fixed him with a steady gaze. "You can't tell anyone about this." When he nodded in agreement, she continued.

"Part of that poor woman's memory lives in me. It's more of an echo. I recognize things I shouldn't, react to things I shouldn't know about and the like. That echo also forces me into actions that I have no control over. At least we think it's the echo. Like when I attacked that trio in the queen's chambers. I was only a passenger in that; something other than me was directing my actions.

So you see, I'm not brave; I've got some serious help. Or hindrance if you want to look at it that way."

"I had no idea. What's it like, living in someone else's body?" His fears vanished as his natural curiosity took over. "What do you really look like?"

"Aside from the echo, it's pretty normal. And for the most part, this is what I look like. Part of me came over, and my consciousness, or something, tried to pull the rest of me through to this world. I do know that the woman had brown eyes, and this hair is quite a bit longer and thicker than mine was. We must have been fairly similar to begin with, because I don't notice that many things that are different."

"And what are you two muttering about back here?" Storm came over to where they sat.

"Just passing the time. Are we close to whatever dreadful place you're dragging us?"

"No, but we should reach it before nightfall tomorrow, providing Crell lets us get moving again." Storm turned to Keanin. "And I want to know what your fascination is with that soldier, Marta. I've seen you staring at her. I didn't think you went for soldiers, old friend."

"I don't." Keanin shot a warning glance to Jenna. "She looked familiar. But I've realized I was mistaken."

"Why do I think I'm missing something?" Storm looked from one to the other with a bemused smile.

"Oh, come on, Keanin, tell him. Or I will."

"Now I'm truly curious." Storm gave Keanin his full attention.

"It was a mistake," Keanin stated. When Jenna gave an indelicate cough, he continued. "All right, Marta approached Jenna and I when we were out on our tour of the city. She propositioned me, I turned her down, she kissed me, and then left. End of story."

Storm looked to Jenna. "Shall I?" she said it innocently, but with a mischievous gleam in her eye.

Keanin folded his arms and turned away.

"Well, it seems that our tall soldier woman has no recollection of me, Keanin, or the kiss. I'm afraid it quite unnerved him."

Storm held his mirth in check for a few seconds, then gave up. "Oh, Keanin, what is to become of you? First Jenna refuses to give in to your courting ways, and now you've been seduced and abandoned by a soldier."

"Now come on, would I laugh at you, either of you, if you'd lost your talents? If Corin couldn't fight or Jenna couldn't do magic? Each of us has our own gifts. Mine happen to lie in a different direction than yours." He turned away with a sniff.

Storm smiled at Keanin's melodramatics. "We're teasing you. Besides, I don't fight well every day, and Jenna can tell you how sporadic her magic is. It's about time that your talents, as you call them, fluctuated."

"You don't have to find it so damn amusing." Keanin stalked off and stayed near the back once they started moving again.

◆

At the evening camp, Jenna attempted to reach Ghortin, but there was no response. She gave a disgusted snort as she prepared to lay out her small tent. What was the use in having a mentor if he only showed up randomly? She knew she was being unfair, Ghortin's situation was far from normal, but she couldn't help it. Everything was making her jumpy and she was wondering where these strange ideas were coming from. So far the commands and Power were on her side. But what if they didn't stay that way? What if there was something more malevolent than a mild echo in her mind?

"I'm sure wherever you put it will be fine." Jenna looked up to see Edgar grinning at her. She realized that while she'd been lost in her worries, she had been holding her tent.

"Sorry. I must have looked silly waving this around."

"Not at all. I informed the troops that you were simply having an argument with Ghortin as to the best location."

Jenna looked down sheepishly. "Thanks. I'm afraid this was just me this time. I was thinking."

"That kind of thinking can only be serious."

"Not really," Jenna lied. She certainly didn't want to parade her paranoid fears in front of a knight. Even if he always looked more like his alter ego of spymaster. "I was letting some unlikely scenarios run away with me."

"This must be quite a change for you."

Jenna looked up sharply.

Edgar went on. "Quite different from being stuck with that old mage in his forest."

Jenna gave a tiny sigh of relief. For a moment she thought that everyone knew she wasn't from this world.

"I'm afraid this isn't anything like I'm used to." A thought dawned on her. Ghortin might not be willing to hazard a guess as to the origins of the attacks on the land of Traanafaeren, but maybe someone else would. "Do you have any idea who, or what, is behind all of these attacks?"

"That is a serious discussion. And as such, should be discussed around plenty of food and drink." Edgar looked over to where Kern's second lieutenant was taking a mess of birds off the spit. "And I do believe our repast is prepared. If you will join me, my lady, I will be more than happy to share my humble thoughts on the origins of our nemesis." He led the way to the mess area.

"Nothing is quite as good as derawri cooking," Edgar said happily as he dug into one side of his bird once they'd settled in.

Jenna was surprised that he took a whole one, but then reconsidered. Along with their ability to heal faster, kelars also seemed to require a lot more food than other folk. Even a relatively small one like Edgar.

"Now, what was it you wanted to know?" He wiped the grease away from his chin.

"I was curious if you had any clue as to what we're up against. All these things keep happening, and yet no one seems able to say who's behind it."

"Most people probably aren't sure. I'd say it points to the followers of Qhazborh. Except that they've not been up to much for at least eighty years, and back then it was small aggressions, nothing large. Also, they rarely worked with animals, and the ertin and sciretts are definitely involved. Based on the level of magic used when the king was taken, we are dealing with a mastermage. Like the one that took the king. Except that no single person alive, even a cuari, could hold that kind of Power long term." He shook his head, black eyes glinting in the firelight. "And Ravenhearst being involved pulls in Strann. He could be acting alone—but with the clout he carries in his country, I doubt it. And then, of course, there are things still darker."

Jenna looked up at his drop in volume. "Everything you've said so far, I've heard about. What darker things?"

"Folk tales mostly. Which is why you may not have heard of them. Living with Ghortin and frequenting castles isn't going to expose you to much of the common people. The tales have to do with the cuari."

Jenna waved a piece of bread at him. "But I thought the cuari appeared when the world started." Part of Ghortin's exceedingly long history lessons had been about the cuari. A species of only one hundred—one of which, Carabella, was Ghortin's mother.

"Since the dawn of time, people have speculated on what life was like before the three species came. When it was just the cuari." He ripped off another piece of the roasted bird. "Some people say that the cuari weren't supposed to be here. That this world belonged to something else and that the cuari got rid of it. Maybe that something else is coming back."

Jenna couldn't fight the shiver that went up her back. This man would be great at telling ghost stories around a campfire. "But that was thousands of years ago. If the story is true, wouldn't whatever was out there have come back a long time ago?"

Edgar spread his hands wide, his grin reaching the tips of his pointed ears. "I didn't say I believed it, I told you what some people think. Personally, I think that tale was made up to frighten children."

Jenna looked at him for a few moments, trying to figure out what he believed. But for all of his open friendliness, Edgar was a closed book when it came to his true thoughts.

"Thank you. At least now I know it's not just me who has no idea what's going on; no one else does either." She stretched as a yawn overtook her. "I'd better get to sleep, or I'll never make it tomorrow."

"Good idea. Although I think I might make a detour over to Crell's tent. She usually has something along to shake off the winter chill." He got up and gave a little bow. "Good night, fair lady." For that one second, Jenna could see him as a knight of the realm, then he winked, and the spy persona reappeared.

CHAPTER TWENTY-FOUR

———◆———

THE NEXT MORNING, THIN SHEETS of snow covered the ground like a scattering of crushed diamonds. It was less than an inch in depth, but it was enough to make Jenna wish for heavier clothing as she disassembled her tent. Although these single person tents were lighter than silk, they held heat amazingly well. Now if she could find someone to make her a jacket out of one.

Jenna spent the first few hours of the trip south trying to contact Ghortin. They were getting close to the temple island and she couldn't tell them she had no idea why she'd made them go there. They'd never trust her on anything again. She was hoping that even if Ghortin didn't suggest it to her, he might be able to come up with a plausible reason for their being there. If he would just come back.

Storm and Edgar had been scouting ahead and waited for them at the shore of a large lake at the edge of the woods.

Frantically, Jenna doubled her efforts to reach Ghortin. Just as they were coming out of the woods an irate, but welcome, voice sounded in her head.

"*What now? I just left you.*"

Jenna almost yelped with joy at the cranky voice. "*No, you didn't. It's been a full day and a half since you showed up last time. And I've got a problem.*"

Ghortin was silent a moment. He came back subdued. "*That long? I swear I feel like I've been gone but a few min-*

utes."

"*Right after you left last time, I had this strange urge to visit a temple of Irissanta. That wasn't a parting shot from you by any chance, was it?*"

"*No. At least I don't think so. But then I also didn't know I was out of things for so long, so who knows.*" He paused. "*How long was I gone earlier, after we got Tor Ranshal and Edgar up to Maggie's?*"

"*Two days.*"

"*I was afraid of that. It didn't dawn on me when I saw the camp. About this urge to go to the temple, you don't know why?*"

"*No. Storm asked if you gave me a clue as to which way to travel. I started to tell him that you left without a direction when a temple of Irissanta flashed to mind. We're almost there, and I should have some reason to give them for this detour.*"

"*True. Or they'll think one or both of us has lost it. Which isn't that unimaginable,*" he muttered. "*But for now, tell them that I wished to meet with the seeress. She and I go quite a ways back and it would be good to talk to her. Yes, that's actually a good idea. Tell them we'll spend the night on the island.*"

Jenna stepped forward to pass on Ghortin's words when the sight of the lake stopped her.

What she thought was a simple lake terminated in a magnificent waterfall. One so high that its bottom was lost in the rising spray. But more stupendous than the glorious fall was the citadel perched on the brink of it. What they called Cathedral Island was completely artificial.

Twin towers rose from opposite ends of the low walled castle. Gracefully curving arches, easily several feet taller than Storm, were everywhere. Jenna realized with a start that they were windows. Larger versions could be seen further back, acting as gateways to the myriad of short walls seen within. The entire collection of buildings, for upon closer inspection it would be difficult to call such a thing a castle, was covered with a pearled white stone which glistened brightly in the afternoon light.

At first she thought the graceful structure lacked defense. This wasn't a populated area and would be prone to bandits. She couldn't believe that the clerics relied on good will to protect them. Then she understood. There was no visible way over to the island; any attacker would be flung off the waterfall. Which posed another problem. How were *they* going to get to the island?

"Does Ghortin need all of us to go over? Or just you?" Storm had approached silently, as usual.

"Oh." Jenna jumped as she came out of her little world. The temple drew her in. "Ghortin wants to talk to the seeress. I don't think everyone needs to go." A thought hit her. Like the original one to come here, it was quick and elusive. With a mental sigh, she gave in to it. Ghortin hadn't seemed unduly concerned that it might be something bad. She just wished she shared his confidence.

"But you at least should go, and Keanin." She held up a hand before he could speak. "Don't ask, I'm only the messenger." Of course, she wasn't sure *who* the message was from. But they didn't need to know that. Not yet, at any rate.

"So I'm to be dragged along again. Don't I have a say in anything anymore?" Keanin gave a long-suffering sigh that probably could be heard in the distant temple.

"No," Storm and Jenna said in unison.

"I do have one question, how do we get over there?" She looked at the rough fall.

Storm walked over to a small shed. "Over here."

Jenna followed with more than a little curiosity. Inside the shed was a small table.

"Lay your hands on the table and think of the temple."

Jenna shrugged and did what Storm said. A feathery tingle filled the palms of her hands as she thought of Ghortin and the temple. A faint chime sounded above her head.

"We are most pleased to welcome such august company. Please stand ready by the staff and we shall send for you." The voice was soothing, but Jenna couldn't tell if it was a man or a woman.

Storm seemed satisfied and headed back outside.

"Are we sure we want to do this?" Keanin sounded edgier than usual. Jenna couldn't understand why. Surely he'd had plenty of contact with Storm's sister, Kaytine; she was a cleric of Irissanta, and he'd been raised with the royal family.

Storm, however, seemed to understand. "I know you're uncomfortable, but if Jenna thinks you should go, you should go."

Jenna stepped back and pulled Storm with her. "Why is he so upset? These are the same clerics as your sister, aren't they?" She had a horrible vision of getting the wrong type of cleric.

"Yes. In fact, this is where Kaytine normally spends most of her time. Keanin doesn't feel comfortable with the seeress. She made some predictions about him when he was young, and he's still unnerved about them."

"What were they, and is she always right?"

"He wouldn't share them. Yes, but not always literally correct." He shrugged. "We tried for years to convince Keanin he had nothing to be afraid of. The seeress herself admitted that what she sees is just one possible path. But he still hasn't gotten over it."

Jenna went back to the auburn-haired kelar and slid her arm around his slender waist. "I don't know what she told you so long ago, but we're all in this together. Storm and I, and even Ghortin, won't let anything happen to you."

He was silent for a moment, and then hugged her tightly. "Thank you. Logically, I know that; but here, in my heart—" He shook his head.

Storm came up. "Good, I wouldn't want to have to

carry you to the island. Hold on a moment, I'll tell Crell and Edgar what we're doing."

As he turned away, Jenna remembered Ghortin's words and called after him. "Tell them we'll be staying the night, most likely in the temple." Keanin shuddered at her words, but didn't say anything.

As soon as Storm came back, a thin line cut through the water from the citadel. It glowed lightly as it reached toward a long wooden staff set into the ground near the cabin. Following about a foot behind the glowing line was a small, flat boat. A figure was poling it, but for the most part it seemed that the line was pulling the boat.

"Greetings, travelers." The green-clad cleric paused when he noticed the rest of their party behind them on a hillside. A frown creased his plain face. "Forgive us, we thought there were only three of you. Shall I send for more boats?"

Storm stepped forward. "No need. Just the three of us will be going with you. The rest of our companions shall await us here."

The man nodded and smiled. "Very well. Are you ready?"

Again, Storm answered for them. "I believe so. I am Corin, brother to cleric Kaytine. This is apprentice mage Jenna and Lord Keanin, both of Lithunane."

The cleric bowed. "I am pleased to meet you. I am called Redge. Please, my boat is small, but it is swift, and the seeress awaits you."

Although he meant that to be a favorable thing, Keanin's face developed a green tinge. Storm took Keanin's pack from his tight fingers and led Jenna to the boat. After a few moments Keanin came muttering after.

"I'm sorry, did you say something?" Storm asked.

"I said," Keanin said through gritted teeth, "that with friends like you two, I don't need any enemies." He reclaimed his pack and joined Redge on the boat.

Cleric Redge helped them aboard, not appearing to notice Keanin's tight-lipped face. Or perhaps he was too diplomatic to say anything.

The boat itself was made of a richly stained dark wood. It was bigger than it looked from the distance, although it was completely flat. Jenna took one look at the raging falls not far enough away from them and forced herself to not panic. The cleric made it out to them fine; obviously the boat didn't need heavy sides to keep them aboard.

As the boat began to move, it became clear that its movement was coming from the strange line that now preceded them to the constructed island. The cleric was pushing his staff down, but much slower than their progress. Jenna looked into the water and was surprised at the depth. What was he pushing the pole against? Just as that thought crossed her mind, the cleric reached out with the long pole again and touched an underwater boulder. She hadn't seen them at first, but hundreds of them lay just below the surface. She looked away, trusting that this man knew what he was doing. In doing so, she found her gaze taken over by the waterfall. It was an eerie, yet wonderful, feeling, pacing along the rim of a fall. Certainly it didn't compare to anything she'd ever done before. She couldn't help but lean over a little, hoping to catch the marvelous view below them. She caught herself as she teetered a bit.

"Easy there. I don't think I'd want to explain to everyone that you went flying overboard." Storm caught hold of her waist and pulled her back.

"Sorry." Her face went hot. "It's so beautiful, I guess I got swept away. Almost, anyway." She noticed that while Storm didn't seem to think she was going to fly off the boat anymore, his hand lingered on her back.

They grew silent as they reached the island. The boat followed a small waterway under an alabaster and gold arch. The waterway seemed to run through the entire structure, but Redge took them to the nearest dock. He tied up the boat, then bowed and made a small gesture with his right hand in front of a small, vaguely feminine statue.

He then turned to them with a bow. "Would you like to rest first or go directly to the seeress?" He paused, cocking his head as if listening to something beyond their hearing. He bowed again and turned back to them, chagrined. "Forgive me. The seeress has said that of course you must rest, and for me to ask was to imply that it was an imposition. Please, if you would follow me, I shall lead you to your rooms." He started down the walkway then turned with a smile. "She says you will be staying the night."

Keanin turned greener.

"If you don't watch it, they're going to think you're mocking the goddess's colors," Storm said to his friend.

Keanin narrowed his eyes. "You made me come on this trip and you made me come out here against my will. I'll turn whatever shade I wish to, thank you."

Storm chuckled. "Maybe now you won't make fun of the way I feel during court functions." Keanin glared and stalked past him.

The walkway they followed was covered with flat, tiny, glittering white pebbles embedded in its surface. The walls glimmered as they went by, and every once in a while Jenna spotted a hooded cleric in meditation. She couldn't understand why Keanin felt so ill at ease here, even if he did hear some bad news long ago. The place exuded peace and serenity. Nothing could harm anyone here. Jenna fought a brief, but nearly overwhelming urge to pledge herself to the goddess and stay here forever. Then she thought of Ghortin among these peaceful souls and almost burst out laughing. No, this wasn't her place.

Cleric Redge stopped in front of a wooden door. He faced them again with a bow. "Honored guests, here are your rooms. If you need anything, please but ask. And when you have rested, just call, and we shall present you to the seeress." He bowed again and left as the wooden door swung open of its own accord.

Storm pushed the door open fully. Jenna followed him, with Keanin reluctantly bringing up the rear.

The room was airy, but quite plain. Two low couches sat in a corner next to a small table. A pair of simple wooden chairs sat against the far wall. A narrow hallway led to a pair of small rooms, one with a single bed, and the other with two cots.

Jenna went into her room, meaning to lie down for a second. Ghortin's internal muttering woke her up an hour later.

"*Thank goodness. I thought I was going to be trapped in here forever. Didn't you get any sleep last night, child?*"

Jenna tried to shake herself awake. An hour wasn't enough to sleep, but long enough to disorient. "Not really. I guess I'm not used to this outdoor lifestyle. We're here, and I still have no reason why." Speaking out loud was easier than mindspeaking when no one was around to hear her one-sided conversation.

"*Yes, I know. I've been rummaging around while you slept. I thought perhaps I could take over and get things done without waking you, but it seems I need for you to be awake. Don't you think it's time to see the seeress now?*"

"But wait, I have some questions about this whole thing."

"*I'm afraid they'll have to wait, child. We must get to the seeress. Now go wake up your two companions; I'm sure they're asleep also.*"

Jenna was annoyed at his abruptness. She didn't feel comfortable not knowing what was going on, and even worse that someone inside her own head did know but wouldn't tell her.

She kept her grumbles to herself as she padded into

Storm and Keanin's room. As Ghortin predicted, both kelars were out cold. Obviously she wasn't the only one who'd been having trouble sleeping. Keanin woke slowly, fighting her the entire time. Storm woke before she touched him, his wide blue eyes sharp and focused. Jenna felt a stab of envy for that immediate awareness.

"I don't see why I have to go with you two. Jenna and Ghortin are the ones that want to see her; why should we be going at all?" Keanin said peevishly once he'd awoken.

"We aren't going for a seeing, Keanin," Storm said, finally becoming annoyed. "We're all going to go in, pay our respects, then leave." The kelar prince turned and left the room.

Ghortin spoke before she did. "*May I?*"

"*Go right ahead, I've no idea what to say to him anyway.*"

Jenna felt that strange tingle that told her Ghortin was in charge of her body.

"Keanin, I know you're frightened, things are going on that are scaring the hell out of you. Believe me, my boy, you're not alone. I need to introduce Jenna to the seeress and share some words with her. It won't take long. Actually, after you greet her, you could probably be excused out of exhaustion."

Ghortin was gentler than Jenna would have thought he'd be.

Keanin took a deep breath. "All right. But I'm leaving after I've paid my respects. I've nothing against her personally, you understand. I just don't like what she does."

Ghortin/Jenna nodded. "Fine. Shall we?"

Keanin rose from his cot and started to take Jenna's arm. He hesitated and looked at them closely. "Ghortin? You don't mind if I escort the two of you? It's kind of odd, what with you being in Jenna's body and all."

Jenna felt Ghortin hold out one arm. "Escort away."

Storm was in the doorway of the main room talking to a cleric. At first Jenna thought she was seeing Kaytine's twin. The kelar woman looked almost exactly like her, except that she had wide, brown eyes. And those upswept eyes were fixed on Storm with unmasked adoration.

"Yes, Prince Corin, I know your sister well. But she never said how handsome you are." The young woman's eyes went wider as she realized what she'd said.

Storm looked down at her kindly, but Jenna noticed a slight crimson blush along his high cheekbones. How someone who grew up both royal and attractive could be so easily embarrassed, Jenna still hadn't figured out. "Thank you, novice Ljasda." Storm looked relieved when Jenna and Keanin walked in. "I think we are ready to be presented now."

The frantic novice looked from one to another, mortified at what she'd said, and even more at possible witnesses. "I'm sorry, Your Highness. I didn't mean—" She put her hand to her mouth.

Keanin dropped Jenna's arm and stepped forward smoothly. He took the shaking novice's hand in his own. "There, there, my dear. What has this wild prince done to you? Corin, you've made her cry. For that, *I* get to walk with her." So smoothly did he step in and take control, that the young novice forgot her blunder and led them to the seeress calmly.

CHAPTER TWENTY-FIVE

———◆———

THE TEMPLE OF THE SEERESS was elegant in its simplicity. The walls and floor were white marble with gold veins and copper flecks catching the light from triads of glows set around the room. It lacked windows, except for two wide bands of clear glass that ran along the ceiling.

The seeress herself was not in sight, and the novice disappeared hastily, carefully avoiding looking at Storm.

The three of them had been standing there for a few minutes when Ghortin moved her to the center of the room.

"Come on, Sarisa, you're not impressing anyone." Jenna was surprised at his tone. Even more worrisome was that it was coming out of her mouth. She didn't want the seeress thinking it was she who was being so forward.

From the far end of the room, a faint outline of a door appeared. A tall, slender woman came through it as it opened.

"So, it is true. You've taken over this poor child's body." The woman who stepped forward was willowy and graceful. She was neither young nor old, and seemed to be a kelar/human hybrid. Long silver hair flowed down to her ankles, but the amount that was caught up in the elaborate knot on the top of her head made Jenna realize that it was much longer than that. As the woman came closer, Jenna noticed that her wide, semi-tilted eyes were almost clear; their pale blue tint looked like an after-thought.

The seeress took Jenna's hands in her own, looking down fondly. "Hello, old friend." After that, all Jenna heard was some mental whispering, not unlike wind in the trees. A few moments later, the woman spoke to her directly.

"Greetings, Jenna. I am glad that my friend has you to give him shelter during this trying time." She froze, tipping her head to one side intently. As Jenna watched, her eyes misted over. When she spoke, it was halting, as if she was working to say it.

"I see you have come far. There is much to do to fix what has been made wrong. The way will be dark; it was not meant to be, but the path was not intended for you. You must learn quickly and take what help you may receive. Be wary of the rift. Know that Power can destroy with as much ease as it can save." Just as quickly as she slipped into the trance, the seeress slipped back out. The mistiness of her eyes vanished.

Jenna was stunned. She hadn't the slightest idea what the woman meant, but she'd felt a spark trigger inside her. Something she'd said hit a nerve. Jenna wished she knew whose.

Keanin stepped back a bit as the seeress turned toward him and Storm. Ghortin took over the introductions; which was fortunate, since Jenna wasn't sure she would be able to sort out her tongue at this point.

"May I formally present Prince Corin and Lord Keanin?" Both bowed low, and Keanin refrained from any of his normal flourishes. The seeress' eyes misted over again.

"I see your path is long, my prince. Your heart longs for two things; one will always be your destiny, the other is already out of your hands. Sometimes we must let go of that which we hold most dear. Other times we are too ready to do that same thing. One must know which time this is."

Storm's face was somber, but he nodded his thanks. Jenna wondered briefly what the second thing was that he wanted. The most important thing to him now was the return of his father. The seeress turned to Keanin as the handsome noble started to shake.

"Forgive me, gracious seeress. I seek not a seeing. I've just come to pay my respects."

The seeress' face brightened and lost some of its otherworldly appearance. "Lord Keanin, you have feared me for too long. Just because you fear something does not mean it is bad for you. All I will say is this; your path doth lay with these three. Be brave and true; many will be depending on this."

Keanin nodded, but kept his head down. "Thank you, my lady. May I leave you now? I am not used to long travel." His voice caught in his throat.

Sadness filled the seeress' face. "Go, my son, and try to be in peace."

Keanin bowed and left as quickly as etiquette would allow.

The seeress turned back to them, and Jenna noticed that her eyes had gone back to normal. "Forgive me for sharing your readings. All of you are tied in to something beyond my ability to see the end of, but you will be together. Also, I felt that I should try to soothe young Keanin before he fled." Her face remained sad for a moment then she took Jenna's arm, motioning for Storm to come to her other side.

They were walking outside toward a small patio when the seeress froze. Her eyes went unimaginably wide and, unlike the previous time, a thick white film completely blocked them out. The voice that came out of her now was low and rich, but still feminine.

"Thy new host does not suit thee, Master Ghortin. I think that thou would be better pleased back in thy original vessel that doth now lie in the Cave of Sorrows.

Abandoned there by thine enemy as an empty shell."

Jenna felt the shock go through Ghortin's consciousness at the seeress' words. Then she realized it wasn't just the words that surprised him. With a start, she realized this must be the Goddess herself. Before anyone could say anything, the presence was gone, and Storm had to catch the seeress before she crumbled to the floor.

Storm looked up at Jenna from where he cradled the seeress. "What happened to her? Will she be all right?"

"I think so," Ghortin said. However, Jenna felt tendrils of worry crawling through his mind. "Bring her over here." He led Storm with the unconscious seeress to a cushioned bench.

"Sarisa? Here you go, dear. Wake up," Ghortin said as he took her from Storm.

The seeress stirred, and then finally opened her light eyes. "Ghortin?" She closed them briefly again. After a few moments she opened them with more conviction.

"Oh my. She hasn't done that in a long time. Did she say anything important?" She struggled into a seated position.

"Just where my body is. No wonder I couldn't sense anything if it is in that tomb of a cave." Ghortin's disgust at this mysterious Cave of Sorrows was strong.

The seeress looked surprised. "She told you where it is? What cave?"

"Excuse me, but what happened?" Storm interjected gently. He looked as bewildered as Jenna felt.

"I'm sorry if I frightened you. The goddess spoke through me directly that last time. Something she hasn't done in nigh on thirty odd years. It took me by surprise. Normally I interpret what I feel from people, and her faint images." The seeress looked at Jenna with a smirk that she knew was directed at Ghortin. "Maybe you are as important as you've always said, old man. She clearly didn't want to take a chance on any mistakes with that information."

"I'm not familiar with the cave she mentioned. Is it nearby?" Storm asked the question Jenna was about to mentally ask Ghortin. She couldn't help the surge of relief the mention of Ghortin's body sent through her.

"It's very old and forgotten now, but the Cave of Sorrows is located deep in the Scareani Mountains. It will add a week or so to our journey, but my apprentice seems to feel it's justified." Jenna shot him the mental equivalent of a dirty look.

"I see her point. I know I wouldn't want you lurking about in my head." The seeress' smile was wry, but Jenna felt a warmth flow through her. Jenna guessed that, at some point, there had been something more than friendship between the two. Ghortin tried to block his feelings, but she blithely told him it was too late.

Storm's face grew serious. "Do you think my father is there?"

Ghortin shook his head. "I doubt it. From what the goddess said, my body was left there because the monster who took it decided it was empty."

Storm's face fell for an instant, then he caught himself. "Then the only thing for us to do is to get your body back and get on with our trip."

The seeress smiled warmly and took Storm's hand. "Things are unfolding as they should. Change is necessary for the world to progress. But I know this does not bring you comfort." She turned and clapped her hands. "I think it is time for old friends to go and tell old tales, and the young to go make memories. At least for tonight."

Two novices arrived in answer to her clap. Ljasda looked away from Storm almost immediately.

Storm looked awkward, but didn't say anything. He wasn't as good at handling unwanted female attention as Keanin was. Of course, with Keanin, little of it was unwanted.

"Please bring me the vase I readied, Karnia. Ljasda, will you please bring me some water?" If the seeress caught the hasty glance the novice shot at the kelar prince, she gave no sign. At least until both novices left on their errands. Then she turned to Storm with a small smile.

"I see you've already captured the heart of one of my novices, Prince Corin."

Storm looked more uncomfortable. "If I did, it was not my intent, I assure you."

The seeress lifted one perfectly sculpted brow. "Why? Is there something wrong with my novice, Your Highness?"

Jenna saw through Ghortin that the seeress was playing with him.

Storm, unfortunately, didn't see it. "No, mistress, not at all. It wouldn't be appropriate for me to go around luring maidens who have given themselves over to the goddess."

"I'll wager you and Keanin will break many such hearts this eve, young Corin." She was laughing now. A sound that was more like small bells than human laughter. "Fear not. My clerics all have free will; the goddess doesn't want them to give up their lives. Look at your sister." She looked up as the derawri novice returned bearing a small gray vase.

"My thanks, Karnia. Please set it down next to our guest Jenna." The novice complied, and then stepped back. A second later, the nervous Ljasda reappeared bearing an intricate goblet of water. Wordlessly she handed it to the seeress.

"My thanks to you as well, good Ljasda. You two may return to your studies."

The novices bowed low, and then disappeared into the building.

"Now, Jenna, how would you like to be free of this old rogue for the evening?"

Ghortin was still in charge, but Jenna sent him her answer with what she hoped was the proper amount of enthusiasm.

"My apprentice is giddy with the thought. But we wonder how you can do such a thing," Ghortin said.

The seeress looked at him smugly. "Ha. For once I have knowledge that you lack. That vase near your feet is from a cuari archaeological find. It can hold your essence in a state that can still communicate for twelve hours. I thought that you and I could reminisce, while the children celebrate."

Jenna felt his surprise. The seeress *had* gotten one up on him. But he refused to let on.

"What celebration, oh devious one?"

"Has it been so long that you've forgotten?" She turned toward Storm with a smile. "Whenever the goddess blesses us with direct contact, for whatever reason, there is a nightlong celebration. I'm sure you will find it most intriguing, Prince Corin." From the sly look on her face, Jenna wondered what this celebration was.

"As for you, young Jenna, you will be free to enjoy yourself. With your companions, or others. Without Ghortin along for the ride."

Jenna had a brief flash of bacchanalian revels. Ghortin caught the thought and spoke directly to her.

"Not that bad, I assure you. Yet you might want to stick close to Storm until you feel comfortable."

The seeress rubbed her hands together, looking for all the world like a conjurer preparing her favorite trick. "All right, first I need you to pick up the vase. Ghortin, when I begin, I want you to start thinking about pouring yourself into the vase. That's all, nothing tricky. Corin, stand close to Jenna. When Ghortin leaves she's liable to feel a little faint."

Jenna wanted to ask about the safety of such a thing, but Ghortin soothed her fears. He had nothing but respect and trust for the beautiful seeress.

Jenna felt him brush her thoughts with a farewell, and

then he was gone.

Her vision faded, and Storm's strong arms steadied both her and the vase.

"I must admit, Sarisa, this is a most unique feeling. Can't see much though." Ghortin's voice came from the vase. Storm tightened his hold on her briefly. It was rather odd hearing the mastermage's voice coming from a small vase, but Jenna was too disoriented at that moment to dwell on it.

The seeress patted the bench next to her as she sipped slowly from her water goblet. "Sit her down here; she'll be fine in a few moments." Her voice was weaker now.

Storm sat Jenna down, and then turned his attention to the seeress. "Are you all right? Should I send for some help?"

She waved a hand at him vaguely. "Thank you, but no. I'll be fine. I underestimated the amount of Power involved, that's all. You're heavier than I suspected, old man." She directed the last at the vase.

"Three thousand years of clean living will do that to you."

Jenna's vision started to clear, and she had to admit the sense of freedom of not having Ghortin in her head was fabulous. "This is kind of you, but how will he get back?"

"Oh, don't you worry. In twelve hours his presence will revert to where it was." She fluttered her hands at the two of them. "Now you two scoot. Go have a good time. I've told my people to bring you celebration robes, and I'm sure your red-haired friend is dying to know what's going on. Go, be happy." With that, she turned back to the vase and began conducting a rather strange conversation with the piece of cuari pottery.

Storm helped Jenna up and they went back to their rooms.

"Are you sure you feel all right? Because we don't have to go to the celebration if you don't want to." Storm stopped in front of their door.

"Don't tell me you're afraid of that lovesick novice." Jenna looked up at him with a wicked smile.

"No, not at all. I'm concerned for you. The clerics of Irissanta are the kindest, gentlest people you will ever meet. They also are *friendly* about their affections when celebrating. At least, that's what I've heard. I just don't want you to feel uncomfortable."

Jenna caught something different in his voice. "So you're concerned about me, for my own comfort? Nothing else? Keanin will be there, you know."

Storm looked down at her, then away quickly. "No. I mean, I'm sure he'll be off somewhere and not watching out for you."

Jenna raised an eyebrow as he fumbled. She tugged on his shirt. "You're certain there's no other reason?"

He did another quick glance down, then looked away. "That's all. Since I found you, I feel responsible for you."

His tone annoyed Jenna. If he had feelings for her, why didn't he say so? It wasn't like his engagement to Mikasa was real; Keanin said as much. And for once Ghortin wasn't around. She certainly wasn't going to figure out her feelings until he resolved his engagement situation. But it would be nice to know if he felt the same.

She abruptly let go of his shirt. "I don't need a protector. I'm going to the celebration with or without you, or Keanin." She spun around and pushed open the door to their rooms.

Storm sighed, then followed her in.

Keanin wasn't in the rooms, but the robes were. They were of a thin, gauzy material, and rather short. Jenna held one up cautiously, and then looked down at the layers of winter clothes she was presently wearing.

"Just where are they having this celebration? We'll freeze in these."

Storm slowly picked up a deep blue robe. It was larger

than the one she held, but wouldn't cover all that much of either of the two long-legged kelars. The matching shorts would at least give them a modicum of modesty. "More than likely, in the main hall. From what Kaytine has said, they'll keep it warm." He looked at her again. "Are you sure you want to go?" Storm sounded forlorn. From the look on his face, his reasons now had as much to do with the costume as with her.

"What, and pass up a chance to see you in that? I wouldn't miss it for the world." She took her bright pink robe and matching shorts and sauntered to her room.

———◆———

Storm looked at his robe with a growing sense of unease. He didn't like this sort of thing, and even less when there wasn't much of a costume involved. He continued muttering under his breath until Keanin finally came back to the room. He was much more at ease than when he'd left the seeress.

"Corin. You won't believe what they're doing tonight." He pointed to the robe in Storm's hand, noted the look of apprehension on his face, and burst out laughing.

"You already know. What did she say?"

"Yes." Storm tossed down the robe. "She told Ghortin that his body lies in the Cave of Sorrows, someplace in the Scareani. And because of that, we have to dress up in these."

Keanin rushed forward and scooped up a dark green robe and shorts. "And for this you are upset? Think about it, if ours are this short, think of what the women's will be like and Ljasda told me there aren't that many handsome young men in the temple at this time of year." He poked Storm in the ribs.

Storm shot him a look of pure disgust. "I'm supposed to be engaged you know."

Keanin shook his head. "You and I both know that you

will find a way to break that." His eyes opened wide and he smacked himself in the head. "My stars. How could I have forgotten?" Motioning for Storm to stay where he was, Keanin rushed down the hall. Moments later he returned bearing a tattered parchment.

"Edgar gave this to me last night, he suggested I wait until we were over here to give it to you. He wasn't sure the best time to give it to you, and he wasn't happy about carrying love notes." He flashed an evil grin. "It's from Mikasa. She made him promise to bring it to you when he and Tor Ranshal were leaving Lithunane."

Storm stopped his hand in mid-reach. "She made Edgar carry a *note* to me?"

"I was hoping that if she annoyed you anew, you'd relax and take a look around you. Maybe even enjoy yourself."

Wearily, Storm took the tan envelope. It had Mikasa's wax seal on it. Love birds and flowers. It was almost as annoying as the woman herself. He turned away from Keanin, then slit the envelope open. It began with her usual sappy self. She loved him more than life itself, and the recent tragedies made her realize how vulnerable such a gallant prince truly was. Since she loved him so much, and since she would die if anything happened to him, she was finding it necessary to break off their engagement. She went on to add that he would always live in her heart, but she needed to find someone safer to marry.

As Storm re-read the letter to make sure it was saying what he thought it said, he began to laugh.

"What says the lady fair?" Keanin asked as he held up the two robes, deciding which suited him better.

"Here." Storm tossed the letter at him. "Read for yourself. The lady has left me."

Keanin's eyes flew wide as he quickly read. "She is sappy, isn't she?"

Storm nodded as he took the blue robe and shorts

out of Keanin's clutches. "Lamentably so. If I'm going, I might as well get dressed." He left, smiling to himself. Jenna was probably going to look quite nice in that tiny robe, and now he could notice without feeling guilty.

———◆———

Jenna came out into the main room as Keanin finished re-reading the letter. "What was Storm laughing about? He certainly wasn't in a laughing mood a few minutes ago." She self-consciously patted down the edge of the robe. It was like a short Grecian robe; one that did little to conceal her legs, even with the shorts underneath. Thank goodness it wasn't as see-through as it had looked.

Keanin grinned and bowed. "Ah, my lovely flower. That robe suits thee amazingly." At her blush, he went back to the letter. "Our royal friend has been dealt devastating news. His beloved Mikasa has called off the engagement." He managed to keep a straight face through most of it.

"What? Why?" Jenna told her hormones to calm down. She was glad that Ghortin was presently somewhere other than in her head or she would never hear the end of it. Surely a prince had many other important admirers, and another engagement would be made soon. Besides, she refused to throw herself at him.

Luckily for her, Keanin failed to notice Jenna's reaction. "It seems she has decided that the royal prince leads too dangerous a life."

"And I'm sure he's just—" She stopped as Storm came down the hall. The short robe and shorts covered only a little more of him than hers did of her. His long muscular legs seemed quite at home on display though. Jenna admitted to herself that he was a damn attractive man. She was surprised to realize that she didn't think of him as being so alien anymore.

Storm did a brief walk through, showing off his new garment. "Did you tell her the news?"

"Yes, he did." Jenna found she couldn't take her eyes off Storm. Rather than make him look feminine, the robe seemed to accent his maleness. Mentally kicking herself, she forced her eyes away. "I must say, you're handling a broken heart well." She looked back at him, giving him a raking once over. "And you actually don't look half bad. I think you may give poor Ljasda fits though."

Storm did look awkward about that. "I think she'll be okay, especially if she's distracted by someone else." He gave Keanin a pointed look.

Keanin shrugged. "Who knows? It's that whole brooding prince thing, makes it darn hard to compete." As he spoke, Keanin disappeared down the hall, only to reappear dressed in his robe.

Jenna let out a low whistle; Keanin was absolutely breathtaking.

"Thank you, my lady." Keanin held out his arm to Jenna then turned to Storm. "As for you, you rebel heartbreaker, I'll thank you to behave yourself tonight."

Storm shot his friend an evil look, then rang for their escort.

CHAPTER TWENTY-SIX

JENNA AWOKE FROM THE PREVIOUS night's festivities with a dull throb of a headache. Noting with dismay what sleeping in it had done to the thin temple robe, she bathed and slid into her normal clothing before wandering out to the front room.

Storm looked up as she entered the living room where he was picking at a huge breakfast.

"Do you know where Keanin is?"

"He didn't make it back last night. I'm sure he's fine." He stopped as the door opened.

"Speak of the devil," Jenna said, as a bedraggled Keanin stumbled in.

"But do you have to speak so loudly?" Keanin whispered irritably.

"You didn't forget that we're leaving today, did you? Retrieving Ghortin's body is going to increase our travel time, so we'll need to start at once," Jenna said.

Keanin collapsed onto one of the sofas with a groan. "Can't you leave me here?" He forced his eyes open. "No, on second thought, don't leave me here. I never thought I'd meet a religious order that could out celebrate me."

Jenna was about to say something snide, when a tingle overtook her. Storm reached out to catch her before she fell.

"*Ghortin?*" She said inside her head.

"*Yes, child, I'm back. Did you have fun?*" He took in Keanin's condition. "*Well, I see that someone did. Are you going to give him something for that? Or are we going to have to listen to him moan for the next two days?"*

She turned toward the stricken kelar. Mentally she began pulling together the Power for a healing spell. She turned to Storm with a sigh.

"Can you get some of the dried Salf leaves from my pack? Ghortin's back and he says I have to make Keanin here travel ready."

Keanin's eyes held a hopeful gleam. Storm, who knew full well the taste of Ghortin's concoctions, smirked as he left.

Within minutes, Keanin was presented with a swirling purple and orange beverage. The Salf leaves themselves were colorless, and so was the chaotic magic they were infused with. But Ghortin taught it to her with these colors added and she found they added something to the presentation. As long as she wasn't the one forced to drink it.

"Are you sure I'm supposed to drink something that's still alive?" Keanin asked as he tried to focus on the swirling currents in the glass.

Jenna masked the glass from his sight with her hand. "Then don't look at it. Drink it all."

Keanin took a tentative sip and choked as the entire drink crawled down his throat. His reaction was similar to Jenna's first, and fortunately only, experience with this concoction. He tried to spit it back up, and failing in that, threw the glass across the room and clutched at his throat.

"What poison have you given me?" Keanin rolled on the floor in mock agony. The fact that he was able to do so was testament enough to the drink's curative abilities.

"Well, if this is all settled, I'm going to eat." Jenna sat down, taking one of the chairs next to the food.

Storm came over and took the other seat. Keanin meandered over, still looking a trifle green. He picked out a single hard roll, and then wandered back to his sofa. They ate in silence. For once Keanin wasn't in a talkative mood, and both Jenna and Storm were lost in their own thoughts.

Storm was at any rate; Jenna was trying to pass along the previous night's events, in a censored manner, to her mental roommate.

Within an hour they had finished eating, packed, and said their farewells to the seeress. Unlike the previous day, she had no visions for them. Keanin stayed at a distance nonetheless.

Redge came to take them to the small boat to deliver them to the mainland.

Their group was where they had left them. Crell, Edgar, and Captain Kern were arguing about which would be the safest and fastest way to get to Lithunane.

Crell waved as they came closer. "Storm. Good to see you three are back. These two," she pointed to the men with a derisive snort, "are being beyond idiotic in their plans."

Storm held up his hands to forestall another verbal battle. "We have to go through the Scareani Mountains. Ghortin can tell you exactly where."

"What happened over there? Keanin looks a little pale," Edgar said, as he took in the condition of the usually flashy kelar.

"Suffering the leftovers from his wild night of celebration. I think we'll want to keep an eye on him; he didn't get much sleep last night." Jenna came up and dropped her pack. She went over to Edgar's things and removed her bow, quiver, and dagger. The knives she had kept with her.

Storm buckled on his long sword. He started to hand Keanin his throwing knives and long bow, then shook his head and repacked them with his own gear. Jenna glanced over at the auburn-haired noble. Keanin looked like he was in no condition to carry his weapons, let alone use them. She was certain her curative had more than compensated for his over-indulgences, but maybe it was better if he didn't have anything pointed on his person for a while.

"The goddess made a surprise visit," Storm said in answer to the unasked question. "She said Ghortin's body was abandoned in the Cave of Sorrows. I've never heard of it."

Crell and Kern let out low whistles at the name. Storm may not have recognized it, but they certainly did. Jenna wasn't sure if that was a good thing or a bad thing.

"Are we certain this isn't a trap?" Captain Kern asked. "That cave is not some place you go to without a good reason. We'll be exposed to the elements, and worse, for the last day of it; there's no cover at all."

Jenna felt Ghortin's presence, so she mentally stepped aside.

"I understand your concern, Kern. And it is well founded, let no one forget that. This is not some lark we go on. I can assure you that it was a true visitation. My body has been abandoned by those who took it. Once we get it back, we may have more of an idea of what we're up against."

The captain didn't say anything, but his jaw was still tight.

Crell nodded and dusted off her hands. "Can't say I've ever had reason to go to that place, although I've heard plenty of rumors and whispers about it. None good, by the way. But if that's where our mage lies, that's where we go." She flashed Jenna a smile. "And I'm sure you'll be more than happy to get that wily old man out of your head, eh, Jenna?"

Jenna laughed inside, but Ghortin was still in charge of the outside.

"Why does everyone keep saying that?" He grumbled.

Storm looked up from finishing his pack. "Probably because they know you." He motioned around at the waiting group. "Shall we?"

After consulting together, Edgar took point, Kern and his guards took the center, with Crell and her band bringing up the rear.

Jenna and Storm stayed near the front, while Keanin kept drifting further behind until he hit Crell's group. Unfortunately for him, the short warrior woman was in a jovial mood, and took great pleasure in poking fun at him and his discomfort. Jenna could hear her jibes all the way up at the front.

They had to go around the temple lake and follow a path that looped around the north rim. There was a small trail that lay outside the forest, but far enough away from the lakeshore that they weren't walking on soft sand. The day was sunny, if not warm, and the soothing pine-like scent lulled Jenna into a relaxed state.

They made it three quarters of the way around the lake and were starting to cross southwest, when one of Kern's men was struck by an arrow. There had been no sounds before it happened, and the archer wasn't visible. Within seconds, all of the party had taken cover. Even Keanin found his reflexes coming back to life.

After dragging the mortally injured man with him into the brush, Captain Kern gravely removed the arrow from his man's chest. "Look at this shaft and fletching. Peasant bandits. Although I never would have thought any of the local gangs were big enough to try for an armed group our size." He carefully closed the dead man's eyes.

"Why would bandits strike us? It's pretty clear that we're not merchants," one of Crell's people said from the base of a tree.

"Only one way to find out." Crell grabbed her sword and edged out into the open. "Show yourselves, you cowards. Or are you afraid of an honest fight?"

Her words were met by silence as she slowly stepped toward the distant line of trees. As she moved, Jenna noticed that the archers in her group moved behind her, but stayed close to the tree line. Their bows were drawn and held ready. If anything was fired at their leader, a dozen arrows would be the response.

Not that the response would stop Crell from becoming a pin cushion. Jenna thought the fierce derawri woman was taking a huge risk. She was now completely in the open, a good ten feet of open ground separated her from any cover. Jenna looked toward Storm, but he didn't seem the least disturbed by Crell's antics. She readied a few defensive spells and kept an eye on Crell.

The silence grew tense as minutes passed. For all her calm facade, Crell's grip on her sword was getting white knuckled.

Suddenly Crell sprang into action. Her sword and body were no more than a blur as she swung her arm up and her body to the side. Jenna didn't see the two arrows until they'd struck the ground almost exactly where Crell had been standing.

Her people answered with their own arrows the instant that the enemy archers exposed themselves by firing. At least seven screams were their reward. With the general positions given away, Crell's people, Kern and his group, and Storm and Edgar charged forward in a rush. Keanin held back; clearly he had no intention of chasing anyone. Jenna held back because she wasn't sure what they were doing. The ambushers had the advantage, in her opinion, and she didn't want her inexperience to get in the way.

Jenna crept around to where Keanin was huddled. She may not be able to help with their defense, or whatever it was the rest of them were doing, but she could at least protect Keanin.

"Are you okay?" At Keanin's tense nod, she added. "What are they doing?"

"Trying to get themselves killed," Keanin whispered back. "That's Crell's strategy. She charges ambushes. It works for her people because they've trained for it. But to pull in outsiders like that is wrong." He let his voice trail off in anger and distress.

"They didn't look like they'd been pulled in to me. I think they went vo—" She broke off as a blood-smeared bandit appeared directly behind Keanin.

The bandit lifted a wickedly curved blade to swing at Keanin's unprotected head. Jenna reacted instinctively. She mentally pulled in Power from the chaos, releasing it as she flung a ball of fire at the bandit's face. He dropped his saber and frantically clawed at his burning skin. With a fluid movement she reached into her boot and threw one of her knives into the injured man's chest. He clutched at it with one hand before collapsing. She let the fire burn out, then she slowly slid to the ground as her actions caught up to her. This was the first time she'd killed someone without being in her mysterious rage. She couldn't look at the body, and kept her eyes down until Keanin came and took her shoulder.

"My god, Jenna." His voice was weak. "Are you all right?"

Jenna forced her eyes up to his face. "I never killed anyone before," she whispered, looking into the brush where the body lay. Keanin gave her an odd look. "The other times, it wasn't me. I mean, it was, but not all me. The other times I've fought, something else took over." She wrapped her arms around her knees.

"I can imagine it's not easy." Keanin laid an arm around her shoulders.

The two sat there in silence until the others returned. Most of them seemed to be all right. Two of Kern's guards and one of Crell's archers were injured, but only one needed help to walk.

Jenna held her feelings in check. She was upset at the way they had all so mindlessly run after the ambush, but at the same time she didn't know what the proper procedure for attacking an ambush was.

"Is Ghortin there?" Storm asked as he came to where they were sitting. He hadn't noticed the body yet and Jenna didn't feel like pointing it out.

"No, he seems to have left again," she said before a familiar voice sounded in her head.

"*May I, lass?*" Jenna gathered by his tone that he was aware of what happened.

"*Be my guest.*" She let him take over.

"I'm here, boy. That was a damn foolish thing all of you did, running into that ambush. I'm glad to see the damages weren't worse."

Storm looked down briefly. Obviously he realized that it hadn't been the best reaction, but he was too proud to say it. "We had to do something; besides, it's over."

"And next time you damn fools will do the same thing. Ki' Crell's people are trained for such maneuvers, the rest of you are not. And I won't have this campaign endangered because you young idiots keep thinking you're invincible." Jenna felt Ghortin's indignation and was pleased that she hadn't said anything. It came out with much more force when it was from him. Even when it was coming out of the same body. The tension in him eased a bit and she felt a light flutter as if he mentally hugged her. "And if you'd pay attention, you would see that these two companions of yours are ill at ease and that there is a dead bandit in the grass behind us. Jenna had to kill him unassisted. It was her first, and she's taking it hard."

Storm jerked his head up and finally saw the body. Grimly, he pulled out the knife and wiped it on the grass before handing it back.

"I'm sorry. But what do you mean 'it was her first'? She's killed others, I've seen her."

"Not really. I haven't been able to pinpoint the source, but something seems to take her over at times. It appears to be in events of high stress. It might have something to do with the echo, or something else entirely. Whatever it is, it didn't happen this time. She did it on her own. However, she will have to grieve later. What did you find out about the bandits?"

"That they weren't good at their job and there were only twelve of them. They were all killed, so we couldn't interrogate anyone. Edgar thinks they weren't local bandits at all, but a trap set for us."

"I'd say he's right; Edgar is rarely wrong on such things. I'd say whatever forces are behind these attacks are finding multiple ways to get to us. I think we should try to put as much distance between us and here as we can. I'm giving way to Jenna, she needs time to process things. However, I'll be back when we set up camp; don't think you young fools are getting away with that stunt you pulled."

Storm started to defend himself and the others, then realized it was Jenna before him and not Ghortin. Sighing, he helped her and Keanin up and the three of them went to join the others.

CHAPTER TWENTY-SEVEN

———

THE WARY GROUP CONTINUED ON for another two hours after the injured were sent back to the temple. Not a single bush was passed without close scrutiny, but no one else attacked them.

True to his word, Ghortin stayed out of contact with Jenna, leaving her to dwell on the dead bandit. No matter how many times she told herself that he would have killed Keanin and herself if she hadn't done it, or that she had killed before, it didn't matter. She kept seeing the horrified look on his face when she threw the fireball at him.

They'd found a suitable camp and she was almost finished getting her tent up when Crell paid a visit.

"Heard you got a nasty surprise earlier. I wanted to see how you are holding up." Her open face was lit with a compassionate smile.

Jenna forced a tight smile of her own. "I think I'll be all right. I feel foolish going to pieces because I had to kill a single bandit. No one else has lost it, and they've had to kill many times." She didn't want to try to explain her strange situation to Crell, especially since she didn't know how much she was supposed to tell anyone.

Crell laid a small weather-beaten hand on her arm. "I know, lass. I'm not sure I understand how or why, but Storm made it clear that this was the first time you'd been aware when you killed someone. I'd like to tell you it gets easier, but I don't believe in lying." She paused, searching Jenna's face. "My people have a custom. After a young warrior has had their first kill in battle, a seasoned warrior befriends them, and they talk. Not so much about the killing, but about life. It strengthens our ties and helps us get through a difficult time. I would like to help you, if you'll let me."

The offer was sincere. Jenna knew that if she said no, the derawri warrior would leave without ill will. But Jenna realized she wanted someone to talk to. Someone other than her two brooding kelar companions. She covered Crell's small hand with her own. "I'd like that."

As Crell nodded and sat down, Jenna thought of one question that had been on her mind which had nothing at all to do with killing or battles.

"Why do you call Corin, Storm? I thought only Ghortin and I did."

Crell leaned forward with an appreciative smile. "Very observant. And a good way to start an eve of talk." She pulled out a small silver flask and offered a sip to Jenna before continuing. Jenna took the offered sip, and managed to hide her grimace as the fiery liquid burned down her throat. Crell nodded and took a much larger sip.

"I've known Storm since he was a wee lad. He's always been a terror, never fitting in and whatnot. My family is tied to his; my line is sworn to protect the royal family. Since I was the youngest in our line, I was given the children to watch. That young Corin was a hellion. He knew that if he got into trouble he wouldn't have to go to the boring court events, so he got into as much trouble as possible. He'd whip through the chambers like a boar in rut, knocking things all around. I never caught him, but I had a pretty good idea who was doing it. I also had a good idea why. So, whenever they'd ask if I knew who did it, I'd say some storm must have been through here." She laughed and took another long draw from the bottle. "That boy would get so mad at me since I wouldn't say it was him. The first few times he tried to tell people it was him. I said I'd been watching him, and he'd done no such thing. I wasn't going to make it easy for him to shirk his courtly duties, even at that age. He finally gave up trying to claim credit, but took to just answering to the name Storm." She shook her head with a wry grin at the memory. "That lad was a handful, but I respected him for it in a way; so I've called him Storm ever since. And now there are two of us. I'd say that's a fine place to start a friendship."

Jenna nodded in agreement as she watched the rest of the group settle in for the night. She felt a little bad about not helping set things up, but she reasoned she would volunteer to set up magical protection around the camp once they'd settled. She wasn't yet skilled enough to hide a group this large and spread out, but she could at least set wards a distance from the camp that would tell them if something dangerous was coming. The other mage in the group, Frankon, a thin, dreary man of Kern's guard, said such a thing was a waste and below his abilities. Jenna surreptitiously probed him magically and could tell he wasn't much above apprentice level himself. He also lacked her innate Power, and more than likely would never get much higher in his life. She left him alone after that, doing the things that she knew he couldn't.

"*Thinking of me again are you?*" Ghortin's voice echoed cheerfully in her mind. He sounded much better than he had when he'd left.

"*Only indirectly. We've settled camp, do you want to chastise them now?*" She'd noticed Edgar and Storm shooting questioning glances her way for the past hour or so. They both knew that Ghortin would be giving them hell for their role in the morning's attack on the bandits, and they didn't want to be caught unaware.

"*Yes, if you don't mind. It won't take too long.*" As he spoke, Jenna mentally stepped aside to let him do his worst.

"Fair Ki' Crell, could I trouble you for a few minutes? I

have some foolish idiots to talk to, and I think you should be part of it."

"So that's why Jenna's face went slack all of a sudden. I'd thought she'd taken too much drink. I assume you're going to be yelling at Storm, Edgar, and the rest?"

"My dear, I do not yell, I discuss."

Jenna gave a snort at that, one that was echoed by Crell.

"You forget, old man. I've heard your discussions. Been on the receiving end a few times. Don't go too hard on them, they fought well, and it was my fault as much as theirs. I should have told them to stay clear."

"I haven't forgotten anything." Jenna gave Ghortin a mental poke, then he amended, "Well, not much any-way. Or so we hope. Actually, what I want you to do is get those lumps working together. We have too many separate things going on here. We'll all be together until Lithunane, perhaps longer. We need to be a cohesive unit."

Ghortin still hadn't let anyone in on what his plans were once he returned to Lithunane.

"So you've decided to do something?" Crell said.

"Why does everyone always feel they have to know everything that's going on? I'm not able to know for certain how long this will go on; not until we've reached Lithunane at any rate. But, who knows? We have just begun our journey, and no one is able to say where they will end up. Now, if you would be so kind as to bring our friends over here, I can get this over with and give my poor apprentice back her body."

Crell nodded with a smile and dusted herself off. "Your wish is my command."

She returned a few minutes later with Storm, Edgar, and Captain Kern. Lagging behind, and trying to look like he wasn't following, was Kern's thin mage, Fran-kon. He seemed fascinated whenever Ghortin made an appearance and usually endeavored to be somewhere close by.

Crell bowed. "Your victims, my most powerful mage."

"I'll keep this brief, but don't think that I'm not serious. If any of you pull something like that again, I'll send you back." He grimly forced each one of them to meet his eyes—or rather, Jenna's eyes. "We're not yet sure what we're up against, but it all points to something big. Something that we can't afford to lose against because of juvenile heroics. Those bandits were untrained, and I think someone put them together quickly for our benefit. The next time they may get better help. And we can be assured there will be a next time. I think that someone doesn't want us going to Lithunane, which is all the more reason to get down there as quickly and safely as possible. I want all of you to work with Ki' Crell and her people. They are trained for this type of fighting. If she says hold back, you hold." He studied all three faces to make sure he'd gotten through. Jenna was surprised that none of them protested in the slightest. Then she looked at them through Ghortin's perception.

All three were experienced fighters; they realized how close that ambush had been to doing serious damage to them. Ghortin wanted to drive the point home and get them working under a single command. None of them would question any command Crell gave them, at least not during this trip.

"I'll leave you to Ki' Crell, but don't think I'm not watching you all. And soon, goddess willing, I'll be back in my own, much larger, body, if you take my meaning."

Jenna felt him slip away, and found four sets of eyes, five if you counted Frankon, trained on her. She raised a hand and shrugged. "Don't blame me; I'm just a body in this."

Everyone relaxed when they realized that the master-mage was gone. A minute later Jenna was completely alone, although Crell had only left to get food for the two of them.

Jenna was straightening out her sleep sack when she felt eyes upon her. Turning, she caught Frankon giving her a strangely hungry glance. He dropped it immediately, but didn't move away.

"Good eve, apprentice Jenna," he said stiffly. "I was wondering if Ghortin was around."

Jenna held her snide comment in check. She'd been trying to hide this moron's lack of skills, and here he was, treating her like she was nothing more than a servant.

"Not at present. I'm afraid he keeps his own schedule."

She expected him to be disappointed and leave, but instead he edged closer.

"I was wondering if you could tell me some things then." His smile barely lifted the corners of his mouth. "I was wondering what it was like to have so much Power at work inside you. Can you truly do everything that the mastermage could?"

There was a decidedly unhealthy gleam in his eyes, but Jenna didn't know what was causing it. So she decided to play it safe.

"I believe so. We haven't come across anything yet that we couldn't handle." She gave the mageling a closer look. She didn't feel any danger from him, and Ghortin said he seemed harmless, but she couldn't shake the weird, skin crawling feeling she got whenever he was around.

"Is there anything we can help you with, mage?" Crell said sarcastically as she returned. She only liked a few magic users, and Frankon wasn't one of them. The undernourished-looking mage jumped out of his skin when she spoke from behind him.

"No." He composed himself, straightening out his robes slowly as if he hadn't been surprised by her appearance. "I was inquiring as to the status of her mentor. Good eve, apprentice." With a dismissive nod, he walked away briskly.

Crell chuckled at his retreating back. "I love being able to do that to him. That man is such a mole dog." She came forward and handed Jenna a small bowl of stew and some flat bread. She also laid a canteen full of water next to her, for which Jenna was eternally grateful. That fiery stuff that the derawri fighter preferred might seem mild to her, however it was anything but, to Jenna. Now she knew where Storm had gotten such a strong tolerance for the drink.

Jenna looked around the camp as she and Crell ate in silence. Looking back toward Storm, a question popped its way out before she thought about it.

"Has Storm ever been in love?" She looked away from Crell as soon as the words were out, hoping vainly that the sharp-eared warrior hadn't heard her.

"Now where'd that come out of all of a sudden?" Crell looked up with a twinkle in her eye. "Could it be our young prince has caught the eye of a fair apprentice?"

"No, I thought…" Jenna stumbled, thinking frantically; she had no reason why that came into her head. Aside from some personal thoughts that she wasn't up to dealing with yet. "I was thinking how sad it is that he was almost married to someone he didn't love, and that he'll probably end up in another forced match."

Crell almost choked on a piece of bread. "What do you mean, 'he was almost married'? Did something wonderfully awful happen to that wretched Mikasa that I haven't been told about? There is something evil lurking behind her simpering, mark my words."

Jenna kicked herself. Maybe Storm hadn't wanted anyone to know. But surely he wouldn't mind one of his oldest friends knowing.

"It happened at the temple. Actually, it happened back in Lithunane, before Tor Ranshal and Sir Edgar set out. Mikasa gave Edgar a note for Storm. Edgar gave it to Keanin to give to Storm on Cathedral Island." She paused for a bit of dramatic effect. When Crell looked ready to take the words from her by force, she continued. "It seems Mikasa was troubled by the recent violence and has decided it's too dangerous to love a prince. She broke off the engagement."

Crell gave a whoop, one that was toned down, but yet gave Jenna a taste of what it could have been if they had been in a safe environment.

"That scamp. He didn't mention it. Well, I suppose we've been a bit busy today, so I'll forgive him. I think this requires a celebration." She unstopped her flask and took a long draw.

"Let's go find our newly single prince." She pulled Jenna to her feet and took off after the unsuspecting Storm.

Storm was leaving Edgar when Crell grabbed a hold of him. She swung him in a circle, gleefully laughing at his confused expression.

"You scoundrel. Why didn't you tell me of your joyous news? It's not every day you get unengaged you know." She turned to Jenna. "You wouldn't have been exposed to her much, but she was a vicious little thing to anyone who couldn't advance her status."

Storm rubbed his face as he realized what the reason for the commotion was. "You heard? I didn't think it would be proper to be seen celebrating such a somber situation." He tried not to smile, but failed.

Crell thumped him in the leg, and he gave up trying to look serious. "Since when did I raise you to be proper? I think we should celebrate." She handed her flask to Storm, who took a long pull. He started to give it to Jenna, but she waved him aside, as Ghortin popped in with a few mental reminders.

"Thank you, but no. As Ghortin so kindly reminded me, we've a ways to travel tomorrow, and I'm not going to waste all my energy healing hangovers. Besides, I have to go set the wards."

Crell swung her around. "How about a small celebration? Don't forget, you and I are still going through your rite of warrior-hood."

Jenna started to shake her off, then gave up. From what she'd seen of Crell so far, the small woman would make an interesting debate partner for Ghortin. It was difficult to say which one was more stubborn. "It's a deal. I'll meet you back at my tent after I set the wards."

Crell nodded and wandered back toward the center of camp with Storm.

Jenna gathered a cloak of chaotic energy around her in preparation for her spell. It wasn't a difficult one, but it had to be perfectly balanced or one side would draw energy from the other, leaving one side unwarded. She decided to set the boundaries a little ways out. The first night Frankon had argued that such distant wards were a waste of energy. Jenna countered by pointing out the uselessness of a ward that warned you only when the enemy was upon you. Crell sided with Jenna, and the matter had been decided. She let the Power of chaos mingle with the words of the spell for a few seconds. This 'pre-mixing', as she liked to call it, seemed to give her spells more definition. Although Ghortin said it was an odd way to go about it, he hadn't been able to find fault with the results.

When she'd given the chaotic Power a chance to know what it was to do, she began to ease it out into the air around her. She was so proud that the spell seemed to be settling nicely that she almost missed a small tug on it.

By the time she sent her consciousness along the spell to find out what it was, the source was gone. She would mention it to Ghortin when he came back, but would keep a close eye out herself. It could have been nothing, or it could have been someone pulling away from her spell.

Satisfied that the spell would last the night, Jenna wandered back to her semi-celebrating friends. For some reason she couldn't tell the difference between semi-celebrating and real celebrating.

CHAPTER TWENTY-EIGHT

——◆——

TEN DAYS LATER, JENNA SWORE as another blast of freezing air stabbed through her cloak. Just when she thought she was as cold as she could get, some misfit of the wind gods came to prove her wrong. Ghortin had made it very clear that magicking up some more supplies in this situation would drain her magic.

It had been getting steadily colder the past ten days, as they moved into the Scareani Mountains. For the last day and a half they had been crossing snow-swept plains, with nothing more than undernourished shrubs for protection from the stinging cold. Everyone's nerves had been on edge, which, combined with the bitter winds, had made for a quiet trip.

A few hours after mid-day, Crell held up her hand, motioning to stop for the night's camp. It was an early stop, but they were near the base of Taria, the largest of the mountains that made up the Scareani range. Crell's scouts had found no better place up ahead, and the small grove of bushes and paltry scraggly trees that Crell was standing in front of would offer at least some protection from the wind.

Keanin wandered miserably up to Jenna, letting his pack drop from frozen fingers. "I may never forgive Corin for this."

The formerly flashy and flamboyant kelar walked with his head and shoulders down, barely moving his legs any further than absolutely necessary to keep him from falling too far behind. And from the steady stream of complaining that had been spewing from him, it was clear he felt he was the most maltreated individual in the universe.

Jenna looked around for someone to pawn him off on. "Why don't you go hang out with Aireys? I thought you two were close." She looked around for the archer Keanin had been snuggling with as of late.

He gave a rude snort. "There's something off about that one. I think I should talk to Crell about her archers."

Jenna grinned as signs of the old Keanin peeked through. "She got tired of putting up with your evil ways, eh?"

"Me?" His golden eyes went wide. "I'm the perfect paragon of virtue, as always. Actually, I think she got to talking with Marta." He looked around to catch any eavesdroppers. As if anyone would care, or have the energy to care, about Keanin's love life.

"I think Marta does remember me; she watches me sometimes at meals."

Jenna hadn't noticed. Although she *had* noticed Keanin still glancing at the tall soldier. Which would account for Aireys' cooler reception, particularly if she too noticed Keanin's wandering eye.

"If that were the case, don't you think she would have made some sort of move toward you?" She looked at the ground before them and selected the least lumpy section she could find and started to lay out her tent.

"Not necessarily. She might be shy."

Jenna almost dropped her tent at that. "Are we talking about the same Marta who damn near kissed the life out of you, a total stranger?"

"That was the drink. It could be that—"

Jenna cut him off with a wave. "Forget it. You know I won't believe you. In fact, *you* don't believe you." She looked up to see Storm bearing down on them. "I doubt even Storm, your lifelong friend that he is, would believe you."

Keanin puffed himself up in defense but Storm cut him off.

"I don't want to interrupt, but don't you think Ghortin might want to make an appearance? We'll be reaching Mount Taria and the cave tomorrow."

Jenna hadn't told anyone, but Ghortin's contact had been weak since the ambush ten days ago. Each time he did appear, Ghortin said he couldn't tell any difference in his connection with her, so he hadn't been much help.

"I'll give it a try, but he hasn't been sociable the past few days." She closed her eyes and concentrated on contacting her mentor.

"*Are we there already?*" Ghortin sounded coherent, but his voice had a distant tinny sound to it.

"*No, we're still a day away, but—*"

"*Then why are you bothering me? I've got things to get ready. I'm not completely sure how this transfer thing is going to work, you know. Now, leave me alone until we're there.*"

"*Ghortin, they want you to take charge of this final leg. It is your body after all.*" His response, or rather lack thereof, was worrying. She would have guessed him to be chomping at the bit to get to his body. She knew *she* was anxious to get rid of him.

Ghortin was silent for a few minutes, but Jenna could feel him pulling in his resources. Even if he wouldn't admit to having problems, he was aware of it. When he came back, his voice was steadier, but still slightly echoing, like there was a bad connection.

"*I don't think I should. We're being followed,*" he said.

It was common knowledge that someone, or someones, had been following them since the ambush at the lake. That none of Crell's expert scouts had been able to get a glimpse of the skulkers said more than enough of their ability. Whoever was behind them wasn't of the same ilk as the untrained bandits they had fought off before.

Ghortin continued with a heavy sigh. "*The person track-*

ing us has magecraft. They haven't used magic yet, except to shield that they have it. I am barely able to sense the shield, but it's there. All I can tell you is that the mage who set the shield is Powerful. I don't think I should make an appearance until we've got my body in hand, so to speak."

Jenna tried to marshal some argument, but soon gave up. Ghortin was still coherent enough to be right. She let him slip back into the dark regions of her mind.

"I'm sorry; Ghortin doesn't feel he should come out until we arrive at the cave."

"What's his problem now? Doesn't he feel it's worthy of him to help find his own blasted body?" Storm was more irritable and edgy than she had ever seen him. Jenna hated to think what they would be like by the time they got out of this winter wonderland. They wouldn't have to worry about enemies stalking them, they'd kill each other.

"For once, I agree with him. Ghortin said our mysterious follower is mage-gifted, but he can't tell anything more than that because their block is too good. He doesn't want to show himself until we're at his body." She hesitated, and then decided to tell Storm the other reason. "And he's not sure how to get himself back into his body. I think he's trying to work something out as we go."

Storm looked up into the gray sky, mumbling curses barely louder than the wind. "When was he going to tell us this? When we fought our way to the cave and he couldn't do anything?"

"No," Jenna snapped back. Sometimes Storm forgot that other people might have reasons that he hadn't thought of. "Ghortin is who he is. Not only would his pride be injured by admitting ignorance, but his reputation could be as well, possibly fatally. You know a mage relies on how other people think of him. It's almost more important than actual skill."

Storm frowned, but relented. "Fine, I understand. But you get to tell Crell we're without Ghortin on this. I'm sure not going to." As he spoke, Storm took hold of her arm and propelled her toward the flame-haired warrior. Who, like most of the crew at this point, had a deep frown on her face.

Crell arched one perfect brow at the mode of Jenna's arrival.

Jenna shot Storm an evil glare as she pulled her arm free, then turned back toward Crell. "Storm wants me to tell you that Ghortin isn't going to be much help at all until we get to the cave. The person following us has magecraft, and Ghortin doesn't want them to pick him up magically."

"I can't say I like it, I was counting on that—" Crell cut off as a figure came running down the mountain slope in front of them and stumbled into their camp. Dragging Jenna with her, Crell ran forward, shoving onlookers aside. The man was one of her scouts that she'd sent to check the next day's march. He had a bloody gash down his entire left side and his right hand hung shattered from his shredded arm. His face was barely recognizable.

Jenna rushed forward with Crell. They realized that he had lost too much blood to live. His final act had been to warn them. The ravaged face opened an unfocused eye at Crell's touch. Fighting fiercely, he managed to unclench his teeth long enough to whisper her name. Crell tried to quiet him, but he doggedly continued. "Ki', you must know. Came out of nowhere. Got Hjard. Controlled sciretts. Vanished after."

There was a look of profound sorrow on Crell's face as she gravely listened to her man's last report. Jenna knew Crell had seen more death in her life than she would ever wish upon anyone; as Crell had said before, it never grew easier.

Jenna went into her healing trance without thinking.

The man was too weak, but she couldn't let him give up and die. Reaching out, she tried to pull in some of the raging chaotic Power all around them. At first the Power came. Then a wall of brutal darkness slammed into her mind. Blackness threatened to engulf her as she fought to draw in magic the way a drowning woman tries to draw in air. And like a drowning woman, all she did was make matters worse. Forcing her panicking mind to calm down and go slow, she managed to break free of the magic black hole.

She opened her eyes, and weakly took Crell's hand. "I'm sorry, I can't help him. I can't reach any Power."

Crell continued to look at her scout's face, barely hearing Jenna's words. "Don't worry, he's beyond help now." Still dry-eyed, Crell lowered the dead man's eyelids.

After a few moments, Storm helped Jenna up and led her to her tent. She nodded her thanks, and sat in numbed silence for a while. She couldn't focus on anything. The sciretts that attacked Crell's men must have had a mage with them. One powerful enough to cause a magic block in his wake. They didn't want the man revived and they tried to take out anyone who would have tried to heal him.

Once she'd shaken off the numbness, she realized that Crell needed to be told about the mysterious magic block. After a moment's thought she realized Frankon should be told as well, she wouldn't want to be responsible for him being skewered in a battle because of that debilitating block.

Jenna went over to where the group was gathered around a camp table looking at a map.

Crell was holding a strategy meeting. "Most of the trails in the deep Scareani are thin and twisted. A more perfect place for an ambush couldn't be created if they tried. They were probably waiting for us."

"Crell, I think we've got another problem." Jenna nodded to the rest of the group. "Something went wrong when I tried to heal that scout."

Crell's face changed from worry at Jenna's initial words, to relieved sisterly concern. "Now, don't you go blaming yourself, or your magic. He was dead before he hit the camp. You tried, that's what counts."

Jenna shook her head. "That's not what I mean. When I tried to call up Power to heal him, I was blocked. I don't know if it was something to do with his attackers or his injuries or something of this region. But I was almost pulled under. I think we should assume that whoever is traveling with and controlling those sciretts has magic well beyond mine."

"Or whoever is following us feels we're getting too close," Storm added grimly. From the looks on Kern and Edgar's faces, they had already been apprised of the situation with Ghortin.

"That's possible," Jenna granted, although for some reason she didn't think it was the case. The person following them had been careful not to use magic so far. She wouldn't even know they were a mage if Ghortin hadn't told her. "Either way, I don't think Frankon or I will be able to fight with magic if we're attacked."

Crell's frown grew deeper. "Thank you for the warning. We'll pass it along." A look of disgust crossed Crell's fine-boned face. "Could you warn Frankon? I doubt if he'd believe anything I tell him."

Jenna nodded as the others went back to their plans. She didn't mention that the sickly mage more than likely wouldn't believe her either. But, pompous conjurer or not, he deserved to be warned.

Unfortunately, Jenna was right about how the thin mage would take her warning.

He took her hand as she tried to drum the information into his head and gave her a patronizing smile. "There, there. Now I know this whole situation can be trying for one so new in the arts. I'm sure it was a little case of emotional blackout. Has Ghortin been in contact since then?" As Jenna shook her head, he added condescendingly, "Then I can tell you what he would tell you. Just rest and regain your strength. I'm sure you'll feel fine in the morning."

Jenna unclenched her left hand and repressed her overwhelming urge to punch the idiot. She'd given him his warning. Three times in fact. If he was too stubborn to take it; well, that couldn't be helped. With a tense nod, she went back to her tent.

CHAPTER TWENTY-NINE

———◆———

THE ATTACK ON CRELL'S TWO scouts had forced a change in direction to get to the cave. Unfortunately, as Ghortin pointed out, there were only two ways to the Cave of Sorrows—their original way and the way they were now planning on going. Those were the only options.

Keanin and Jenna were chatting as they trudged up the steep mountainside. She'd figured out that asking him about royal gossip—any royal—kept him from whining about the terrain and weather. She was rapidly becoming an expert on people she'd never met, from lands she'd never heard of.

She went silent as they came around a sharp turn in the trail. They had climbed fast and hard as soon as day had broken, but she hadn't realized how high they'd gotten until she looked out from this bend. A valley lay hidden within the close-knit mountains. Like the mountains themselves, and the plains behind them, the small valley was cloaked in a dusting of white. From this distance and angle, it was absolutely breathtaking.

"I do hate to interrupt this sightseeing, but I believe we should be quite near the cave. So, if you wouldn't mind?"

Jenna didn't bother to acknowledge Ghortin's irritated request; she did, however, start walking again.

"We'd better get there soon; his crankiness is driving me crazy."

"He's still at it?" Keanin shook his head.

"Who's still at what?" Storm asked as he came up to

them, readjusting his pack. With all of his weapons sticking out of his bundle, he looked like a prickly turtle.

"Ghortin. My mental companion has been getting edgy as we get closer to the cave. He wants this to be over."

"I can't say that I disagree with him," Storm said. "I don't feel comfortable up here. Like we're intruders or something."

Jenna grinned up at her tall friend. "What? The great, fierce, fighting prince showing caution?" She faked a swoon into Keanin's arms. "Catch me, I may faint." Her sarcastic comment ended in a scream as her eyes happened to glance straight above.

Hanging high above them, like so many racks of beef, were well over a dozen corpses. All three species were represented, along with some odd-looking animals. The corpses were encased in a gauzy shroud type covering—one that wasn't enough to hide what was up there. The ice and the odd fabric must have blocked the smell. At ten feet above the trail, the bodies should have been quite pungent.

Storm swore, drew his sword, and made ready to climb the steep mountainside to reach the trees and their grim burdens. Crell was on him in an instant, pulling him down.

"I *know* you weren't thinking of doing anything as stupid as climbing up there." She held on to his tunic tightly, clearly fearing he'd try again.

"We can't just leave them." Storm waved his sword in a wild arc above his head.

"We can and we will. It galls me as well. But more than a few creatures know how to use the dead as bait for the living. 'There's no use killing them that's still livin' for the sake of them that's not.' That's what my Da always said. And I agree with him. Now get down, and keep walking." She turned around to face the gathering group.

With a sigh she freed one hand from Storm to point up to their grisly find.

"Look well. This is what can happen to you. So pay close attention to the trail and your mates. Now, we've a task to finish, so, ladies and gentlemen, if you will kindly move it."

Hauling Storm along like an errant child, she stalked back to the front of the line. She also ignored Storm's requests to be let go. It wasn't until they were a good half hour away that she released the annoyed, but no longer irrational, prince.

Jenna noticed a horrific odor not too long after that. She shot a furtive look up, half afraid more bodies would be dangling overhead, but there was nothing. However, the further up they went, the worse the smell got. Soon, most of the people behind her were coughing and lagging behind. Crell was walking faster now, and Jenna found it difficult to keep pace with the much shorter derawri.

A twinge told Jenna they were close. She caught up to Crell. "The cave is nearby. Ghortin can tell."

Crell looked grimly ahead to the next bend. "I was afraid you were going to say that." She frowned, her nose wrinkling up at the awful smell. "Well, there's nothing to do for it except to find out, I suppose."

The two women rounded the corner cautiously, with Storm and Edgar not too far behind.

The rest of their people held back, ready should they be needed.

The bend led them to a small cave opening, set a good two feet above the trail. The mouth was wide, probably about four feet across, more or less in the shape of a circle. From Ghortin's response, Jenna knew that this was the Cave of Sorrows. Less fortunate was the fact that it was also the location of the putrid odor.

"Don't tell me, this is the mysterious Cave of Sorrows,"

Edgar said as he came closer. The wiry kelar had a pained look on his face as he looked at Jenna for confirmation.

"Unfortunately, yes. At least Ghortin says this is where his body is. I suppose I should go in and get this over with."

Crell stepped forward and stopped Jenna before she took a step. "I don't think that would be a wise idea. We've no idea what else is in there. Or what that smell is that's gracing our presence."

She turned to Edgar, motioning to the group behind them. "I'll need two of the strongest fighters with the best stomachs to go in and get Master Ghortin."

Storm stepped forward. "I'll be one."

Crell looked up into his blue eyes intently, a small frown creasing her brow. "Are you certain? It's liable to be hideous in there."

"I'm certain. If anyone gets the opportunity to drag that old mage out by his heels, it should be me."

Crell looked at her one-time ward with a serious eye. "I suppose you'll do. Edgar, just find me one. Preferably someone of the same stature as Storm here. It'll make carrying Ghortin's body out easier."

Edgar nodded and disappeared, only to reappear moments later with a familiar face in tow.

Marta nodded to Crell in lieu of a formal salute. "I'm ready to help."

Crell gave her a nod. "I've no idea what else is in there, but we do know that Ghortin's body is in there somewhere. You just need to grab him and get out."

"What about me?" Jenna asked quietly. "Ghortin says we should go in; there may be a spell hiding the body."

She wasn't anxious to see what was making that smell, especially after their gruesome find back down the trail. But Ghortin's urging was almost obsessive.

Storm frowned and shook his head. "That's not a good idea. It's not safe for you. Or for Ghortin." He seemed to add the last part as an afterthought.

While Jenna thought his concern for her was sweet, she also knew Ghortin wasn't going to let it go any other way. "I don't have a choice. I *need* to go in."

Crell ran her hand through her hair and threw a worried look over her shoulder toward the cave mouth. "I'm not trying to make light of your abilities or training, but what if you collapse? I don't think even these two giants could get you and that monster of a mage out in one shot."

"I'm not going to pass out. If something starts to happen, I'll leave. I don't want to do this either, but Ghortin thinks it's necessary."

Crell took a deep breath. "Okay, but at the first sign of something bad, or if you start feeling odd, I want you out of there." She waved the three toward the dark entrance.

The cave was pitch dark and Marta pulled out a small glow light that the army members all carried. Wordlessly, she stepped ahead of Storm and crawled up into the cave. He and Jenna were close behind.

The first few feet of the cave were dry and tight, but taller than the opening. They could all stand and, as long as they stayed single file, they didn't hit the sides. The smell was almost overwhelming here, but so far there wasn't any sign of the source.

Jenna heard Marta gasp as she reached a deeper section of the cave. Storm was silent as he approached. But a shudder ran across his broad shoulders. Preparing herself for the worst, she moved forward and around Storm to see ahead.

She hadn't braced herself enough. The light of the glow fell upon a sight so wretched that nothing could have stopped her from running back out of that cave. Almost nothing. Across the gruesome chamber lay the one thing that could, and did, stop her: Ghortin's empty body.

Unfortunately, the ten or so feet lying between them

and his body was something out of hell itself.

The room's floor was a good two feet lower than the path they were standing on. It was buried in torn apart bodies. They seemed to form a grisly offering to a sick and twisted deity, with Ghortin's untouched body as the crowning piece. That the entire cave was some sort of sacrificial altar was obvious, even to Jenna.

Jenna steadied herself and forced her eyes away from the awful sight. Marta was already scouting around for the easiest way to get to Ghortin's body, and Storm was trying to find some sort of identifying marks from the less mangled body parts.

"Damn," he swore as he identified tattoos on a shoulder and an ankle sticking out of the macabre pile. "We found at least one of the lost villages, or some of the former villagers."

Jenna laid an almost steady hand on his back. "From the Markare?" They were hundreds of miles away from the desert, yet somehow she knew in her gut that these poor souls had made the trip alive. Which raised a good question. "Why would they have been brought this far to be killed?"

"I don't know why they were killed." Storm turned away from the sight with a pale face. "This is beyond even the horrors of Qhazborh's followers. Does Ghortin have anything to say?"

Jenna searched inside her head for a moment, but came up empty. She could tell he was still there, but she couldn't reach him. Most likely he was readying whatever spell he thought to use to get him back to his body. Providing they could manage to get it out.

"Ah-ha." Marta waved to some dark shapes off to the side. "We can use these." As she spoke, she held up two wide planks for them to see.

"Why would they have those there?" An answer hit Jenna as she spoke. She sent a probing spell over the twisted bodies. She kept it low level so she wouldn't distract Ghortin, but she got her answer all the same. The seemingly freshly killed bodies were actually being maintained by a protective spell. They were being held in stasis from just after death.

Rather than Ghortin being there first and the bodies added, it was the other way around. The two planks were used by whoever took the mage's body to place him above the grisly tribute.

Storm was also confused by Marta's find, until Jenna explained her probe to them. With a grim nod, he took one of the huge red oak planks from the soldier and gently laid it across the mangled bodies. "If it worked for them, it'll work for us."

He and Marta made their way, slowly but steadily, to Ghortin's resting place. Jenna started to pull up a spell to make sure no traps awaited them, but she couldn't seem to remember how. Shaking her head, she tried again but found herself lost in a mind fog. She thought she noticed Marta turning toward her with an odd look, and part of her mind screamed in warning, but the look and the scream evaporated as soon as they reached Ghortin's body.

His body was crisscrossed with a myriad of intricate protection spells that had Ghortin's own signature. That explained why his body was offered here but not destroyed. His attackers could move him, but they couldn't hurt him.

She was about to shout a warning anyway, so they'd be aware of Ghortin's spells, when they reached the body and unceremoniously lifted it up.

Storm and Marta made it back to Jenna without trouble. They were almost to the cave's mouth when an odd rumble came from behind them. Jenna looked back at the spot where Ghortin had lain. She couldn't remember why she hadn't checked for spells around Ghortin's body, the fog she'd experienced blocked out that entire few minutes. If his kidnappers couldn't put a spell on him, it would be logical to bespell the inanimate material beneath him. Jenna swore as a spell glimmered under her probe.

"Run! Something's been triggered and I can't stop it!" She pushed the others until they were free of the cave. Looking back she saw what the spell had triggered. The dead body parts were moving in a weird disjointed dance. And they were flopping toward the cave's mouth and the outside. In a whirl, Jenna formed and aimed a disruption spell at the roof of the cave. She held it steady and pulled it toward her as she backed out of the cave, forcing the entire mountainside to collapse on the remains of the unfortunate villagers.

Jenna tumbled out of the cave mouth just before the hillside completely collapsed down on the opening of the cave. Storm and Marta barreled down the hill as fast as they could without jarring their precious cargo. Crell took one look at their faces and ordered the rest of the troops to follow. Edgar hung back with her and they half dragged a dust-choked Jenna down the trail as soon as she rolled free of the landslide.

***

Once Crell decided they were far enough away, she slowed down and Jenna motioned to the side of the trail. Crell helped her over as Jenna fell to her knees and became violently ill.

Edgar and Crell exchanged concerned glances over Jenna's heaving back, but said nothing. Both of them had enough magesense to have felt the sheer amount of Power she'd sent into that cave roof. For whatever reason, Jenna had risked herself, and the others, to keep something in that cave. Thinking of the rancid smell that had come from the cave when they approached, Crell didn't want to ask, but she knew she had to find out eventually.

Leaning forward, she gently rubbed Jenna's back. "Easy, honey. It'll be all right. Let your body do what it has to, and don't fight it."

Jenna coughed once more with a shudder, then reached out and pulled some of the long trail grass. Crell thought for a moment that Jenna had finally snapped, when she realized she was wiping her mouth with it. Finally, she turned to face Crell and Edgar.

"I'm sorry I didn't warn anyone, and I hope no one was hurt. But I couldn't take the chance that even one of those things would get out." She shuddered again, and for a brief moment looked like she was going to be ill once more. The spasm passed without incident. Taking a few deep breaths to calm herself, Jenna went on. "We found Ghortin's body in the middle of some sort of religious altar. There were mangled body parts all around it. Storm said the bodies were from some of the missing villages near the Markare. When he and Marta removed Ghortin's body, they triggered a spell." She paused; the look of disgust that crossed her features was directed inward now. "A spell I didn't think to look for. It animated the body parts of those poor people. I had no idea how strong the spell was, so I had to use everything I could to make sure they didn't get out." She hung her head. It was obvious to Crell that Jenna had thrown everything into that spell; and was willing to trap herself in there if that had been the only way to stop it.

Crell looked up as Storm came back up the trail, minus his cargo.

"Is she all right?" he asked, as he saw Jenna near the trail.

As Crell nodded, she happened to see his eyes. Whatever the tie was between Storm and Jenna, it was a strong one. She'd not seen that much concern on her former ward's face for anyone for a long time. Interesting.

Jenna raised her head. "I'm fine." Her voice was weak, like she'd just run ten miles backward. "Someone has to go back and make sure nothing got out."

Looking at the lass, Crell seriously doubted Jenna would be able to do anything about it if something had made it out, but decided she most likely knew that as well.

Storm squinted through the slowly settling dust up the trail. It was clear, even at this distance, that the collapse had been huge. "I'll go make certain." He drew his sword, more for effect than any real sense of danger. "Wait for me here."

Crell had Jenna standing by the time Storm returned.

"You did it. Everything in that cave is now flatter than a pressed flower; half of the hillside filled it in. How about I give you some help down?"

Jenna looked ready to shake him off out of pride, then stopped with a wince. "Thanks. I'm afraid I'm overburdening Crell here."

The diminutive fighter smiled wryly, "Not at all, my dear. I've lugged bigger and taller ones than you off a battlefield. But I'll be the first to admit that I lack the grace of our young giant here." She smiled up at Storm. "She's all yours."

As Crell stepped aside, Storm moved in to pick up Jenna. With a sigh of resignation, she slid her arms around Storm's neck.

CHAPTER THIRTY

CRELL COMMANDED JENNA TO REST before she attempted to contact Ghortin. Jenna agreed, but had only meant to rest her eyes. Therefore, she was more than a little surprised when she finally stirred at the muted sounds of the first watch changing over to the second.

"Goodness, child, I thought you were going to sleep for days." Ghortin's mind voice was so quick to acknowledge her that she had a feeling he had more to do with her awakening than the guards outside.

"Well, I'm sorry," she snapped back. *"It may happen to you on a regular basis, but that's the first time I've had to pull down an entire mountainside."* She grimly refused to think about what she'd pulled the mountain down over.

"Yes, yes. I searched your memories while you were asleep. I must say, you are quite a bit of a powerhouse. It wasn't exactly the way I would have done it, mind you, but quite effective nonetheless." He paused. *"If you're ready?"*

Jenna mentally pulled back. How could he possibly be ready for the transfer so soon? Shouldn't there be preparation of some sort? Ghortin snorted with laughter when she asked him. What, he inquired cheerfully, did she think he'd been doing since they heard of the location of his body? No, he ewas quite ready, she had regained her strength, and it was best if they did this before anyone knew she was awake.

At Ghortin's insistent urging, Jenna left her cot and stepped over to the cot that Ghortin's body was in. Ghortin's body took over most of the small cot, so she slumped down on the ground next to it.

"*Now reach out with your magic. Just enough to activate the spells of warding I've laid.*"

Jenna did, and met again with the brightly woven strands of Ghortin's protective spell. "*Now what?*" She fought to keep the tension out of her mental voice. Ghortin might be confident that this would go off without a hitch; she, however, was not.

"*Now you sit back and feed me Power. Actually, it would help if you concentrated on me being back in my body.*" He came back with a word of caution. "*But don't think of any spells. Even if you think you know what to do, or if that other presence shows up. This is going to be tricky enough without worrying about overlapping spells.*"

"*I don't have any problem with that; but I can't speak for the echo. If it shows up, I'll try to make it understand.*" She paused as movement from outside the tent flap caught her eye. "*Are you sure we shouldn't at least call in someone?*"

"*I'm sure. Nothing against any of them, but they'd be a hindrance. I'm starting the spell, so relax and pull in Power.*"

She threw herself into pulling the chaotic energy into her body, amazed at how quickly Ghortin was using it. She couldn't see the entire spell, even though it was going on inside her head. The making was intricate; it felt to her like thousands of lace circles merging.

She kept drawing Power, careful not to go wandering into the chaotic realm, but she found that she did need to go a little past its fringes. The bright colors and strange shapes amazed her anew and she almost forgot what they were doing. Until she heard Ghortin's voice. Out loud and no longer part of her mind.

Her eyes flew open. "Ghortin? Are you in there?" She hardly believed it, but she didn't feel him in her head anymore.

"Y-yes," he said weakly as he forced a smile up at her. "We did it, lass. *Now*, you can go call the others."

Storm, Crell, Edgar and Captain Kern all managed to get into the tent once Jenna notified a guard to find them. Frankon hovered right outside, as usual. Ghortin was still weak, but he managed to sit up with assistance.

"I can't tell you how good it feels to be seeing you with my own eyes." He let his eyes linger on each of them, with the longest pause on Jenna. Then he nodded to Crell.

"I'm afraid this took a larger drain out of me than I would have thought. I won't be ready for travel for at least a day or two. I'm glad to say that I don't know how Jenna feels, but I'd guess she's in the same state."

Jenna smiled. It was odd not having his presence inside her brain. But what with the echo, and the outside spell-using entity, she decided she wouldn't be lonely. "Good guess, oh, wise teacher."

Crell looked from one to the other. "Done and granted, we will rest for a few days. First watch thinks our shadow is back." She shrugged, sending a ripple down her mane of red hair. "I guess whoever it is isn't fond of the Scareani; for which I can't say I blame him." She started to help Jenna back to the other cot, then stopped. "Storm, could I prevail upon you? We need to get Jenna back into her tent and your stuff over here."

Storm moved toward Jenna, then Crell's words sunk in. "My stuff? Where am I going?"

"We're short a tent." Crell waggled a small finger at him. "You don't think I'm going to spend the night with this cantankerous old sod, do you? That's what you young 'uns are for. Now scoot."

Storm rolled his eyes, but picked up Jenna and did what he was told. "And people say *I'm* stubborn."

Jenna was almost asleep again by the time he got her set up in her tent. The way he was being overly gentle with her, he probably thought she was asleep already.

"Thank you," she managed to mumble.

Storm smiled. "I was going to tell you to get some sleep, but somehow I don't think that's going to be a problem." He pulled a blanket up around her. "I'll see you when you get up."

Jenna tried to raise herself to respond, but couldn't do more than nod before she completely fell into a dark, dreamless slumber.

"You know, for an all-powerful mage, you certainly can't control your snores. I'll wager all of Lithunane can hear you," Storm growled at the loudly sleeping Ghortin as he roused himself for the last watch. For the past two weeks, he and the mage had been forced to continue their shared living arrangements since there weren't enough tents. While he didn't think it was as bad for him as it must have been for Jenna while Ghortin had been in her head, he also knew she didn't have to listen to his snoring. It was all he could do to refrain from throwing something large and potentially dangerous at Ghortin's head. Storm held himself in check; they were a few hours out of Lithunane's main gates. He'd be free of his unwanted roommate then.

"Good evening, Prince Corin. Rather, good morning. I think I'll catch a nap before true morning." The guard he was relieving looked like he had been ready to take that nap a while ago. Storm wished him pleasant dreams and took his post.

The early morning was quiet, not that he'd expected it to be any different. Their mysterious follower had left them two days ago. Crell theorized that it was obvious at that point where the group was heading, and whoever it was had no wish to go into the city themselves.

That brought up a sore point in Storm's mind. He and Crell had an ongoing argument about what they were to do now that they were within Lithunane's reach.

Storm wanted to rush in, get Ghortin's mysterious book, gather a good-sized fighting force from within the city, and flee before Resstlin could gather himself enough to react. Ghortin had declared that he felt a strong unease in the Markare and in the Anterian Plains that lay between Traanafaeren and the Markare. Ghortin wouldn't bet on it since he hated to wager, but he believed that the King was with that force. Storm's plan was to rescue his father first, and find out what their mysterious enemy was up to later.

Crell agreed that it appeared they would have to go out to the desert, but she disagreed on their tactics. She had tried to convince Storm that stealth would be better than force. Resstlin was sure to have heard about their unauthorized jaunt by now.

Storm knew his oldest brother didn't think much of him. Resstlin grudgingly admitted that Storm was one of the best swordsmen in the kingdom, but Storm's habit of leaving whenever he could, and his blatant dislike of court life, left little love between them. This latest escapade, coupled with the lack of family around to act as intermediaries, might be very bad for Storm. If Resstlin caught him, he most likely would lock him in his chambers for a very long time. So, even though he could see Crell's point, he refused to sneak into his own home. He still believed that he could get in, get the book, gather some fighters, and get out without Resstlin catching him.

Finally, in the early morning darkness, Storm admitted to himself that Crell might have the right idea. Resstlin did have a black temper, and there was a chance that he would be caught.

Storm kicked a rock into the forest as he made up his mind. As much as it galled him, stealth would be better for all concerned.

"Did that particular rock offend you, or were you thinking of someone else?" a low voice said softly behind him.

Although he hadn't heard Crell until she spoke, Storm gave no indication of surprise. He slowly turned and favored her with a grin.

"Just myself. I've decided you're right about sneaking into Lithunane." He sighed and ran his fingers through his long hair. "I hate being sneaky."

Crell chuckled at his look. "Good thing we've got Edgar with us, then. I'd bet he could sneak in and out of the realm of death without being noticed."

"Actually, I think I have upon occasion," Edgar's voice came out of the darkness behind them. "Or at least it seemed like it at the time."

Crell gave his entirely black outfit and alert face an appraising glance. "Now, I know I didn't put you on watch tonight."

"I was doing a little freelance work. Thought I'd see what I could about the city."

Storm raised a brow at that. Lithunane was still a few hours away. Edgar must have taken off as soon as they set camp.

"And?" Crell prodded.

"And it's been a long trip. Mind if I sit?" The lean spymaster folded gracefully to the ground. Crell glared, then followed suit. Storm stayed standing, his eyes on the dim woods around them. He could listen to Edgar's report without compromising his watch duties.

"Ah, better." Edgar stretched out his legs, studiously ignoring Crell's evil glare. Finally, he acknowledged it.

"Lithunane is under guard. Much heavier than I've ever seen it. But it's still open." He snorted in disgust. "Resstlin has no concept of adequate protection. An apprentice assassin with the Mark on her face could get in past those guards. We should have no trouble tomorrow." He nodded toward Storm. "You've straightened things out with His Highness, I presume?"

"If you mean, has she beaten some sense into me about our sneaking in, yes," Storm answered.

"*Our* sneaking in?" Edgar said.

"I hadn't brought up that part yet, thank you." Crell spoke with such tension that Storm turned back toward her.

"What part? What are you two talking about?" Storm turned back to the woods, but his attention was on Crell.

Crell's voice dropped. "We thought that since most of us won't be going in, it would be good if someone of importance stayed here. Someone who, by his own admission, doesn't like sneaking around."

"What?" Storm turned and glared down at her. "You want me to stay here? While you and the others prepare for our battle?"

Edgar held up a placating hand. "Easy, big fella. We're not preparing for any battle yet. Slip in, get Ghortin's ratty old tome, and slip back out. Nothing more."

"But there will be a battle. You know what we've got to do once we get that book. Something's happening in the Markare, and we have to stop it." Storm crossed his arms and frowned at the two of them. "Or were you planning on leaving me out of that also?" The last people he'd thought would try to keep him out of the loop were Edgar and Crell.

"I swear, sometimes your head is nothing more than rock encased by long hair and a handsome face." Crell stood up and fixed him with one of her better glares. "No, we were not going to leave you out on that one. Aside from your possibly getting killed, there isn't a good enough reason to exclude you from whatever we have to do in the Markare. Unlike the trip to the castle, where there is a good reason not to have you there. And not a single reason for you to be there. We can't risk Prince Resstlin seeing you and shutting us down." She poked at his ribs with her tiny fingers. "Besides I need someone to go with Jenna to the town outskirts. She said something about Tor Ranshal telling her to find that hearth witch, Rachael. I thought you could do that."

Edgar raised a brow at that, but said nothing.

Storm agreed with Edgar's unspoken words, this was most likely a placating gesture thought up at the last moment by Crell. But at least he would be doing something.

He sighed, giving a great show of giving in. "All right. You win again. I'll track down Rachael with Jenna. Does she know why we're supposed to find her?"

"No, I'm afraid our good seneschal was his usual obtuse self. Whatever the reason, you and Jenna could leave at first light. We'll be leaving a little later, but you two won't need nightfall to go into the outskirts. But take care. It won't do to have some farmer say he spotted the missing prince in the poor part of town. Now off with you, I'll finish your watch."

Chapter Thirty-One

———

STORM AND JENNA WERE TRYING to leave at first light. However, Ghortin clucked over his apprentice like a mother hen until she was ready to travel on an empty stomach just to get away from him.

"I'll be fine," Jenna growled for the umpteenth time as she wolfed down her rations.

"Well, in case you run into anyone who—"

She cut her mentor off with an icy glare. "We aren't going to run into anyone who will do anything. We're going to the far side of town, having a talk with Rachael, and then leaving."

"It may take a while. Rachael sometimes goes wandering." Storm came out of his shared tent.

Crell waved them off. "Take your time; we've no idea whether Ghortin's going to remember where he put the book, let alone what spells he put on it. We'll be trying to hide and let him sort it out at the same time. Good thing it's a big castle."

Ghortin nudged Crell with a booted toe. "Be still, woman. At least I think I recall the blasted thing now. Have a bit of faith." He turned back toward Jenna with a frown.

Jenna knew he was going to return to his earlier tirade, so she moved rapidly to follow Storm as he practically ran out of the encampment.

Ten minutes later Storm continued to stride like the bats of hell were behind him.

"Would you slow down? Wearing me out isn't going

to get us there any faster you know." When Storm still showed no sign of slowing down, Jenna stopped in her tracks. "If I collapse, you're going to look pretty stupid carrying me all the way to Lithunane."

Finally he stopped and turned. "All right, I'm waiting." When Jenna simply folded her arms but didn't move, Storm held out his hands in supplication. "I'm sorry; I shouldn't be taking it out on you. I promise to show the utmost kindness and consideration to you from now on." He tilted his head. "Well?"

She started walking again. "I suppose that'll do." Jenna's mind wandered as she looked at the patchy woods around them. The trees here were healthy enough, but there were large areas that they simply refused to grow in. She thought of faery circles and almost started to laugh. She sobered up when she thought of her own situation and realized that little folk with wings were probably more likely than her present life. It was hard to believe that it had only been eight months since she'd been dragged into this world.

She was still pondering that when Storm brought her up short. She didn't notice he'd stopped until his outstretched hand hit her arm. "What in the—"

Storm shook his head and motioned for her to be quiet. He was straining to hear something behind them.

He finally motioned for them to continue walking. After a few moments, Jenna ventured a whisper. "What were we listening for?" She briefly thought of her fanciful thoughts of faeries, but Storm's face was serious.

He kept his voice low and kept moving as if he'd heard nothing, "I think we're being followed. Whoever it is, they're good. I don't think I can catch them before we reach Lithunane."

Jenna let her eyes roam through the woods. That she didn't see anything didn't surprise her. The entire time they had been followed by the mysterious tagalong up north, she hadn't heard or seen a thing.

"Could it be the same person who was following us after the visit to Irissanta's temple?" She kept her voice low.

"Possible. Although we thought they had disappeared a few days ago. If it is, then at least we've narrowed down who it is they are tracking." He grimly looked down at her.

"Me?" It came out little more than a squeak. "Why not you? You are a prince and all."

He shook his head. "A relatively unimportant prince. You, however, have had some unhealthy interest shown in you before."

Jenna started to shake him off, until she remembered that afternoon she'd cornered Ghortin in his lab. He'd told her that someone, or something, had been hunting women who matched her description. Either she looked like the one they were after, or, more likely, she was the one they were after and the other unfortunate women looked like her. She hadn't thought about it when they were being followed before. "But why?"

Storm was silent for so long Jenna wasn't sure if he was thinking about it or didn't want to tell her. "I'm honestly not certain."

Jenna mentally asked the echo if it knew about this. If it did, it wasn't saying. Or she had imagined the whole other being concept and was losing her mind even as they spoke. Unbidden, another answer came to her. "The mindslave."

Storm looked up sharply at Jenna's tone. "What? Here?"

"Not here. I just made a connection. They are after the former mindslave that this body used to belong to." It wasn't the cheeriest of answers, but it was the most plausible.

"That could be." He automatically reached for his sword even though it wasn't there. That had been another fight, this time between he and Edgar; Storm wanted to bring his sword. "But unlikely. Besides, why go through all this to kill her? Unless…" He broke off and looked down at Jenna. "You've never gotten any solid information from the echo, have you?"

"No." A cold finger went down Jenna's spine. "But that's probably it, isn't it? That mindslave knew something."

Storm dropped his intense look. "No, that wouldn't work. I may not know much about the ways of magic, but even I know nothing of the mind survives the sacrifice into mindslave." He shook his head. "There must be something else that we're not seeing."

Jenna nodded glumly and they continued in silence.

Lithunane looked the same as she remembered. After they entered the gates, they would take the far outside roads to Rachael's home to lessen the chances of being seen.

Jenna wiped her hands on her leggings, surprised at how sweaty they were. It was warmer down here, but not warm enough to warrant sweaty palms. She wasn't sure if they were caused by a fear of being caught, or concern about what Rachael would have to say to her. She had a sinking feeling it was the latter.

She had truly liked the strange old woman, even with her odd predictions. But there had been a weird nagging in the back of her mind ever since Tor Ranshal had told her to seek her out. Something that she had seen in his eyes for the briefest of seconds.

Storm pulled up his hood and shuffled slower as they approached the gates.

Two burly guards stood at attention while a third questioned incoming traffic of their intentions within the city walls. "As if a thief or assassin is going to announce himself. They aren't stopping anybody." He kept his voice low nonetheless.

"Intentions?" the bored guard asked.

"We come to look for work." He gave a nod, making sure the hood he wore stayed low over his face.

"Laborers." The guard grunted out, managing to make it sound like a swear word. Another guard, hidden to their sight previously, scribbled it down, and motioned for the two to enter.

They stopped once they were out of sight of the gate. "I'd say they aren't too clear on security. I mean, what's the point of keeping track of who comes in if you don't verify what they say?" Jenna shot a despairing look back where the guards were.

"Exactly. I thought my brother had more sense than that." Storm spared a brief glance back the way they had come, and then headed them out toward the poor section. "It's as if he's not taking the attack seriously."

Jenna had only seen the fringes of the poor section on her previous trip through the city. Now she was being afforded the opportunity to explore the squalor in depth. More than the poor were the number of criminal types watching them with far too much interest.

Storm walked by, seemingly not noticing, but his jaw was tightly clenched and his hand stayed near his knife.

"Has it always been this bad?"

"No. Resstlin's not watching down here either."

It was a longer route to Rachael's house than the way they went before. Storm was taking the most out of the way streets he could find, and twilight was falling when they reached it.

"Rachael, it's us." Storm knocked softly on the door, then harder when she didn't answer.

"Something's wrong." Pulling out a small pick kit that he must have borrowed from Edgar, Storm broke into Rachael's home.

The small place was ransacked, and a faint bloody trail led toward the back door.

"Storm, is she…" Jenna let her words fade at the look

on Storm's face.

Without saying a word, he ran out the back door.

Jenna started to follow, then froze when a horrific stench hit her. With a piece of her tunic held over her nose and mouth, she crept forward.

Storm stood over a decomposing body. "I don't know who this was, but it wasn't a woman, nor a kelar."

CHAPTER THIRTY-TWO

JENNA STARTED TO ANSWER WHEN a ghostly image hit her. Rachael facing a group of thugs who were attacking her. Jenna couldn't see the fight, but the thugs who survived had fled. And Rachael went toward the countryside. "She's okay; she fought them off."

He moved next to her, as if she was seeing something in the wreckage that he'd missed. "I don't understand." Storm's voice held a tentative hope as he voiced the same thought that was floating in her own head.

"Neither do I." She shook her head, trying to clear it. This wasn't the time, or the place, for deep searches into magecraft. "Somehow I was able to See what happened. A group of people attacked her, but Rachael fought them off and got away. I can't explain it better than that, because I haven't figured it out myself. But she's alive, and we need to go that way." She pointed toward the direction she'd seen the image go, out of the city limits and into the open countryside.

Storm looked the way she pointed, then looked back at her. "Are you sure it's not a trap? Something set by the bastards who did this?"

She wished she could explain how she knew, but she couldn't. It was an intangible certainty, the same way you know your own name. It just was. "It's not a trap. I'm not sure of too many things in this strange world of yours, but I know this."

With a shrug, Storm led them out toward the edge of town, he peered out over the darkening plains. Night would fall soon. "There's not much out there in that direction; are you ready?"

Jenna checked her pair of knives and took a deep breath. "I guess so. We need to go toward the right." She wished she knew where they were going, instead of just telling Storm when to turn. But nothing more than a general direction would come no matter how hard she concentrated.

Storm led them across the street. They slipped through the city's dark side. Soon they were at the low wall that served as a barrier for this end.

"Isn't that kind of pointless?" Jenna asked as they shimmied over the five foot wall.

"We haven't had any reason to worry about anything from this side since my family's been in Lithunane. I guess Resstlin didn't think of this end when he set up guards."

"Wonderful." Jenna took hold of Storm's hand as they headed out into the night. "We go that way."

Storm pulled back on the hand she held. "Are you certain? There aren't any farms out there for miles."

Jenna felt his concern. She was exhausted already. And they certainly didn't have any supplies for camping out in the wilderness with them.

"Yes, she's over there somewhere." She used the hand he held to point, so he'd have an idea where it was. Storm squeezed it once, then started walking.

The moon was high overhead when Jenna finally had to stop. "I'm sorry, I have to rest. I can't—" She froze as a change in the wind brought a strange humming to her ears. From the look on his face, Storm heard it also. Someone was entirely too close to them.

"Back this way, there was some cover at the last hill we crossed."

Jenna ran with him, amazed at how much energy fear gave.

The cover Storm referred to was little more than a

large clump of bushes. The two crouched low to the ground as the odd humming came nearer. Jenna couldn't make out the shape, but it stopped right in front of them.

Jenna swore she heard a low whiffing, and the shape swayed from side to side. Jenna readied a spell and Storm freed his knives.

"Oh dear, this won't do at all. You two sneaking around like this. Well, two handsome young people sneaking around at night is understandable, even commendable. Alas, I fear your reasons for slipping around out here aren't romantic. Are they, my boy?"

It took Jenna a few moments to recognize the voice, but Storm caught it immediately.

"Rachael?" He waited until she finished her rambling.

"Now who else could track down the prince of hunters out in the wilds? Come, come, the night is full, and it would be best to get inside."

Without waiting to see if they followed, Rachael headed off into the darkness.

Storm and Jenna followed close behind. A small cottage lit up against the dark sky was visible as they rounded the hill. Jenna had no idea why they missed it before. Unfortunately, she was so tired, her mind only thought about the strange house for a split second before it connected house with bed, and bed with sleep.

Rachael led them inside, keeping her hood up until they had shut the door on the night. The cottage was small, but quite neat and tidy inside. A small side room with a huge fluffy bed in it took up Jenna's attention. She was so caught up in thinking of sleep, she failed to notice Rachael when she took off her hood.

Storm pulled back with a curse, whipping out one of his knives as he did so. "Who are you? Why have you brought us here?"

The woman under the hood was a wicked-looking old crone, down to the wart on her nose and a snaggletoothed grin.

"Easy, my fine Prince. It is I, Rachael." As she spoke, she held out her hands in a soothing manner. Jenna felt dizzy, as if the woman was shimmering out of reality right in front of her eyes. The features melted and changed. Within a few seconds, Rachael stood before them.

Storm kept his knife up. "That proves nothing except that you're mage-gifted."

Jenna disagreed. That did prove something more; that she was *incredibly* mage-gifted. But she kept her thoughts and fears to herself. Had the real Rachael died in the attack and this thing set a trap for those who would follow?

"Oh, pish. Corin, you young hooligan, I've known you since you were no bigger than a toadstool." She waggled a finger at him. "This is why I never transformed in front of you before. You have no acceptance for people changing on you; always want everything to stay the same."

Jenna was staying out of this; she doubted that her simple truth spell would work on someone who could change form.

Storm still looked wary and his knife didn't waver a bit. "Make me believe you. Tell me something no one but the real Rachael would know." His eyes were narrow and suspicious, and he now had a knife in his other hand as well.

Rachael clucked at him like a mother hen with a wayward chick. "Very well. But it won't be pretty. Your first love was an upstairs maid. Her name was Rubela or some such. You had snuck away and kissed her in the pantry and were sure you had to marry her. I do believe you were twelve at the time. Shall I go into more private details of other first-time affairs?"

Storm had already slid the knives away with a crooked grin. "I had forgotten Rubela. That was quite a long time ago." He stepped forward and engulfed the small kelar woman in a hug. "I'm sorry we were so suspicious, little mother. Strange things are happening."

Rachael tipped her head back to get a good look up at him. "Such as a member of the royal family going about Lithunane, when he is supposed to be in Irundail?" She turned to include Jenna in her smile, and frowned. Disengaging herself from Storm's arms she came to her side.

"Things have been happening to you, young one. Oh my, have they." Slanted eyes peered closely. "But your mysteries, as well as my tale, shall have to await until morning. You are almost out on your feet."

"No, I'm fine." A yawn gave her away.

"Nonsense. Corin, you and Jenna shall have to share the bed. I was only expecting one of you, although now I'm not sure which one. Now to bed with you."

Storm shook his head. "I'm not that tired. And where will you sleep if we take your only bed?"

Rachael peered at him expectantly and he gave a huge yawn. "I thought so. The two of you, to sleep. I have many things to do before morning. Fortunately, sleep isn't one of them. Now scoot."

Jenna looked toward Storm. She was dead on her feet, but if he felt they shouldn't sleep until things were settled, she'd follow suit. He shrugged and motioned toward the bedroom. "Right side or left, my lady? There will be no arguing with her tonight."

CHAPTER THIRTY-THREE

THE SMELL OF ROASTING BACON brought Jenna out of a deep sleep. She turned over to see that Rachael hadn't completely magically induced Storm's fatigue; he was still sound asleep. She took a moment to study his lean face. So relaxed in sleep, yet still so graceful. Everything about him was more gracefully masculine than any other man she'd ever met. He was beautiful without being feminine.

Thick black lashes dusted his skin. His tapered ears were the only thing outside of his elegant grace that looked alien. A lean but well-muscled arm had slipped free of the covers. With a grin, she forced herself out of bed before the temptation became too great to see if more than his arm was bare.

Rachael was in the small kitchen, studiously poring over a gray book much like Ghortin's, but smaller and slightly lighter in color. Rachael looked up and nodded with a smile.

"Good, good. I did so only want to deal with one of you at a time. Now I can find out why Tor put his sigil on you without that dear boy asking all sorts of questions."

Jenna smiled back, realizing that the book had disappeared without her noticing. She thought it best not to ask about it, at least not yet anyway. Prior to his mentally losing the thing, Ghortin had been highly evasive about the book he carried. Rachael might feel the same about the one she had.

"What do you mean, 'sigil'?"

"Oh, nothing to worry about. Tor wanted to make sure I could find you." She gave a little chirping laugh. "Or, in this case, you could find me. Now settle right here and let me have a look at you."

Jenna settled at the wooden table on a bench Rachael had pointed to. She wasn't sure what to do, and was about to ask, when her stomach gave a demanding rumble.

Rachael burst forth with another laugh. "Oh, dear me. It seems the physical is going to take precedent over the magical yet again." She scurried to the pan hanging over the fire and gathered a huge plate full of food. Eggs were mixed with vegetables, bacon, and a few herbs. The smell was absolutely amazing. Jenna started in practically before Rachael's hand left the plate.

"Sorry. Didn't realize I was so hungry. I'm afraid it's been quite a while since I've had real food." She managed to get out between bites.

"Hush. I should have realized that and fed you first off. Now you eat up; I don't need your attention to see what he marked you for. Unless, of course, he told you?"

"Actually, I think it had to do with this strange echo in my head. Only now there's something else in there too."

As clearly as she could, Jenna told Rachael about her encounters with the echo, and the odd presence, and the actions it had been taking with or without her approval.

Rachael quietly absorbed it all; her frown deepening with every new turn.

"Things *have* been happening, haven't they?" She shook her gray head slowly. "Tis my fault. I should have paid more attention to the first sighting I had of you. And we should have told Ghortin more. We've always done things with a small group, safer to keep the information secret. That is proving to be a bad choice."

The hearth witch drifted off in her own musings. Jenna didn't want to bother her, especially when she looked so serious, but she needed to know what was happening. Or more importantly, what had happened.

"Tell Ghortin more what?" She pushed aside her now very empty plate.

Rachael shook herself as if she'd forgotten she had an audience. "Oh, I'm sorry, child. Drifted off I did." She led Jenna over to the sofa.

"We should have told him more of what was behind this world. It was thought, centuries ago, that having only a few who knew the truth would make things safer." She shook her head. "But that's neither here nor there. We were wrong, so I'll tell you what we should have told Ghortin." Her eyes took on a sudden intensity. "What do you know of the Books of the cuari?"

Now it was Jenna's turn to shake her head. "I'm afraid I've never heard of them. I've heard a few stray things about the cuari themselves. Ghortin's mother was one."

"Carabella. Oh, she's a cuari all right. Well, I'm going to start at the beginning." She paused and looked up expectantly toward the doorway to the bedroom. Storm's half-clad form filled the doorway almost immediately. He hadn't put his shirt back on, and Jenna would have drooled if she didn't have an audience. He was drop dead gorgeous. Even if he looked like someone who'd been woken out of a deep sleep by an alarm clock. Up, but a bit shaken and disoriented.

"Did I miss something?" he asked groggily as he made his way over to the food. He helped himself to a huge plateful, then scooted Jenna over and sat next to her.

Rachael nodded at something only she saw. "Not yet. I was about to explain some things to Jenna, and I think it would be best if you heard them as well." Her tiny face grew serious. "Ghortin needs to be told of the situation. If one of you doesn't make it back to him, the other must tell him."

Jenna looked to Storm, one of them not making it back wasn't something she was ready to think about.

Rachael began her story. "In the beginning, there were only the cuari. Oh, they were a full species back then, far more than the hundred around now. Their people filled the known world. Even beyond the seas, to lands we've yet to visit. They were a gifted but greedy people." She took a sip of water from a glass that Jenna swore wasn't there moments before.

"They sought to change the essence of the land. Mold it to their liking. The cuari of that time were more powerful than they are today, and far less ethical. Against the advice of the gods, their strongest mages joined their Power to open a portal through to the universes. They sent any creatures they didn't want in their perfect world through the portal.

"The cuari mages refused to listen when the gods and goddesses asked them to stop. When one of the lesser gods—Typhonel—tried to reason with them in this plane of existence, they threw him into the portal."

Silence filled the room as Storm and Jenna digested her words. Jenna hadn't been taught much about the religions of this world, but she had thought there were three deities and each had their own religion. Ghortin had explained that Irissanta was a good goddess, DOL was a neutral, gender-duo deity, and Qhazborh was of the evil side. And that, for the most part, the deities stayed out of people's business.

"How many deities were there?" Jenna was becoming more confused with this explanation, not less.

Rachael gave her an odd little smile. "I am sorry, I'm jumping ahead in my story. The deities, oh yes, there were more of them back then, or rather, they were more separate back then." Rachael looked carefully at each of them, and Jenna wondered if she looked as confused as Storm did.

"I suppose I'd better go into that a bit. Oh dear, there is so much that's been forgotten. I'm afraid the Guardians have made poor choices over the years. Back in the beginning, the deities were in contact more often with the worlds. They watched over more than our little world; and there were many gods and goddesses. After what happened with the cuari, some of them left and hid themselves on planes known only to them. Those who remained divided themselves into three groups. Basically good, evil, and neutral. Those beings that are now worshipped as single deities are actually groups of deities. Makes it easier for them to keep their distance that way."

Storm looked like he'd been struck. "You mean the goddess Irissanta doesn't exist at all?" Jenna didn't think that Storm was a particularly religious person, but the idea was clearly unsettling.

"Not in the sense that she is believed to exist, no. She is the embodiment of all of the remaining gods and goddesses who work on the side of good. Just as DOL is for the neutral deities and Qhazborh is for the evil."

Storm wordlessly opened and shut his mouth a few times. But the poleaxed look stayed on his face. Jenna could sympathize. She had lost her world, now his was being turned upside-down.

"As I was saying about the cuari. The remaining deities decided that the cuari would have to pay for their crime. After a mighty war, the portal was obliterated, and almost all of the cuari population was destroyed. Floods, famine, and pestilence claimed most of those who survived the war. Finally, the goddess Irissanta, or the group for good, stepped forward and said that was enough. They took the remaining one hundred cuari and set them the task of watching this world. The events of what had happened were wiped from their memories, except for one cuari scholar who managed to write it all down. He alone of the cuari understood what would happen if the portal reversed itself and all knowledge of how it could be closed again was lost. He wrote the Books of the cuari, and it is believed the gods let him, for they could have stopped him had they wished it. They did wipe his mind clear of the event after he was done. Then the gods created three new species of beings, each with the full range of goodness and evil that the cuari had tried to erase."

Rachael stood up and paced around the small front room. "A group drawn from the three new species was also given the task of watching over the new world. Unlike the cuari, these Guardians had knowledge of what had truly happened and the Books of cuari. As well as how to use both when the portal opens again. But in thousands of years, knowledge and books can be lost."

Jenna felt like she had been struck with too much information at once. "But why worry about the portal at all? I thought the gods destroyed it."

Rachael slowly shook her head. "They could only destroy the physical aspect of it. Without the unique set of skills from the cuari who created it, they couldn't will it out of existence. It still exists, even though we cannot see it." A small frown creased her face and she looked down for a moment. Then she shook it off. "And they still hoped that their lost brother would be able to return."

Something finally connected in Jenna's overloaded mind. "So you think that this portal is coming back. And that things are going wrong because of it."

"Yes. Tor Ranshal and I are two of the Guardians." She waved a hand at their startled expressions. "Don't look at me like that. Unlike the cuari, the Guardians are not immortal. The post is handed down when the time comes." She slipped a quick smile to Jenna. "In fact, I had hoped that your coming might be my time. I've been on this world for quite a spell, far longer than any of my kind has lived before. But I see now that something else has shaped your destiny."

"What do you mean?" That didn't settle Jenna's nerves at all.

Rachael resumed her pacing around the small rug. "It is said in one of the books that there is a special Guardian, a protector incarnation. One who will show him or herself when the time is at hand. One who's Power will be unlike any other. Like the other Guardians, this one will not be immortal, but will be passed down through the generations, to come forth when needed. I think, somehow, you are that protector."

Now it was Jenna's turn to drop her jaw. "But how could I be? I'm not from this world." She paused as a chill crawled up her back. "Unless the mindslave was the protector incarnation?" If the mindslave was some sort of savior, and whoever had made her into a mindslave knew that— "That's why they've been following me." She whispered it more to herself than the others.

Both sets of sharp kelar ears picked it up however.

"Who's been following you?" Rachael asked as Storm said, "That could be."

Jenna looked from one to the other as the insight solidified briefly in her mind. She wanted to say her idea before her mind dumped it out of terror. "Someone's been looking for me, or rather, this body. My coming over here modified this body somewhat, but I still might be recognizable to whoever destroyed that poor woman.

"If this woman was the protector, and if whoever killed her knew that; they'd fight like hell to make sure she hadn't come back somehow. Like the women who have been killed that looked like me, and the one who's been following us. And Ravenhearst must somehow be part of it, that's why I kept seeing him."

Luckily, both Storm and Rachael were sharp enough to keep up with her ramblings.

As she nodded her approval of Jenna's assessment, Rachael raised her hand. "One thing more, whoever controls the portal, should it come back into physical existence, would wield an unheard of amount of Power.

Enough to change everything we know, should they wish it. But they'd also have to deal with who, or what, comes through once it is opened."

Jenna struggled with the implications. "What would be coming through?"

Rachael gave a small shrug. "We're not sure. Things that were sent in there originally, like the ertin. Perhaps it does link to other worlds, and peoples from them could come through. We've truly no way of knowing. We do know that most of the life here on this world now would perish in the cataclysmic changes that the fully opened portal would bring to this world. The worlds are not meant to be open to each other."

"Wait a minute, what do you mean, like the ertin? What do those creatures have to do with this portal thing?" Storm had managed to overcome his shock.

"The portal was in what is now known as the Mark-are." Rachael favored him with a smile, as she fixed them all cups of tea. "Haven't you ever wondered how a natural desert could be almost a perfect triangle? Each of the three groups of deities held a corner when they destroyed the portal. The ertin are the first ones that we know of to have come back through after the destruction. A new species doesn't pop up out of nowhere. But after they appeared, or reappeared, there were still no indications that the portal was open. The Guardians noted it, but there was nothing we could do."

She waved her hands, trying to dispel the gloom. "Now don't think that everything's lost. The portal isn't open. We are sure of that much. We've kept a close eye on it. There was a group of kelar mages who tried fiddling with it many years ago. They died of their own folly before they could do any real harm. But if someone should find out how to open and control the portal…" She let the rest of her thought fade out.

The three of them sat in silence for a long time.

Finally Jenna screwed up her courage. "So, the followers of Qhazborh want me, because somehow I may be able to open this thing? Could I have come through it?" That thought frightened her almost as much as the rest of the morning's conversation had.

Rachael took her hand gently. "They want you because you can close it. Or so they fear. And I don't think you came through the portal. Corin found you too far away from the Markare. But someone may have been trying to create a new portal, or experiment with Power, and inadvertently pulled you from your world." She turned to Storm. "Was there anything odd about the area where you found her?"

Storm started to shake his head, then stopped.

"Yes, there was. I had gone out to check a strange sighting near one of the villages." He shuddered. "The village had been completely destroyed. Ghortin said he thought it was by a single blast of Power. She wasn't more than a few hours from it."

Jenna shook. She'd had a feeling there had been something about her arrival that Ghortin and Storm hadn't told her, but she had no idea that she might have been the cause of death for an entire village.

Rachael kept a tight hold of Jenna's hand, keeping up a soothing rub as she held it.

"Easy, lass. I know what you're thinking, and I can say you're wrong. You were probably the unexpected result of what happened to that village." She nodded slowly to herself, as if something had finally been settled.

"I think I can make a fairly accurate guess at what happened. Whoever is trying to reopen the portal, and all signs point to someone doing that, has been experimenting with Power sources. Necromancy is the fastest way. This person was testing to see how much Power they could get by destroying a small village. They must have brought their slaves with them, including a mindslave.

Which of course supports the theory that the followers, and possibly the deities, of Qhazborh are involved." She nodded to Jenna. "This wasn't an ordinary mindslave; the mage user behind this must have known she was the protector incarnation, which would explain why this mage possibly kept her with them at all times. Somehow they generated a partial portal, one to your world."

Jenna sat there while a stunned coldness crept over her. "Am I supposed to take over where she left off?" How could she save an entire world? If she had the knowledge the original woman had, instead of only her echo, she might have a chance. But without it?

"I think that's what has to happen." Rachael peered into her eyes. "I'm afraid you haven't had any choice in this whole thing. However, I will give you a choice. You can stay here, fight, and possibly die, to save us. There won't be another protector incarnation in time, I'm afraid. They are born when needed. A new one won't be born until you die, or are gone from this plane." Her wide blue eyes grew brighter. "Or I can send you home."

The kelar witch said it as if it was the simplest thing in the world, and Jenna felt a momentary thrill. She meant it; she could send her back. Somehow, Jenna knew she could go back to her world.

Then she turned and looked at Storm. She'd grown more than fond of him. And more importantly, how could she let this world go? She was a part of it when she worked her magic. And if she was as important as Rachael claimed, her leaving might end up destroying it.

The vision of the cave where they'd found Ghortin's empty body collided gruesomely with the faces of the people she'd grown to care about.

"No." She shook her head at their startled looks when she said it louder than intended. "Sorry, my thoughts kind of escaped." Another deep breath. "I'm staying. It wouldn't be right to run off on you. Besides, this is my home now."

Storm gave her a quick hug, his eyes saying things she wasn't sure of. Rachael beamed. "I'm pleased. For more than a few reasons. One of which is that your former world may be in danger as well. Obviously, it isn't too hard to reach. That rogue mage was able to do so. They would have physically been there to cause you to be pulled through."

Jenna hadn't thought about that. If the portal was like a hall, the worlds closest to this one were more likely to be affected.

She drew herself up straight. "What do I have to do?"

"First, we have to find my father," Storm said, as he too straightened up, but Jenna felt his arm still protectively close. "I don't know why he was taken, but odds are whoever kidnapped my father is the same person who's trying to open the portal."

At first it looked like Rachael was going to disagree. Then she gave a small nod. "Although, I think it would be wise to stay out of the Markare until we know more of what is happening. And until we find the third book of the cuari."

Third? They already had two of these mysterious books? Jenna's question must have been transparent.

"Yes, child. We have two of the books already. Or rather, I have one and your master has the other." She scowled. "Or will have once he gets it back. Although he doesn't know it."

"That gray book?" Storm and Jenna exclaimed at the same time.

"Yes, that would be it. I'm afraid Tor Ranshal and I felt it best if no one outside of the Guardians knew of their existence. I'm not sure where Ghortin found the one he has; it sort of showed up with him one day. Which is why you must make sure to tell Ghortin everything. Once you get back from freeing your father, we must regroup and plan our strategy. I'm afraid our fight hasn't even begun."

Chapter Thirty-Four

As it turned out, Rachael's concern about their trip back was unfounded. Of course they also took an unexpected and twisting route back, and avoided going through Lithunane itself.

The attack upon Rachael was mostly glossed over, but she did say she had people tracking down whoever was behind it. They'd all been out of towners, and even though only one died there, the others wouldn't have survived long.

She wouldn't go deeper than that, but said she was completely safe out where she was. Then she admonished them to watch out for each other, gave them one of her bright smiles, handed them packs filled with food, and shooed them out the door.

The trip back had been quiet for the most part, with Storm and Jenna each lost in their own thoughts. When they stopped for a meal break, Storm finally broke the silence.

"I'm glad you're staying." He hesitated; looking like that hadn't been what he was going to say. "Not because of what you may or may not be able to do. I've grown fond of you; I wouldn't want to be without you." Storm grimaced as the words came out stiffly.

"Thank you. I wouldn't want that either." Jenna looked at him closely; was that a blush? It was hard to say with Storm, he was so forthright in some ways, and so closed off in others. Chances were if she pushed the issue now, he'd clam up. "Well, you really are stuck with me;

Rachael's made us each other's wardens. That will teach you to rescue foundlings in the forest."

"Ah yes. I've always had a soft spot for weak, helpless females." Storm had composed himself and he looked her over appraisingly.

"Somehow, I think that once you, Ghortin, and Crell are done, that won't be a term that will apply to me." She wiped the breadcrumbs from her lap. "How much of what she told us did you already know? I know Ghortin never said anything about any of that to me."

He pushed a stray hair free from his face. "To be honest, I hadn't heard of anything that she spoke of before. It was as if she was speaking of a different world, not mine."

Jenna nodded slowly. That hadn't made her feel any better. "What will we do now? After we get the king, I mean."

"I'm not sure. Once we get my father back, I'll fight wherever they tell me." His look was thoughtful as he turned and looked out into the woods.

"You think it will be a war?" These skirmishes and odd attacks had been unnerving enough, but the idea of a full-scale war, with both magical and physical aspects, terrified her.

"It's hard to say. We have to assume that whoever this mage is, he's got support somewhere—at this point we can't exclude that he is either a follower of Qhazborh or is working with them. Even the most powerful mage in the world wouldn't take on everyone at once without support." He looked down. "I wish I knew why they took my father. Ghortin I can understand, they probably thought to drain his Power. But no demands have been made for my father."

"Is your father mage-gifted?"

"Slightly, but not enough to be of any value in that respect." He ran his fingers through the new knots in his long hair, more as an act of frustration than any real hope of untangling it. Jenna didn't envy him getting his long hair knot free this evening, although she was tempted to offer to help him with it. "That mage must have known we'd not let him take our king without a fight."

Jenna's mind slowly came up with a partial answer. "Maybe he was counting on it." She waved his confused look away. "No, think about it. We shouldn't have known what we learned from Rachael about that portal. And if we didn't know better, we'd go blazing into that desert."

"But why set a trap? What could we have—" He broke off and looked at her sharply. "You. You can't go with us." He said it so matter-of-factly that Jenna's temper rose.

"Oh? How could the mage be assured that I would go traipsing after the king in the first place? And in the second place, weren't you listening to what Rachael said at all? I have to go."

He shook his head. "No. You have to be there later, when we've figured out what we're supposed to do to shut this portal."

"How do you know that this isn't an important part of that?" She stood up and dusted herself off. "I don't think we have a choice here."

Storm followed suit, but his movements were stiff. "Look, you can't go, and that's final."

"And where are you going to put me? The only safe place would be Ghortin's cottage, and even I know it's in the opposite direction from the Markare. Or were you planning on sending half our group with me?" She tried to calm down. The look in his eyes told her he wasn't doing this to be difficult, he was worried. But so was she, and she knew they had no choice; she had to go. She hadn't been happy to hear Rachael's words, but she had to admit they rang true.

Different emotions warred with each other across his lean face. Finally he gave in. "You're right. But it doesn't mean I have to like it." He turned away and stalked down the path.

They continued in silence for the final portion of their trip. Once she calmed down, Jenna was flattered at Storm's determination to protect her. It was sweet, if a little pig headed.

A small meeting was called once they got into camp. It didn't take as long as Jenna had thought to tell them of Rachael's startling revelations. Ghortin asked a few questions, but for the most part stayed quiet. He'd known a bit more of the tale than Storm and Jenna had, but not near enough. And that clearly disturbed him. Jenna was more worried by his silence than any rants he could have had.

The others had made it into the castle with minimal glamouring from Ghortin and good disguises from Edgar. Ghortin managed to find his hidden book; luckily he often hid things in the realm of chaos, something Jenna wouldn't have thought possible. But with that being his favorite hiding place, it hadn't been hard to find the book. Even if he still had no memory of it.

Jenna asked to see the book. It seemed much more ominous since they knew a bit more of its importance. Unfortunately, you had to be familiar with its spells to open it. While she could access some of the spells previously, actually opening the book had always been done by Ghortin.

"Could the mage have been trying to get the book when he attacked you at the ball?" Keanin asked.

"I may not remember anything about this Book of the cuari, but I do think it wouldn't be something I'd be carrying on my person at a ball. I'm afraid we're not going to be sure what our friend is after until he does it. At least for now. What is our next course of action?"

"I'm going after my father." Storm kept his voice low, but his eyes were steady and woe to the person who tried to stop him.

Ghortin studied him for a good two minutes, then reluctantly nodded. "You're right. As much as I fear this is a trap, you're right. We must get the king back before we do anything else. Jenna, now that we know—"

"Don't even think about it." She waved him off. There was not going to be a repeat of the disagreement she'd had with Storm. "I already had this discussion. I'm going too. We don't know if this is what I was brought here for or not. And we can't spare the people to protect me separately from the rest of you."

Ghortin tilted his head. "Actually, I was going to say that we could probably work on some more offensive spells on the way out. I wouldn't dream of meddling with Rachael and Tor Ranshal's plans."

Jenna's face went red. She had assumed that Ghortin was going to try to protect her. And the little flush in her mentor's craggy face when he mentioned the two Guardians told her how he felt about their duplicity, regardless of their reasons.

With a heavy sigh, Ghortin turned toward Crell. "Tell the captain we move at first light."

CHAPTER THIRTY-FIVE

THE SHOCK WAS CLEAR ON all of their faces; even Storm wouldn't have thought to leave that soon.

"But, how can we? We need more troops, we need supplies, and we need—"

Ghortin cut Storm off. "We've more people on the way. Some will be here in the morning and another group will meet us en route. The soldiers that will be here at first light, with supplies and horses for us, were handpicked by Edgar and me from the capital regiment. Crell's extended troops will be meeting us on the road."

By mutual agreement, Kern and his people hadn't been told much of what was really going on. Ghortin had explained their private meeting as one concerning magic, which had been a good excuse to turn away the captain. Ghortin felt Kern was a good man, if somewhat rigid, and more than likely could be trusted. But he couldn't vouch for the captain's people.

Ghortin had given Frankon a magically induced headache severe enough that the mageling had to respectfully withdraw from the opportunity of joining the meeting. He didn't completely trust Frankon, but it wasn't enough to fight to exclude him from the trip itself.

A group of fifty mounted guards and mages arrived shortly after daybreak with over one hundred horses. After a few words with Edgar and Ghortin, they linked up with Kern's contingent. Kern and his people appeared relieved at the newcomers' arrival. Not because of the extra fighters, everyone knew this trip was going to survive on stealth, not strength. The guards relaxed because they recognized the new arrivals as good, highly trained guards and mages, who would follow Ghortin's orders without question, as any of them would. More than a few of Kern's people had wondered aloud why they hadn't received orders from Resstlin directly, since they were so close to Lithunane. Ghortin had danced around the issue, but now they seemed to accept it. Surely the mastermage and his companions couldn't be doing anything bad if new troops, fresh from the castle itself, had come to help them.

Kern's people had no way of knowing that this hand-picked group all had strong ties to Ghortin and the king directly. That when given the chance to help them, all had jumped at the opportunity, even if it meant going against the heir's wishes.

As the reinforced group began to move, Jenna looked around for her friends. Ghortin was in a last-minute conference with Edgar, who would soon slip ahead for reconnaissance. Keanin was slinking around the fringes, eyeing any fresh prospects.

Storm had taken command, at Crell's request. The kelar prince assumed a different bearing now, more regal and authoritative. He might not be fond of his royal lineage, but there was no denying that he had it.

"I think there may be hope for that boy yet." Ghortin settled his chestnut horse into pace alongside Jenna and her gray gelding.

Jenna glanced back. She and Ghortin were ahead of the group, in hopes they'd be able to detect any magic traps before any of the troops set them off. Storm rode ahead of the rest, but still a bit behind Jenna and Ghortin.

Jenna turned back to the present situation. "So, are you going to start teaching me more offensive magic now, or wait until my hair turns gray like yours?"

Ghortin looked ready to spit out a suitably rebuking

response, then shook his head. "I think we need to build a stronger base first."

He wouldn't give her the spells yet, saying that she needed to become relaxed with the formation first. It had been a boring and frustrating day for her, similar to spending an entire day pulling back a bow without being allowed any arrows.

She was extremely happy when the company called a halt for the evening.

Keanin rode up alongside her as she dismounted, and he did the same. "Do we know what the plan is? I can't get near Corin or Crell, and no one else takes me seriously."

"I'm afraid I don't know any more than you. Ghortin's kept me doing finger exercises all day." She stretched slowly; just thinking about the repetitive exercises was making her stiff again.

"Maybe if we ask Corin real nicely?"

"Ask me what?" Storm inquired, appearing behind Jenna. His broad grin said he was pleased at the jump he'd gotten out of her.

"You know, one of these days you're going to do that, and I'm going to fry you," she snarled. "And it might be by accident." Her fingers curled and uncurled as her mind released the spells she had grabbed.

Keanin tsked his friend. "Corin, Corin. How many times do I have to tell you that scaring beautiful women is not a good pastime?" He turned to Jenna with a sad smile. "I think the boy's a bit daft."

"Daft, am I? Then I suppose you don't want to talk about our plans?"

"Plans that include me going home?" Keanin flashed his most charming smile as he fumbled around with his tent. "I wonder if you three plan on having your tents up by nightfall." Ghortin's voice broke in from behind them.

Jenna shot him an evil look. "My hands would work

better if they weren't cramping up."

Ghortin shrugged, but didn't look sympathetic. "The exercises are done for a reason, maybe enough practice will keep you alive."

Keanin stuck his head out of his set up tent. "Must you always be so damn pessimistic?" He climbed out of his tent and busied himself by wiping imaginary dust from his tunic.

"It's not pessimistic, it's survivalist." Ghortin narrowed his eyes. "I believe you could do with some training as well."

Keanin had looked exhausted as he'd flung up his tent, but his eyes went wide at Ghortin's words. "Ya know, I recall that Crell needed me over there." He was gone before Ghortin could respond.

Ghortin and Storm started talking plans for the approach on the Markare and the other troops who would be joining them on the way. Jenna tuned them out as she finished her tent and then started thinking through the day's lessons. Ghortin's practicing had left her almost ready to dive into bed right then.

"Now I am concerned. Maybe it's just me."

Storm's voice brought Jenna out of her thoughts. Looking around, she saw that Ghortin was now gone.

"About what?" She asked as she made a show out of inspecting her tent.

"Ghortin was gone no more than a few seconds, and you drifted off again." He was trying to look angry and hurt at her missing what he said, but wasn't succeeding. The corners of his mouth kept fighting to pull upwards.

"No, I didn't." She couldn't have missed anything; she was only thinking for a second. "I didn't miss anything."

Storm's left eyebrow inched toward his tattered hair band. "Oh, really? It's all right with you, then?"

Jenna should have suspected something by the look on his face, but she was determined to play this thing through.

"Why yes, I think it's a perfectly lovely idea." She folded her arms.

Now Storm's right eyebrow disappeared into his mass of hair. "Well, you don't think it will cause a scandal? I am newly removed of my betrothal after all." As he spoke, he narrowed the space between them until it was less than a hand's breadth.

Jenna was reminded how tall he was as she had to pull back to see his eyes.

"I, ah well—no, I think it would be," she floundered, racking her brain for what she had missed. He was acting as if—no, he couldn't have offered her his company for the night? And she missed it?

"I can be back here right after first watch." As he spoke, he lowered his face down closer to hers until she thought they were going to bump noses. She nervously licked her lips, then stopped and gave a weak smile. She didn't want him to think—well, she might want him to think that— but then again, she might not.

Storm drew a deep breath and slightly parted his lips. "You should pay more attention to what's going on around you out here," he whispered as he delivered a quick peck on the top of her head, then stepped back with an insufferable grin on his face.

It took a second for Jenna to sort it out in her mind. "You. You made me think—"

"Is it my fault that you have terrible survival skills? You let people sneak up on you, and you drift off and believe the most ridiculous thing anyone claims you agreed to."

Jenna felt an irrational stab of hurt. He felt that she and he would be ridiculous? She wasn't completely sure how she felt about it, but that wasn't the word that came to mind.

Storm shook his head as he watched her face, "You know what I meant. Do you think, if I wanted something like that to happen, that I would drop it on you in normal conversation? Hi, Jenna, how's the weather, and how would you like to share my bed for the evening?"

Jenna felt her face grow red. There were times when she would willingly strangle him. "Of course not. I was trying to stall you until I could figure out what you'd said." She looked down, feeling completely foolish. "I knew that you'd never suggest that kind of dalliance."

Storm was silent for a moment, and then he stepped forward and lifted her chin up. All traces of humor were gone from those magnificent eyes. "Don't say never with such certainty. I said I would never say it in such a way. And I wouldn't during a time like now. But I never said I wouldn't say it." He leaned down and brushed her lips with his gently, lingering long enough to send a shudder completely through her. "Now I think I'll go before I get myself into any more trouble. Sleep well."

He disappeared into the forest around them before Jenna had a chance to respond. She almost went after him, then realized it might not be the best idea at this point. She had enough to think about for one evening.

CHAPTER THIRTY-SIX

———

JENNA HAD BEEN UNCERTAIN OF her feelings toward Storm before that embarrassing evening. A week later she was even more confused, and there wasn't anyone she felt comfortable talking it over with. Crell might have been a possibility, but the derawri warrior was focused on battle strategies.

Talking to Keanin or Ghortin about it would be worse than if she ignored the entire thing. And since she hadn't been around Storm much after that night, she decided ignoring it for now would be the best option.

Of course her mind still drifted around a bit, and not always concerning Storm. Now it was Ghortin who took her to task for it, not the prince.

Unfortunately, his disapproval was physically painful.

Jenna collapsed on one knee as a wall of blinding light engulfed her mind. She pushed herself back up from the ground, blocking the light in her head as she did so, and glared at Ghortin.

"Now, what would have happened if I were the enemy? I'd have killed you or taken you before you could have done so much as scream." He walked around her, shaking his head. "Not to mention cast a spell. You. Must. Stop. Daydreaming." Each word was punctuated by the magical equivalent of a poke in the back.

Jenna whirled on him, anger clouding her vision. She couldn't stay on guard all the time. Damn it, they couldn't expect it of her. But at the same time, she couldn't think of a good defense for her inattentiveness, and whining would earn her another attack, or worse.

She latched on to their most recent lesson. A spell so powerful that it had to be taken from the center of chaos directly. She slipped into the magically chaotic level and drew the Power to her. Forming the spell in her mind, she flung it at Ghortin. If he was as ready as he expected her to be, he should be able to deflect it. If not? Well, she should be able to pull the reins in enough for him to save most of his skin.

Ghortin was somewhere in-between in readiness. He expected—well, hoped actually—that his student would answer his challenge with one of her own. What he hadn't expected was for it to be the spell he'd just taught her. And formed perfectly, as well.

If it had hit him at full Power, it would have shattered his shields and mind as easily as a bear broke a twig. Fortunately, it felt like Jenna had modified it so it wasn't at full Power, and Ghortin did have some of his best shields up. Even so, it hit him hard enough to drop him like a sack of wheat, leaving his head ringing and vision distorted.

Jenna ran forward, remorse already showing on her face. Ghortin waited until she came close. Ignoring the searing pain in his head, he flung another spell at her. Her face showed shock for a moment while her body was engulfed in flames. Then the moment was gone and she'd put out the flames. A second later, Ghortin was rolling madly on the ground trying to dodge lightning bolts flung from her crooked fingers.

He swore to himself. These bolts were of her own creation. She had modified a simple lightning spell to give her complete control over the firing. And she was a damn good shot. But he knew she would break for Power sometime.

Ghortin waited until that telltale lag in her firing told her she was tapping into the Power. He timed his own blast for that moment and sent her flying across the clearing on her rear. To her credit, she was up in a second, her body instinctively going into a fighter's crouch as she let loose an incapacitation spell.

Ghortin let the spell roll over him, then nodded in defeat. He couldn't move any more than that. She was getting good; too good. When this entire situation was over, as much as it galled him, he might have to send her to the council for further training. If he could get her to stop dipping into the realm of chaos in the middle of a fight. That was one thing he couldn't understand. She had more innate Power than anyone he'd ever heard of before, yet she always went back to the realm of chaos. And more than once he'd caught her staring off into space. He knew her mind was swimming among the colors and sounds of chaos.

"Truce?" Her tense voice broke through his thoughts. She hadn't come any closer, and still held her hands up.

But she had loosened her spell. Ghortin forced his body to sit up. "Truce." He clutched his head. It felt like it had been shattered into a thousand pieces. He looked at his student with new respect.

"Good job, my dear. But…" He tried rolling to his feet.

Jenna stepped forward to help him. "But what? I got you down, didn't I?"

"Yes, you did. But you shouldn't have had to wait so long. I shouldn't have been able to get through your shields when you went for Power. Drawing Power is supposed to be a fluid thing." He shook his head as he dusted off his vest. "You run like you're holding your breath, then break everything to grab a breath of Power. Draw as you go, take it from the space around you, not just the realm."

"That's how it works for me. I can't do it any other

way." She shrugged.

"You had better learn to. And soon. I can't say that you would have been able to hold me off permanently. As much as it saddens me to say it, I am not the most powerful being around. That point has been made quite clear by Rachael's revelation, if I doubted it before. Those of us who were so certain of our worldly knowledge have just had that understanding turned upside down." He paused, taking a different tack. "You see the lines around us every day, right? The chaotic Power that every living thing generates?"

Jenna bit her lip and looked around at the trees surrounding them. "No, I don't see anything like that."

"Nothing? Nothing at all?" He was stunned. He'd never thought to ask her that simple question. He could see how the Power was drawn to her. The lines bent in her direction no matter where she walked. He knew she had been having some sporadic problems with her magic, losing control of it completely from time to time and the like. Fortunately, the loss of control had made the Power disappear, not burst out randomly. But he'd never thought to check her perception abilities.

"Jenna, I want you to look carefully at those two trees over there." He pointed to two slender pines across the clearing. The Power emanating from them was quite substantial. Nature's chaotic Power was often found in groupings. If a mage needed a big burst, they went directly to the realm of chaos. Otherwise, they drew what they were able to from the general flow of the world around them.

Jenna stared at the two trees. Finally she shook her head. "Still nothing. What, exactly, should I see?"

Ghortin quickly flung a spell at Jenna. It dissipated into nothing as her shields deflected it.

"Well, your magic is still working, that's good. Where did you pull your energy from?" Maybe if they backtracked enough he could find the weak link.

"From the chaotic plane."

"But you didn't tie into it."

"From my memory of the plane. For simple things all I need are the colors. Isn't that what you—" she paused and peered closely at him. "What's wrong?"

"From the memory? How can you—but how?" He shook his head. "Then why did you break concentration in mid-fight to pull Power?"

"For bigger things I prefer to go back there. I usually can use the memory, but I like visiting." She shrugged and looked embarrassed, "I guess my subconscious takes over in times of stress and takes me there. I realize I shouldn't, especially not in a battle." She broke off and frowned at him. "Why are you staring at me like I just grew two heads and fangs?"

Ghortin smiled weakly and looked around for a place to sit. Finding none close by, he settled on the ground with a thud.

Jenna folded her arms and glared. "Oh, come on. I can't be the only one who likes visiting that place. I know I shouldn't do it in a fight, but I don't see why you have to act so strangely about all this. So I can't see something magic in the trees. So I visit the chaotic plane because I like it. I'm still a mage, aren't I?"

Ghortin ran a shaking hand over suddenly tired eyes. "You shouldn't be." It was little more than a whisper, but he spoke louder as Jenna leaned forward. "You shouldn't be working magically at all. But you do, and you are going from what your mind remembers of the chaotic realm. Can't see the natural Powerlines, even though they *love* you." He gave a weak laugh. "You know, we might have a chance in this upcoming battle, if we can get you trained without blowing all of us up."

Now it was Jenna's turn to sit down heavily. "What do you mean, blow us up? Have I been doing something wrong?" Her face went pale.

"Tis my fault, lass. You latched on so quickly to the gift, I never thought to see how you were using it. I can't say about Rachael and Tor Ranshal, but maybe that's how you Guardians work. I've never heard of someone who attracts magic like you do, who can't see it, but can pull Power from a memory of the realm of chaos. You shouldn't be able to do that. And if it could be done, you should have burnt yourself to a cinder almost immediately." He waggled a thick finger at her. "Although your magic shutdowns could have been a result of this."

His initial shock was wearing off and excitement at this new development took its place. The rash young mage who had fought all rules and tamed a vortex was rising to the surface. "Now, we'll have to take things slow, but with extensive retraining, I think we can make you into one of the deadliest mages this world has ever seen. Including the cuari."

Jenna rubbed her arms as if cold. "I don't know if—"

Jenna's words were lost as a blast of pure Power ransacked Ghortin's head. He felt like his mind was being forced out of his ears and his eyes were about to explode. Jenna had curled over, obviously in the same predicament.

As suddenly as it came, the pain was gone, leaving a dull throbbing in its wake.

Ghortin recovered first, although his head still felt like a cracked vase. "Come on, we've got to get back to camp." It took him three attempts before he was successful in getting up. Jenna had to be hauled up and they leaned heavily on each other as they made their way back to camp.

***

Storm laughed as Ghortin and Jenna staggered toward him. "Have you two been drinking already?" His joking stopped when he got a good look at Jenna's pain-twisted face. He rushed forward and took her from Ghortin. Ghortin swayed a bit and adjusted himself so that he could lean upon Storm's shoulders.

Wordlessly, Storm led them into the center of camp. It was clear that every mage-gifted person in their group was in similar straits. He helped them to Ghortin's tent and tried to make them comfortable. He didn't know who could help them, but he knew he had to look.

Stepping outside, he stumbled on a prone figure that wasn't there when he brought Jenna and Ghortin inside. He was shocked to see it was Keanin. He looked no better than the rest of the mage-gifted; in fact, he looked worse. Storm shook his head as he lifted Keanin up. As far as he knew, his childhood friend had no mage-gifts at all.

As he got an arm under Keanin, Storm noticed that Keanin's face was going gray. His breath was coming in ragged gasps, and there was an odd tremor coursing through him. Storm hauled him into Ghortin's tent.

Ghortin and Jenna were still stunned, but not nearly as bad off as Keanin. "Ghortin, you've got to come out of it." Storm tried shaking the older man, then finally started slapping him lightly. He wasn't sure if it was a good idea, but Keanin was slipping into something that looked very much like severe shock.

Ghortin fought his way to full consciousness, and weakly stopped Storm's hand in mid-hit. "Easy, I'm here. Someone's not. In pain. Who?" The words were disjointed, but Storm took solace in the fact that he was talking to him. He'd have to hope that Ghortin could understand him.

"It's Keanin. All of the mage-gifted are in the same shape as you and Jenna, but Keanin's worse."

The mastermage's eyes opened at that. "But he's not gifted." He sounded accusatory, as if it was Storm's fault that this strange thing happened.

"Don't get mad at me, I have no idea what happened. But I do know that Keanin's going into shock and needs help right now." He pulled Ghortin into a sitting position.

"How could this have happened? That attack was aimed at mage-gifted individuals." Ghortin shook his head and winced. Storm had rarely seen Ghortin so physically distressed; it was almost more disturbing than Keanin's collapse. Jenna mumbled something unintelligible behind him and Storm leaned back to catch her words, then faced Ghortin grimly.

"She says he is gifted. Something about his family, he didn't want anyone to know."

"Damn his stubbornness," Ghortin swore. "From what I can tell, this backlash is the residue of a spell cast at a particular individual. A gifted, yet unshielded individual. Him." He swore to himself under his breath. "Keanin must have been like a welcoming beacon to whoever cast that attack. Worse yet is that it was targeted *at him*. Whoever cast it knew that Keanin was gifted, despite him being able to hide it even from me."

Storm didn't think Keanin was going to be happy when he recovered; the look on Ghortin's face wasn't boding well for the noble once the crisis was over.

Setting his hands on the sides of Keanin's angular face, Ghortin put himself into a trance. "I can't get him to hold on. His lack of training is making his mind too slippery."

Jenna pushed Storm aside and laid her hands on Keanin's head. Storm could hear her murmuring softly and it looked like Keanin's color was returning. After a few moments, Jenna and Ghortin backed away.

"Will he be all right?" Storm thought Keanin looked better, but it was hard to tell. Neither Jenna nor Ghortin appeared to be in great shape either.

"I think so. I don't understand what happened though." Jenna rubbed her head.

Ghortin slid back down to the floor with a sigh. "Someone found a weak spot, that's what happened. And from what I gathered before they slipped away from Keanin's mind completely, that someone is waiting for us on the Acaras Plains. I think we go into battle now."

CHAPTER THIRTY-SEVEN

"WHAT DO YOU MEAN, WAITING for us?" Storm tore his gaze from Keanin's pale face. "Was this a trap?"

Ghortin rubbed his chin as he studied the sleeping noble. "No, I don't think the attack on Keanin was to set up a trap. The thoughts I caught were improperly shielded; it's impossible to fake that. But they *are* waiting. Somehow they knew about Keanin having the magecraft ability, even when I didn't." He looked at Storm intently, maybe he had missed something, or perhaps he had been misled. "Rachael didn't say anything to you two about this, did she?"

"No," Jenna said as she picked herself off the ground. "Keanin told me back in Irundail, but he made me swear not to tell anyone. It has to do with the way his parents died, they were working in the Markare when it happened." She shrugged with a frown. "To be honest, I'd forgotten about it."

Ghortin started tapping his fingers. "His parents must have been mages, there's no other way a group that small could have hoped to set up camp in the Markare. Okay. But how in the seven hells of the abyss did whoever just attacked know that Keanin would act as a transfer?"

"A what?" Storm and Jenna asked at the same instant.

Ghortin didn't want to lose his train of thought, but he tried to answer them clearly. "A transfer. The mage used Keanin to get a spell in under our shields. Fortunately, we were shielded heavily." He nodded to Jenna. "At least you and I were, and I think we can assume that we were the targets."

Pulling back the tent flap, Ghortin stared outside. Darkness would fall within the hour. "We have to be ready to travel quickly tomorrow at first light. Earlier than that if we can. We need to use our knowledge to our advantage."

Storm shook his head with a frown. "But we aren't ready for a battle. Look at the two of you, not to mention Keanin and the rest of our mage-gifted."

"That's why we must do it now. They know where we are. They know we're coming their direction. They'll believe that they've hurt us enough to slow us down significantly, enough to give their reinforcements that I sensed time to get there. We've got to get there before then." They needed to conserve their energy, not waste it on infighting. "Storm, your father is there with them. I picked up that also."

The change in Storm was immediate. His jaw tightened and his hand gripped his sword hilt. "We'll leave by first light if I have to carry Keanin out of here myself." He rose to his feet. "I'll leave him in your hands for now. If you two will excuse me, I've troops to ready." With a curt nod, the prince strode from the tent.

"Don't worry, the Storm you know is still in there," Ghortin said as he leaned over Keanin for another check.

Jenna turned. "That obvious, eh?"

Ghortin sat back from Keanin's sleeping form. By some miracle the noble seemed to have gotten through the attack with his wits intact. Although how many of those wits would still be there when Ghortin finished with him, it was hard to say. No matter how painful it was, Keanin was going to have to be trained; untrained, his gift was a danger to them all.

"Storm is an odd boy, always has been. But he's fiercely loyal. He'll fight through hell and back for a friend or a loved one. In a way, that's one of his hindrances as a prince—despite the heroic way it makes him look. Extreme devotion sounds romantic in the bard's tales, but it can hinder a true leader." He nodded toward the darkening sky visible through the tent flap.

"You'd better get some sleep. Somehow our hardheaded peacock here made it through the attack. Oh, he'll have a headache all right, at least until we reach the plains, but he should be fine. I'll watch him through the night to be certain."

Jenna stood inside the tent flap. "How long will it be?"

She didn't say what it was she spoke of, but Ghortin knew. "I fear we shall have more trouble on our hands than we want by three night falls from now. Sleep well, it may be the last real sleep you'll be getting for a while."

<hr>

After two and a half days of hard riding, Edgar and the scouts came back to report an enemy encampment less than an hour's ride ahead of them. Ghortin held a conference with the mages, while Storm called a halt for a brief rest. They had only been riding for a few hours that morning, but he wanted them completely regrouped and rested before they engaged in battle. From what the scouts had reported, their enemy had about twice as many fighters as they did; and although they weren't slacking off, they also hadn't expected their foe to be so close. Surprise would give their troops the edge they needed, if they could marshal themselves into a single fighting force.

Across the camp, Jenna was losing the battle, but she wasn't giving in without a fight.

"Having us in the back is one of the most asinine things I've ever heard of." At a sharp cough by Keanin, she amended her words. "All right, having *me* in the back is asinine."

"Who is going to protect Keanin if we're all up front?" Ghortin paused in his pacing, but then began a new round. "Should we paint a target on him inviting their mages to have their way with him? Unless he's well shielded, they could use him to get under our shields again. All of ours."

"I think that with you and I both out in the open as targets, their mages aren't going to have time or energy to go around looking for someone else. You said yourself he's not as open as before." A new thought hit her. "Have Frankon guard him. I don't trust that man, and this way Keanin can keep an eye on him too." She grabbed hold of Ghortin's arm. "You know I'll be more help than him." She stepped back as Ghortin quickly looked away.

"Or is that it? You're afraid I'll blow it, or blow everyone up; aren't you?" She admitted to herself that she had similar doubts, but at the same time she knew they needed her, and, more importantly, that she could hold herself together.

"I know you wouldn't mean to, but—"

Edgar cut him off as he joined them. "We've no choice. Ghortin, I'm afraid we can't let someone with Jenna's abilities hide in the wings. I wouldn't even let Frankon do it, but I agree with Jenna; there's something damnably odd about that one." He sat down and grinned at Keanin. "How's the head?"

Even after almost three days, Keanin still complained of a headache. "I keep hoping it will fall off. Makes me almost want to go find the gentlemen and/or ladies who gave this monster headache to me. *Almost*."

Ghortin waggled a finger at the spymaster. "Now I wouldn't be telling you how to use your spies. You don't realize what could happen if she has a backlash or loses control out there. She'd not only wipe out herself, but possibly everyone around her."

Edgar's sharp face grew uncharacteristically serious.

"No, I can't imagine that. But I do know what will happen if those mages of theirs get through. Our people won't stand a chance. We've little choice, and we can't leave without the king."

Ghortin resumed his pacing. Jenna could tell he was trying to think of a delaying tactic. The whole concept of her magic wiping out everyone was terrifying, but Edgar was right; the mages they were up against would shred their forces without enough protection.

Ghortin continued to mutter, but Jenna knew that he also realized Edgar was right.

An hour later Jenna, Ghortin, and the other ten mages sat atop their horses five hundred yards from the enemy camp. Dispatching the perimeter guards had been 'disgustingly easy' according to Edgar. The spymaster was now circling the exterior of the camp, looking for more prey. The rest of their troops were behind them; Keanin and Frankon were in the rear.

The plan was simple. The enemy was at the edge of the plains. Two sides ended in steep cliffs that dropped two hundred feet to the ocean. A small group of Crell's people would charge on foot from the third side, forcing them to run into the main fighting force.

"Now what are you so worried about?" Ghortin whispered. "We've got the advantage; they don't know we're here."

"I still don't see how Crell's people are going to get them running," she whispered back. She knew he was trying to keep her mind loose. It was minutes until the trap was sprung.

Ghortin gave a wink. "That's because you've never been on the receiving end of Crell's fighters."

A swarm of that deep green and brown was pouring out from the foothills less than twenty yards from the enemy camp. Shouting filled the air as the scattered enemy ran for their weapons and horses. Ghortin was magically sending words of panic to the poor tethered beasts. Ghortin held his mind control of the horses a second longer, then released it with a grimace.

"Their mages are faster than I thought. But it won't help them with their horses." He nodded toward the mass coming toward them. The enemy was giving no thought to anything other than saving themselves from Crell's troops. Jenna had to admit that part, at least, was working. She nudged her horse off to the side with Ghortin and the other mages. Then Prince Corin, for that was surely who he was at that moment, led the charge into the fray.

Storm the brash young hunter was nowhere to be seen as he swept through the outnumbering enemy like an angel of death. At least ten had fallen on his first pass. He and his people had the advantage for the moment. As long as their mages could hold the others at bay, they might stand a chance.

Instinct took over as one of the few mounted foes blocked his way. The man was scarred, his lean face haggard and deadly. He was kelar, but only one ear tip poked free of his short gray hair. Storm's innards went cold. The land of Khelaran marked their most violent murderers in such a way. Just before they were drawn and quartered, the tip of their left ear was removed. Storm had a split second to wonder how this man had gotten free before he was engaged.

The black sword of his opponent flew with unnatural speed. Storm found it almost impossible to keep up and missed a block. The sword slid into his left arm, and the light, magic-enhanced armor he wore was the only thing that kept it from severing the limb completely. Storm pulled back in pain, sweat stinging his eyes. He made a desperate swing back, but pain ripping through his wound made him misjudge the blow. The gray-haired kelar snarled and raised his bloody sword.

Suddenly a small dark shape flung itself from the ground onto the assassin's back. The tip of a derawri dagger jutted out from the gray-haired kelar's breast before he could react. With a strangled gurgle, the black sword dropped from his numb fingers and he slid lifelessly to the ground.

Crell grinned without humor. "Thank you for letting me take your kill. Your father is in that tower; we killed everyone who was running toward it." Without waiting for an answer, she jumped from the horse's back and into the melee.

Storm gathered five fighters with him; no more could be spared until the fight was better contained. After doing a quick field dressing on his arm, they made their way toward the tower near the cliff.

The tower was ancient, of a design that Storm wasn't familiar with. It was no more than twenty feet high, with one small opening that was being guarded by three edgy-looking men. They must have realized that their reinforcements weren't coming, and that they would have to fight alone.

The two thin ones on the ends looked ready to bolt, but the bear of a man in the middle grabbed both of their tunics before they could move. By the time he'd finished dressing them down, Storm and his people were upon them.

Storm stayed in the lead, and he singled out the heavier man as the most obvious threat. Fighting on horseback would only give him a marginal advantage against a foe that hung close to a building, so he slid off his horse, and ran to meet the huge human.

His people made quick work of the other two. The man Storm faced was a good fighter; he wore a tattered uniform from the Strann army, and he was well trained. But there was an unstable gleam in his eyes that told

Storm how far the man had gone from his days as a soldier.

Even with his injury, Storm was able to get the large swordsman off balance enough to defeat him. It took longer than it should have, and if his opponent had been sane, perhaps he would have had a problem. As it was, Storm was exhausted by the time he managed to get a killing blow in.

After dispatching the other two, his people had held back, knowing that the prince would want to be the first to go inside. Silently, Storm limped to the tower door and, surprised to find it unlocked, he shouldered it aside.

The small room at the base of the tower was musty and unused. At first Storm's heart fell as he believed it to be a trap. Then he saw a thin trail in the dust that led up the narrow stairs. Motioning for the men behind him to stay at the bottom, Storm made his way up the curving staircase. The first landing was empty, with nothing disturbing its coat of dust but the trail that continued upwards.

The top landing ended at a heavy door, and Storm felt the hair on the back of his neck go up. Not only would this be a perfect trap, it had a feeling of wrongness about it. He tried, but couldn't narrow it to anything beyond a general feeling of unease.

He finally took a deep breath; wincing for a moment at the surge of pain the movement brought his battered body. Then he slowly eased the heavy door open.

The floor of this room was clean, with a few odd whirls of dust to imply that the cleanliness was due to movement rather than actually being cleaned.

As the door swung farther open, Storm let out his breath, just realizing that he'd been holding it. Ahead of him lay a shabby cot, with manacles coming from the legs. Sitting on the cot, too weary to look at what he most likely thought were his captors, was the king. With an inarticulate groan, Storm stumbled forward and fell at his father's feet.

———◆———

As the battle began, Jenna watched the charge forward. Storm's long hair flew behind him like a banner as he led them into a clash of steel with the guards of an odd gray tower.

Once Ghortin had pulled free of his horse-riot incitement, they launched a full-scale magical assault on the mages within the other group. Jenna was a little surprised to find that while there were over twenty of them, none of them were very Powerful. They'd been able to use Keanin because he was unprotected and they had worked in a tight formation. In her mind, she felt them scrambling to pull their magic together in such a formation again.

Thinking hard about a puzzle flying apart, she directed a burst of chaos into the forming nucleus of the enemy mages. Their dismay was tangible as they were suddenly without their tight formation.

Opening her eyes, she took a quick look at the field. People were down in bloody heaps, skittish horses from both sides were running off; the war-trained ones standing still, but lashing out at anything that moved too close. She could make out Storm fighting in the middle of a cleared area. His opponent was a large man who moved like a kelar. Jenna sucked in her breath as the swordsman got a full blow to Storm's left side. She almost broke off to help him, when a small shape flung itself at the enemy swordsman.

"Don't lose your concentration now," Ghortin growled behind her. "They may not have much strength, but they've still enough to cause problems."

Jenna shook her mind free of Storm's situation; for good or ill, she couldn't help him now. Two of their own mages had fallen to the ground, one no more than a blackened husk, the other moaning softly. Jenna traced the killing magic from the dead mage and found a trio of attackers at the opposite end of the enemy's camp. The formation was almost an exact duplicate of the one that had attacked the queen in Irundail.

The Power of this triad was so tightly linked that she couldn't force it apart. It was as if they had merged into a single being. She lashed out at what was the weakest link, only to receive a major attack on her shields. She held on through the attack, firing back a searing bolt through the magical link they had. She was rewarded with a stunned jerk as the bolt hit home. But her relief was short lived. They hadn't released the line to her, and they were coming back.

Fear dug in as she realized she was trapped; they were going to do to her what they'd done to that blackened mage on the ground, and there wasn't anything she could do about it.

Suddenly, there was a new presence at her side; two actually, one fighting with the other. She forced her eyes open to see Ghortin struggling to hold back a distressed Keanin. Keanin seemed to be in great pain as he reached again for her.

Ghortin clearly feared this was part of some compulsion that had been planted in Keanin's mind. Jenna didn't think that was the case, but she knew she was doomed without his help. Reaching past the others, she grabbed Keanin's hand.

A renewed burst of energy hit her. Power, pure and raw, flowed through her. Modifying that Power, she sent it slamming back along the link that led to her would-be executioners. She was rewarded with a mind-numbing scream as the trio burst into flames, taking down a dozen of their guards.

Jenna enjoyed the vengeance for a brief second before she crumbled to the ground.

CHAPTER THIRTY-EIGHT

———◆———

IT HADN'T TAKEN LONG FOR the remaining troops to disperse the enemy regiment. However, it took a bit longer for some of the main participants of the battle to regain consciousness.

Ghortin rushed forward when Jenna collapsed, intent on prying Keanin's hand off of his apprentice, even if he had to cut it off. But as he reached forward, he felt a strange tie between the two. Somehow, Keanin had formed a crude version of that odd, and potentially fatal, link the trio of enemy mages had used. Feeling better about Keanin's role in whatever had happened to Jenna, and unsure of the best way to separate them, Ghortin satisfied himself by carefully dragging both of them a safe distance from the fighting.

———◆———

At the far end of the plains, Storm awoke slowly, blood loss, exhaustion, and shock leading to his collapse. He opened his eyes, half afraid that his father wouldn't be there. That it had been nothing more than a cruel trick.

But it wasn't, or if it was, the illusion was still with him.

"Father?" The king was battered and had more gray hair than he'd had before, but it was him. At first the king stared at him blankly, then he gave a jerky nod, and a tear broke free.

Storm engulfed his father as well as he could considering his injuries, and held him until Crell found them.

"And so we found them, each one too weak to stand, and both denying it completely." Crell finished her tale with a wry look at their royal faces. Father and son had never been closer than they were right at that moment.

They were lying in a makeshift hospital tent, surrounded by equally damaged subjects. Jenna smiled at the sight of the two headstrong kelars trapped in their cots.

She and Keanin had come out of their battle without any lasting damage. They also had what Jenna could only equate to the grandfather of all migraines.

Keanin was complaining to all who would listen that he wanted nothing to do with magecraft in any form. All it did was give him the worst hangover he'd ever had, without the enjoyable trip getting there. He wasn't sure why he had done what he did, let alone how he did it. Jenna herself found it difficult to think of anything more complicated than her name without her mind threatening to scream out of her ears.

Ghortin had held still while Crell recounted her finding of Storm and the king, but he resumed pacing soon after. "I don't like it. This was too easy."

With indignation, Keanin gave a groan as he made an aborted attempt to sit up. "Easy? I'd like to know what you think is hard. I'm not sure what I did, but those people were about to kill Jenna. I'd not call that mess 'easy'."

Crell looked thoughtfully at the auburn-haired noble. "I think that those who died would agree with you, Keanin. And their lives were not given in vain. However, I also agree with the mastermage. Why go through all that trouble to get the king, and then just have a few hundred men guard him? Even if they had more coming, they shouldn't have been so unprepared for this. I think we're missing something." She shook her head and sat down next to the injured king.

The king gave a slight grimace, and then forced it into a weak smile for the derawri warrior. "My thanks to all of you. You could be correct. I think the mage who grabbed me—I regret I never got a clear look at the villain—was trying to hide something in the Markare. He vanished a week ago, and from what I heard, that was where he went." He nodded toward Jenna. "Those mages you fought were highly regarded by him. It took a long time to get them to function as a unit. I believe he counted on them to either slow you down or destroy you completely. Once he realized I wouldn't help him in his plans, he decided I would work as bait." His weary eyes looked into Ghortin's. "Think about it, old friend, it makes sense."

Ghortin rubbed his chin. "Well, I suppose it will have to do for now. We haven't come up with anything else." He turned to Crell. "I'd like you to take command of all the troops. Sweep the area for any stragglers we may have missed. I'd like at least a few live ones, if you can find them."

Crell nodded, bowed to the king, then she was off.

Storm struggled to rise. "I should go with them. She's going to need help."

Ghortin forced him back onto his cot with nothing more than a glare. "Not from you. All four of you have managed to pull through this, but you need rest, or all of Healer Otillin's work will be undone. Trust me; none of you want an irate derawri healer on your hands. Now sleep." He turned toward the door, then back again with an evil grin. "Or shall *I* fix something for you?"

By the grimace on the king's face, even he hadn't escaped Ghortin's concoctions.

Ghortin smiled, knowing that all four were sufficiently cowed. "That's better. Oh, there will be a guard out front. For your own protection, you see. And he's under orders to refuse all royal commands. Sleep well."

The king gave a weak chuckle. "I think we'd better follow orders. I never could overrule him." With that he rolled over and drifted off to sleep. Within moments the rest of them had followed suit.

Jenna woke with a start a while later, a sticky feeling filled her mouth and she couldn't sort out where she was. She was coming out of a strange dream that had hovered on a nightmare. An odd, dark-cloaked man had been reaching across a great gulf to find her, and at first she couldn't see his face. Then it became her father, then, as she looked harder, it became Ghortin, then Storm, finally settling on a twisted version of Keanin. Or rather, someone who looked like him. As she looked closer, she realized it wasn't him, but someone who was close enough to be his cousin. The figure was linked with two others, and they were calling great Power. Power that could rip open the universe if completed. She was about to yell a warning, although she wasn't sure whom to, when she awoke in a cold sweat.

The king and Storm both appeared to still be asleep. At first she thought Keanin was as well, he was laying so still. Then she realized his huge golden eyes were locked open.

"Keanin?" she whispered.

The handsome kelar jerked with a start, then slowly turned toward her. Relief showed on his face once he realized who had called him. "Thank the stars. I was afraid they'd finally learned my name."

Jenna looked around but didn't see anything out of the ordinary. "Who?" she finally ventured.

Keanin flushed. "It was a dream." He gave a shudder. "I'd rather not talk about it right now, if you don't mind. Maybe later when we're warm, safe, and far away from the Markare." He sat up slowly. "Do you think they'd let us out now? It's either dusk or morning."

Jenna rose. He was right; the light coming through the slightly open flap was faint. "I'd say if we've slept the entire night away, they couldn't stop us."

They stole to the tent flap and poked their heads out. There was a guard all right, but it was also clear that morning was almost upon them.

"Where's Ghortin?" Jenna whispered to the dozing guard.

He jerked himself awake. "Asleep in his tent I would think. Now you get back in there."

"I'm his apprentice, it's vital that I see him now. You wouldn't want to interfere with a magic crisis, would you?" Jenna did her best to sound extremely worried.

The guard wasn't awake enough for serious thinking. "No. You can leave for that. But why is he going?" He woke up enough to nod suspiciously at Keanin.

Jenna leaned forward with a whisper. "He's the magical problem I've got to talk to Ghortin about."

The guard pulled back, looking at Keanin like he'd grown fangs. He stepped aside. "The mastermage's tent is on the far side."

Jenna hid her smile as they slid by the now fully awake guard. "See, I told you they'd let us out," she said smugly.

"True, you got past a sleepy guard. But what about her?"

All the self-congratulations went out of her sails. Crell was bearing down on them. "Damn. Think she'll fall for the same thing?"

Keanin sadly shook his head as the derawri warrior came to a stop in front of them. "Now I know you two wouldn't have snuck your way out against orders, would you?" She tilted her head up as she looked intently at them.

"It was all her fault. She made me go." Keanin shrugged at Jenna. "Sorry, Crell has methods of torture you couldn't imagine."

Jenna shot him a withering glance. "Actually, we thought that we'd get some fresh air. And Keanin wanted to tell me how he knew I needed his help yesterday."

Crell raised one deep red eyebrow at them. "I don't believe either of you for a second. But as it turns out, your little escapade yesterday is what Ghortin would like to go over with you." She gave Jenna a questioning look. "That and something about his book. He's waiting for you in his tent. Now, if you don't mind, I'll be going to mine for a rest."

Jenna and Keanin said their good nights, or mornings as the case was, and walked over to Ghortin's tent.

Jenna kept a tight grip on Keanin's arm after he almost wandered away a few times. She could sympathize with her friend; he was obviously terrified of his odd ability. That made it all the more necessary for them to explore what his limits were and get him trained.

Ghortin was settled on a folding camp seat, sipping sage leaf tea when they came in. He motioned for them to take up seats on the ground before him. "Very prompt. I'd thought it would have taken Crell a bit longer."

Both of them wore innocent looks and Jenna nodded. "We came as fast as we could. We were anxious to learn what you found in your book." She decided she'd give Keanin a chance to relax before Ghortin started magically dissecting him.

"Ah, yes." He set his cup down, then reached under some covers on the cot, and pulled out the gray book. The one that they now knew was one of the three Books of the cuari.

"I still haven't recalled it, or what I knew of it. Which strikes me as damnably odd. You'd think one of their offspring wouldn't forget something so important. Anyway, I did manage to break the spell on the cover, although I can't get past the first page."

Something clicked in Jenna's mind. "I think that

could be the problem, you *are* of cuari blood. The cuari can't remember anything about what happened during the before time. Including the books." At Ghortin and Keanin's continued blank looks, she elaborated. "Your non-cuari blood was able to understand it when you initially were working with it. But when you were pulled out of your body, your cuari blood, the part of you that couldn't have anything to do with the book, erased its existence in your mind. As you're returning to your former balance, you're able to deal with the book."

Ghortin frowned. "I don't think I like the idea of my body splitting up like that. However, I admit it makes sense. I'll have to give it more thought." He shook himself and forced a tight smile. "Now, about this front page." He held open the book to show them.

The inside was ash gray, and in it was a detailed drawing of three people holding hands together. In their center was a glowing light, one so bright no form could be seen within it. For some reason Jenna *knew* there was a fourth person in there. The three figures surrounding it were representatives of the three species.

Underneath, in an ancient flowing script that she could barely make out, it read:

"With the three that are one, the one who is three will have Power against all and will be the link between the worlds."

"Three that are one?" A thought hit Jenna. "Like that trio we came across yesterday?" Her stomach made a few unsettled flips.

"You might be right, this could be a warning against them, or more like them," Ghortin began his usual pacing. "Or something else entirely."

Keanin looked at them perplexedly. "I could have sworn that you said we destroyed that trio, so why are you two looking so concerned?"

"If they could link like that, then they have the ability

to form others." Ghortin increased his pacing. "Actually, they already have. Those three that you fought in Irundail were of the same ilk, if my sense of that night is true."

"Why wasn't I ever taught to link like that? Is it something forbidden?" Jenna could still feel the immense amounts of Power the triad had been able to pull. It was terrifying, but also seductive.

"Not forbidden, just unheard of. I've never heard of two mages working like you two did yesterday, let alone three. Which reminds me—"

"Don't tell me you were making plans without including us?" The voice from the other side of the tent flap was weak, but there was no doubting it belonged to a king.

A second later, Storm's hand came through, holding back the flap as he helped his father enter.

Ghortin's surprise at the king's appearance showed on his face, but he quickly recovered and motioned for Storm to set his father down on the small cot.

"Daylin, you stubborn scoundrel. Why aren't you still in bed? We aren't going anywhere right now, and you know it."

A brief spasm of pain flashed across the king's handsome features, followed by a look of grim resolve. "I can't waste time, and neither can you. We have to go after the mage behind this; he mustn't complete whatever he's doing in the Markare."

Jenna started to tell the king about the portal, but something in Ghortin's face made her hold her tongue. There was a concern there that looked like more than just worry over the king's health.

"Now, I'll agree we can't let this maniac go, but we don't have the personnel to mount a desert campaign right now—we lost too many yesterday through death or injury. You, of all people, should realize that," Ghortin said.

The king's hands tightened at his sides. "We haven't a choice. What have my people changed into in my absence that they would be afraid to sacrifice themselves for the safety of their kingdom? We must strike now, before he realizes what we are doing."

Storm watched his father carefully. "I think Ghortin is right, Father, we need more people; and the mages are mostly dead or injured. Resstlin needs to know what's gone on."

The king was silent for a moment, then went on as if neither of them had spoken. "Here's my plan. Ghortin, you lead Crell's fighters around through the Dorga Pass. My boy here and I will lead the rest straight through to—"

Ghortin grabbed the king's hand. "What in the stars has become of you? Didn't you hear anything we've said? We can't go in there like this. Give us a week; we could mount a hasty attack if I can contact someone in Lithunane."

"I *have spoken*. We ride tomorrow morning. I will give you instructions then." Ignoring the looks of disbelief and worry on the faces around him, King Daylin imperiously stood up and grabbed Storm's shoulder. "I will be making plans in my tent, if any of you feel like coming to reason."

Storm looked as shaken as everyone else as he wordlessly helped his father out of the tent. The remaining three all looked at each other in stunned silence.

"He can't be serious." It was Keanin's subdued voice that finally broke the silence.

"Maybe he knows something we don't?" Jenna ventured quietly. "After all, he was with them for a few months."

Ghortin shook his head, his dark eyes unfathomable. "I don't think so, or he would have told us. Besides, regardless of what he knows, it would be suicide to go in so weak and ill-prepared." He turned toward Keanin. "I want you to go find Kern, tell him I order a guard put on the king at all times. No questions. Tell him I fear magical tampering."

Keanin grimly nodded, then was gone.

"Do you think that's not the king?" Jenna wondered how she was staying so calm about this. She hadn't been sure what would happen once they rescued the king, but she was certain this wasn't it.

"No, it's the king of Traanafaeren, I'm afraid it may not be *our* King Daylin." Ghortin shook himself off, and then held up his hands. "No time to waste. Until Keanin gets back, we'll work on your sight of Power on this plane."

Jenna let out a small sigh. It was going to be a long and tedious day. With any luck, tomorrow would be one as well.

They'd gone away from the tents and had been working on her efforts to see Power on this plane for most of the afternoon. She didn't feel like she was making much progress, but Ghortin kept pushing at her.

By the time they were interrupted by a soft cough behind them, Jenna was seeing colors everywhere except for where they should be.

"Sorry to interrupt," Edgar said as he studiously ignored Ghortin's annoyance at being disturbed, "but the king is still convinced that we're leaving tomorrow. Corin's trying to talk some sense into him, but it's having no effect."

"Tell him to give up." Ghortin's stomach gave an involuntary rumble as the first whiff of dinner from the main fire wafted over them. "In fact, if you two would be so good as to retrieve our prince and that missing young peacock, we could meet back in my tent. And find someone to bring us some supper as well; I fear we may be in there for quite a while."

A short while later they'd gathered in Ghortin's tent and were just beginning to discuss the day's events when

Marta appeared, bearing food. One of her fellow guardsmen was helping her.

"I hope this will be enough. We hadn't realized Keanin was here as well." She gave him an odd look, and then quickly turned back to the food.

Ghortin glanced briefly at the food. "Yes, that should do nicely. Thank you," he pointedly added when the guardswoman didn't immediately depart.

Jenna lunged for a juicy leg of bird before the tent flap closed. The others, with Ghortin trying to maintain order, were right behind her.

CHAPTER THIRTY-NINE

VIOLENT TREMORS SHOOK JENNA OUT of a deep sleep. Forcing herself to stay calm, she opened her eyes to figure out where the safest place in a tent during an earthquake was. She was more than a little surprised to find that Ghortin, rather than an earthquake, was responsible for her shaking.

"Wha-I'm awake. Stop it." She made a swing for his arm and found that her hand moved like it was made of rope.

Ghortin took the attempt for what it was and stopped his rousing. "You must start moving around. I fear there's still too much of whatever we were given in your system."

Jenna shook her head as two Ghortins bloomed into being. The shake brought them back together again.

"What?" She wished her mind could come up with something else, but it seemed like the most important thing to say at the moment.

Ghortin ignored her question and lifted her up. Supporting her with one arm, he marched her up and down outside of her small tent. Jenna looked around as best she could, but her neck was stiff and immobile. She thought that quite a number of tents were missing, but her vision was still having trouble as well, so she wasn't certain.

"Now, how's that? Feel better? Think you can stand on your own?"

At her tentative nod, he slowly released her. She still shook a bit, but as long as she didn't make any sudden moves, she was able to stand on her own. After a few moments, she ventured her question again.

"What happened?"

"We're not certain, but I can make a good guess. We were drugged."

Jenna anxiously looked around for attackers, but she found none, unfortunately she was certain there were only a few tents now.

"Why drugged? Where is everyone?" Her mouth was still working a bit on the slow side. Which wasn't so bad since her mind was as well.

Ghortin ran his hand through his unkempt hair with a frown. "The two are linked, although I'm not sure why. I awoke myself not more than a half hour ago. Let's go join the others; they should be a bit better off than they were when I left them."

Jenna was dismayed at how few 'the others' were. Ghortin, Storm, Edgar, the injured, the mages, as well as Crell and her fighters were the only ones left in camp. The rest had taken flight, or been taken, while they slept.

"Was it our enemy? Did their reinforcements arrive? Could they have carried everyone else off?" Jenna asked quietly. She was glad that most of her friends were here, but she was worried about Keanin's absence.

Edgar shook his head slowly. Like the rest of them, the master spy was still recovering from their little sleep aid. Jenna had never seen him look this out of sorts. He also looked furious. She guessed that he'd never found himself on the receiving end of a drugged coup. "And take their tents as well? No, most of those that we fought yesterday were mercenaries, kidnapping isn't their style. I think everyone left of their own accord." He looked over to Storm with a frown. "I think the king made good on his threat to leave."

Storm's jaw tightened and Jenna got the distinct impression that this conversation had been going on before she arrived.

"I can't believe that my father would drug us just so he could have his way. And Keanin would be one of the last people to go venturing off into the Markare without us. He's terrified of that place."

"He has a point." Crell nodded stiffly. "I've looked the grounds over, our people went voluntarily, regardless of whether Keanin did or not."

"There's one person who could have gotten them to do that," Ghortin added.

"But why? And why would he leave us?" Storm shook his head.

Ghortin looked up thoughtfully. "Because we—even you—disagreed with him. Something horrible happened to Daylin during these past few months. He's not himself. He drugged those of us he knew he couldn't convince to go along with his plans, and then he led the rest away. I'm sorry, lad," Ghortin looked down at the brooding prince, "but that's what it points to."

Jenna stepped into Storm's silence. "But why take Keanin? Granted, he couldn't have stopped the king, but he certainly wouldn't have gone along quietly."

"Maybe he didn't." Edgar tapped one slender finger on the crude table as he quickly sorted his thoughts. "There are some rare poisons that act as a delay for other poisons. If someone mixed some of those into our food, the meal we all ate in Ghortin's tent, it wouldn't have kicked in until much later."

"That would mean that Keanin ate it too," Jenna said.

Edgar nodded. "Yes, for some reason Keanin was taken, even though he was unconscious."

Ghortin shook his head. "Perhaps Daylin thought that he could use Keanin's mage abilities. He carefully left all the rest of us mages, but because he raised Keanin, he might have felt he could trust him." He gave Jenna a wry look. "Except for Frankon. Maybe he thought to try a combination of Frankon's skill, such as it is, with Keanin's raw magical strength."

"But do you think Keanin would help him? I mean, once he woke up and we weren't there?" Jenna couldn't imagine her friend giving up on them.

Storm's lean face was dark. "He would if my father convinced him that he had no choice. Once they get into the middle of the Markare, with no help in sight, he might give in to anything."

Jenna noticed that he no longer argued that his father hadn't been the cause of the missing people. As much as it tore him up inside, he had accepted his father's actions.

"Which brings us to the question, what do we do now?" Edgar's words quieted the tent.

Storm looked up grimly. "We have to go after my father."

Ghortin frowned. "I don't think that would be wise. We may have lost all of them already, I'd not like to lose the rest of us, even for the king. We took a big chance coming out here in the first place; I say we go back and get help."

Crell shook her head. "I'll not argue with you about the danger, but my fighters are furious about the deception and the drugging. My scouts said the tracks were still fresh and that we might be able to cut them off at Narrows' Pass. I say we go." There was more anger in her green eyes than she was letting show in her words.

"I have to agree with Crell," Edgar said. "We might be able to turn them around. Make the king see reason, and I'm sure that most of those who went would have been unaware of his drugging us. I think he moved in with a fast story to get them to go."

"I don't think we should go into the Markare so unprepared. And undermanned. Remember, we've got all the injured." Ghortin got up and paced. Jenna was amazed that he didn't dig a pit with the number of times he walked his tight little circle before he spoke.

He finally turned with a long sigh. "You may be right; we should at least see where they are headed. But," he held up a warning hand, "if we don't find them in one day, we go back for help."

Now that he'd decided what the action was to be, Ghortin became a commanding general. "Crell, you and Healer Otillin move all of the injured who can't ride into the tower. Leave him, and two of your fighters in it as well. Tell them—" He paused, looking out across the near empty camp. "Tell them to hold it against any who come, unless one of us is with them or they come directly from Lithunane. We can't trust anyone who left with the king until we know what happened. The rest of you, get ready. We ride within the hour."

It didn't take long for Jenna to gather her possessions; she hadn't taken anything out last night. She looked away from Keanin's empty tent space. There must be another reason the king took him, something she wasn't getting. Storm had her worried as well. He'd accepted his father's betrayal poorly, his face now cold and unmoving. She wondered what would happen if they did find the wayward king.

How did they know that the king was wrong? His actions were drastic, but a madman hadn't held any of them for three months. Maybe he did know something about what he was doing. A shiver went down her back. Could it be the time for her to do whatever it was she was in this world for?

"You know, it's easier to pull out the stakes from the bottom."

Jenna jumped and found herself face to face with Edgar. The spymaster had donned light clothes and wrapped a cloth around his head. At her confused look, he nodded toward the tent corner she'd been pulling on without notice.

She shook her head. "Sorry. I was thinking."

"Don't apologize, it's your tent. What were you thinking so intently about?" As he spoke, he started taking down one side of the tent. Jenna finished on the other.

"I was wondering if this was what Rachael was talking about. If we're being brought into the desert for a reason."

"Can't say." He looked at her intently, as if she might hold secrets she couldn't speak of. "Do *you* think this is it?"

She paused for a moment before answering. "No, I don't think so. I mean it could be, but I'm not exactly sure what this whole thing is, even after Rachael's explanation. I don't feel ready, that's for sure. And I think…" she paused, searching Edgar's black eyes for an answer that wasn't there.

She gave a little sigh and looked away. "I think more has to happen. I think there would be more disturbances if someone was actually ready to open that portal."

Edgar let out his breath. "Good to hear that. I know I'm not up to a battle for the world today. Or tomorrow for that matter. Now, the tent is packed, you're packed, and I see by his impatience, Ghortin is ready to ride. Shall we, my lady?" He gracefully bowed and led her to the horses. It would have been more charming if he wasn't looking deadly in his spy garb.

Crell's scouts were in the lead, easily keeping ahead of the horses. Every once in a while Crell would drop back and tell Ghortin of a change in direction or of any obstacles ahead of them. The trail was fairly clear, and Crell wasn't the only one who had a feeling the king, or someone with the king, wanted to be followed.

"Why do you think he's making it so easy?" Jenna asked as she rode closer to Ghortin.

He shrugged. "I can't be sure. It isn't a tactic I taught him. But we can't be certain of whom he was making it easy for."

The words struck an ominous tone in Jenna. "Do you think the king is working with someone?"

"Now, I didn't say that." Ghortin tried to look gruff, and for once Jenna wished she could still hear his thoughts. "The king may not be aware he's leaving such a trail; he is quite out of sorts. Or it could be that someone else is suspicious of his behavior and is leaving it. I'm not certain at all." He looked up as the spymaster rode up to them.

"I think I can pinpoint the area they are headed to. There's only one safe stopping point within a day's ride. The Shadon. It's a small wash with running water." Edgar looked concerned about something. "It's odd. That's where they're heading, but they've taken the longer route. They're on the old caravan trail. There's a new path that would cut about five hours off their travel time." He shook his head sharply. "I don't understand why the king is taking the old route. It makes no sense."

Ghortin nodded as if it made perfect sense to him. "Ah, but it does, and it ties in with the mystery of why the trail has been so clear. Kern is providing directions to the king." He gave a laugh, "I always knew that man wasn't as unimaginative as he acted." He motioned toward the other two as if they were errant students.

"Kern went along with Daylin because he felt he couldn't disobey a direct command. But he's been leaving trail markers and taking an old, slow route on the chance we'd be coming along to straighten things out. It could be someone else's doing, but Kern would be the best guess."

He gave a nod toward Edgar. "Don't sit there, man. Tell Crell to change direction to the newer trail. If all goes well, we'll catch up with our wayward king before nightfall, have a nice sleep, and then be on our way for Lithunane in the morning." Ghortin was positively beaming as he urged his horse to a faster pace.

The shorter caravan trail worked. They crested the last hill in sight of the king's camp as it was being set up.

CHAPTER FORTY

O NE OF THE LITHUNANE ARCHERS who had fought alongside Crell during the battle for the tower was the first to spot them. "Thank the Lady you're here. I'm not certain what's going on, but something is horribly wrong."

Crell nodded. "What's happening?"

The tall archer flicked a look over her shoulder at the settling camp. "King Daylin told us we were to be part of an advance group and that backup would follow. Captain Kern kept asking him questions that he couldn't answer. It soon became obvious that this was a plan of his alone, and that no support would be coming." She looked at the small group with a sigh. "Unless, of course, you happened to have brought more people with you? Who are hidden at the moment?"

Crell shook her head. "Just the rest of those who can still fight. They're around here somewhere. Pasha, tell me, does it seem like someone is controlling him?"

The black-haired archer shrugged. "I don't think so. Captain Kern doesn't think so. But he does think something is wrong with the king. He seems to lose touch with reality from time to time. Forgetting who our true enemy is." She gave a pointed look at Storm and Ghortin.

"He's told people we're the enemy?" Ghortin was surprised at that. Storm said nothing, but a tight white line appeared along his jaw.

"Not really. He let it slip around Kern on the way here. That was how Kern figured that things weren't as the king said. Kern tried to leave a trail in case you were following, and he convinced the king that it would be safer to take the old route." She snapped to attention. "What now?"

"I think you should stay out here as guard. The Markare isn't a safe place, even this close to the border. One way or another we're going to convince the king to come back with us," Ghortin said as he moved his horse forward. The archer gave Crell a small nod, then faded into the woods.

The camp itself was neat and orderly under the guidance of Captain Kern.

"Ho. Mastermage Ghortin, Prince Corin. I'm glad you made it. You found the trail?" Kern's eyes were bright, but he wore a slightly haggard look. It must have been hard to keep the king happy and still leave markers for them to follow.

"Yes, and thank you. It made our trip much easier. Where is he?" There was steel in Ghortin's voice that no one could miss. Jenna knew her mentor was at the end of his patience.

Kern sighed and wordlessly pointed toward the large healer tent. Ghortin motioned for the others to follow a bit behind him as he marched to the tent.

The recovering king was on a cot with Frankon and three guards huddled in conference. Sitting dejectedly in one corner was Keanin.

Keanin's face lit up at the sight of them, but he said nothing. The king must have caught his intake of breath however, for he looked up at that moment. A frown was quickly replaced by a calculating smile.

"Ghortin, my good man. You made it. Good, good. Now, we've been working out a plan. If we break up into groups of three or four, we can have this quarter of the desert covered by—"

"What are you talking about, Daylin? Why did you

leave us behind?"

The king's smile vanished. "My actions are not to be questioned by anyone, even you. Now you can go along with us and our plan to track down the mage who abducted me, or I can put you under guard and send you back to Lithunane." His eyes took on a pleading gleam. "I'd much rather have you with us. And, of course, the rest of you." He nodded toward Edgar, Storm, and Jenna but it seemed that his bright eyes lingered on her for longer than necessary. The kindly looking man she had briefly seen at the ball all those months ago was a far cry from the feverish man huddled in front of her.

"This involves magic of the highest order. Do you want me to overrule you in front of these people? I will." Ghortin looked down at the king with unflinching resolve. "This isn't the right time. We'll do nothing but die."

"Are you so afraid to die? We die for a cause." The king's face was becoming unnaturally flushed.

"If we die, they win. I don't intend to let that happen." Ghortin stepped forward. Daylin shrunk back, and then hung his head.

"Perhaps you are right. Let me sit for a while, then I shall come out and announce my decision." For a brief moment he looked like a tired old man. "You will let me keep some dignity, won't you?"

Ghortin smiled at his old friend. "I could never take that from you. We'll wait outside."

The king's eyes searched Storm's tight face for a brief second before Storm turned and stiffly followed Ghortin out.

Crell had waited outside to give the call to her fighters, who were circling the camp, should the need arise. "Do we fight?" She stood at attention.

Ghortin shook his head. "No, he's decided to come back with us. But I'm going to let him tell these people.

You might as well call all but a few scouts in."

As he spoke, a strange wailing flowed over the camp. It took but a second to realize that it was coming from the king's tent. Jenna tugged on Ghortin's arm as a sickly force hit her magic senses.

"It's Frankon, he's pulling in Power for something like those triads."

CHAPTER FORTY-ONE

JENNA FRANTICALLY LOOKED AROUND AND realized that Keanin hadn't followed them out. "Keanin's still in there. Frankon must be using him, pulling Power from him the way Keanin helped me before."

Before Jenna could run for the tent, Ghortin was in front of her, pulling in huge amounts of Power as he ran. He was slammed to the ground an instant later as an uncontrolled discharge of the Power building in the tent exploded.

"No. Get away from me!" Frankon's scream was followed by the mage himself a split second later. His eyes were wide and bloodshot, his pupils unnaturally small and his body shook uncontrollably as he fell to his knees, a knife dark with blood falling from his hands. He stretched those same hands out to Ghortin, but it wasn't the mastermage he was seeing. "Help me, Lord Ravenhearst. I didn't know what they were. They aren't—" His scream was cut off abruptly as his head was sliced off by a huge battle axe.

Frankon's body tumbled to the ground as a snarling Marta stepped forward from the side of the tent. A cut on her arm oozed sickly green ichor; identical to the color blood shed by the demonspawn. Two other guards stepped forward with the king, no longer looking frail, behind them.

"Too bad the idiot figured things out faster than we expected." Marta dropped the axe, and pulled a sword out from a dead man behind her.

Ghortin released a massive firestorm spell, one that should have wiped out not only the demonspawn Marta, but everyone with her. The flames abruptly vanished a foot in front of her.

"Always predictable, aren't you, cuari spawn? Even now, you have no idea what is about to happen." The king spoke; it was he who had stopped the flames with little effort.

Storm went pale and he gripped his sword tighter. "What have you done with my father?"

The look on the king's face proved without a doubt that he was not Storm's father. "Oh, I'm still Daylin, well, what's left of him anyway. I'm sure you'll last much longer before *your* mind explodes."

A subtle movement gave him away and Jenna threw herself physically and magically in front of Storm. The spell had been brutally strong, but was meant to ensnare, not kill. For some reason, the demonspawn king wanted Storm alive.

The false king pulled back in surprise and regarded Jenna closely. "This is interesting, and oh so unexpected." The look on his face was nothing short of horrifying, with a death's head grin, he closed his eyes and began pulling something to him. Five demonspawn appeared out of thin air behind him, and more were trying to come through. Jenna frantically pulled in more Power than she had ever held; constructing it as she drew it into a new weapon. She piled layer upon layer on it, hoping at least one would get through. The false king was somehow opening a passage to whatever hell his kind came from. Colors burst in her head, momentarily blinding her as she cast the spell at the false king. Her eyesight cleared well enough to see him stagger under the spell's attack.

The newly formed demonspawn were still there, but the gaps for the ones still trying to come through closed with loud pops. The false king turned and stumbled back into the tent.

Jenna took a shuddering breath and found a sword hilt being shoved into her hands by a numb-eyed Storm. That was a good idea on his part, she didn't think she had any Power left at this point. He nodded once she had the sword tight, then turned and faced two of the demonspawn guards. Jenna struggled to hold her own with another, as Ghortin flung spell after spell at Marta. Crell joined in and made short work of the guardsman Jenna had been trying to fight.

Fighting broke out all around them as those who had followed the false king into the desert attacked the demonspawn that he had been able to pull through.

Jenna and Ghortin ran toward the tent as Keanin let loose a horrifying scream.

Ghortin almost shredded the tent trying to get inside, but he pulled back immediately once he did. The former king bore no resemblance to Storm's father now. His skin was cracking in dozens of oozing green sores, his eyes flashing red as he looked up at them. Jenna pushed past Ghortin when she saw Keanin lying unconscious next to the false king. She froze when she realized that the thing had one hand on Keanin's heart, the other on his head. Keanin's face grew gray and wan as a transport spell flickered around him and the demonspawn.

"We can't let them go." Jenna reached for a spell only to find nothing remaining. The look on Ghortin's face said he had nothing left magically either.

The demonspawn released the hand he had over Keanin's heart and reached it toward Jenna. "Come with me, child; my master will welcome two such worthy prizes."

As he spoke, Jenna found her feet moving toward him in an odd shuffling step; nothing she did halted her movement. Ghortin reached for her, but he was frozen in place.

Storm came in and stood next to her with a look of terror on his face as he took in the tableau before him. He immediately raised his sword and charged forward, only to be locked in place by the same spell holding Ghortin immobile.

"Stay there, boy. Join your pretty friends."

Storm stumbled, but took a step forward. Jenna realized the thing before them had been able to stop him, but controlling herself and Ghortin was causing a drain on his Power. She didn't think it would be able to control Storm for long. Storm's sword raised higher as he took another step forward.

"I gave you that sword for your fiftieth year coming of age; you can't kill me with it. You won't kill me with it. You'll come with me to my master; you can have the girl when he is finished with her."

As he spoke, the demonspawn king removed his other hand from Keanin, moving away with arms raised as if to show how little he feared Storm. Even though the thing before them didn't look like King Daylin to her eyes, to Storm it must have been brutal. That the demonspawn had his father's memories was terrifying.

Storm took another step, but Jenna saw the pain in his eyes. He shook himself off and took yet another step, tears coursing down his face as he closed in on the thing that had been his father.

Jenna fought harder to push against the invisible bands holding her. From the strain on his face, Ghortin was trying as well. An instant later the hold broke on Storm and he ran forward, spearing the false king in the heart.

Jenna and Ghortin both dropped to their knees as the creature's spells broke when the sword pierced his heart. Storm stumbled back and dropped down next to Jenna.

The dying demonspawn king lifted his head enough to look at them all, his gaze fading as he glared at Ghortin. "You have won but a small victory, Ghortin. Slowed us down, nothing more. And we will know more for next time."

A chill crept down Jenna's back as the voice faded along with the thing's life.

Ghortin shook them all back to awareness. "Come on, help me get Keanin and let's leave here. I want this all burnt to ash."

Jenna and Storm helped each other up. Crell came into the tent to help him wake Keanin. Unfortunately, Keanin wouldn't wake and they finally had to carry him out.

The scene outside the tent was almost as grim as the inside had been. The remaining demonspawn were all dead, but not before they took out half of the fighters from Kern's group and half of the additional fighters from Lithunane. Kern and Marta were found a few feet from the tent, locked in a bloody death grip that neither had survived.

Ghortin separated the bodies carefully. "It's as I feared; like the false king, this demonspawn didn't change back at death. Demonspawn always revert to their true form at death. I have no idea what they are, but they are far beyond normal demonspawn."

No one said anything; everyone was too heartsick and injured to speculate on what form of demonspawn they had been dealing with. Ghortin looked them over briefly, and then nodded. "Crell, gather our people. We need to take those who will live back to Lithunane as soon as we can travel. We need to burn the remains of those demonspawn. That thing back there," he pointed at the tent, "was right; our victory is not what it should be, and it cost us much. As soon as everything is ready, we ride. We need to make plans with King Resstlin; the war has begun."

THE END

D EAR READER,

Thank you for joining in on the flagship adventure for the Books of the Cuari trilogy. I hope you enjoyed it as much as I enjoyed writing it.

The second book, DIVISION OF CHAOS will take off early 2021. The battle is just beginning for Jenna, Storm, Keanin, and the rest.

If you're also interested in space opera, please check out the first book in The Asarlaí Wars trilogy- WARRIOR WENCH.

Magic, mayhem, and drunken faeries run loose in THE GLASS GARGOYLE, the first book in The Lost Ancients fantasy series.

Like steampunk?
Try A CURIOUS INVASION.

THE GIRL WITH THE IRON WING is the first book in a fast moving urban fantasy thriller if your interests go that way.

I really appreciate each and every one of you so please keep in touch. You can find me at www.marieandreas. com.

And please feel free to email me directly at Marie@ marieandreas.com as well, I love to hear from readers!

If you enjoyed this book (or any book for that matter ;)) please spread the word! Positive reviews on Amazon, Goodreads, and blogs are like emotional gold to any writer and mean more than you know.

Marie

About The Author

Marie is a multiple award winning fantasy and science fiction reader with a reading addiction. If she wasn't writing about all of the people in her head, she'd be lurking about coffee shops annoying innocent passer-by with her stories. So really, writing is a way of saving the masses. She lives in Southern California and is currently owned by two extremely pushy cats—who often like to walk across her keyboard.

When not saving the general populace from coffee shop shenanigans, Marie likes to visit the UK and keeps hoping someone will give her a nice summer home in the Forest of Dean or northern Wales.

More information can be found on her website http://marieandreas.com/